ANTHONY: UNSHACKLED

by
JOAN VASSAR

Special thanks to my readers, I love you all. To my editor, Felicia Murrell, thank you for your dedication to this project. I so appreciate you. To Karyn Wilkerson, Ja' Nair Wilkerson and Carla Wynn, thank you for test reading.

PROLOGUE
The Hen House
New York, September 1862

THE BLUE ROOM had a canopy bed large enough for five people. There were pillows everywhere, and the satin sheets were a powder blue. Anthony had two drinks in his ass, enough to dull the pain, but not enough to put his dick to sleep. He was seated in a blue, velvet-upholstered chair that put him in the mind of a throne. Standing before him was a brown-skinned, curvy woman, he figured to be about twenty summers. He had been to Miss Cherry's House of Comfort once or twice. The woman before him was fresh, not hard in appearance like the women who worked the pussy parlor back home.

Anthony didn't want to talk; he wanted to ease into her body and feel something other than pain. He didn't even want to know her name, but he *would* keep her all night. She stood about five-feet, six-inches. Her hair was braided in one thick French braid with a blue ribbon at the end. She had dark eyes that seemed void of emotion, a small nose and big juicy lips. She lingered by the door and he liked the illusion of her innocence. She wore a black, gauzy gown that clung to her beautiful body. Her nipples were visible, and he thought her striking.

"You gonna help me undress?"

"Yes," she responded, her voice throaty, but hesitant.

He watched the sway of her hips as she moved toward him. When she was close enough, he reached out for her. She accepted his hand, and he pulled her onto his lap. The woman smelled of roses, but it wasn't overpowering. He kissed her, and she accepted his tongue. When she whimpered, he pulled back and gazed at her. He touched her lips with the pad of his thumb, and she smiled nervously. He leaned in, kissing her again, and she was even more receptive. He groaned.

Anthony stood to his full height of six feet and allowed her to slide down his body. He removed his guns and placed them on a small table next to the chair. She reached up and unbuttoned his white shirt. When it fell to the floor, he removed his own trousers and boots. He was already hard, but he would pace himself. She was his for the night.

His manhood jutted out between them, and he took her by the hand and showed her how he wanted to be touched. The action caused him to close his eyes and revel in the feel of her fingers wrapped about him. It had been a while since he had been with a woman, for he had been immersed in grief. He was in danger of spilling his seed where they stood. Backing away, he lifted her night dress over her head and carried her naked body to the bed. He climbed right between her legs and kissed her deeply.

Leaning down, he allowed his tongue to play with a brown nipple. She cried out, and Anthony found that while he did not want to know her name, he wanted her to know his.

"My name is Anthony," he said against her ear.

When he took her other nipple into his mouth, she panted, "Anthony—Anthony."

Hearing her chant his name almost brought him to conclusion, but he had a plan. He would sink deep within her, take the edge off and then enjoy the rest of the night. Placing himself at her core, he could feel the promise of her heat, and he pressed forward. Taking her mouth in a stormy kiss, he plunged deep within her sweetness, until he was buried to the hilt.

"Shit," he hissed as she pushed at his chest trying to dislodge him.

"Ohhh," she cried out. "Anthony, ya hurt me."

Backing out of her tightness caused him to ache. He had not expected to find a virgin at a damn whorehouse. Dazed, he rolled off her and tried to collect himself.

"What's yo' name?"

He lay facing her as she looked up at the ceiling. "Emma," she answered.

Anthony allowed her to pull the covers over her, but not before he saw the blood on her thighs. She cried softly as they lay in silence. He started to rise from the bed not feeling good about the situation.

"Please give me another chance," she whispered, "I'll do betta."

He sighed. "How you come to be here?"

Emma looked afraid, but she did not answer. He stood and walked over to the window, naked. Looking down onto the dark street, he knew he needed to leave this place. He also knew he couldn't leave the girl. His mind was going through the floor plan of the gentleman's club on the first floor. Turning away from the window, he grabbed his clothes from the floor and began dressing. Emma sat up in bed wrapped in a sheet, watching him.

"Please," she said. "Are you gonna complain?"

His eyes narrowed. "How old is you?"

"Twenty summers."

He was relieved. "Get dressed."

She went to reach for the nightgown, and he asked, "Do you has anything else to wear?"

"No."

He stopped moving and glared at her. She looked away.

"You will leave here wit' me. This ain't no place for you."

"I cain't leave. They owns me," she answered anxiously.

"Who is 'they'?"

She didn't answer, but he wouldn't leave her. He went back to dressing himself and when his guns were in place, he moved to the bed and yanked the sheet from the mattress.

"Cover yoself," he ordered.

Emma did as he asked, and he took her by the hand, leading her to the door. She pulled away from him.

"I cain't leave here; they will kill you."

Even if she wanted to stay, he wasn't going to allow it, but he asked anyway, "Ya wanna stay here?"

"No."

Anthony nodded, and then backed away from all emotion. Taking her by the hand once more, he pulled the door open and stepped into the dimly lit corridor. An oil lamp sat on a table to the left of the door and just beyond the light, he could hear the moans of a satisfied customer. On the opposite end of the hall, he heard giggling. He moved toward the stairs with Emma in tow. The combination of piano playing and plush carpet helped drown out the frenzy of his footfalls.

At the top of the landing, he looked about. The steps curved to the right at the bottom, giving way to a well-lit parlor. The Hen House was an upscale brothel, and colored women were the main attraction. His back was to the wall as he dragged Emma along in his wake. Her steps faltered twice, and he had to stand her back on her feet. Holding her with his left hand kept his right hand free for business. He moved into the curve of the staircase, and out in front of him was the saloon. A few tables dotted the area. Beyond the tables, male patrons sat on overstuffed couches while scantily clad women vied for their coin.

Left of the bar, an older colored fellow played the piano

accompanied by a young, dark-skinned woman who sang. She was dressed in nothing but yellow feathers. If the situation had been less stressful, Anthony would have appreciated the scene before him. His eyes fell to Jeremiah, who stood with his back to the bar. E.J. sat at a table a few feet away speaking with a white man in a dark suit. When Jeremiah spied him on the stairs, he moved, ever so slightly, away from the bar.

Anthony stepped down into the saloon and moved toward the entrance. He could see Frank posted up at the door, but not Lou. Still, Anthony knew Lou wasn't far. A white man wearing a brown suit stood and stepped forward. He had blond hair, small eyes and lips that were proportionate to the rest of his face. The man looked to be about forty summers, and his speech was educated.

"Boy, where is it you think you're going with Moonbeam?"

Anthony did not answer the question, countering with his own question. "How much for the girl?"

"You can't afford her," the man replied. "You aren't the first patron who has fancied himself in love with one of our girls."

E.J. walked over. "I will pay for the girl. What is the price?"

The man in the brown suit never took his eyes from Anthony. "Moonbeam isn't for sale, gentlemen. Let's stop here and go back to having a good evening."

Anthony glanced at Jeremiah who had turned his back toward his brother. The black cracker spoke calmly to the bartender. "Get yo' damn hands on the bar."

The man in the brown suit looked at Emma. "Moonbeam, honey," he said in a patronizing tone, "look at the trouble you're causing. Get back upstairs until I come for you."

Anthony's grip tightened on her wrist as he made for the front door. The music and singing stopped. The woman dressed in the yellow feathers disappeared through a door behind the piano.

When the man in the brown suit reached for his gun, Anthony drew his weapon and shot the older fellow twice in the chest. Emma screamed and began hopping up and down. Anthony stepped to his victim and shot him once more, making certain the job was done.

He dragged Emma toward the door as Jeremiah brought the bartender down with one shot between the eyes. E.J., in the meantime, shot a man seated on the couch with two women. Jeremiah went over to E.J.'s companion still seated at the table and knocked him unconscious.

"This way!" Frank called out.

They all made for the door, and Lou was out front with a carriage he had stolen. Frank drove, and Lou covered him. Anthony, Jeremiah and E.J. climbed into the carriage after tossing a shrieking Emma inside. The darkness engulfed them, still men pursued them on horseback. Stray bullets rang out, but Frank kept the carriage moving. They broke away, headed for upper New York, with the men inside the carriage taking turns shooting into the darkness from the windows.

The carriage continued at a breakneck speed. When they thought they were in the clear, one of the horses collapsed from a gunshot. Frank yelled, "Oooh shit!"

The other horses stumbled over the fallen animal, causing the carriage to shift violently to the left. Suddenly the cab itself began rolling, and Black's first rule popped into Anthony's head. *Business and ass don't go together.*

The carriage came to an abrupt and brutal stop against a tree. Anthony heard the girl moan as he lay in the blackness of the cab taking inventory of his own person. When he found he wasn't injured, he asked, "Emma, ya alright?"

"I think so," she whispered.

"Jeremiah–E.J.!" Anthony called out.

"I'm good," Jeremiah answered.

"Yeah," E.J. said.

Jeremiah climbed out of the carriage; Anthony followed and called out for Frank and Lou.

Both brothers answered to his relief. They needed to keep moving. Frank put two of the horses down. The other two animals were cut loose and taken along. They headed on foot to the nearest farm where an old white man sold E.J. a rickety carriage and two older horses. The price he paid was robbery, but he couldn't haggle. The old man's wife took mercy on Emma, giving her a dress and boots that were too tight.

Lou took over driving the new carriage, and Frank covered him. The small posse headed for Canada. They had been traveling for about thirty minutes when E.J. asked the question everyone was thinking.

"Which one of us is going to explain this shit to Black?"

1

September 1862
Fort Independence

BLACK LEANED AGAINST his desk, legs stretched out in front of him and crossed at the ankle. His arms were folded over his chest as he assessed the men before him. The twins stood to his left–Lou with a bandaged arm. Jeremiah and E.J. stood to the right; E.J. appeared uncomfortable. Directly in front of him stood a young, brown skinned woman staring up at him from her place at Anthony's side.

The room was silent as Black tried to gauge the trouble that would come. Exhaustion was still deep in his bones from the last time they rode out. Elbert and James stood behind him–closer to the window. Black held back from questioning Anthony, so as not to embarrass the woman. But if he'd heard correctly, Anthony had stolen her from a pussy parlor. A shoot out had ensued, in which the cousin of Fernando Wood, mayor to New York City lost his life.

Everyone present was waiting for a response from him, and it was everything Black could do to keep from sighing aloud. He had received two deliveries of the *New York World* newspaper. One from

Frederick Douglass and the other from Camille. The paper explained in great detail how Hugh Wood was murdered in cold blood while taking a brisk evening stroll. If the news were to be believed, the mayor had issued a reward for facts leading to the capture of his cousin's killer. This did not bode well for Fort Independence.

Black had been about to suggest that the woman be taken to Big Mama, but before he could voice his thoughts, there came a knock at the door. The tension in the room seemed to thicken, still he called out, "Enter."

The door swung open with purpose and to Black's disappointment, it wasn't his mama. Jake, one of the men added to the eighteen when Morgan became with child, appeared. In the younger man's hand was yet another package. As he ambled forward, Black noted the grave expression on his face. Jake reached up to swipe at the sweat that dripped from his dark skin. When Black assessed him further, his black trousers were dusty and his white shirt was wet at the armpits. It appeared Jake had been running.

"Another package come for ya."

Wordlessly, Black reached out a hand and the action caused Jake to reciprocate–the russet paper crinkling as the package dangled from his fingertips. The players in the New York debacle were quiet as they awaited Black's displeasure. When the parcel changed hands and Jake turned to leave, his eyes fell upon the woman at Anthony's side.

Jake's breath caught as he whispered. "Emma, that you?"

The woman's eyes widened–surprised; she breathed. "Jake?"

"How ya get here? Where ya come from? I looked for ya–thought I'd never lay eyes on ya again." Jake continued.

"I come with Anthony–he brang me."

As Black watched the scene unfold, the gravity of the situation began to weigh heavily on his person. The woman, Emma, was going to be a complication that Fort Independence could do without. Black gauged her as she stood next to Anthony while facing

Jake. She was lovely and the innocence that dripped from her only added to the trouble.

Jake's eyes bounced up to meet Anthony's glare. "Where ya find Emma?"

Black noted that the question Jake posed was benign. Still, Anthony offered no response and his silence carried threat. Behind them, Black heard Elbert cough. In front of them, Jeremiah chuckled. Anthony would never again speak on where he found the woman and there was no mistaking the possessiveness emitting from him. Jake, who was oblivious to the storm brewing, stepped in as if to hug the Emma woman.

James, sensing the severity of the matter, moved with the swiftness from his position at the window to stand between the woman and Jake, essentially blocking Anthony from the shorter man. Jake stumbled back and Anthony reached out a large hand, palming the nape of Emma's neck.

"Jake, come on wit' me." James said, his back to Anthony and the woman. "I needs help down at the barracks."

Black, who was thankful for James' quick thinking, cleared his throat before speaking sharply. "Jake, I'll send for you, if I need you."

It was Black's tone that got Jake's attention. The shorter man then stepped to the left of James to look at Anthony before abruptly exiting the study. Emma, herself, also looked relieved as she leaned into Anthony's touch. When the tension loosened, Black had several new issues to address; he would speak to Jake to find the connection between he and the woman. Next, he would house the woman in one of the upstairs bedrooms until he got to the bottom of the Emma conundrum. What Black did not need—no, what Fort Independence did not need was dissension in the ranks.

James and Jake had been gone for only moments when the study door swung open. Big Mama stood just inside the doorway wearing a brown dress with a stained white apron. Her gray hair was styled in two large plaits, pinned neatly to the top of her head. Mama spoke with authority when she addressed the woman. "Emma–honey, come on wit' me so's I could get ya settled."

Black noted the hesitation in Emma's eyes as she looked to Anthony, who nodded. She turned to Big Mama with a nervous smile and answered, "Yes, ma'am."

As the study door closed with a soft click behind the women, Anthony offered his full attention to Black. The younger man, who had been closed off and aloof since Luke's death, was showing signs of life. Today, Anthony showed volatile.

Black was thinking on his next words when Jeremiah spoke up. "It was us or them."

"I woulda paid to keep her, but they ain't wanna bargain." Anthony said, his tone harsh.

Black had questions that could only enflame. He was at a loss as to how to present his thoughts without soiling the woman or making Anthony appear weak for pussy. In the end, Elbert stepped away from the window and asked what could only be interpreted as fighting words.

"The pussy parlor is make believe–ya get that right?"

"I gets that." Anthony replied; his demeanor bored–closed off. He offered no insight to his actions.

"Your actions will affect the fort. I want answers without having to ask questions." Black had become salty.

"I woulda bargained, but the innkeeper reached for his weapon–weren't nuttin' else to say." Anthony shrugged.

Black unfolded himself from where he leaned on the edge of his desk. Standing to his full height, he looked Anthony square in the eyes. His thoughts wandered to the people of Fort Independence, the folks he had sworn to protect.

"The girl ain't belong there." Lou offered as he moved in behind Anthony.

In the face of Black's rising anger, Anthony backed down; still the fight wasn't completely gone from him. "Was her first day–her first time. She's mine."

Jeremiah chuckled.

Elbert whistled before adding. "Shit, it's a first time for everything."

Black sighed aloud at Anthony's words. Next to him, Elbert confirmed what Black was thinking. "I woulda stole her ass too."

A vision of Elbert burning down Boston's waterfront in search of Will Turner popped into his thoughts and Black had to shake his head to clear it. Yes, his brother would have taken the girl as well. Anthony interrupted his musings.

"I ain't tryna make trouble. I can take Emma and leave."

Black could feel the room collectively holding their breath. "Your departure will leave us down a good man and will not change the fate of the fort."

Anthony nodded.

"We will meet again tomorrow." Black said, dismissively. "The woman will stay in this house–Big Mama will handle all things concerning Emma."

Anthony stared at Black for seconds before conceding. Turning on his heels, he followed the men from the study. When the door swung closed, Black moved around his desk seating himself. Using the silver letter opener to his right, he cut the string holding a package together. As he unraveled the plain brown wrapper, Elbert looked on in mild curiosity.

In the middle of the packaging lay the *New York World* newspaper. This was now the third copy that had been sent to him. On top of the newspaper was a missive written in a perfect hand.

My Friend,

I believe a matter has come to light that you will find interesting. Please let me know if there is anything I can do to help.

Sincerely,

A L

Black shook his head; the president was offering his assistance.

This could mean only one thing–he had underestimated the enormity of events that had taken place in New York City. He didn't voice his thoughts; instead he passed the note to Elbert, who shook his head after reading it.

"The fallout from this will be great."

Elbert replied, his grin wide. "I say we ride out."

"And if we can't fix the matter?" Black asked.

"Then we burn New York City to the damn ground." Elbert answered without hesitation.

Black thought of his wife and children–there could be only one response to such a statement. "I'll bring the match sticks."

"I'll get the men together while you figure on keeping Anthony from killin' Jake." Elbert quit the study, leaving Black to glare after him.

Anthony stepped onto the porch of Black's house and into the September heat. The sun beat down on his ebony skin as he walked in the opposite direction of the barracks and the men. He didn't seek Emma out because he wasn't up for facing Big Mama. The old woman could be meaner than her sons and he was thankful to never have been the one to stoke her anger.

He needed a moment to collect himself and his thoughts. Luke's death had changed him from good-natured to ill-mannered; the transformation was unnerving–even to himself. He'd lost his best friend in the war on slavery and his vexation with the world ran deep. Taking the woman gave him something to focus on and there could be no compromise. Emma belonged to him.

In his not so distant young–ignorant days, Fort Independence seemed impenetrable. He hadn't understood what it meant to be Black or the men who rode out to face the dangers of abolition work. The fort was a sanctuary that was now compromised because of his actions. Still, if he had it to do over, it would be done the same.

He walked until he came upon the cemetery. He was frozen in place for moments before averting his gaze and moving toward the swimming hole at the back of the fort. Dust from the path kicked up with his every step as he tried to get away from the reality of Luke's demise. As grief chased him, Anthony found he couldn't run fast enough.

Down past the storage structures and just beyond the thicket was his safe place. Anthony stood at the muddy bank of the small pond contemplating his troubles. The woes that could result from his choices would be big; but he would continue to live by his new boundaries. If any man should raise his hand to do violence against him, then Anthony would kill that man. And he would do so without hesitation-without regret. Life had changed and he had made the necessary adjustments to survive.

There was movement to his left, and Anthony turned to catch sight of James walking toward him. Casting his focus back to the water, he offered no immediate conversation as James came to stand beside him. When he finally did speak, his thoughts bordered on trivial if one didn't look too deep.

"Luke and me used to love swimmin'– we wanted to see the girls' dresses cling to they bodies." Anthony chuckled at the memory.

"Swimmin' and chasin' after the womenfolk is the life of a boy." James countered.

"Don't I know it. Shit ain't easy no mo'."

"No, but many hands makes for light work. Black is right when he say we must labor together to make this thang work." James explained.

"I agrees wit' Black, but Jake cain't have Emma."

James sighed. "Ain't no one finna take the woman from ya. But think on this, ya took Emma and that was the easy part. Now she yours to look after and that be the hard part. Jake is small in all this–what's big is you understandin' ya needs the men on this fort to help keep her safe. Is ya man enough?"

Anthony was hoping James wasn't looking for a response, because he had none to give. In truth, he hadn't thought beyond removing her from the pussy parlor and possessing her. His eyes did not move from the water, which made it easier to speak. Yet, he stepped away from the topic of Emma and Jake to offer clarification of his actions.

"I wanted to pay for her – tried to negotiate – but the man from the cathouse reached for his damn gun. Any man draw on me betta be quicker than me. Either we talkin' or we shootin'."

When James didn't respond, Anthony glanced his way to find him staring out over the water. He turned back to the small waves lapping at the bank and waited. James didn't disappoint.

"Ya ain't answer the question. Is ya man enough?"

"Yeah." Anthony countered.

"Good–cause ya shot the mayor of New York City's cousin. Shit finna get bad fore it gets better." James said, his voice matter of fact.

"I wanted Emma–not the worry."

"Can ya be a family man witout worry?" James asked.

"Guess ya askin' cause it ain't possible." Anthony replied.

"Black got a lot on 'im from running the fort to Sunday and the new babies. He also gotta keep the group of cutthroats under his command straight. Don't make him have to manage the differences betwixt you and Jake."

James' words hit Anthony like a sledgehammer. But before he could confirm his understanding, James walked away. He was being left to face his manhood and all that it implied. After reviewing the events and himself, he turned, heading for the barracks. As he made his way to the heart of Fort Independence, Anthony set aside the boy he used to be in order to embrace the man he had become; he would start with the Jake fiasco.

Off in the distance men worked the fields, while the barracks went through a shift change. But it was the sight of children playing at recess that caused him dread. Some women worked the vegetable gardens and still others hung laundry. Fort life was bustling with hard work and freedom. He wasn't man enough—no matter what he told James.

Anthony had to stop himself from spinning about like a damn visitor. He was seeing life from the standpoint of protector; the observation caused feelings of inadequacy and angst. His brain faltered, but his feet did not. When he reached the barracks, he pressed through the throng of men clustered about the main entrance. Just as his booted feet crossed the threshold, someone shouted his name. He no longer needed to seek Jake out—the problem had come to him. Turning, he found Jake moving toward him and damn if he didn't look man enough.

They stood to the left of the main entrance eyeing each other. Anthony felt his temper and jealousy burning hot. He worked at self-control, waiting for Jake to speak.

"Antney, we needs to talk."

Anthony didn't respond verbally; instead he jutted his chin out, pointing toward the backdoor that was also open. At his words Jake turned and began striding down the aisle, leaving Anthony to awkwardly trail him. They moved past the front desk where Elbert, Simon and James stood handing out supplies. James glanced their way, then turned back to the task at hand.

When they reached the backdoor and stepped through, the commotion inside the barracks became background noise. On a warm breeze drifted the smells of cornbread from the mess hall and animal sweat from the stables. The combination often overwhelmed the senses. Anthony stared at the large oak tree nestled between the bathhouse and mess hall while trying to gather his words. Jake spoke first.

"Where ya get Emma from?"

Anthony's eyes bounced from the oak to Jake; his voice even when he spoke. "Don't question me, Jake. I ain't finna speak on Emma wit' you or no other man."

Looking away, Jake took a deep breath. "I been to New York City a few times for Black. He takes care of Miss Camille and little Curtis, the blacksmith's son. There also be the colored orphanage on 42nd Street–Black sends coin to them. I saw Emma at the orphanage."

Anthony did nothing more than stare. He had already made clear the boundaries of this conversation. Jake needed to back off or the situation would become violent. He didn't care where Jake met Emma. He had been her first–she belonged to him. Crossing his arms over his chest, Anthony gave nothing.

Jake coughed before conceding. "I ain't mean to step on ya toes."

Anthony nodded.

Jake stepped back before heading for the backdoor. "Imma get on back to work."

When Jake would have disappeared into the barracks, Anthony said, "Don't question Emma–I won't see past the offence."

Jake stopped mid-stride to look at him. The shorter man curtly nodded and then he was gone. Anthony leaned against the wall and inhaled. The exchange had not gone well, and he prayed Jake would stop pushing him beyond his limit. Anthony was sure the next test he would fail.

❈ ❈ ❈

Black stood staring down into the bassinet, where his twin boys lay sleeping. His wife had dubbed them Benjamin and Daniel Turner before passing out in complete exhaustion. Four months later, his wife was still weak from the birthing and he was beside himself with worry for her. Big Mama, Iris and Cora were helpful, but there was the issue of his wife not producing enough milk. He dreaded the feeding hour for it left him feeling helpless.

As if his thoughts conjured them, Iris and Cora appeared; Cora spoke first.

"Ya mama got Nattie. We'll take the babies to Sunday."

"That Ben-Ben sure can eat." Iris said on a giggle.

Black offered a ghost of a smile as he watched each woman take up a bundle and leave. Leaning back against his desk, he crossed his arms over his chest. He was deep in thought about his wife and children when Mama stepped into his office. Nattie stood to her left fisting Mama's skirts. He beamed at the sight of his daughter in yellow pajamas. This was their time together before she was tucked in for the night.

"Dad-dy." She squealed as she ran to him on sure feet.

Black scooped her up, kissing her cheek. "There's Daddy's girl."

Nattie was a busy child; so as fast as she was picked up–she was trying to get down.

He laughed as she rushed off to the corner of his office where Paul left newly carved blocks. It was early evening and he wondered after his wife.

"Sunday?"

"She wit' the boys, helpin' to settle them for the night." Mama answered.

"I haven't seen her all day."

"I been makin' her rest," Mama said.

"She's still weak."

"She gainin' strength. These thangs take time." Mama countered.

"Is she eating enough? Why can't she make enough milk?"

"We done worked it out so's the babies and Sunday is gettin' enuff."

He was about to ask another question, but Mama shook her head. The message clear, she was telling him to stop worrying. She turned to leave and over her shoulder, she called, "Brang Nattie to me in a few."

Black was still staring after his mama when Nattie threw a block and started crying. He felt like crying too. "What's the matter, baby girl?"

"Up," she demanded.

Picking her up, he began pacing the office; Nattie was asleep within moments. All Black wanted was to spend time with his wife. He didn't want to think about New York City. The very idea of being separated from Sunday was unthinkable. He tried not to focus on the problems facing the fort, but the truth was plain to see; he could not be Nat because the circumstance called for Black.

He went in search of his mama, while Nattie snored lightly against his shoulder. Big Mama was seated in a chair by the window plaiting her hair. "Put the chile in my bed. Come mornin', I finds her curled up next to me anyways."

Black did as Mama instructed before heading off to his own quarters. He almost expected her to stop his departure, but she didn't. The door to his room sat ajar as he approached, and he could hear one of his sons wailing. Black could also hear his wife's soft voice crooning to their babe. Pushing the door wide, he found Sunday breastfeeding Benjamin and Callie breastfeeding Daniel; his son's dark curls peaking from beneath a yellow blanket as Callie gently cradled him. On the bed lay Miah, Callie's daughter with Jeremiah, who was fast asleep.

"My love." Sunday called to him. "Is Nattie in bed?"

He had figured on a wet nurse to help with the babies, but he hadn't known the identity. Clearing his throat, he answered his wife. "She's sleep in Mama's bed."

"Good." Sunday said with a smile.

Black's eyes bounced over to Callie and she whispered. "Mister Black."

"Miss Callie." He responded with a curt nod.

Before any other words were exchanged, Black backed out of the room. When he stepped onto the porch, Jeremiah was coming up the stairs as he started his descent.

"Callie?" he asked.

"She's in with Sunday." Black answered, before coughing uncomfortably. "And the babies."

Jeremiah nodded, stopping his ascent. "You headed to the barracks?"

"Yeah."

"I just come from Elbert's–Anna got Otis." Jeremiah said. "Tryna help out wit' my son."

Both men headed for the emotional safety of the barracks. They walked in silence, allowing Black to replay the exchange. It was obvious Jeremiah knew Callie was the wet nurse for his boys; he offered no reaction to the news that his woman was helping Sunday. It had been a trying few months with Sunday not producing enough and the babies unable to hold down milk from Abby or Mary. Still, Black had not known the women settled on Callie.

When they stepped into the barracks, Black found James, Elbert and Simon standing at the backdoor. He headed in their direction and Jeremiah kept pace. Since it would be a while before he could go to Sunday, he turned his mind to Fort Independence.

"Black–Jeremiah." Simon greeted.

"Simon." Both men responded.

James spoke to Jeremiah. "Thought you was comin' for Otis yesterday."

Jeremiah grinned. "Tryna give Miss Abby a break from seeing me. I just come from bringing in water for Anna and helpin' get the boys settled."

James nodded.

"Anthony and Jake spoke." Elbert said, changing the subject. "Tension still thick."

"We's men." Simon said. "Shit gon get thick from time ta time."

Black folded his arms over his chest and listened. He agreed with Simon. James added his thoughts and it was another subject change.

"We needs to scout out the situation in New York."

Indeed, Black thought.

❁ ❁ ❁

Emma sat in a chair facing the window, but the sun had long since gone down. An oil lamp burned brightly in the background, offering the reflection of a sad woman against the glass. She couldn't even appreciate meeting the legendary Black, himself. The occasion was overshadowed by the feeling that Black didn't want her in his home or on his land. And seeing Jake again only served to further complicate matters, if the tensions of the previous day were any indication.

The first time she saw Jake was at the New York Colored Orphan Asylum, when he had come to bring food, clothing and coin. In a two-year span, he had come to the orphanage three times. Ms. Dowling, one of the few colored staff members said he'd asked after her. There was a sparkle in the older woman's eye, and Emma knew she had hoped to match her with Jake. Matching and matrimony almost never happened for colored women. But Ms. Dowling was hopeful, then she died suddenly, and Jake hadn't returned.

The truth is she hadn't really known Jake. And though he had shown interest, it had been to Ms. Dowling about her—not to her directly. Time lapsed and the circumstance became dire; it had been suggested that she consider becoming an indentured servant to a landowner in New England. This is what often happened to colored children too old to stay on at the orphanage. The prospect to Emma, sounded like slavery; she ran away in the wee hours of the night with one of the older girls. If she closed her eyes, she could still see all that happened.

"Emma, wake up." Alice hissed, frantically. "Is ya comin' or stayin'?"

When Emma would have verbally confirmed, Alice placed a hand tightly over her mouth; she nodded.

They made their way through the kitchen and out the back of the children's home. Their paths marred by complete darkness. The air was cool, and the smell of overgrown vegetation pummeled their senses. Alice was taller and cleared the fence with ease. The abrupt sound of fabric ripping followed Emma over the barrier. Once on the other side, they gathered their skirts and ran off.

The young women were armed with hope and a newspaper ad that read:

Governess positions available—Bliss Mansion. Docile/Colored women need only apply.

It had taken them all day to locate Bliss Mansion. When the day got underway, so too did the heat. The fall weather on Manhattan Island was stifling and the horseshit lining the streets only added to their discomfort. The women finally stopped at an imposing brick structure on the corner of 4th Avenue and 61st Street. Behind a stone fence were well-manicured lawns and opportunity—both women were giddy with triumph.

"We could change clothes in the bushes." Alice suggested.

"I ain't wantin' to get caught naked in these white folks bushes."

"We can't ask for a audience lookin' like runaways." Alice rebutted. Emma sighed and Alice rushed on. "Them shrubs over there is good enough."

The sun was beginning to drop from the sky causing Emma to think of bugs and snakes. Still, they climbed the section of fence hidden by two large oak trees; crouching down they headed for the bushes. Emma was sad that they couldn't truly freshen up. The dress she wore was wet from perspiration; she smelled unclean.

"We just need to get the positions." Alice said, as if reading her thoughts. She waved her hands around trying to fight off the tiny bugs flying about. Pulling a different dress over her head, Alice wriggled then smoothed the material. Emma followed her lead; their hair was unkempt and damp from sweating, but they looked better than when they first arrived.

"Leave the sacks here, we'll come back for 'em later."

Alice seemed to have a plan and Emma was thankful. They hurried back to the narrow path that led from the street to the looming front door. Once on the stoop, Alice asked, "How do I look?"

Emma eyed her friend with nervous energy. Alice was light skinned and just shy of white. She had brown eyes, big lips and a flat nose that appeared button like. She was plump, but curvy. Her hair was in one braid, pinned at her nape. The dress she wore was her Sunday best; gray with large mismatched buttons on the bodice.

"Ya looks good." Emma replied, realizing for the first time that Alice was also anxious.

When Alice pulled at the gold doorknocker, Emma felt the banging in her chest. Waiting for someone to answer the door left her nerves frayed. It occurred to her after Alice knocked that they were two colored orphans at a white residence with only a piece of newspaper. There was no date, no reference as to which paper the ad came from and most important...

The door swung wide to reveal a young colored man dressed in butler attire. Emma had never seen one of her own outfitted so well—male or female. He wore black trousers, a matching jacket with a crisp white shirt and gloves. His skin was dark, his white teeth visible against his grimace. The man before them had huge brown eyes, which made the unkindness within him unmistakable. Emma took a step back, while Alice moved forward into the entryway—into his personal space.

"How may I help you?" he said, his stance haughty, his voice polished.

"We come 'bout the ad." Alice replied. "We hard workin'."

"Alice." Emma tried to caution.

"We here cause the newspaper say you has governess posts to fill." Alice hurried on, ignoring Emma's pleas.

The butler's gaze danced between them, before he schooled his expression. Even as he was shutting the door in their faces, he dryly instructed. "Wait here."

"Alice, I changed my mind."

"Emma, it'll be good. We needs this."

"What we shoulda done was think on this 'fore we come here."
Emma countered, then pleaded. "Alice, let's go."

She was backing away when a white man wearing gray trousers
and a white shirt pulled the door open. He had blond hair with small
blue eyes. Unfriendliness radiated from him and it was a contradiction
to the words emitting from him. The man plainly assessed them, as one
might do a horse before purchase.

"The governess positions are still available. Welcome."

"I'm Alice." Over her shoulder, she pointed. "This here is Emma."

"Won't you please come in," the man replied. "I'm Mr. Wood."

Alice didn't move, but she did reply. "Emma and me want to work
at the same post. We ain't looking to be split up."

As Emma watched the exchange, she realized that Alice was
unqualified–she was anything but docile.

"I suppose that could be arranged." Mr. Wood agreed.

Footsteps sounded in the corridor outside the room she had
been given at Black's house. Emma was snatched from her reverie,
but not her thoughts. Indeed Mr. Hugh Wood had kept his promise
of not splitting them up. He had taken them to the Hen House
against their will, and Alice had protested vehemently. On day two
of the tragedy, Alice was removed from the room they were to share,
never to be seen again. Emma remembered being advised by one
of the other women that to survive is to accept male companionship–then Anthony happened.

Unable to stop herself, she wept. She cried for Alice, whom she
was sure was dead. Her sorrow extended to Anthony, who would
soon come to his senses about her. Lastly, the sharp pain in her chest
came from tasting *safety* and realizing that it would be taken away.
It was time to figure on where she would go from here. Staying in
Canada seemed to be the best decision, given she had the death of
a white man hanging over her head.

Emma stood, snuffing out the lamp before climbing into the
large bed at the center of the room. In the morning she would try

to find her way to the nearest town; maybe she could find work as a laundress or maid. Two thoughts troubled her most before sleep finally claimed her. Would indentured servitude have been better than the choices she made thus far? Would Alice still be alive if they hadn't been naïve enough to chase work meant for white women?

Sleep was a restless endeavor and still when the morning sun spilled through the window, Emma was more rested than she had been in weeks. Across one of the black chairs, lay three dresses, two brown–serviceable and a blue one with a delicate lace collar. On the floor were a pair of black shoes that were more conducive to the terrain. A clunky pair of women's boots meant to protect from the turning of an ankle. Looking about, Emma figured Ms. Cora must have come and gone quietly while she slept.

In the corner of the chamber on a wooden nightstand sat a white pitcher and basin. On the left of the night table lay a brown cloth; she sighed at the thought of freshening up. Removing the too small clothes she wore–she wiped her face and body down. Beneath the dresses she found several undergarments. Emma had never been so thankful. Once fully clad, she found that everything fit perfectly, even the shoes. Turning to survey the now messy room, she set about putting everything to rights. It was the least she could do before leaving.

As she worked on straightening up the room, there came a knock at the door. She furrowed her brow, but she didn't answer; had she ever given anyone permission to enter before?

"Emma, child, you in there?"

"Y-yes, ma'am." She answered.

The knob twisted and in stepped Ms. Cora. The older woman was dressed in a blue dress with a white apron. She was smiling as she balanced a tray of food.

"Mama sent breakfast for you."

"Thank you." Emma whispered. "When can I see Anthony?"

"The man workin', girl, you'll see him soon enough." Ms. Cora replied. "Come eat, I'll be back later for the tray."

Before Emma could inquire about the next town or where she might find work, Ms. Cora quit the room. The mouthwatering smell of breakfast was only proof that she had come and gone. Emma sat down to grits, eggs, biscuits and a cup of coffee on the side. She never cared for coffee, but this morning the rich aroma was enticing.

She ate with gusto and a real lack of manners, so hungry was she. Her belly filled quickly, and she had to breathe in deeply in order to fit more food in her stomach. When she was stuffed to capacity, Emma wrapped one biscuit in a table napkin for later; the next town might be far. Looking back on her travels, she was sorry she hadn't paid more attention to her surroundings.

Removing a pillowcase from the chest at the foot of the bed, Emma rolled up the second brown dress, along with pantaloons and a shift. She placed the clothing and the food in the sack and headed for the bedroom door. Once in the hall, she stood for a moment to get her bearings. At the top of the stairs she could hear voices and laughter. The hour was still early, but the house was alive.

The hallway was dim, yet at the bottom of the steps the front door sat open. She hesitated, before finding the courage to make her way down the stairs. If nothing else, she knew where the front gate was located. She would start there and ask for directions to the nearest town. Emma didn't look back toward the kitchen or the voices; instead she stepped into the brilliance of a sunny new day. Her feet picked up speed as she crossed the porch. She was about to descend the stairs when a deep voice floated from behind her.

"Good morning, Miss Emma."

She didn't have to turn to recognize Black's voice. Clutching the sack to her chest, she spun to face him.

"Good morning to you, Mista Black."

Black was well over six feet tall and drenched in sunlight, he appeared even more striking than he had the day before. He wore tan trousers with a white homespun shirt. His skin was dark–smooth. He was bald with almond shaped eyes that never left her. The weight of his stare made her take a step back. She stumbled and was about to fall to her death, but he caught her just in time.

Placing her gently back on her feet and away from the stairs, he grinned. "You going somewhere?"

Emma felt as though she had been caught committing a crime. She answered his question based on guilt. "I only took two of the dresses and a biscuit."

Black cocked his head to the side, studying her. She held his gaze… waiting. Finally, he asked again. "Are you going somewhere?"

"Ahhh." She stammered. "I was going to town to see if I could find work."

"I see."

"I am free to go, ain't I?"

Black didn't bother to answer. Lifting his eyes from her, he stared off to the right of them. The action caused her to do the same. On the path from the barracks, a group of rough looking men were walking toward them. Emma recognized Anthony, Jeremiah and the twins. She felt the same tensions of the day before, but it was more intense. Turning back to Black, he offered a curt nod toward the door. He waited for her to proceed him into the dim hall.

They walked through the kitchen where Ms. Cora, Mama and Ms. Iris sat drinking coffee. The older women stared at her strangely. She didn't know what to say and luckily, she didn't have to do any of the talking.

"Emma will be in the meeting with us." Black said from behind her–then he offered instructions. "Keep on down the hall."

She entered the office and stopped, unsure where to stand. Black took her elbow and led her to stand in front of the large desk. Behind them, the men marched in seating themselves on the gold couch and floor. Others stood about with their arms folded over their chests; when she looked up, all eyes were on her and Anthony was moving through the crowd in her direction.

He wore brown trousers with a tan homespun shirt. Emma noted Anthony's muscular frame; his dark skin was without blemish and there was no smile on his face. Low chatter filled the room as Anthony came to a stop in front of her.

"She was trying to run off to the nearest town." Black said, his voice holding amusement.

Anthony's eyebrows popped and his gaze fell to her. "You ain't allowed outside the gate alone."

Emma found herself standing between Black and Anthony. All conversation had stopped and when she peered over her shoulder at Black, he shrugged. Turning back to Anthony, her speech shook when she said. "I thought ya said the people here were free to come and go."

"Not you," he replied, and there was no salt in his response.

Anthony reached out, twining his fingers with her own before tugging her toward the window to stand next to him. Black turned, addressing the men, authority dripping from his every word.

"Our first order of business–Miss Emma is not allowed off the compound."

The men nodded, accepting the rule. Emma gasped.

2

September 1862
New York City

FERNANDO WOOD SAT in the receiving parlor of his Manhattan estate listening to an accounting of his cousin's last moments. He had been inundated with the company of fallen women–colored whores to be exact. In his quest for the truth, Fernando found himself unable to think of his political career. His family had suffered a blow in the face of Hugh's death, and he'd lost a great friend.

Seated behind a large oak desk, Fernando allowed his eyes to bounce from person to person. Standing before him were three harlots and all three were lying. The women had given their names, but such details were inconsequential. The mayor turned to Liam Quinn, his latest henchman and nodded. It was the signal to continue untangling the mystery of his cousin's demise.

Pretending to lend his focus to the picturesque view and the river beyond, Fernando waited for the inquiries to resume. Liam asked, "Where were ya when the shooting started, lovey?"

The taller of the women spoke up first. She was dressed shabbily in brown skirts and a matching brown overcoat to ward off the

September chill. The woman was black, there was no other word for it. With large lips and wide eyes, her hair was braided in tiny plaits all over her head. In the mayor's opinion, she was chubby and offered little appeal. Yet, he had been assured that she brought in lots of coin. She looked out of place in his well-furnished parlor.

"I was wit' a payin' friend. I ain't see nothin'," she said. Then pointing at the women next to her, she continued. "Pearl and Florence ain't see nothin' neither. They was wit' payin' friends, too."

The women standing on either side of her began nodding with conviction. The woman to the right was thin and light of skin with brown eyes. She was dressed in blue skirts with a brown overcoat. Her mouth was heart shaped and her hair was plaited in two large braids. She emitted a meanness; the whore gave Fernando the willies. The third of his unwanted guests was dressed in brown, the same as the first with an orange, stained overcoat. She was brown skinned with unkempt hair and a small frame. Her eyes were perceptive and on her lips was a smirk. They were mocking him. Fernando wanted to kill them, but the thought seemed counterproductive. They were, after all, his merchandise.

The Hen House was a business venture, now passed on to him in the wake of Hugh's passing. Seized by his own feelings, the mayor almost missed the taller woman's derisive comment.

"We's at the Hen House to be on our backs—we ain't there to look after the men that comes and goes."

Angry, Fernando pushed back from his desk and stood. Two of the three women retreated a step at the fury rolling from him. Rounding the elegant furniture, his booted feet echoed against the hardwood floors—then muted abruptly when he reached the burgundy area rug to face them. The mayor's words were clipped and directed at Liam.

"Get them from my sight, lest I forget my gentlemanly nature."

Liam, who was just shy of six feet, but taller than the mayor came forward. "Come, whores."

Catching his breath, Fernando turned as Liam's burly form began ushering the women through a hidden door along the back wall. In a tight voice, he snapped. "Send in the next interview."

Liam's shoulders stiffened, but he offered nothing verbal; the mayor appreciated the quiet. Clasping his hands behind his back, Fernando strolled leisurely around the cream-colored settee to stand before the window. From the rear of the parlor came the sound of creaking hinges, making the hidden entrance obvious. The mayor turned to find a white man dressed in a blue suit, his hands anxiously clutching the rim of his hat. Moving forward, the man introduced himself; his voice shook with the effort.

"Clifford Jones at your service, Mayor."

Fernando did not feel like niceties. "Mr. Jones, I'm told you were on hand to witness my cousin's end. I want the facts, sir. It would be detrimental for you should I be sent on a wild goose chase."

The other man paled before clearing his throat. "I was given the connection through a business colleague and friend, Archibald Stone. Mr. Hunter wanted to purchase horses. I believe he wished to contract with the Union army. We didn't get far in our talks before Mr. Wood was shot and I was rendered unconscious."

Fernando watched as the other man nervously crushed the rim of his hat. "Where is Mr. Hunter from—where does he live?"

"I'm unable to say for certain, but his companions were slaves. The lot of them were more organized than the union army." Clifford replied, reverently.

The mayor moved closer to the window, his mind racing. This was not the first time he had been told that slaves were responsible. Organized niggers—the very concept was outrageous. Hazarding a glance at his guest, Fernando detected awe from Clifford Jones. He was sure the wonderment he was witnessing was for the slaves that had terrorized and ended his best friend's life.

"Help me to understand, Mr. Jones. Are you saying that you

were content to do business with a man you knew nothing about?" Fernando asked, accusingly.

"This was a deal that would have been open and shut. Cash at the time the horses changed hands. As for where Hunter came from... I believe the south, based on his accent. We met at the Hen House because I thought it would be safe. Where he rests his head nightly, I couldn't say."

Fernando continued in his scrutiny of Clifford Jones, when movement at the back of the parlor caught his eye. It was Liam waiting on the periphery of this tragedy for instruction. While the mayor tried to surround himself with gentlemen, at times life called for the likes of Liam Quinn. Hugh had in the past tried to disguise the burly man as a servant; but no one in the mayor's circle believed such a tall tale. Even dressed in tailored suits, the man looked the part of a ruffian. In the case of Liam Quinn with his red hair and blue eyes, he was a book that could be judged by its cover.

"Mr. Jones," The mayor said dismissively. "My manservant will show you out. Thank you for your time. I'll be in touch should I have more questions."

His guest appeared confused–then relieved. Turning, he headed in the direction from which he came. As Clifford Jones drew nearer to Quinn, his steps faltered. Fernando chuckled to himself for the sudden rigidity of his guest's shoulders indicated that he understood his situation. Though the circumstance was calamitous, Fernando was a politician–a gentleman. Mr. Jones wouldn't be killed, but he *would* wish he were dead.

When the door clicked shut behind him, the mayor began to pace. He was swallowed up by grief. But what troubled him most–the fact that he lived in a country that was trying to free the slaves. His very own cousin and friend had been murdered at the hands of a slave. Damn the president for taking such a stance on servitude and damn the people of this nation who wanted to arm slaves.

Niggers more organized than the union army, the mayor of New York City would never believe such foolishness.

❊ ❊ ❊

Business at the Hen House had not decreased, even with the murder of its proprietor. The corner of W. 10th Street and 6th Avenue marked a visual change in the community. Other more upscale establishments sat along the avenue, but it was the Hen House that supported them all. At first glance the place appeared to be a normal residence situated in the merchant district. Upon further assessment, one realized it was a whorehouse specializing in dark meat.

The lower west side was a blend of cosmopolitan and rural. Around the Hen House were well-kept lawns and on either side of the porch sat box shaped shrubs. The back of the property housed several chickens, a goat and eight horses. The main structure itself was white with green shutters, two stories high and just shy of mansion status. Hugh had been efficient in his running of the place. The women cooked, cleaned and tended the outside, while servicing the never-ending stream of male patrons.

Fallout from Hugh Wood's demise started in earnest on the docks of Lower Manhattan, stretching through Five Points like a blaze on a windy day. There were no exceptions to the unnecessary roughness. Hardworking citizens—the shipyard worker, the blacksmith and the steel worker alike—were manhandled for information. It was simply unacceptable to claim ignorance, even if one were telling the truth.

This course of action produced an expected result, for everyone knew the murder was committed by runaway slaves. The racial divide only deepened with each passing day as white folks in Lower Manhattan were saddled with a new goal—finding a killer. The implications were clear, the death of the mayor's cousin was every person's problem. And the violence would only intensify as

Fernando Wood transitioned from his post as the mayor of New York City.

Liam Quinn served at the mayor's pleasure and he did so effectively. Fernando loved that he only had to speak to an idea, even if not well thought out, and Liam would make it happen. He needed that at a time like this; it made his sadness tolerable. Seated in the darkness of an unmarked carriage, Fernando submerged himself in the clip-clop of horse hooves against the cobblestone. When the vehicle lurched to a stop, he listened as the driver set the stairs.

"Sir?" Liam's voice floated through the murkiness of the cab. "Ya ready?"

"I am."

The carriage door was suddenly yanked open, leaving the mayor no choice but to step down into the chilled September night. He glanced about, gauging his chances of being found at a sex den. Visiting such an institution was beneath him but essential to getting at the truth. The hour was late, yet for those seeking debauchery, it might as well have been midday. Striding up the walkway, Fernando didn't get the opportunity to knock; the door opened as if by magic.

All eyes were on him as he made his way into the gentlemen's lounge. The bar was against the far wall and plump couches sat about the room—in colors of brown, gold and black. On the left of the parlor, next to the stairs was the grandest of pianos; the bench was empty. Taking in the scene before him, the mayor smirked. The crowd was divided in two—whores to the left, patrons to the right. Fernando couldn't think of a time when he felt truer to a task.

As his focus bounced from right to left, the mayor waited in silence. The customers totaled fifteen white and five black men. Liam stepped up to do his bidding while directing the gunmen securing the patrons.

"Gentlemen," Liam said to the room at large.

Fernando snorted at the use of the word. He raked his gaze over the assorted patrons and shook his head. Several were men he knew from more respectable circles, yet they pretended not to know him, and he did the same. There was the shipping tycoon, Leslie Bonnar and the proprietor of the general store, Merkle Patton. Hiram George, the pastor of the local church was also present; he had come to save those who had fallen hard from grace.

The pictures on the walls were of high quality and rich in color. One canvas was of fruit, another of water pouring from a lovely vase and still more portraits were of scantily clad women. Fernando made a mental note to remove anything of value from the house. Looking to the women, he found his collection of whores worthy–though he did not dabble. He feared disease and it was enough to keep his pecker in his britches.

"A fortnight ago, one of our own was murdered. We aim to get answers." Liam continued. "Which of ya was here the night we speak of?"

The men all started talking at once; the women remained mute. Fernando didn't want this to be a wasted exercise. "Quiet!" he yelled, gaining control of the room. "Who was here the night of Hugh's demise?"

"Who da 'ell is 'ugh?" A man wearing worn brown trousers and a threadbare overcoat asked. He was missing several teeth, his blond hair unclean.

Fernando didn't answer, instead he turned to Liam. "Send the women to their rooms. There will be no services rendered this night."

There was more grumbling from the patrons, but that soon stopped when the men used as heavies began separating them–and *not* by order of importance. There was no rich or poor in this arena, there was only information and Fernando aimed to get it.

Five men stood holding guns on the group and they, like Liam, were well dressed. Two looked like Fernando's manservant and were obviously family. The other three were rough in appearance and the mayor did not doubt their ability to do violence. In the gentlemen's lounge, a gold couch sat facing the bar with the pillows blown out from apparent gunfire. Liam ordered the couch be left where it was as a visual to help matters along. Fernando walked over, seating himself to the right of the hole. The first man to protest was dragged from the throng of patrons and put through the paces; his blond hair plastered to his head from sweat.

"Had ya ever seen the slaves—what was here the night Hugh got done?" Liam asked, his tone conversational.

"I ain't never seen them runaways 'fore... never."

"How do you know they was runaways?" Liam asked.

"Ain't all niggers runaways?"

There was a cough to conceal laughter, causing Liam and Fernando to focus on the disgruntled customers. In the second row, stood a white man of average height with black hair and perceptive blue eyes. He was dressed in coarse brown trousers and a white shirt. Fernando thought him a dock worker, but his speech elevated him a station or two.

"Somfin humorous about this eve?" Liam asked.

"Forgive me, but all slaves don't see themselves as slaves." The man explained, then added, "My name is Mitchell Houser."

Fernando stood and rushed forward. "And what are you, Mr. Houser, a free thinker?"

"I beg your pardon, Mr. Mayor... a free thinker? No, just a thinker." Mitchell replied. "I was here that night and what I witnessed was frightening."

"Frightening?" Fernando echoed.

"They were organized, and it was alarming to behold. I had hoped that you would triumph in seceding New York City from the union; armed colored men cause my blood to run cold."

"Flattery, Mr. Houser, will not work." Fernando scoffed.

"How can you be flattered in a place this far beneath your station? Hire me and I will do your bidding. I will see to the running of the whores and leave you untainted to handle more pressing matters." Houser countered.

"What the 'ell..." Liam hissed.

Fernando held up his hand, muting Liam. "Mr. Houser, this way, we need to talk."

"Wait..." Liam called out.

"I will deal with Mr. Houser and you will complete our task." Fernando snapped as he walked off with Houser in tow.

As the mayor headed for the office, he heard his manservant yell. "All righty, boys, everyone of ya out back!"

3

October 1862
Fort Independence

EMMA STOOD IN the center of the cabin she now called home. It was a simple dwelling with a full-size bed in the corner of the one room. The quilt dressing the mattress was multicolored; still the dominant color was yellow, adding life to the dimness of the chamber. At the foot of the bed was a black trunk that kept her clothing dust free. A scarred wooden table rested to the right of the fireplace, with two matching chairs. Over the back of one chair hung a brown cloth. The table itself was crowded with an oil lamp, a white, chipped water basin and a black pitcher.

Just off the beaten path were five cabins separated by small patches of grass and a well-tended garden. Emma's home was situated between Molly's cabin and where Frank stayed with his woman, Carrie. Two of the rudimentary structures were unoccupied; tall trees lined the pathway behind the buildings offering a seclusion that Emma couldn't get right with. Being an orphan was lonely enough without the added issue of feeling closed off from everything. This truth made her ever thankful for Molly's kindness and friendship.

Each cabin was equipped with two windows, one in the front to the right of the door and one in the middle of the back wall. Emma's panes were covered by heavy, dark drapes to ward off the morning chill that came with Octobers in Canada. Early morning was her favorite time of day and though cold, she couldn't wait to stand on her makeshift porch to watch the sun ascend to the sky.

Wrapped in a spare quilt, Emma lumbered onto the porch; the wood beneath her feet creaked. She shivered, then smiled, while taking in the blends of pink, orange and blue. Dawn was lifting and Emma appreciated the bright promise of a new day. The cabin door to her right squeaked, then slammed with a thud as it did every morning. Turning, Emma found Molly standing on her porch, shaking from the cold.

"You ain't for early time. Why you up?" Emma asked.

"Tryna figure on why you likes this time a day." Molly countered.

"I don't wanna be missin' nothin'." Emma giggled.

Molly huffed out a laugh. "Ain't a thang back here but trees and some old log cabins."

"Ya say that every mornin'."

"It ain't changed nothin'. We still be out here the same as every mornin'." Molly said, then added, "I gots warm biscuits."

Emma didn't respond right away, instead she stepped down from her porch and made her way over to Molly's cabin. When she was closer, she muttered. "It don't pay to show folks yo' weakness."

Molly laughed as she turned leading the way into her home. The smell of biscuits and coffee danced around Emma's head. She loved food and she had been told on several occasions that it was a wonder she wasn't plumper. Emma would smile, but she never shared the fact that if not for Black, the children at the orphanage might have starved. Here at Fort Independence, the food appeared to be never ending.

"Have a seat and help yoself." Molly said, gesturing to one of the two chairs at the small table by the fireplace.

Molly kept a spotless home. There was a full-size bed with an orange covering; at the foot was a black chest that Emma was sure housed her clothing. In the left corner was a woodburning stove, which added to the coziness of the cabin. Directly in front of the stove was a large tin tub. Next to the fireplace was a wooden stand that held spices, an oil lamp and a smaller tub of soap water. Even in all its neatness, the cabin felt lived in.

The heavy drapes were drawn not to keep out the light, but the morning chill. Emma helped herself to eggs, a biscuit and a cup of warm milk. Between them burned two candles and she observed that Molly wasn't eating much.

"This ain't ya last, is it?" Emma asked, alarmed.

"No... no. Lou brangs me too much. I's happy to share."

"Why don't Lou live here wit' you? I thought you was his." Emma inquired, before realizing the question might be too forward.

Molly's smile disappeared, before she dropped her gaze. Apologetically, Emma rushed on. "I'm sorry... really. You gon have to make me mind my manners. I gets meddlesome at times. You can say I ain't wantin' to speak on it."

When Molly finally got the courage to look up once more, she appeared troubled. She was a brown skinned woman, and if Emma had to guess–a little younger than herself. Molly had large round eyes, a tiny nose and big lips. Around her left eye was a slight discoloration of the skin that appeared permanent. The same eye was also a tad smaller than the other. She wore her hair in two cornrows and Emma was impressed by her braiding skills; coming from an orphanage, she had braided a lot of hair. It was the older girl's job to keep the younger children neat in appearance.

"I don't find ya meddlesome." Molly answered, her voice soft–sincere. "Lou lives at the barracks. We... ahhh—"

"Anthony lives at the barracks." Emma stated. It was her attempt at letting Molly out of an uncomfortable exchange. "I ain't sure what to call us."

"I's sho on what to call you and Anthony. You's his—I sees it in his eyes." Molly said.

Emma had just eaten a spoonful of eggs and almost choked at the other woman's words. When she would have responded, the sound of booted feet on the porch caught her attention. There was a loud knock and then a deep voice.

"Molly, girl, it's me—Lou."

Hastily, Molly stood, smoothing her hands over the brown dress she wore. Emma giggled, causing her new friend to mock glare at her.

"Come on in, it's open." Molly called out, a shy smile on her face.

Lou pushed open the door, then looking back over his shoulder, he yelled. "Ant, yo woman is ova here wit' mine."

Both women chanced a glance at each other while trying not to laugh. Emma's heart started banging around in her chest at the sight of Anthony in the doorway behind Lou. His face was shaved, though his hair was thick and unkempt. They were both dressed in all black; Lou was shorter.

"Good morning, Miss Molly." Anthony said, then directing his words to Emma, he continued. "I come to walk ya to Black's house."

Emma found herself smoothing her dress and hair. She wore blue today and she did not look at Molly, who she was sure would have a smug expression on her face. Taking another mouth full of eggs, Emma headed to the door.

"Mawnin', Miss Emma." Lou drawled.

"Mornin'." Emma replied.

He stepped aside allowing her to exit; her quilt wrapped about her shoulders. When she turned back to wave at Molly, she witnessed Lou placing a kiss on her forehead. Embarrassed, Emma turned away allowing Anthony to help her down the two stairs. Behind her, Molly called out. "See ya later on."

Emma didn't answer; the presence of the men had her tied in

knots. She followed Anthony; his gait was leisurely. They moved off the path and into the thicket; the leaves were colorful, while some trees were bare, permitting sunlight to pour through the foliage. Underfoot the ground crunched with their steps and like every morning for weeks, Anthony said nothing. Their lack of verbal communication made Emma feel unwanted; still, he came every morning to escort her to Big Mama.

He took her a different way each day, as if familiarizing her with her new home. This morning they came upon a swimming hole and to Emma, the air felt cooler. She pulled the blanket tighter about her as she took in the beauty that surrounded her. Anthony hung back, as always, offering her time to think. She realized she would have to start the conversation in order to free him of his entanglement with her. Emma wanted him to know that she appreciated being saved from the Hen House, but he wasn't stuck with her.

The water shimmied on the breeze and lapped at the bank, while her breaths came with frost. There was still an awkwardness that lingered, and Emma was sure it was because of how they met. The clumsy coupling they shared was background noise that happened each time they came into contact. He had breached her physically, yet they were strangers. The intimacy of their first encounter had not eased the tightness of their dealings with one another. His silence when with her only added to her feelings of mortification. Sadly, she couldn't see what Molly saw in Anthony's eyes, because she couldn't hold his gaze.

After a time she walked back to where he stood, leaving the peace of the pond. He had been about to turn, heading for Black's house, when she took a deep breath and spoke. Anthony's eyes were intense as he stared at her, offering his undivided attention.

"I know ya feels like ya has to take care of me, but ya don't. I can figure on how to move forward from here. I sure 'preciate all ya done for me."

Anthony didn't respond right away; instead his eyes bounced

away from her to the pond and the thin mist dancing above the water. She was thankful that she wasn't his focal point, so she could study him. There was plenty of anxiety where Anthony was concerned. She often tried to reconcile the killer she met that fateful night with the quiet man she faced daily. Try as she might, Emma couldn't see the two men being one–but they were one in the same. She was deep in thought when his words penetrated her musings.

"I'm tryna give ya time to get used to me. I ain't finna keep on at the barracks. Better for you if ya use this time to understand that you is mine–anythang else is a waste."

The statement was delivered in such a matter of fact fashion, if Emma didn't know better, she would have thought him uninterested. Anthony didn't frown or show temper, it seemed he was offering sound advice. Everything about him seemed easygoing, but his eyes were a direct contrast. Emma looked away. She didn't know how to proceed.

"I… Anthony…"

"Come." He said, cutting off her attempt to take a stand. "Mama waitin' on us."

Bringing her gaze back up to his, she tried to find the words. Anthony must have sensed that she had more to say, because he shook his head as if forbidding her to speak. Nervous energy caused her to drop her gaze once more.

"Emma." Her name floated on the crisp air; his voice was husky–thick. "Look at me."

Anthony stood before her, arms crossed over his chest and feet spread apart. She had to work at not fidgeting while bearing the weight of his scrutiny. Emma was consumed by his maleness and her body's reaction to him. His stance relaxed as she gave over her attention, but a sharpness was now manifest in his next assertion.

"Ain't no other man for you."

Emma couldn't breathe nor could she reply. Abruptly, he turned walking back the way they had come; she followed. In her head she thought to tell him that he was not her master, but he seemed prepared to argue the point. She wasn't ready.

❀ ❀ ❀

Anthony lay flat on his back, arms folded behind his head staring at the ceiling. He occupied one of the many cots pushed neatly against the wall to the left of the great room. All the wooden bed frames were clad in a pea green blanket–pulled tight; it was military life. The sound of booted feet, Simon giving orders and the men laughing grated on his sleep deprived mind. Both the front and back doors were thrown wide, allowing the morning chill to take hold. He never noticed these annoyances before, but this day…

As the barracks bustled with activity, the men worked through a shift change. The feeling of wellbeing that came with life in the garrison disappeared with Luke. Normally, the noise of the men didn't keep him from sleep. Now, Anthony couldn't turn his head off. Rest had become unattainable and Emma's presence at the fort made him even more vigilant.

Swinging his legs over the side of the bed, Anthony strode from the barracks by way of the front door. He trekked through the trees and along the foot paths until he found himself at Emma's cabin. The modest weather-beaten structure needed repairs and he needed to quiet his anger. He assessed the place before backtracking to the shed by the chicken coop for tools. When he returned, he started with the loose floorboard on the top step.

Working with his hands aided him in organizing his thoughts. Anthony's mind went to his earlier interaction with Emma. He realized that he was leaving her too much time to think, and he had not offered the direction she needed; his quiet nature was being misconstrued. Emma thought him uninterested and nothing could be further from the truth. Other than their walks to and from Black's house, he left her to her own devices.

After the meeting with the men the morning that Emma had

tried to run off, Black spoke with him giving the smallest amount of guidance. Anthony could still see the exchange in his head. Black had moved behind his desk and taken a seat. Dressed for his name, he was every bit the leader of Fort Independence; still he looked tired.

"I think we have given Miss Emma the impression that she is not welcome." Black had said.

"She ain't finna leave me or the fort."

Chuckling, Black went on. "It seems our concerns about New York have caused her to blame herself. We have not done well with Miss Emma; pick a cabin, move her in. See to it that she understands you will keep her safe and the men on this land will help you."

He stared at Black for moments before he turned for the door. "I'll pick a cabin."

When his hand landed on the knob, Black added. "Lou's woman Molly is a sweet thing. I think she and Emma will get along nicely. There is an empty cabin next to Molly's. Big Mama and Iris can use help during the day."

Anthony only nodded before going to do Black's bidding.

"Shit." Anthony yelped when the hammer came down on his finger rather than the nail. The mishap yanked him abruptly from his reflections. He stood shaking out his fingers while wishing the pain away. Looking around, he found that he had been at it for hours; still, judging by the sun's position in the sky, he had time before picking up Emma. Surveying his handy work, he made a mental list of the fixes that needed doing before winter.

Testing the sturdiness of the new railing to the left of the door, Anthony placed both palms to the wood offering his weight. When it held, he gazed out toward the thicket. His thoughts traveled to Luke who had been the talkative one between the two of them. Together, they had gotten into plenty of mischief. It had always been Luke's quick tongue attempting to talk them out of trouble. He talked much in Luke's presence, but with the other men, he was a mere observer. Replaying his discussion with Black brought into focus his need to engage Emma.

Anthony cringed when yet another thought became clearer to him. Both Black and James thought him not up to the task of caring for a woman. James' words came to life in his head. *Ain't no one finna take the woman from ya. But think on this, ya took Emma and that was the easy part.* Anthony sighed; it seemed he would have to do more than escort her about. He would have to be her man. What James and Black did not say—*Give her to a man that could care for her if you ain't up for the job.* He would be damned if he allowed another man to have her.

❄ ❄ ❄

When Emma entered Black's home, she turned her thoughts from Anthony. She was shaken up by their daily contact, while he appeared unfazed. The routine helped her step away from the embarrassment of how she met him. Each time she looked into his eyes, she relived their naked encounter. And though she feared the fallout from the white man's death, she could muster no sorrow for his demise. Alice's blood was on Hugh Wood's hands. Emma was sure of it.

Refusing to replay Anthony's warning in her head, she went about her day. Emma didn't think she would enjoy her time at Black's house, but she did. Her two favorite pastimes were the babies and Big Mama's cooking. Everyone was kind and she seemed to blend well with the ladies. She worked closely with Big Mama and Iris to keep the place clean and orderly. While she hated dusting, the task gave her time to admire the magnificent paintings that adorned the walls. Emma had been amazed to find that colored folk lived in such luxury.

Miss Cora herded the older children with Emma helping to chase and keep up with them. Elbert Jr., Nattie and Little Otis could be a handful. She also assisted Sunday and Callie with the new babies. When her chores and baby tending were done for the day, she would venture into the kitchen. There she aided Big Mama and Iris in cooking for the household. She often tasted and nibbled so much that she couldn't sit down to a plate. The older women laughed as she fell into a chair patting her flat belly.

"Emma 'bout bad as the doctor. Both of 'em can eat." Mama said, shaking her head.

"Sure can." Iris agreed on a giggle.

Emma took no offense; she was only too happy to be where there was food in abundance. "Chicken and dumplings is now my favorite."

"Chile, ya said that yestaday 'bout the beef stew and cornbread." Mama replied.

"And I meant it." Emma said with sincerity.

She had been about to say more when from the hall leading to the kitchen came the voice of Dr. Shultz.

"Mama–Iris, is that chicken and dumplings I smell?"

Emma and Iris keeled over giggling, before Iris whispered. "He will eat wit' us, then go home and eat what Mary cooked. It's a wonder 'im not fot."

"Hush, you two." Mama said, shaking her finger at them.

Emma loved Iris' accent, and it served as a lesson that colored folk have a history beyond America. She had just managed to school her expression when Dr. Shultz stepped into the kitchen, dressed in all black, gun holstered to his left side. He pushed his glasses up his nose, then brushed brown hair away from his face. Upon noticing Emma, he grinned.

"Miss Emma, how are you this fine day?"

"I's wonderful, Doctor." She answered. When she would have turned her attention back to Iris, Anthony stepped into the kitchen behind Shultz.

"Anthony, how is ya, son?" Mama asked, greeting him with a smile.

"Good, Mama, ya lookin' well. Miss Iris, how is ya?" He responded.

"Well." Iris replied.

"Is ya hungry, son?" Mama asked.

Anthony's eyes fell to Emma as he replied to Big Mama. She couldn't breathe. "No, thank ya. I come to fetch Emma."

"I bet ya did." Iris mumbled and Anthony's gaze bounced to the older woman. His lips twitched, but he didn't smile.

When his gaze landed back on her, the weight of his scrutiny caused Emma to drop her eyes. But not before she noted that he had changed clothes and looked as though he had come from the bathhouse. He was now dressed in brown trousers, a tan shirt with the sleeves rolled up and black boots. Somehow, she knew he wouldn't be escorting her home and leaving her to her own devices. She hazarded another glance at him and in his dark eyes, she saw intent.

Time stood still, even as conversation continued around them. The air between them throbbed, and Emma was sure the others felt it too. She wanted to escape this moment, for it was too intimate. As she plotted her getaway, Anthony spoke only her name.

"Emma."

The one word offered direction and warning. Gathering her courage, Emma peered up at him only to find him reaching out a hand to her, palm up. The illusion here was that she had a choice, but he was without a doubt commanding her to come with him. She looked around for an excuse–for help from the older women. She thought to tell him she wasn't finished with her chores. What she found was Mama and Dr. Shultz discussing the ingredients used in this evening's meal. Looking to Iris, she hoped to find a friend, but a smirking Iris encouraged.

"You, young folks go on–me and Mama got it from here."

Iris was a brown skinned, thin woman with a head full of gray hair, braided in two fat plaits. She stood nearest to the table wearing a blue dress with a white apron tied about her waist. Her chestnut eyes were filled with mischief. Emma could think of nothing to say and unable to trust Iris, she nodded.

There was no way out. Emma didn't look at Anthony as she placed her smaller hand in his. When his work roughened fingers closed around hers, she felt a burst of energy zip through her middle. She inhaled a shaky breath just as he said to the room at large.

"Doc, Mama, Miss Iris–y'all have a good evenin'. Emma won't come tomorrow, we has plans."

"No worries, man." Iris replied.

"Sho' nuff." Mama answered, while never looking away from the doctor.

The natural light was fading; Paul, Iris' husband, who also cared for Black's home, began making his rounds to light the oil lamps and candles placed strategically about the house.

"Good evening, Anthony–Miss Emma." Dr. Shultz said as he stared over into the pot Big Mama was stirring.

Formalities out of the way, Anthony led her toward the front of the house. The hall leading to the porch was now lit by an oil lamp that flickered from a small polished table midway between the kitchen and the front door. As they stepped onto the porch and into the setting sunlight, Emma wondered if she had pushed him too far by trying to disengage from him. She tried to pause before allowing herself to be ushered down the stairs, but he gently, yet firmly, tugged her along.

As they began walking, Emma noted the men leaving the barracks, heading for their homes and families. Children played between the cabins, while the womenfolk pulled laundry from the lines and tended their vegetable gardens. Turning her mind from the agitation that lingered in the air around them, Emma waited until they were off the beaten path. Once away from prying eyes, she tried to pull her hand back from his. He would not let go.

She stopped moving, but her gaze never lifted to his face. On the ground were different colored leaves, evidence of autumn. The air was dry and crisp, the chill just bearable. She had forgotten her blanket; she had no coat. The best she could do was say her piece and head back to her cabin to warm up. Emma found her voice but not the strength to accompany her statement.

"I … ahhh think it's best if'n we go our separate ways, Anthony. Just causin' we… ahhh–I don't hold ya responsible for me. After all I was at the Hen House."

Emma sucked in another wobbly breath, thankful to have the words out. She realized he was still holding her hand; he hadn't spoken. A slicing wind blew and the leaves rustled, followed by an eerie silence. She chanced eye contact. His facial expression was intense, and she recognized the man who had purchased her for pleasure. In her head she could see the lit match that was his arousal fall to the dry earth igniting everything around them.

"I been inside ya, woman–another man won't trail me. You is mine." His voice was laced with threat and desire. "Is it Jake you's after?"

"What… no, I ain't after a husband. I's tryin' to see thangs as they are–is all."

The grueling travel in a too tight dress and boots distracted her from the complication of them. Meeting Black and experiencing Fort Independence further sidetracked her from the potency of him. But when the dust settled and her world began to calm, their first encounter played over and over in her head. It had been the carnality of his stare, the thickness of his voice and the heat of his skin against her own that confused her. As he had so nonchalantly stated, he had indeed breached her. Yet, the loss of her innocence had not removed her ignorance of menfolk.

At her confession that she didn't want Jake, Anthony's rigid posture eased. Emma took advantage of his receding tension and pulled free of his grasp. It suddenly felt as though the sun dropped from the sky unexpectedly leaving them in the dark and cold. Wrapping her arms about herself, she took a step back for clarity. Emma struggled to rid her senses of him, but to no avail. The sharp wind carried the scent of coarse soap with a hint of cinnamon. The murkiness of the evening did nothing to take away the imposing figure Anthony cut. And when he spoke, his words enflamed.

"I figured on givin' ya some time. But when ya speaks, ya seems further from the truth."

"Further... from the... ahhh truth." Emma repeated, hesitantly. Anthony strode forward with purpose and Emma retreated until she was backed into a tree.

"I see what I ain't see at before."

"Anthony..." she managed.

"You fixin' to be my wife–tonight."

"What?" Emma was confused.

"Come."

They started in the opposite direction of her cabin. His strides were long and offered no patience for her slighter steps. As they walked back through the heart of the fort, it was transformed by darkness and quiet. Anthony kept the pace until the barracks came into view. She noted men standing about, while several lanterns lit the space between them. The great door was pulled back to reveal organized activity. Emma had finally gathered her thoughts and was about to speak when a booming voice called out.

"Antney... somethin' wrong, son?"

"Philip, ain't nothin' wrong. I just needs the twins and please get my coat."

"Sho' thang." Philip replied, before disappearing down the aisle between the cots. The older man lived in the barracks and helped with the day to day operations.

Turning to Anthony, Emma hissed. "We cain't marry."

He didn't respond to her because Frank and Lou had joined them. It was Frank that spoke first. "Philip say ya needs us."

Lou handed Anthony a too large brown overcoat, then asked, "What chu' needin'?"

Taking the coat from Lou's hand, Anthony turned and wrapped the garment around her. Emma almost sighed at the relief it provided from the increasingly cold night air. She had been about to thank him when Anthony began talking to the twins.

"Emma and me is headin' to Herschel's cabin."

Lou barked out a laugh and Frank grinned. She could tell them apart; Frank had the scar and Lou had long locks, thick as a buffalo's mane. Emma was sure that without those physical markers, she wouldn't have been able to tell who was speaking. She wanted a moment alone with Anthony, but that no longer seemed possible. Allowing herself to be tugged along, the four of them moved down a path, cloaked by blackness. She couldn't see her hand before her face; then several cabins came into view and the flicker of candlelight from the windows confirmed life on the inside.

The small structures sat in a clearing, blanketed by the night sky. A full moon hung low and appeared as though it touched the treetops yet offered no visibility. Booted feet sounded on the creaking wood before a banging caused Emma to startle. The door swung wide and a stout, short white man moved into the entrance way. He looked disheveled, though the hour wasn't late.

"Gentlemen." The man greeted.

"Herschel, thank Anthony needs ya dis eve." Lou said, the mirth in his tone unmistakable.

"Come in… come in," the man invited.

Backing away from the door, Herschel waved them in. Frank entered in first, then Lou. Taking her hand, Anthony led her onto the makeshift porch and into the cabin. Herschel closed the door before turning to face the room at large. When his eyes landed on her, he smiled warmly.

"Dis here Emma." Anthony explained.

"Good evening, Miss Emma."

"Sir." She replied anxiously.

She tried to tunnel further into Anthony's coat to ignore the scene unfolding before her. Emma thought about Ms. Dowling, who would have been pleased. The older woman wanted a match for her; but did she need a husband now that she was at Fort Independence? Could she stay on indefinitely if she refused to heed Anthony's commands? All the men seemed to think she belonged to him, so if she wanted a husband it wouldn't happen while living here. In truth she wanted him, but his actions were high handed.

"Emma."

Anthony called her name, and she was so deep in her head that she jumped from the force of his voice. She had clearly missed pieces of the conversation happening around her. Refocusing on the room and the men, she noted that Herschel was standing by a small round table with two chairs. The twins stood in front of a green sofa and when she chanced a glance at Anthony, he was glaring down at her.

"Herschel ready to marry us." Anthony said, his voice tight.

"I ain't wantin' to marry."

Herschel coughed. Emma was sure the sound came from the older man since Frank and Lou wore neutral expressions on their faces. Lou looked away as if he disapproved of her declaration. When she looked up into Anthony's face, a muscle ticked in his jaw. Behind them, Herschel cleared his throat.

"Why don't you, young folks—"

"Emma here in a family way, so ain't no reason to wait on marryin'." Anthony said, his tone even. She gasped at his forwardness.

Herschel's eyes bounced back to her and his cheeks tinted. Emma could see his mortification even in the poor lighting. Oh how she wanted to kick Anthony. Meeting his stare, he arched a brow as if daring her to dispute his words. She could argue that she wasn't in a family way, but that was what he wanted. Anthony wanted it known that he had breached her–damn him.

"Yes... well, that said..." Herschel couldn't seem to finish a sentence.

Picking up the bible, Herschel came to stand in front of them. Anthony reached over, removed his overcoat from her shoulders and tossed it on the sofa. He took her hand, before turning them to face Herschel. Everything became hazy as the next words from the older white man's mouth described the rest of her life.

"Dearly Beloved, we are gathered here this evening to join this man and this woman..."

She heard Anthony say with confidence. "I do."

When Herschel would have addressed her, Emma turned to Anthony panicked. "Wait, what's yo' full name?"

"I's just Anthony." He said with a shrug, then countered. "What's yo' full name?"

"I ain't never had but one name... I been *Emma* my whole life."

Anthony nodded, then instructed. "Give her my name."

"Do you, Emma, take Anthony to be your..." Herschel continued.

"I does." She answered shyly–nervously.

"I now pronounce you, Mr. and Mrs. Anthony."

Before Emma could react, Anthony leaned down and kissed her chastely on the lips. She heard Lou and Frank clapping. The old man chuckled, then moved in to slap Anthony on the back. She was still turning her new name in her head, *Emma Anthony*, when her husband pulled the overcoat around her shoulders once again.

"Thank ya, Herschel." She heard Anthony saying as he maneuvered them toward the door.

Once outside, he began walking away from Frank and Lou. Pulling her along, Anthony shouted over his shoulder. "I needs both of ya in the mornin–I has to go to town!"

"Sho thang." Emma heard one of the twins respond, but in the dark their voices were the same.

She almost had to run to keep pace with Anthony. When they came to her cabin, instead of leaving her at the front stairs as he'd always done, he continued inside. Emma stood by the door listening as he fumbled around in the blackness. Suddenly, the hiss of a matchstick and then the lighting of three candles and an oil lamp brought the one room to life. He didn't spare her a glance as he moved on to the task of building a fire. In the weeks that passed, when he escorted her home each evening, these chores were already done. Never once had she walked into a cold or dark cabin.

Anthony gave her his undivided attention when he finished tending the fire. Emma couldn't bring herself to step away from the door. A nervous feeling plagued her, and her hands trembled as she held tight to the coat wrapped about her. She maintained eye contact, trying to read his facial expression. There was nothing left but to give him her truest thoughts.

"Ya shamed me into this marriage." She whispered.

"Shamed?" The incredulity apparent in his voice.

"Ya told that white man I was a soiled woman."

His eyebrows were pressed together; Anthony was pensive. When he spoke his words were candid. "I ain't never touched nothin as sweet as you. Any man can see yous far from soiled."

He took her breath away; still she hadn't ventured any further into the cabin. Emma was unable to articulate her emotions.

"I cain't figure on what comes next," she murmured.

"Next is you gettin' used to me being here."

She anticipated as much. Dropping her gaze, she tried to collect herself.

"Come sit, Emma."

The sound of her name on his lips caused her head to pop up. Anthony had removed a chair from the table and placed it before the fire.

"Woman…" His voice thick–gruff. "Come talk to me. Please."

Gracelessly, she stepped away from the door, seating herself by the fire. He joined her, moving the second chair from the table. As he sat, Anthony reached down and grabbed the leg of her chair, pulling her to face him.

"I ain't fo' sho." He said, his demeanor casual. "But I thinks I's about twenty-five summers."

"Ya just might be younger den me." She said on a giggle.

"Naw. I could tell when I crossed outta bein' a boy."

And just like that—she was back to feeling shy. Emma didn't look away, there was no sense in trying to hide. He had her chair pulled snuggly between his thighs.

"I come from a plantation in Georgia. When I was a youngin', Black brought me here; been here ever since."

The warmth of the fire relaxed her. "I ain't sure where I's from. The orphanage been my onlyist home."

In all their interactions, Anthony never appeared uncomfortable. Suddenly, he began rubbing at the back of his neck and dropped his eyes. It was a move she had done many times with him, so she recognized his discomfort. She couldn't bring herself to inquire on what was troubling him. Emma was certain if it made him uneasy, the matter would do the same for her. Moments passed while he gathered himself.

"That night… at the Hen House. I was a brute."

"I ain't blamin' you. I was at the Hen House after all."

Anthony finally pinned her with his stare before he went on. "I handled ya rough. I's sorry for that."

The shyness she felt was unnerving. Still she held his gaze when she admitted, "I ain't never wished another harm, but the man ya shot…"

"How you come to be at such a place?" he asked.

"I's too old for the orphanage. They was wantin' me to become an indentured servant. Me and Alice answered an ad what said they's lookin' for a governess. We had an audience wit' Mr. Wood and he brang us to the whorehouse. Neither of us was wantin' that kind a work."

"Alice?"

"She was like a sista to me. We growed up together at the orphanage. Alice refused to take a patron to her bed. They come and dragged her from our room one day. I's told by one of the women that to survive I needed to accept male companionship. I never seen Alice again."

"So they killed yo' sista." Anthony stated, his reply blunt.

Emma sighed, then shook her head as if to clear it. His candor struck her hard. She had surmised as much, but she had been unable to verbalize the thought. Alice meeting with a violent end because of their naivety gave Emma the faints.

She was thankful for his change of subject until she focused on what he said. "Come let me help ya undress."

"Undress?"

"Ya needs rest, been a long day." He countered.

"You leavin' for the barracks?"

Anthony cocked his head to one side and studied her for long seconds. Patiently, he said. "No."

Emma looked around the one room alarmed, "Can we snuff out the candles and lamp?"

"No."

Anthony decided that he wouldn't allow them to dawdle in awkward silence. Leaning over, he lifted one of her feet and removed her boot before dropping it with a clunk to the planked floor. Doing the same with her other boot, he stood, pulling her to her stockinged feet. His big fingers were clumsy as he maneuvered the small buttons of her bodice. When the fabric loosened, he pushed the dress from her shoulders until it puddled at her feet.

He took in the lovely sight of her standing before him in a white shift with thick gray socks covering her toes. Emma wore her hair in two cornrows with a decorative comb holding the ends in place. The orange, red and gold hues of the firelight seemed only to enhance her beauty. She clenched her plump bottom lip between her teeth as she stared up at him; her dark skin and eyes called to him, yet he understood that tonight he could not be the man from the whorehouse.

Stepping back from her, he removed his boots, shirt and trousers. He wore long tan underwear and no undershirt. Once they were disrobed as far as he dared to push, Anthony snuffed out the candles and oil lamp. Taking his sweet wife by the hand, he led her to the bed. Pulling back the quilt, he permitted her to climb in first. Emma paused for seconds, then scrambled in pressing herself against the wall. As the bed creaked under his weight, he settled in and faced her.

"Imma take ya into town in the mornin'." Anthony said, his causal tone returning.

"Town... oh."

"I needs to pick up a few thangs." He explained. "I has an errand to run for Black."

"I would love to see the town."

Anthony narrowed his eyes. "Dis here yo' home—you gets that right?"

His wife stared at him offering no response for a time before asking, "Did we marry causin ya feels stuck wit' me? I ain't in a family way."

"We married cause ain't nothin' sweeter than you. We married cause you was wastin' time tryna be free of me. We married to keep me from killin' Jake." He countered.

Emma gasped and he laughed out loud; he was coming to recognize when she was overwhelmed. His hilarity turned to an involuntary groan when he pulled her into a hug. She began panting at the contact. The press of her smaller frame against his own made him painfully aware of when she stopped breathing. He rubbed her back in small circles, trying to soothe her.

"Emma?"

"Hmmm?"

"Breathe, darlin'." He said, his humor returning.

When she began relaxing into his touch, his dick perked up–unbidden. It was the material of her shift; the softness of her curvy body and the bursts of breaths emitting from her that aroused. Anthony did not try to hide his erection. It was the natural order of things between a man and woman–husband and wife. If he were being truthful, he loved when she gasped in surprise. The sound made him want to try wringing cries of pleasure from her.

"I ain't never slept wit' anyone." She whispered.

Anthony wanted to continue engaging her but concluded it would be better for all involved if he pushed her to rest. "Go on to sleep, Emma, tomorrow gon be a long day."

Emma quieted and quit fidgeting. She eased right into sleep, while he lay awake staring into the fire. Luke popped into his head and Anthony wondered how long it would be before he could think about his best friend without pain. Snuggling closer, his wife must have sensed his hurt. He felt the tension drain from his body at the nearness of her. Closing his eyes, he decided to try for sleep; after all, he hadn't rested in days. It was his last coherent thought.

Anthony was startled awake by a banging on the cabin door. When he could get his bearings, he felt Emma trembling in his arms.

"Ant... it's me, Lou!"

"Gimme a minute!" Anthony hollered back. Looking to the window, he saw that dawn was happening. Addressing his wife, he explained. "Imma handle some thangs and come back for ya."

Emma nodded.

Climbing from the warmth of the bed, Anthony dressed quickly. He stoked the fire, lit the oil lamp, then rushed outside. "You's late." Lou accused.

"I plan on takin' Emma to town–thought ya might brang Molly." Anthony informed and suggested, ignoring the other man's crankiness.

It was damn cold, he thought as he pulled on his coat. Lou's eyebrows popped at the mention of taking his woman from the fort. Anthony was aware that Lou never took Molly outside the gates. Still, he pressed the matter because he thought it might be good for both women. Lou, however, didn't see it the same.

"Me and Frank got yo' back, but…"

Before Anthony could work on changing Lou's mind, Frank walked up. While he hated manipulating Lou, he wasn't above it. "I's tryna get Lou to brang Molly into town wit' Emma and me, but he ain't willin'."

Lou was the youngest and the meanest of the twins, but he could refuse Frank nothing. Being with the brothers made Anthony ache for Luke. He could feel their attachment. Carrie had given Frank a son this past May, but it was as if she had given both men a child. Lou couldn't get enough of little Frank. He stopped by daily to smile at his nephew.

"Thought ya said we was gon take Molly to town." Frank said turning to his brother.

"I don't recollect agreein' on takin' Molly from here." Lou refuted before glaring at Anthony.

"Ya cain't keep on livin' at the barracks and visitin' ya woman ever'day. It's time, Lou." Frank said.

"Shit." Lou mumbled.

Anthony watched as Lou abruptly stalked off toward the cabin Molly occupied. He called out after him. "Imma change clothes, den see Black–be back in 'bout a hour."

Lou stood on the makeshift porch next door to Emma's cabin scowling. Behind him, Anthony heard Frank whisper, "Go on now–fore I has to fight wit' 'im."

Taking the older twin's advice, Anthony rushed off for the bathhouse. He needed to get this day started. Tidying up, he didn't bathe, the chill of the morning was a major deterrent. Once he changed clothes, Anthony headed to Black's house. As he strode up the path from the barracks, he could see Black, Elbert and James standing on the porch. When he reached the bottom of the stairs, Elbert was the one to break the silence.

"I hear ya married last night."

"Hear the twins stood for ya." James added, his voice tight.

Black didn't comment, though he frowned. If Anthony didn't know better, he would swear they were disappointed. "I ain't plan on marryin', but Emma…"

"We woulda stood for ya." Elbert replied, his tone grumpy.

Anthony was at a loss, he looked to Black for help. Black smirked. "I been dealing with this all morning and it's all your fault, Ant. Ever since these two had a child together, they been hens."

James glowered at Black. "You's a fine one to talk–bellyaching that Ant been wit' you since he was a youngin'."

Anthony's eyes bounced back to Black, who shrugged sheepishly. He would have laughed if the three hadn't appeared wounded. The brothers were a menacing sight to behold as they stood about in the morning sun–dressed in all black, guns holstered at their sides.

Sighing, Anthony tried for diplomacy. "I come to you all cause I needs help."

Black's and James' glares lessened. Elbert, however, looked meaner. Anthony cleared his throat, then tried not to sound as nervous as he felt. "Black… I needs to collect on my pay. Emma ain't gotta coat or warm boots for the comin' cold. Elbert, I was hopin' you would ask Anna to make Emma some dresses. Imma get the material today. James–me and the twins is takin' Molly and Emma to town, thought ya might come wit' us for back up."

All three men nodded, and Anthony realized the brothers had been worried for him. Black was the one to break the ice. "Come to my study."

"Imma get a carriage ready for the women." James chimed in.

"I could ride out wit' you all." Elbert added. "We can talk wit' my Anna when we get back."

As Anthony climbed the steps, James and Elbert moved down the stairs and onto the path. Following Black into the house, he could hear Mama, Iris and Cora before they reached the kitchen. The older women looked up from their cups; at the sight of he and Black, they smiled.

"Guess ya meant bidness when ya said you and Emma was busy." Iris said.

"Shol did." Mama agreed.

Miss Cora giggled, and Black continued on to his study. Once inside, Anthony shut the door and waited until Black removed a gray strong box from behind the large painting of Big Mama. Placing the metal container on the desk, he watched as Black began thumbing through a leather-bound ledger.

"How much are you needing?" Black asked.

"What I got?"

"You have in total seventy dollars." Black answered.

"Seventy dollars? That ain't right."

"Seventy is correct." Black confirmed. "Luke had thirty-five dollars as well. I'm sure he would want you to have it."

"Oh." Anthony countered, weakly. "Forgot 'bout Luke's coins."

He broke eye contact with Black and walked over to the window. The fort was coming alive and from the glass pane, Anthony could see the children running about. He heard the school bell and saw the men heading for work in the fields. Surveying the lay of the fort made his chest tight.

"Livin' here made me feel like ain't no harm could come to us."

"The safety of Fort Independence is only as good as the men who live here." Black explained.

"I wants never to think 'bout failin' Luke."

"Did you really fail him?" Black asked.

"Do ya feel like ya failed Otis?"

Unable to speak about the death of his brother, Black changed the subject. "Marrying Emma was best for the fort."

Anthony turned to stare at Black. "Jake?"

"We don't need division between the men. It's better when the lines are clear, so a man knows what boundaries not to cross."

Anthony nodded, then added. "Jake ain't the onlyist reason–I got New York to face."

"We all have New York to face."

There was no anger in Black's tone, and it made Anthony feel worse. "I brought shit home wit' me, feels like I failed twice."

"You ain't alone." Black offered.

"I's terrified for the womenfolk and children. I needs to get Emma set up 'fore I has to leave."

Black was about to speak when there came a knock on the door. "Enter." He called out.

The door opened and Little Otis rushed in followed by Nattie.

"Uncle!" Otis yelled as he ran to Black.

Nattie bellowed. "My daddy!"

Fast on their heels was Sunday pushing a blue carriage that almost didn't fit through the study door. Ben-Ben and Daniel were wide eyed as they watched the older children run to the corner for the blocks and carved farm animals. Sunday wore a green dress and her hair was cornrowed in two fat braids. She smiled when she noticed Anthony.

"Ant, how ya been? Nat tells me ya married last eve."

"Sunday, I's good... Me and Emma... yeah, we married." Anthony answered.

"Nat wanted to stand up for ya. He been grumpy dis mawnin'." She said staring at Black.

Black cleared his throat and Sunday continued. "I means to say James and Elbert was grumpy, not Nat."

Anthony couldn't help it, he laughed and so did Sunday. Black ignored them and plucked his sons from the carriage before seating himself on the couch. It was Anthony's cue to take his leave.

"Black, Imma check the dry-goods store for messages while in town."

"Good." Black replied and he was all business again.

"Imma take twenty dollars…" Anthony said. "Ain't no need for more."

He had been about to leave when Black asked. "How did you get Lou to agree to take Molly out?"

Anthony shook his head. "Frank."

Black nodded and Anthony bid the family good day. When he arrived back at the cabins, James was there with a carriage. Elbert and Frank were already on horseback. He was about to ask after Lou, when Frank pointed to the cabin with his chin. Suddenly, Molly's door swung open and Lou stepped out first, looking anxious. Molly wore a brown dress and overcoat with black boots.

"Miss Molly." All the men said in unison.

Anthony wanting to avoid Lou's discomfort stepped onto his own porch and pushed at the door. "Emma, is you ready?"

His new wife was wearing a brown serviceable dress like Molly's. Anthony was thankful the chill had eased. Upon seeing him, Emma headed for a smaller brown coat dangling from the peg to the left of the door frame. He frowned as she explained.

"Molly loaned me one of her overcoats."

It was the small acts of kindness that made him proud to live at the fort. Anthony was moved. "Come, the men is waitin' on us."

❄ ❄ ❄

The carriage ride was glorious as far as Emma was concerned. Molly, who started out nervous and quiet, was enjoying herself immensely if her smile was any indication. Once they reached the small town and the store called "Everything," the day became sensation overload. The inventory boasted of stoves, bathtubs and clothing. There were even perfumes, soaps and flowers. Emma did so much sniffing of the lady products that her sense of smell stopped working. The establishment also offered sweets and she and Molly surely ate too many peppermints.

Anthony and Lou stayed nearby but managed not to intrude while she and Molly explored. Outside, Elbert, James and Frank stood guard. All the men, Emma noted, were different now that they were away from the fort. In truth, she could feel the hazard radiating from them. Emma would have feared them if she weren't with them.

"Do ya likes the rose water, Emma?" Molly asked.

"I do."

"I believes it would make the cabin smell nice if'n ya bathe wit' it." Molly said dreamily.

"I believes so too."

Emma turned to say something to Anthony, but he had wandered down another aisle. He was speaking with a man Lou had addressed by the name, Virgil. It appeared the white gentlemen was the proprietor of "Everything." Emma heard them mention Black, but their conversation was muffled at such a distance. She had been about to turn away when she noticed Anthony pointing at her.

"Emma." He called out, then waved her forward.

Molly reached for her hand, walking with her over to the men. Anthony made the introductions. "Virgil, dis here is my Emma."

"Good day to you, Miss Emma."

"Yes, sir, good day to you."

Lou never introduced Molly and Emma could feel her trembling as they held hands. The man called Virgil allowed his gaze to touch Molly briefly, but he offered nothing verbal. The day was so bright that the sunlight spilling through the storefront gave Emma the opportunity to really see Lou. He was shorter than Anthony but still a sizable–formidable man. Lou was dressed in brown trousers and a tan overcoat. His skin was the blackest, his eyes a deep brown. The thick locks on his head were tied back by one of Molly's red hair ribbons. He had a tiny patch of chin hair on his otherwise clean-shaven jaw. Emma was sure that though she had not witnessed such, Lou was dangerous. When he addressed Molly, Emma felt it too.

"Molly, girl–come." His tone rough–rusty.

Dropping her hand, Molly moved to grasp his fingers and Lou walked her down another aisle away from where Emma stood with Anthony and Virgil. Sucking in a hasty breath, Emma was sure of one thing–Lou bites. She almost giggled at the notion. Anthony pulled her from her thoughts.

"Emma." He said, holding out a hand.

"This way." Virgil directed.

Once in the small office at the back of the store, Virgil showed Anthony several rings. Emma was shocked when Anthony offered. "Pick one."

Filled with delight, Emma decided on a plain silver band; her husband paid two dollars and she almost cried. Molly *ohhhed* and *ahhhed* over the ring, and while they chatted, Virgil, Lou and Anthony talked business. Emma saw both men give the proprietor money before she and Molly were escorted from the store. Their next stop was the dressmaker; each woman picked several different materials for the purpose of making dresses and underclothes. The men stood outside and spoke among themselves.

The wonder of the day was winding down. Anthony had gone to the bakery and dry-goods store while Lou led them toward the horses. James had just rolled up with the carriage when a group of women burst from O'Reilly's eatery. They were laughing and giggling; the women were without male protection. Their clothing was gaudy, and their faces were painted; they were stunning.

A petite doll of a woman appeared on the boardwalk wearing a red dress with a matching hat. She was light of skin and her slanted brown eyes were fixed on Lou. The strumpet called to him and because Emma had her elbow linked with Molly's, she felt her friend stiffen.

"Lou…" the strumpet purred invitingly–throatily. "I been missin' ya all week. Is ya comin' *again* on Saturday?"

Emma had spent enough time at the Hen House to know that

the woman called Lou out on purpose. She was attempting to sow discord. Lou never looked at Molly; his face was impassive when he addressed the painted beauty.

"Miss Katie… how is ya?"

"I's missin' you, lover. I hopes to see ya again… You know I'll turn the others away for ya–like I done week-fo'-last."

Lou never answered her question, instead he smiled. Frank appeared on the walkway next to his brother. "Ladies, ain't y'all better make it on home? It's finna be dark."

The women simpered and laughed while conversing with Frank. Emma realized that Frank was creating a distraction. Lou took advantage, ushering them to the carriage. James set the steps and once they were safely ensconced in the cab, Molly began to sniffle. After about twenty minutes, the carriage lurched forward, signaling the long trek home. Once they were rolling good, Emma moved to sit next to Molly. They hugged all the way back to the fort while Molly wept softly.

It was dark when the gates finally closed behind the group. James took them straight home. Before the carriage door could be pulled open, Molly gathered herself. Only Frank and James were present. Peering up at their cabins, Emma could see the candlelight flickering from the windows.

Frank walked Molly to her door, while James helped Emma. "Where is my husband?"

James pushed at the door; the firelight casting his features in eerie shadows. His tone was strained when he replied. "A package come for Black, Ant went to handle some thangs."

Emma nodded. "Thank you."

Shutting the door behind her, she listened as the carriage pulled onto the path. She wanted to go next door, but Molly hadn't spoken on the ride back. Emma thought it best to give her new friend some space. She had been hungry, but the day ended all wrong and her appetite was lost.

4

Reality
Fort Independence

BLACK STOOD AT the front of his study staring at the men. E.J., Jeremiah, Frank, Lou and Anthony were present. Brown packaging lay open on the desk, revealing yet another copy of the World newspaper. The headline proclaiming: **Patrons of the Infamous Hen House Found Dead on Blackwell Island**

"Gentlemen, we will meet at the barracks–early morning." Black said, his eyes bouncing from man to man.

"Imma go round and let the men know." Anthony volunteered. Jeremiah spoke up. "I'll help."

Black noted that Lou seemed preoccupied and Frank was fidgeting. He had been about to end the discussion when Tim, Elbert, James and Simon walked in. James asked the question that Black hadn't wanted to touch.

"Did a missive come wit' the package?"

Anthony rocked back on his heels as if punched. Black took control of the gathering. "We are done here for the night. The morning will be soon enough to examine the issues that plague us."

"Time?" Elbert asked.

"After the shift change and things settle at the barracks." Black replied.

E.J. turned and started for the door. "I'll help Anthony and Jeremiah spread the word."

Black watched as all the men began filing out behind E.J. except two. When the study fell silent only Jeremiah and Lou remained. Black already knew what Jeremiah wanted, but he couldn't guess Lou's concern. The black cracker glanced over his shoulder at Lou, then shrugged.

"The meetin' being early means I should leave Callie here overnight."

He looked for it, but Black saw no resentment from Jeremiah about the amount of time Callie spent with Sunday and his children. In fact, she constantly helped with all the children. Much of her time was spent with his three children, Jeremiah's son Otis and Miah, the daughter she shared with the black cracker. Black also noted that Callie still avoided and did not like him. It seemed she had not forgotten or forgiven the fact that he and his brothers tried to kill Jeremiah; yet the adoration she felt for his wife and babies was visible.

Black nodded at Jeremiah's words. In truth, he spent much of his time in his studio, painting. His sons were young and often needed to nurse in the late of night or early morning. Nowadays, Callie slept in his bed with Sunday more than he did. His chamber had been turned into a nursery and the very thought caused Black to chuckle.

Jeremiah furrowed his brows, causing Black to explain. "Sunday and Callie are in charge... speaking to me does nothing for you."

Jeremiah grinned, and Black realized that he was making small talk because of Callie. The black cracker was checking the temperature in the household where his woman spent most of her days. Once he understood the purpose of the discussion, Black was better equipped to participate.

"I'm thankful the women have worked out the needs of my

sons. Callie avoids me, but I have nothing but gratitude for her. I try not to bother her." Black said.

It was Jeremiah's turn to laugh, and Black saw that he had relaxed. "I will go and help Anthony then."

"Yeah." Black said, and then Jeremiah was gone.

The door closed with a soft click. "Lou, what troubles you?"

"I cain't make the meetin' in the mawnin'. Whateva you decides, I has yo' back. Molly is mad wit' me…"

Folding his arms over his chest, Black stared at Lou. "I understand. Frank and Anthony will keep you informed."

Lou nodded and was about to leave when Black asked, "Why is sweet Molly upset with you?"

"The womens from the pussy parlor was out and about while we was in town. Miss Katie asked if'n I was gon come back so'n we can have some mo' fun." Lou answered, his voice tight.

"Oh…"

"I loves Molly." Lou countered. "Frank say when he took her home, she been cryin' a bunch…shit."

"Where you headed?" Black asked.

"Barracks… tryna get my nerves up."

Black smiled. "If you go to the barracks first, you'll find reasons to continue avoiding her. She'll think ya don't want her. Go to Molly and get it over."

Lou was staring at his feet; his head popped up at Black's words. He nodded, sighed, then exited the study. Alone, Black was deciding on whether to read the missive that had indeed come in the brown packaging. As he flipped the thought over in his head, there came a knock at the door. Knowing who it would be, Black crossed the study and pulled the door open. Callie stood with her fist poised to knock again.

The caramel skinned woman before him was nervous. Callie's large eyes dropped to the floor as she mumbled, "Sunday is waiting for you. I will return later to help feed the boys."

She wore a blue dress with a button-down bodice; her hair was pulled back in a big puff. Black could see that Callie wanted to get away, but he had other plans.

"Good evening, Miss Callie."

"Same to you, Mister Black."

"So we still aren't friends." He stated.

"No."

Black couldn't help it, he laughed at her curt response. Her voice was deadpan when she asked, "Have I said something amusing?"

There was no need for him to take offense, Callie still didn't speak to E.J. either. Black reeled himself in, then posed his question. "Why can we not be friends after all this time?"

"You know why."

Black did know why, and it was interesting that she understood that about him. "You still believe I would kill Jeremiah if you give the slightest impression of contentment."

Callie didn't respond to his statement, so Black continued. "Jeremiah is alive because of who he is as a man—not because your skirts are wide enough to hide him from me."

Her eyes widened with unshed tears, and Black cursed himself for upsetting her. Callie whispered. "I cannot be without him."

"The goal here was not to upset you."

"I know the aim of this discussion." She said.

"What is my intention here?"

"You would have me unburdened by a matter only Jeremiah can control."

Callie's intelligence was large. Black added. "I appreciate your help with my sons. You have been a great friend to my wife."

"I don't nurse your sons for Sunday... although I love her. I take your sons to my breasts because you brought me to freedom, because you gave me a safe place to birth my child, because you didn't let James kill the man I love. I care for your family because of you; still the idea of you is too big—you scare me."

Anthony: Unshackled | 65

Black hadn't expected that. "You don't owe me anything."

"I owe you everything." She whispered. "I'm just thankful you expect nothing because I could never repay you."

They stood in silence for moments, with Black at a loss for words. Callie stepped back, then spoke. "Sunday is waiting. I'll be in a room upstairs, send for me when the boys have need for me."

Callie left him standing in the middle of his study well after she had gone. Black finally collected himself, then went to his wife and children.

❈ ❈ ❈

The night air was icy, and his every breath was cutting, but Lou was mentally numb to the elements. His boots crunched against the dry earth as he traveled the scenic route delaying the inescapable. Reaching the clearing, he cowardly turned in the direction of his brother's cabin. Stepping up on the porch, Lou didn't knock; instead, he waited for Frank to come to him.

When the cabin door swung wide, it was Carrie who stood just beyond the threshold smiling at him. "Lou, come on in from the cold."

He had been about to refuse, about to fall back on the impropriety of the hour, but his brother called out to him. "Come rest yo' bones, man."

Carrie moved back from the doorway and Lou stepped into his brother's life. The cabin was warm and smelled of freshly baked bread. Frank sat in a rocking chair by the crackling fire, cradling his son in his arms. Lou approached taking the rocker next to his brother. The men didn't speak, but Lou got the message Frank was sending.

At the table, Carrie sat sewing baby clothes. She was a dark, brown skinned woman with a slender frame; she was much like his Molly. Carrie wore her hair plaited and her small eyes were always sincere–she was right for his brother.

"Lou, could I fix ya somethin' to eat?" She asked, her voice soft. "We has fresh bread and stew."

"No thank ya, Carrie." He countered. "I done ate."

He hadn't eaten, but the thought of food turned his stomach. All he could think of was Molly's pain–the pain he caused. While he was deep in his head, Frank stood.

"Gimme yo coat."

Lou shrugged out of his overcoat and Frank gestured toward the chair he had just vacated. Laying his coat on the rocker, Frank promptly pressed his sleeping son into Lou's arms. His brother walked away and began speaking with Carrie.

"Imma brang in some water."

Carrie nodded and Frank went about his evening chores; Lou sat before the fire rocking the sweetest baby ever born. Junior was a black skinned baby with hair on top of his head and none in the back. The boy looked just like his brother and him; Lou was moved.

Frank made several trips outside for water and firewood. When the door slammed on Frank's latest exit, the baby started to fret. Carrie came to help, and Lou was thankful.

"Time for 'im to eat." She whispered, then disappeared into the back.

Frank's cabin was bigger than most. In the front room was a worn, brown, wooden table with two mismatched chairs. The rockers by the fireplace were new and gifts from Lou to Frank and Carrie. In the corner was a large black wood burning stove with a huge pot of water that was constantly boiling. It aided in moistening the air and keeping the cabin comfortable. At the back of the cabin was an extra wall meant to divide a small bedroom for Frank and Carrie. Lou knew Frank added the wall to give Carrie privacy and make room for him. He loved his damn brother.

Lou shrugged back into his coat and met Frank just as he was bringing more firewood onto the porch. "Junior woke up on ya and got to fretting?"

"Yeah." Lou admitted on a chuckle.

Frank immediately changed the vein of the conversation. "You ain't finna head back to the barracks–is ya?"

"How I'm 'pose to explain the pussy parlor to her... shit."

"Ya has to move past the misuse she suffered. Both of ya has to try." Frank replied, his concern evident. "Ya cain't keep on visitin' ya own home. Molly needs somethin' else to liken against the mishandlin' she endured."

Lou nodded before stepping off the porch headed for Molly's cabin. Frank stood on his own porch and waited until he banged on the door. After a time, the cabin door slowly inched open to reveal a sad faced Molly. Candlelight shimmered in the background as she stepped back to allow him inside. He didn't look back at his brother before entering.

"Lou..." Molly said softly. "Is ya hungry?"

"I needs to speak wit' ya."

He pushed the door shut behind him, but they hadn't moved into the warmth of the cabin. What surprised him was that she didn't look away; meeting his gaze head on, she nodded. He noted that her spine stiffened at his request to talk.

Turning, she moved to stand by the table. Placing her hands on the back of one of the two chairs, Molly waited for him to speak. It struck him that she appeared faint and he directed her to sit. When she was settled, he allowed the silence to linger a bit while he cleared his head. Molly spoke first and her voice was thick with tears.

"I ain't needin' to hear what you do when ya ain't wit' me."

"I wants to be here wit' you–I ain't think you was ready." Lou replied, his tone gruff.

"You needs to find another to call on."

"Molly, girl... please."

Lou could tell the moment she disengaged from the conversation–from him. He supposed it was how she survived the misuse she suffered. But here in this setting, he couldn't allow her to look through him.

"I ain't judgin'–I just think it best. I understand Frank lives nearby. I can find another cabin."

Molly pushed back from the table, stood, then started for the door as if to dismiss him. Lou panicked and dashed around the furniture to grab her roughly by the arm. Spinning her away from the door, he shoved her against the wall near the neatly made bed. He was sure she was frightened, but he too was terrified; he feared losing her.

"Lou." She panted, her voice wobbly. "Ya scaring me."

"Molly–girl, you has me 'fraid, too." He choked out. Against her ear he added. "I loves you… only you."

"I ain't sho' I can give ya what ya needin'. And you ain't sho' neither, else ya wouldn't be seekin' comfort from… Miss Katie."

Lou felt it when she heaved in a breath and began to weep in earnest. Softly, he continued explaining himself. "I ain't know how to ask for comfort from you after all ya been through. Molly–please, I wants whateva you can give."

"That cain't be true." She answered as she buried her face in his shirt.

"Comfort and love–it ain't the same."

"I been givin' it thought long before now–took me a long time to heal up inside. Carrie give Frank a son. I ain't sho' I could give you children."

Lou thought back on the scene at the dry-goods store in Washington, where they'd found Molly and a white woman, naked and shackled in the back room. They killed the man who held them hostage. Still, Shultz made it clear that Molly had suffered much. The days after he made it back to the fort, Lou had been beside himself with worry for his brother and Molly. In the months that followed, he had assisted with her care–bathing, dressing and help-ing her to walk. One morning, weeks after he'd brought her to the older women, he overheard Big Mama telling Iris that she didn't think Molly would ever bear children.

"I has Frank for that–my brother will gimme chilren."

"Lou…"

"I ain't wanna push you–I tried to take care of my own needs witout troubling you. We here now and cain't go back."

She kept her face hidden from him. "I ain't never found comfort in coupling."

Lou didn't know whether to ask questions that were sure to upset him or demand that she understand that she belonged to him. While he was figuring on the best she asked.

"How often you goes to see this woman?"

He wondered if she was asking how often he was going to want to couple with her or how often he went behind her back to the pussy parlor. Shit–he suspected a little of both and it caused him to step back from her so he could see her face. It was suddenly hot, and his overcoat was a burden. Shrugging out of the garment, he laid it across the foot of the bed. Folding his arms over his chest, he tried for eye contact. Molly tried to disengage yet again; the candle and firelight were bright enough for him to see that she dreaded his answer.

"I been to Miss Cherry's House of Comfort three times since you been at the fort."

"I see."

"What you see?" he countered.

"I been here a spell…"

"Coupling don't mean love, Molly-girl. I loves you and we ain't never coupled."

"If'n we did… ummm couple, ya might not like me."

"Ohhh, Molly… I ain't never had the choice of coupling wit' a woman I loves. Imma like you just fine."

"Lou…" her voice was breathy.

"Coupling is so much mo' than me being inside ya. Is that what's worryin' you?"

"I ain't sho' I can take it." She whispered.

"Do ya love me, Molly-girl?"

Lou held his breath as he waited for her response. "Yes, Lou, I loves you… I ain't never loved a man before. I's sorry, I don't know how to be."

"You do just fine." Lou said, his tone drenched with arousal. Her answer caused his heart to bang around in his chest.

There was something in Lou's voice that made Molly's gaze collide with his intense stare. He stepped back from her, eliminating everything physical; thereby enforcing soul searching eye contact. She feared the sex act and all that it encompassed. Her thoughts traveled to a time when he first brought her to the fort. Their interactions had been the most intimate exchanges she'd ever experienced with another human being.

Lou had bathed, dressed and helped her to the chamber pot. The older women tried to relieve him of such duties, but he would not be dissuaded. And when she had regained minimal strength, he moved her to a cabin where there was only him. He had not seemed sexual in light of her dire situation. In hindsight, she now realized he had always been carnal, but she had been too physically and emotionally taxed to recognize it. Molly could see him clearly now–Lou wanted more, and he wanted it from her.

Over the years, she had learned to remove her head from her bodily circumstance. Lou seemed to sense when she was disengaging from him and the situation. There were instances when he would allow her to hide, but tonight wasn't going to be one of those times. He stood before her with his arms folded over his chest, feet spread apart–eyes penetrating her heart. Lou was muscled, dark of skin and male. He was more than she knew what to do with.

Coupling for her had been holding still until the master's son finished his business. It was why she had run only to end up trapped at the dry-goods store in Washington. Once there, she had become carnally enslaved. She wasn't naïve; she had witnessed and experienced brutality before, but never where it seemed unending.

"Molly-girl, come back to me."

Climbing out of her head, she refocused on Lou. "What now?"

"I wanna share yo' bed at night."

His words knocked the breath from her as she acknowledged that she wouldn't be alive if not for Lou. She couldn't ever repay what he had done for her. Would the sex act be the method of compensation between them? Defeated, she whispered, "I don't guess you has to ask; the cabin and everythang in it belongs to you."

"I wants all of ya, Molly-girl, and I wants you to want me. It cain't work no other way for us."

"Lou... I can try." She pressed her back to the wall as if trying to disappear. "You wantin' to start now?"

A low chuckle rumbled from him. "I ain't wantin' you to suffer me, Molly-girl."

"It's you who gon suffer me."

Lou had a sudden burst of laughter before cocking his head to one side and assessing her. Abruptly he stepped away, snuffing out the candles and oil lamp. The room was cast in gloom, but for the fire. When she thought his focus would swing back to her, he began moving the furniture. After pushing the table and chairs closer to the door, he moved the bed in front of the fire.

"I promises to go slow." He said reassuringly.

Molly was guarded when he turned to the table and began shucking his clothing. Lou removed his boots and gun before dropping his shirt and trousers on the chair. He wore long red underwear and though the lighting was lacking, Molly knew the color because she washed and mended his garments. She turned her back to him before unbuttoning the bodice of her dress. Slipping the fabric over her shoulders and past her hips, Molly folded her clothing; she lay everything on the chest at the foot of the bed.

She knew it was ridiculous to feel shy, Lou had seen her naked. If she were honest, he had seen her beaten, both emotionally and mentally. Dressed in a white shift and...

"Is dem my socks you's wearing?" Lou asked.

"If'n you can tell who socks I's wearin', it ain't dark enough in here."

"It's too damn dark." He countered.

She found herself giggling and he went on. "Come by the fire, so's you can be warm."

Molly had been about to tell him that she didn't feel a chill with him nearby. But he turned to his overcoat laying at the foot of the bed and fished something from the pocket.

"Come, Molly-girl."

The roughness of his voice compelled her to move forward. He offered his flask and where she would have refused, she accepted and drank deeply. It wasn't the first time she partook in spirits with him, but that had been for medicinal purposes... now it was so she could be still until he finished.

He reached out twining her fingers with his own, then tugged her into his body. Molly placed her other hand flat against his hard chest to steady herself. Lou's skin was hot to the touch; she thought she heard him stifle a groan at the contact. He allowed her to break the entanglement of their fingers and bodies to find her own steam with which to move toward the bed.

Once she stood between the bed and the fireplace, she looked up at him. "Where is ya wantin' me?"

He stared at her for moments, before saying in a gravelly voice. "Take everything off. Let me see ya."

Lifting her shift over her head, Molly looked past him as she removed her pantaloons. Bending over, she pulled his socks from her feet; when she was completely naked, she allowed her eyes to bounce back up to his face. She waited for his reaction. Molly waited for his need to be bigger than him. The crackling, hissing and popping of the fire was the only sound in the cabin. Lou was quiet, pushing at his underwear until his hard member bobbed free.

"Shit." Molly breathed, using Lou's favorite word.

Nudity between them had been one sided, she had never seen Lou without clothing. His shoulders were wide, his belly bricked, and his legs were thick with muscles. Lou was beautiful–powerful. Molly was awed–stressed. The spell was broken when he took a step forward; in contrast, she backed away.

"You's safe."

Molly stopped moving at the hurt she heard in his voice. She noted that his member had softened with the exchange and she wasn't sure if that was good or bad. He began walking toward her again, and it took all her strength not to retreat.

"I just wants to hold ya." He continued.

When he was close enough, he pulled her into a hug. Molly moaned at the full body embrace and wrapped her arms around him. Unable to help it, she started crying, so overwhelmed was she. They stood like that for a time, with the heat from the fire cocooning them. Lou finally broke the cuddle, stepped back and lifted the quilt. Molly climbed in, scrambling to the far end of the bed. As he settled in next to her, the mattress dipped under his weight. Lou turned to face her; his shoulders eclipsing the firelight.

His features fell into the shadows. Molly reached out and caressed his jaw. She needed to make certain that it was Lou in her bed and that he was the same in the light and in the dark. Conversation escaped her–leaving her ill equipped to intelligently speak her thoughts. He turned his face into her hand and kissed her palm with an open mouth. Molly felt his tongue.

"You ever been kissed, Molly-girl?"

The question was forward and only added to her shyness. She attempted to pull her hand back, but he stopped her. "I ain't never been kissed by a man before ya. Been kissed by the old lady what raised me."

As soon as she finished speaking, Lou leaned in and kissed her softly on the lips. Molly gasped, and he scooted closer before pushing his tongue into her mouth. She was stiff—trying not to move or disappoint.

"Put yo' tongue in my mouth." He coaxed, against her lips. "Taste me, Molly... please."

Awkwardly, she tried to do as he asked. She stuck her tongue out and Lou drew it into his mouth, suckling. Closing her eyes, she whimpered, overtaken by the sensations seeping into her person.

"I needs to kiss ya all over, Molly-girl." He groaned.

He didn't give her a chance to think on what he was saying. Lou shoved the covers back and yanked her to the center of the bed. He pressed her legs apart, then knelt between her thighs, effectively stopping her from closing her legs.

"Lou... please." She panted from fear and an unnamed feeling she'd never felt before.

"Shhh ... sweet-woman. I just wants to kiss ya."

She had been about to say she wasn't ready, when he placed both hands on either side of her head. He kissed her again, then he began applying open mouthed kisses down her neck and across her collarbone. She felt her skin heat up as she followed his movements with her eyes. Lou licked betwixt her breasts, then paused before taking her left nipple into his mouth.

Her moan was involuntary. "Ohhh, Lou."

He licked around her right nipple, never quite touching it with his tongue. The anticipation became too much and she whispered to her shame. "Please... please."

Lou tugged at her nipple, suckling, before moving down to her belly. He kissed the scar leading to her navel; he dipped his tongue inside the button. She arched up to his mouth, but he backed away going lower still. Molly tried to push him away, embarrassment piercing the sensual fog about them. His tongue slid between her folds and her body stiffened in utter ecstasy.

"Shit…" she panted. "Lou…"

He answered by shouldering her thighs further apart and burying his face in her core. She was surrounded by the scent of her carnality and him. Lou smelled of peppermint soap and tobacco. Molly was pushed to the edge of climax and confusion. It was his stubbled jaw against her thighs and the roughness of his tongue caressing her sensitive flesh that shoved her into mind-numbing pleasure.

"Ohhh…" she moaned, as her body trembled with release.

Molly lay spent, her legs cocked wide, her eyes shut–unable to face him. But Lou wouldn't be ignored. He stretched out over her and shared the taste of her arousal with her. She felt the hardness of him pressed against her belly. Panic seized her for seconds. She thought he would enter her, but he moved to lay next to her; his face pressed firmly between her breasts.

It was the way he backed away from her; Lou gave her the room to compare. He was allowing her to see that their coupling would be different–enjoyable even. Overstimulation caused Molly to burst out crying. His head popped up as he gazed down at her, but he never asked a question. Lou seemed to understand her needs.

"Easy, Molly-girl, everythang gon be all right."

She nestled against him, feeling his strength and gentleness. Sleep claimed her and when she woke next, dawn was pressing through the window curtains. The roaring fire was evidence that he had moved around the cabin long after she slept. Molly took a moment to get her bearings; a light snore emitted from Lou, who was snuggled under the quilt at her back. Turning in his arms, her heart squeezed at the sight of him. Emotion not thought caused her to lean in and kiss his plump lips.

Lou opened his eyes, offering her a lazy smile. He allowed himself to be kissed–he did not seek control. Following his example and wanting to give him what he gave her, Molly kissed his chest.

"Molly… you ain't gotta…" he panted.

She kissed his mouth once more, before shoving her tongue between his lips. Molly whispered. "I was wantin you to make me feel good again."

Lou's groan echoed around the cabin. He was about to push her on her back when she continued bashfully–determined. "I wants to try to make you feel good first."

Molly pushed him onto his back and began dropping light kisses all over his face, neck and chest. His maleness jutted between them, blatant and ready. Getting on her knees beside him, Molly wrapped her fingers about his length. Lou, blinded by need, reached out placing his hand around hers; he stroked himself, teaching her what he needed. He arched up into their combined grip and choked on a sob.

Lou was stunning in the throes of the sex act; she couldn't look away. Emboldened by his labored breathing and blissful expression, Molly leaned over and sucked the head of his shaft into her mouth.

"Easy, Molly-girl…" Lou pleaded. "You finna suck my thoughts from me."

She kept up the rhythm of their hands and her mouth. His body shook as his shaft jerked on her tongue. Molly was relentless in her quest to please him.

"I cain't stop it…" he warned. "Molly–I am finna…"

Molly stayed with him until the end, tasting him as he had pleaded only hours before. Later, they held each other in the after-glow of passion. Two days passed–Lou and Molly did not leave their cabin. They talked, slept, ate and orgasmed. Lou pleased her… enormously.

5

Perception
New York City

LIAM QUINN SAT at the breakfast table of his modest E 65th street home struggling through the newspaper. He could piece together enough words on the page to explain the mayor's anger. In black fancy ink, the headline read: **Patrons of the Infamous Hen House Found Dead on Blackwell Island**

The sun shone through the window, spilling over everything and giving the illusion that life was splendid. But circumstances for Liam were anything but grand. He had worked hard for the late Hugh Wood and now for the mayor; yet all his efforts had gone unnoticed. In his more honest moments, when he was faced with the basics of being himself, he admitted to thoughts of wanting to murder Hugh Wood. The problem–he hadn't been ready for the fallout. It wasn't fear by any means that kept him from homicide. Liam just believed in being prepared. Fernando still had the loyalty of the Municipal Police, even though the group dissolved in the late 1850s. In his opinion, there was no difference between him and the mayor. Liam recognized the ruffian that was Fernando Wood.

He sipped his coffee while pondering on how to proceed. Puzzlement racked his person as he tried to figure out why the mayor would be concerned about the press. Surely, Fernando understood that the people of Manhattan Island realized he was terrorizing them. Liam's thoughts drifted back to the night when Mitchell Houser had stolen from him the opportunity to run and own the Hen House.

Liam watched the mayor's retreating back before turning back to the customers of the Hen House. "All righty, boys, everyone of ya out back!"

The customers all started speaking at once which only served to further aggravate matters. In close operations Liam used his two cousins, Francis and Ennis, along with Collin, Brian and Fergie. While he appeared calm on the outside, Liam was seething from his dismissal by the mayor. His eyes locked with Ennis'; he curtly nodded, giving his cousin the signal to be brutal.

Ennis stepped forward, all six feet and two hundred pounds of him. Removing his gun from the holster, he began beating a patron with the handle. When the man dropped to the floor with a dull thud, Collin dragged him through the house and out the backdoor. The throng of men quieted, becoming instantly compliant.

At the back of the house, Liam stood facing the paying customers/ hostages of a business he now knew would never belong to him. The knowledge caused a lack of respect for the consequences, and so he set about giving New York City a metaphorical shake. Liam looked on as Fergie took names and Brian pointed to every other man before ordering. "You go... you go... go."

Francis pulled the paddy wagon around back, scaring the goat and chickens. Ennis carried the torch parting the night; the remaining customers were loaded into the wagon. Liam followed in a separate carriage and when they came to the docks of the East River, his blood started thrumming. More torches were lit, and the sound of the water added sinister to the situation.

Liam stepped down from the carriage in time to see the prisoners lined up on their knees, hands behind their heads. Two of the hostages tried to make a run for it, but to no avail. The light wind blowing off the river was icy against his skin. It was the blackness of the water, the torches emitting light and smoke that reminded him of the constant dirt he did to make other men great; fuck the mayor.

The prisoners were shot point blank and unlike Fernando Wood, Liam removed his expensive overcoat, rolled up his sleeves and helped drag the bodies onto the waiting ferryboat. When the last corpse was loaded, he hefted himself into the boat and took the ride to Blackwell Island.

A soft voice interrupted his violent musings. "May I pour ya some more coffee, sir?"

"No fank ya, Alice." Liam responded, allowing his accent to thicken when he spoke to her. It amused him to watch her try to figure out what he was saying. When she wasn't sure, she erred on the side of caution, never asking him to repeat himself.

Hugh wanted Alice killed because he couldn't break her. Defiantly, Liam brought her to his humble abode, fucked her and kept her. It was with delight that he discovered she was unused. She didn't like him, but she did fear him and thus an agreement was born. Alice was tall and curvy with a mop of wild black curls. She was of mixed race but still considered a nigger. Liam thought her stunning with her button like nose, heart shaped mouth and deep brown eyes. The lass before him had gumption, refusing to whore for a meal. He never before kept a woman; Alice gave him pause.

She wore a serviceable brown dress that worked against her beauty. Turning back to the stove she retrieved the kettle and moved to pour him more coffee. Liam held up a hand. "I said no fanks."

Nodding, she went back to her chores. Liam had no staff for the inside of the house and while he was far from tidy, he wasn't filthy. As Alice stood at the white counter scrubbing the surface, two pot lids on the brown stove began to clink when the contents came to a boil. On the wooden chopping block, at the center of the kitchen, an assortment of vegetables lay, cut and separated. Liam had to admit his house always smelled good now that he had her.

In the kitchen, she covered the large window overlooking the small barnyard with yellow curtains. Liam couldn't have guessed from where she'd have gotten the drapes. In the parlor, she brushed the brown sofa and two matching chairs daily. On the coffee table, as a centerpiece, sat a red book; he couldn't make out the title. The fireplace was small, yet in proportion to the room, it kept things cozy.

The house had two connecting bedrooms, one with a cot for a bed and a nightstand. His chamber was the largest with a four-poster bed and heavy black drapes. In the far corner, a huge tub sat to the left of a colossal fireplace.

"Would ya like somethin' to eat, sir?"

"Liam…"

"Would ya like somethin' to eat…" Alice swallowed hard. "Liam."

"No… I have a meeting."

She stared at him for moments, then cocked her head to one side. He knew she didn't understand his response; still she smiled faintly before turning back to her chores. He chuckled, stood and moved in behind her– crowding her as she stood in front of the window. Alice stiffened, but she didn't dare pull away. Liam had two rules when he brought her to his home. One: you will refuse me nothing. Two: if you run, I will find and kill you. Alice had not offered a verbal exchange on the rules, but she did nod. Most important, his accent was slight when he issued the threat.

The yellow curtains were pushed back, and Liam could see over her head out into the barnyard. It was his turn to stiffen as the unmarked carriage used by the mayor came into view. Fernando never came to his home. Liam had been summoned and loosely invited to the mayor's home, but never the reverse. The carriage door swung open and the mayor stepped down, followed by his new bitch, Mitchell Houser.

Both men were dressed impeccably, with the mayor in a blue suit and Houser bedecked in gray. Liam watched as they were escorted by one of the two stablehands to the back porch. The house was small with no need for a butler. Liam opened the door and did not smile when he addressed his unwanted guests.

"Mayor." He said, ignoring the presence of Mitchell Houser. "Thought we was to meet later today."

"Yes… well, Mitchell and I were already out and about handling business."

The mayor glanced around until his eyes landed on Alice, who was standing at the chopping board. She kept her gaze cast downward. Houser's eyes lingered on her until Liam said. "Gentlemen, dis way."

He led them to the parlor where Fernando sat in one of the two chairs facing the couch. Houser took the chair next to the mayor. Liam sat himself in the middle of the sofa, leaned back and waited.

"Mr. Wood will soon be leaving his post as mayor of New York City. We need to find those responsible for his cousin's demise before he moves on to larger government. The fiasco on Blackwell Island is causing the mayor some political pains. Discretion will need to be a priority moving forward. Do you understand the ramifications of what I am saying?" Houser asked, as if he were speaking to a simpleton.

"Fernando, do you have a problem with the work I do?" Liam asked, offering insult by using the mayor's given name. He cleaned up his speech to convey hazard.

The mayor had the good sense to appear shaken. In his left hand, he held his hat; with his right, he pushed his fingers through his neatly arranged hair. "I have no problem with how you work, but we can't have reporters taking notice. The written word is a powerful thing; it can maim a man's life work."

Liam couldn't read nor did he give a shit what the newspapers spouted. He eyed the mayor attempting to make clear that he did not receive guests. Into the silence the clink of dishes caught his attention. Liam looked up in time to see Alice with a tray in her hand before she placed the food and drink on the table. She poured each man a cup of coffee, pairing the hot beverage with a wedge of pound cake. When she turned exiting the parlor, Liam glared at the men sitting opposite him. They didn't reach for the refreshments and it was obvious that Liam was daring them to partake.

The mayor avoided eye contact and Liam could tell Fernando was seeing him anew. He could smell the apprehension on both men; it was the beginning of respect. The bodies left on Blackwell Island gave Fernando a reason to reassess. Liam bet the mayor had no idea the type of debauchery his cousin had gotten up to. Hugh's presence offered a barrier between reality and where the money really came from. It was an illusion Liam no longer cared to uphold.

"I will find who did this to Hugh, but I ain't takin' orders from the likes of 'im." Liam said as he jabbed at the air in Mitchell's direction with his thumb.

"No…no. You will work with me." Fernando countered, the desperation about his cousin an all-consuming matter.

"I want the 'en 'ouse when I deliver the men responsible for 'ugh's death." Liam demanded falling back on his accent.

Indignant, Mitchell answered with a sneer. "You can't even read… how would the likes of you run a lucrative dwelling like the Hen House?"

Liam offered a smile that didn't reach his pale blue eyes. It was evident that Houser had been gathering information on him. But the fact that he couldn't read was common knowledge. His voice was even, his accent almost gone when he replied.

"No, I can't read, but I can cipher numbers. I excel at problem solving." Liam leaned in, placing elbows to knees, his gaze intense. "For instance, if two men come uninvited to my home and I kill one–then I have one unwanted guest left."

The mayor's lips twitched, but Houser blanched. His attempt

at nonchalance fell short when he tried to rattle Liam in return. "The whore in your kitchen is that the one Hugh ordered killed?"

Liam didn't respond because Houser wasn't man enough to take Alice from him. Still, he did decide to kill Houser and felt better immediately. Fernando intervened trying to ease the tension.

"You can keep the girl. Hugh noted she wasn't worth his trouble—he also realized that you would dispose of her when you tired. The real clue here is that the woman who was acquired with her was stolen from the Hen House by the gunmen. Did you question her?"

"Question her 'bout what? She were gone from the whorehouse for days before all 'ell broke loose."

"Maybe she heard of this group of slaves." Fernando countered.

"Course I asked her about the runaways… I questioned all the whores." Liam replied.

"Where did these women come from?" the mayor continued.

"They applied to the ad for governess."

Fernando deflated at Liam's response. He nodded, then stood as if to leave. Houser followed suit; Liam never moved. His guests could see themselves out. Before they could exit the parlor, Liam added. "Fernando, we will take our meetings elsewhere—yeah?"

The mayor nodded and then they were gone. When the backdoor closed behind them, Liam was up and pacing. His anger almost stifling his breaths. Hugh wanted to move into local government, leaving the Hen House to him. The plan was for Hugh to be a silent partner until Liam bought him out or killed him. Now, all he had to show for his efforts at the whorehouse was a lass who didn't want his touch.

He stopped at the window seeing the mayor's carriage rattle through the decorative gate at the front of his house. The trees in the yard were without leaves and character because of the time of year. A stablehand closed and locked the gate before crossing the brown lawn heading for the barnyard. As the carriage moved easily into 4th Avenue traffic, well-dressed pedestrians strolled the walkway beyond his home providing picturesque moments that clashed with the realism of life as he knew it. Liam would find the man who killed Hugh and derailed his plans; he would murder him.

He would start with the mayor himself and negotiate while offering two deliverables. Hugh's killer for the Hen House. And if Fernando should renege…

"Liam?"

Turning, he found a nervous Alice standing at the entrance of the sitting room. He had forgotten she was present in his space, in his home, in the hell that was his existence. More anger welled up inside him. At times like this, he would pick two whores to ease his tension. Now he only wanted the lass standing before him. He was constantly losing.

"What, Alisss?"

"You gon hurt me when ya get tired of me?"

"If I answer yes, will it make you work harder to keep me 'appy?"

"No," she whispered.

Liam couldn't bite back the grin.

Everything about Liam gave Alice pause, his size, his red hair, his pale blue eyes and most important the danger that overshadowed his beauty. He kept his hair shorn close; his eyebrows were thick angry slashes above large discerning eyes. Liam's jaw was square–strong and rough with a few days' growth. His lips were fat and soft when he kissed her. He was muscled with an almost orange tint to his skin that was otherwise creamy. She hated that she recognized and desired his maleness.

Liam dressed in expensive, yet plain clothing. Today, he wore dark blue trousers with a crisp white button-down shirt. Ruffles seemed to be the fashion for men, but his shirts, though of high quality were simple affair. He stood by the window; the sun magnifying his rage, causing her to remain at the threshold of the room rather than enter the parlor completely.

Alice overheard the conversation between Liam and his guests. She'd even read the paper proclaiming bodies found on Blackwell Island. Her time at the orphanage offered some schooling, but she was primarily taught the duties of keeping house and small children. Still, she could read the written word and life well enough to know that Blackwell Island was his doing.

"Where you and the other woman come from, Alice?"

"I ain't wantin' to be here, sir. When can I leave?"

"Ya ain't leavin' me." He countered; his accent thick.

She understood him, accent thick or no, but she wanted to stay disconnected from him. Alice feigned confusion when he spoke, thinking it would be safest. Yet her struggle to comprehend seemed to amuse him. He talked all the more to her–swinging between an unintelligible and proper accent.

"Where ya come from, Alice?" he asked again.

"Emma was stole from the whorehouse–did ya ever find her?"

"Emma." He said, as if tossing her name around on his tongue. "That her name?"

"I don't know nothin'." Alice held her palms out to show what nothing looked like. "We was wantin' the position of governess–not whore."

She deliberately talked at him. Alice didn't want to point him back to the orphanage. She wanted to leave the children's home out of the mess she made of her life. It seemed the awful man who tricked her and Emma had been killed. Had Emma been stolen or rescued from the whorehouse? If she had to deduce Emma's circumstance, Alice would guess she had been rescued by Black and his men. The mere thought gave her hope–for Emma.

Liam took a menacing step forward and Alice countered by taking a self-preserving step backward. He shook his arms out for the briefest of seconds before clasping his hands behind his back.

Alice trembled as she watched the gamut of emotions cross his keen features.

"Finking a runnin', Alisss?"

"No." she replied, her tone icy. "I wants nothin' more than to be yo' whore."

He glared at her and Alice forced herself to hold the weight of their eye contact. She had already stepped back from him out of fear. There was nowhere else to retreat; Liam had the power and he knew it.

"Careful." He warned, his voice gravelly.

Alice was all over the place with her feelings. She was angry, afraid, and even aroused by him. But when Liam issued a threat, she took heed.

"Sorry for my sharp tongue... please don't harm me." She whispered.

He didn't move to reassure her that she was safe with him. Instead, he clasped his hands behind his back. The gesture seemed to keep him from choking the life from her.

"Where ya from, Alisss?" he repeated.

They both knew it was the last time he was going to ask the question. His voice was deceptively calm; Alice trembled when she answered. "I come from the colored orphanage."

She was a coward. Telling him where she came from only pro-longed the inevitable. He would kill her and dump her in the river soon enough. She had changed nothing for herself, but Emma was free. Alice just knew it was Black who saved her; who else would be so bold?

Black's men came to the orphanage regularly. They brought food, coin and clothes for the children. At times they brought toys; then a great while passed and they didn't come. It wouldn't have been the first time the children's home was forgotten by the more fortunate. She and Emma had run—in hindsight, they'd made a grave mistake.

"Do ya know who took Emma from the Hen House?" Liam asked, his voice startling her; Liam exuded hazard.

"No."

"Ya lie to me, Alice."

It was a statement, he wasn't asking. Still, she answered. "No, sir, I ain't lyin'."

He started walking toward her, causing her to back out of the parlor entrance. She found herself with a wall behind her and Liam in front of her. The corridor was dim, as the natural light didn't reach this far into the house.

His maleness was pressed against her belly as he leaned down to ask. "Ya finkin' 'bout another man?"

She gave the smart answer. "Just you, Liam."

He backed away and stared at her in the gloom of the hallway. "Collin and Brian will remain to look after ya."

Alice sagged with relief when she heard the backdoor slam in his wake.

※ ※ ※

Liam didn't know what he hoped to find at the Colored Orphanage Asylum, but he took the trip to mark the possibilities off his list. When the carriage came to a lurching stop outside a large estate with two wings and four stories, he was impressed. He had of course heard of the home for nigger children, but he had not seen it. The courtyard was filled with children at play; they were all dressed alike, the girls in blue dresses with a white over smock–the boys in brown trousers, tan homespun shirts and blue overcoats.

All activity stopped when Liam stepped down from the carriage. An old white woman in a black dress, accessorized by a bright white apron, came forward to greet him. She was plump with ruddy cheeks, brown eyes and gray hair pulled back in a bun. Her nose was pointy; the air about her was haughty.

"Good day, how may we help you?" she asked, although she was the only person inquiring about his presence.

The courtyard had begun clearing out, leaving Liam and the old woman. On the front steps several others were posted up watching the exchange. Five of the staff were white and three were black. They were suspicious of him and they didn't try to hide it. In the windows, the curtains moved ever so slightly as the children gathered to see what he wanted.

"Good noon." Liam replied, unsure of what to say. "My name is Quinn and I am here on behalf of the mayor."

"The mayor?" the woman repeated, incredulously. "What could Fernando Wood want from a colored orphanage?"

"He seeks to become a benefactor." Liam lied.

"Are you speaking of the same man who proposed the secession of Manhattan Island with the Confederacy? The man who wishes to continue exporting cotton to the detriment of human beings … that Fernando Wood?"

Liam nodded.

"The orphanage has a hard-enough time because the children are colored. Go away, Mr. Quinn, and don't come back. No one here knows what happened to the mayor's cousin." Liam offered no reaction to her words, which in hindsight was a response. She went on. "We read the newspapers and hear the talk. Stay away from my children."

The old woman turned and walked away, never looking back at him. Of course she was correct about the mayor in every way–her attitude was believable; still he was sure he was missing something. As the carriage pulled onto the main thoroughfare, Liam decided the orphanage needed to be watched. He would appoint his cousin Ennis to the task.

6

Fort Independence
November 1862

THE EIGHTEEN HAD now become the twenty-one with the addition of Jeremiah, E.J., and Anthony. If the ambassador should ride out with them again, they would become the twenty-two. Black met with the men the week prior, but he only discussed the tightening of security around the inner and outer walls. The men noticed he gave no detail about the last package received or the missive that came with it. Black needed a moment to collect himself and work through the finer points of their predicament.

Elbert and James were already on the porch, passing a flask back and forth. Black joined them. It wasn't quite four in the morning, which was the best time to meet about sensitive issues. James offered Black the flask and he partook. On a stool to the left of the brothers, a lantern burned bright, which only made the area outside the light darker. A quarter moon stared down at them offering no visibility. The air about them was unseasonably warm and Black thought the weather the calm before a nasty winter.

When the men began appearing at the bottom of the stairs,

Black passed the flask back to James, then turned leading the way inside. They filed quietly into his study so as not to wake the rest of the house. The door was closed firmly behind the last man and Black moved to the center of the room.

"The package was from Mr. Lincoln." Black's voice was strained.

"His message–what did it say?" Elbert asked.

Black produced the missive and read aloud:

My Friend,

I shall travel north to look in on an acquaintance who has suffered a great loss. I hope to see you that we might bridge the gap of time.

Sincerely,

A.L

"When we gon ride out?" Anthony asked.

"I'm sure more thorough instructions will come soon." Black replied. The room went silent; the men waited for his next words. "I think we should ride out now and see for ourselves what goes on in New York."

"I agrees." James said.

"They huntin' me–is what's happenin'." Anthony countered. "And y'all is tangled wit' me."

Black stepped over Anthony's words. "I need you to tell us everything that happened in New York–leave nothing out."

"Travel was without event until we landed on Manhattan Island." E.J. said.

"We seen to Camille and Curtis first." Frank added.

"We ferried from Queens to Manhattan." Jeremiah chimed in.

"E.J. met wit' a Mista Jones at the pussy parlor." Anthony offered.

"It was us what push Ant to the girl. He ain't wanna be bothered." Lou admitted. "Thought he needed to get his head off a Luke."

The story was abstract, coming out in pieces. Black stared from man to man, conveying his bewilderment. Anthony spoke up filling in the missing information, eluding to but not quite touching Emma's place in the tale. What Black had not been ready for was the knowledge that Emma was with another young woman who disappeared from the whorehouse.

"Emma only just told me 'bout Alice; she say they took her away—say she refused to take a man. The girl raised a fuss tellin' whoever could hear they was from the orphanage—not whores." Anthony said.

"She dead." Frank said, shaking his head.

"Or she was gifted to a man that could break her." Jeremiah added. All eyes swung to the black cracker, but he held firm under the scrutiny.

"Ya broke women?" Gilbert asked, incredulous.

Black cut Gil off and addressed Jeremiah. "I saw it the same."

Jeremiah's eyes bounced over to him. Black saw that the ex-overseer was openly thankful for his ability to steer the conversation away from the past. The queen's man lightened the mood by joining the discussion. Black and the ambassador spent months putting together a statement for the queen detailing their time with Lincoln. Bainesworth, who never left the fort to voyage home, was his usual, jovial self.

"Well I can't very well leave for England now. I have sent my report to her majesty, besides this accent can open doors for us. In the states, my pronunciations are considered flowery." The ambassador laughed aloud. "It's almost never caught that I haven't said shit. No... no—you all need me."

The room at large laughed, and the tightness of the situation eased a bit. Black was sure it would tighten up again with his next statement. "In two days' time, I will ride out with six men. The remaining men will come after instructions from Lincoln reach the fort. We will set up camp in Queens—Ravenswood."

Everyone started talking at once, and Black had to hold up his hands to get the group to settle. When the room quieted, James spoke his anger. "We in this room ain't womenfolk. You ain't finna put us off. The fort needs you more than any one of us–no, brother."

Anthony stepped in behind James adding his thoughts and vexation. "Dis is my mess–ya cain't cut me out."

Black sighed aloud before speaking. He wasn't used to explaining his decisions, but the men were volatile–restless. He thought the president would have shown him something more by now. "Who will stay behind to get the instructions from Lincoln?"

"I will." E.J. offered.

"I'll stay and ride out wit' E.J. when word comes." Simon said. "Seem to me like we ain't strong enough to do a simple thang like wait–the womenfolk do ever thang betta. Imma take Jesse, Horace, Shultz, Ephraim, Jake and Emmett."

"We ride out in four days." Elbert said. "If word comes from Lincoln within that time, then we all ride out."

"Give us time wit' the women and children." Frank replied.

"Shit, we finna come home to mo' babies." Lou said on a chuckle.

Black thought Lou correct in his assessment. The last time they rode out several of the womenfolk ended up with child. James had a daughter with Abby, named Jamie. Frank had a son with Carrie, named Lil Frank. Shultz had a daughter with Mary, named Meg. Gilbert also had a new daughter with Hazel, named Gillie. Tim and Sarah were also the proud parents of a new baby girl, named Amelia; then there were his own twin sons with Sunday.

"Four days it is." Black countered, when it seemed there would be no putting his brothers off. He hoped matters would fall into place and if not, they would ride out. There would be no more stalling. He couldn't escape the thought of men from the Hen House being murdered because someone was looking for them. The article described nine men shot at point blank range and left on the shores of Blackwell Island. This matter was critical in the extreme.

❋ ❋ ❋

Anthony left Frank and Lou with the other men talking and planning. He walked home at a brisk pace needing to speak with Emma. Their time getting to know each other had been both awkward and beautiful. He was learning much about his new wife and his heart was full. In the past few days, he added a wood burning stove to their cabin only to find that Emma couldn't cook. He found that tidbit hilarious considering she ate more than he.

"Don't you help the older women cook?" He'd asked her one evening.

"I tastes everythin' they cooks–that is helping." Emma had countered, her eyebrows pushed together.

He hadn't been able to stop laughing. Emma giggled as well. His wife was fast becoming his new best friend. Still, there were days when he felt nothing but pain and the guilt ate at him. Luke would never experience what he was finding with Emma. It hurt to think on the loss at all.

When he approached the cabin, his real concerns surfaced. He was leaving Emma and like Luke, he didn't know if he would survive. Anthony understood what Black didn't say. Nine men had been murdered in the search for the man who killed the mayor of New York City's cousin. They were hunting him, and the innocent were dying in the process.

What never occurred to him was how Alice affected the problem. She had refused to whore, spouting that they were free women. Anthony saw the dread that Black tried to cover. Alice's place in the story made the leader of Fort Independence anxious to see the orphanage for himself. Black wanted to make certain the children were safe. It was enough to scare the shit out of Anthony. He hadn't argued–but he felt the same as Black. He thought they should leave in two days. The woman complicated matters. It would almost be better for the children's home if Alice were dead. Anthony was immediately ashamed of the thought.

Elbert was thinking more clearly than he or Black. Anthony understood that and obviously so did Black. It's why Black gave in and let the men make plans. He'd meet and strategize with the men over the next four days, but he would make time for Emma. Spending moments with his wife wasn't born out of some masculine obligation—he needed her. Anthony found that while he had a sense of family with the other men and older folk, he was still very lonely. What he had with Emma helped to grow his person.

Like Lou, Anthony backed away from the sex act. He realized that he had to separate himself for his wife's sake from the patron at the Hen House. But this morning, as he stood on his makeshift porch in the dark quietly pondering and evaluating, he recognized his need to be buried deep within his woman, seeking all the comfort she could give. The thought that summed it all—being inside Emma would push his fear to the edge of the situation; thereby giving him enough room to act on the tiniest bit of courage he possessed.

Dawn wouldn't happen for another hour, but a lantern sparked to life from the window to the right of him. Emma was up and while he desperately needed her, he didn't want to tell her that he was leaving in four days. Anthony was inundated with conflicting feelings where his wife was concerned. He made it a point to consider her sensibilities at all times, but this morning...

The door creaked on its hinges and a slice of yellow light splashed onto the porch and him. Anthony turned to peer at Emma as she stood with her head poked out from behind the door. She was smiling, until she caught sight of his expression.

"Ant, ya all right?"

He sighed before turning to enter the cabin. The weather being unseasonably warm had him carrying his overcoat. Placing it on the peg by the door, he blurted. "We rides out for New York in fo' days."

"No, Ant."

He had done nothing to prepare Emma for what life was really like at the fort. It was yet another way he failed in all this. She continued. "Why would ya go back?"

Emma leaned against the door as if struck. She was dressed in a pink shift, her legs and feet bare. The cabin smelled of roses and he knew she'd just bathed in the white porcelain tub he purchased for her. He remembered how excited she had been when she came home to find the tub and stove. The extra coin from Luke helped greatly.

The tub had been too heavy for the flooring of the cabin. Lou and Frank helped re-enforce the wooden planks, so it would hold the weight of the tub and water. Next spring, he planned to add to the structure. He got lost in safer thoughts, but Emma pulled him back to the present.

"Anthony?"

"I left a mess in New York. I has to ride out wit' the men." He said.

"I thought since ain't no one from New York come after us–we was safe."

"You is safe." He explained. Then, using Black's words, he continued. "The fort is only as safe as the men what live here."

His wife's beautiful face mirrored his own fear. Anthony worked hard to appear untroubled in his demeanor. "Imma miss you is all."

"Can I come wit' you?" she asked.

The very idea of Emma coming with him to New York was appalling. He didn't allow his voice to indicate his real feelings, but his statement showed his worry. "Promise me you won't try leavin' the fort."

"I wanna come wit' you," she whispered.

"Emma, ya cain't come–now promise me."

She stared at him for weighted moments before her shoulders slumped. "I won't leave here. I'll wait for ya, Ant."

It was his turn to study her for sincerity. When he was satisfied, he nodded, and then looked away. He mumbled. "Good–good."

The awkwardness of their first ever meeting occupied the space between them–or so he thought. While he was figuring on begging her to lay with him, she asked. "Will ya visit a different whorehouse when you's in New York?"

Anthony's eyes went wide, and a sadness washed over him. Emma still saw him as the man from the Hen House. He supposed it was fair. Lou's situation with Molly hadn't helped matters. Emma avoided Lou, speaking to him only when there were no other options. She was always polite and Lou… well he behaved as though he hadn't noticed.

Unclear what to say, he went with the truth. He was sure it would get him further away from the goal of intimacy. "I ain't never had a woman that was mine."

More staring happened until Emma shrugged her shoulders. She stuttered. "A…All right."

She tried to step around him, and he caught hold of her wrist. "It's a pussy parlor nearby–I ain't been goin'."

He was frustrated, giving her honesty like strong whiskey with no chaser. She gasped and he supposed it was at the vulgar falling from his lips. He let his head fall back to glare at the ceiling. This was not going the way he planned. Releasing her wrist, he started for the door. They were arguing and this wasn't how he wanted to spend his time before riding out. He was about to yank the door open when Emma's soft appeal stopped him.

"Ya never ask 'bout couplin'…" her words trailed off and Anthony kept his back to her waiting for her next thought. Emma didn't disappoint. "Molly say she was mistreated, so Lou ain't wanna ask. Why you don't ask? Do ya not want me now that we's married? Should I ask you? I ain't fo' sho'."

His wife was now offering him reality with no chaser. When Anthony finally got up the nerve, he turned to study her. Emma appeared innocent and stunning all at once. Her femininity along with the scent of roses caused him to harden in his trousers. She kept her beautiful brown face turned down as if to prevent rejection. Did women who weren't whores ask for coupling? Shit, he wasn't for sure either.

"How would ya ask me?" he inquired.

Slowly, she raised her eyes to his. "I guess livin' wit whores even for a short time–well, I just might be soiled."

"Ask me."

"I was wantin' us to finish what we started at the Hen House."

Anthony had to close his eyes for moments to keep from spilling his seed in his trousers. No woman other than a paid whore ever asked him for the sex act. His head was swimming, and he forgot to answer his wife.

"Ant, we don't have–"

"Help me undress." He countered, cutting her off.

She walked over to where he stood by the door and getting on her tiptoes, she cupped his face, then kissed him. "Come."

She took him by the hand and led him to a chair by the small fire. He sat, and Emma knelt before him, helping him remove his boots. Placing them together by the table, she climbed into his lap straddling him. His wife leaned in and kissed him, before assisting him in pulling his shirt over his head. Anthony reached down to palm her ass where her shift had ridden up; Emma was bare assed, and he groaned with delight.

Abruptly, she backed away and pulled her shift over her head, standing before him unabashed. "Take yo' trousers off."

He did as she asked dropping his trousers and long underwear to the floor. His dick bounced free and he wondered if his wife would lose her nerve. She stepped forward and wrapped her hand about him.

"Shit… easy, Emma. I'm 'bout to shoot off like a rifle wit' a hair trigger." Anthony said, panting.

But his lovely wife didn't ease up; instead she leaned in, kissed his chest, then licked his left nipple. Anthony was beside himself with wanting her. He hadn't come close to release since that fateful night with Emma at the Hen House; he couldn't wait–he had no play in him. Snatching Emma up, he carried her to the bed and tossed her in the center. He climbed between her legs and shoved himself inside her.

"Damn, woman, yo' pussy tight. I ain't gonna last."

"Anthony… ohhh, you's big."

He couldn't hold back, he banged up inside her three times hard and at the last he buried himself to the hilt. Dick pulsing, he groaned. "Ya feels so good, Emma… so damn good."

Abruptly, he pulled out, pressing her thighs further apart, then latched his lips onto her clit. He tongued, licked, nipped and kissed her to conclusion.

"I's dyin', Ant… ohhh, please don't stop."

And he didn't. Anthony stayed with her until she stiffened and began trembling. As she started coming down from orgasm, he climbed back over her and entered her again. Their second coupling wasn't hurried, yet still frantic. They climaxed together calling each other's name. Later, as they lay snuggled up, Anthony was dozing when his wife spoke.

"Ant?"

"Hmmm?"

"Is you gonna cook? I's awful hungry."

Anthony laughed at his quirky wife. "Ya bet not be tellin nobody that I does the cookin."

"I wouldn't dare." She whispered against his chest. "Ya cooks better than Big Mama and Iris."

He laughed, then got to work. Anthony made scrambled eggs, grits, bacon with biscuits and gravy. They ate naked while propped up in bed, sharing the same plate. He was in love with his wife; he was sure of it.

❋ ❋ ❋

The black cracker pulled his timepiece from his pocket. He was almost late. Following the path leading to the center of the fort, he veered left, walking four lanes over. Three cabins sat side by side and he approached the middle. It was midday with an overcast sky, but the warm temperature seemed to be holding. Stepping up on the porch, he knocked, then waited until she called out.

The old woman wore a brown dress with a cream-colored sweater. Her hair was freshly braided in two fat cornrows and her smile for him was wide.

"I was thanking ya forgot me." She said.

"No, ma'am." He replied. "You ready?"

"The weather is good."

"It is." He answered.

The old woman, Ella, had a little cabin situated between Sonny and E.J., Jeremiah's white brother. Sonny lived with Eva; his brother lived with Nettie and Suzanne. Nettie had given E.J. a son, whom they boldly named Edward Hunter III, after their father the old plantation master. Suzanne had given him a girl who was proudly named Lizzy, short for Elizabeth.

The cabin was simple; a full-size bed sat in front of the fireplace. In the far corner sat a black stove and to the right of the room was a table with six mismatched chairs. Every Sunday, his brother and uncle piled into Ella's cabin to eat and be with the old woman. She fussed over the children and basically over fed everyone. During the week, weather permitting, she went socializing and it was his job to escort her.

Freshly baked apple pie filled the cabin and his mouth watered. Turning back to the table, Ella reached for a dish covered with a red and white checkered towel.

"You taking the whole pie over to Miss Olive's?"

"Yes. I's meetin' Big Mama, Cora and Iris at Olive's cabin." His grandmother giggled. "I left another pie on the stove. Come has some afta ya takes me to Olive's."

"I gotta go to New York with Black," he muttered.

"Oh."

"I'll be gone for a time. You'll look after Callie and the children?"

"Sho' will."

"E.J. and me ain't ready to move on the land we bought. You'll be safe here." He said reassuringly.

"Ya told Callie?"

"Not yet." He answered.

"When?"

"Four days." He said, and he could see she wasn't pleased.

The old woman's eyes watered, and he was unsure what to do. Their interactions of late were strange now that he knew she was his grandmother. Ella liked to be the chief of their time together; she liked telling him what to do. He also did his best to get along with Sonny. His uncle was amused by the shift in power and often used it to his benefit. Jeremiah stayed annoyed, but he didn't complain. Both Eva and Callie laughed when they thought he wasn't looking. His thoughts wandered to the Sunday before last.

Sonny was seated next to Eva, chatting. When Jeremiah reached for the dish holding the last piece of pie, his uncle pushed the piece onto his plate with his fork. Leaving him holding an empty dish.

"I was gonna eat that." He growled.

"Mama, can I has this piece a pie? I thanks Jeremiah was wantin' it."

"Jeremiah know I'll make mo'—go on and eat it, Sonny. He ain't frettin' 'bout no pie." Ella explained on his behalf.

He could still see Sonny's smug expression.

"Ya needs to speak on this wit' Callie."

Backing away from thoughts of killing Sonny, he said. "Imma speak wit' her this evenin'."

"Good… Sonny will come for me when I's done at Olive's; be safe, man."

"Yes, ma'am."

When they stepped out onto the porch, Jeremiah spoke with petulance. "I ain't sharing no pie wit' Sonny."

His grandmother stopped and glared at him. She shook her finger in his face. The black cracker gazed about to see if anyone saw him getting scolded. "Save some for ya uncle–stop being mean."

He mumbled. "Damn Sonny."

The old lady giggled as they made their way to Miss Olive's. When they reached their destination, Big Mama, Iris and Cora were approaching from the opposite direction on the path. James and Little Otis were with them.

"Daddy!" Otis yelled.

His son ran to him and Jeremiah lifted him into his arms. "You heavy."

"He been eatin' all day." James said on a chuckle.

"Papa, gimmie some pepmins." Lil Otis explained.

Miss Olive had one leg. Paul and Sonny built a small slope for her porch. This made it easy for her to move about on crutches. Otis ran up and down the ramp.

"He gon tire his little self right on out." James whispered.

After the older women were settled, Jeremiah walked back to Black's house with his son and James. Otis still called Elbert Mama, and James Papa, but he now called Jeremiah Daddy. The boy ran out ahead of them.

"Not so far." James called out

"I ain't told Callie yet." Jeremiah said.

"No matter, she knows." James countered and Jeremiah stopped walking.

"Come on, Daddy!" Otis yelled.

James guffawed. "Callie is smart; she 'bout live in Black's house. Ya really thank she ain't figured it out?"

He knew James was right. But once in front of Black's house, he kept on to the barracks after kissing his son. James delivered Otis to the women and met him later. They worked through a shift change and when night fell so did the temperature. It wasn't icy, but there was a nip to the air.

Jeremiah stepped out the backdoor of the barracks. The night was clear, the large oak's bare branches were suspended before the pale moon. Stars dotted the sky. He couldn't face Callie. They hadn't had much time together of late. She worked constantly with the children and Sunday. Most of his time was spent alone or at the barracks. He needed her, but he didn't want to complain. Soon they would ride out.

The backdoor sat ajar with a slice of light spilling into the night, along with the laughter of the men. Jeremiah breathed in deeply–he was conflicted. This was the opportunity of a lifetime, riding out with the legendary Black. Living as a colored overseer, his entire life had been spent on the Hunter plantation. E.J. went away regularly, but Jeremiah's lot had been to await his brother's return. Although his brother shared all his experiences, nothing could have prepared him for true freedom.

If he were honest with himself, he felt some jealousy about Callie living in Black's big fancy house. Black represented everything he was not. Though he would never ask, he knew Callie thought Black impressive–in his thinking and his maleness. Breastfeeding Black's children was her way of repaying what he could not. While Black had his complete loyalty, he couldn't help the way he felt. He loved Callie more than his next breath. His woman slept in Black's bed, and even though it was with Sunday, the concept was more than he could bear.

The twins were starting to be weaned, so maybe he could have Callie back when they returned from New York. Part of him didn't go to her because he was afraid to find that she didn't care he was leaving. E.J. having two women didn't help his thought pattern; if ever there were a man who could handle two women it was Black. He shook his head to free himself from self-pity and envy.

Behind him, the men inside the barracks grew quiet; the lack of sound was deafening. He heard someone address Black, then all conversation resumed.

"Jeremiah's out back." Another male voice clarified.

Black was the last person he wanted to see right now. The large door inched wider and out stepped the leader of Fort Independence. He was dressed for his name with a black fur hat on his head. Black didn't address him, instead he looked back over his shoulder and called out.

"He's out here."

Callie's little frame stepped out the door behind Black. Her voice broke when she said, "I been waiting for you to come to me, Jeremiah. I made Mister Black bring me to you."

"I figured you was helping wit' the children." He answered lamely. Black snorted, making his answer that much weaker.

Callie wore his big brown sweater pulled over her gray dress. Her eyes were bright with unshed tears. The lighting was just enough for him to see her pain. He tried to think of what to say, but she threw herself into his arms before he could get the words out; holding her felt good.

"I don't want you to go. I love you, Jeremiah."

Over her head, he watched as Black turned and walked away.

Callie loved Jeremiah more than her next breath. She worried he'd found some other woman to occupy his time. Life had been hectic with the children, but always she ached for him—*for time with him.* He broke into her thoughts.

"Let me get ya back to Black's house. It's nippy out here."

"Sunday and me is trying a new thing with the babies. I want to go to our cabin." She replied. "Do you not want me?"

"Oh, Callie—I want you so bad, woman. I ain't want to complain."

It was dark behind the barracks, so she couldn't enjoy the beauty of his maleness the way she needed. Still, she reached up on her tiptoes and kissed him deeply. Jeremiah tasted of peppermints and masculinity uncut. He was a heady flavor. She smiled against his lips.

"Lil Otis gave you peppermint."

Jeremiah chuckled. "He did."

He twined his fingers with her own and led her around the side of the barracks until they came to the front. James, Elbert and Black stood about speaking with each other. The front door was closed against the slight chill. Upon seeing them both, Elbert and James addressed her.

"Evenin', Miss Callie." They said in unison.

She offered no eye contact. "Gentlemen."

"I'll be back in the morning." Jeremiah said.

"Yeah." They all responded.

When the darkness swallowed them up, Jeremiah swung her up into his arms; she giggled. They reached their cabin in record time. A fire blazed in the hearth, while an oil lamp added to the ambiance.

"Who?" he turned questioning eyes to her.

"I asked Sonny to ready the cabin. He said you been at the barracks mostly."

"I still wanna kill him."

"Cause of the pie?" She laughed out loud.

"Damn Sonny." He muttered, then chuckled.

She moved toward the fire and began removing her clothing. First the sweater, then her boots and dress, leaving her crisp white shift and pantaloons. Boldly, she pushed the pantaloons down until the garment pooled at her feet. Turning, she found him gazing at her.

Callie's breath caught. This is what she longed for—the sight of the black cracker in all his glory. Jeremiah had removed his sweater and shirt. His muscled form was even more defined with the work he did at the barracks. The fly of his trousers was unlaced, revealing no underwear; the fine hairs at his navel trailed down into his pants. Against the rough fabric his maleness was hard–brazen. He had cut the hair on his head in the heat of the summer, but it was growing back–wild and black as ever. On his jaw was about two days' worth of growth forming neither a mustache nor beard. Jeremiah was her everything.

She pushed her shift down over her hips and loosened the binding that she and Sunday had wrapped about her breasts. Callie felt self-conscious because her breasts were larger. They ached and she was starting to leak. She was frustrated; she wanted to be as beautiful for him as he was to her.

Awkwardly, she whispered. "My breasts are leaking; this would be feeding time. Me and Sunday is trying to wean them. I'm sorry–"

"Can I taste?"

"Ummm… I…" she was at a loss and Jeremiah grinned.

He shucked his boots and trousers, then crossed the room to her. Swinging her up into his arms he carried her to the bed, placing her gently in the center. He climbed between her thighs and she thought he would kiss her. Instead, he leaned down drawing her left nipple into his mouth. He suckled, deeply drinking her milk then switched nipples doing the same. The feeling was arousing and alleviating. Callie moaned aloud. He repeated the process several times until she was panting. And when she could no longer think straight, he leaned over and kissed her senseless.

Pressing her thighs apart with his knees, he eased into her and groaned her name. "Callie… Callie."

Pulling out and reangling, he slammed home–roughly. Her eyes watered as she told him. "I love you… can't live without you."

They found a rhythm that was immensely pleasing. Callie opened her legs wider and his hips stuttered from the intense pleasure. His words were broken when he sobbed. "I ain't nothing without you, woman."

Their confessions of love tipped them over the edge. Orgasm gripped them; she felt his maleness jerk and pulse within her. He pressed his nose against her cheek; his whiskers scraped her skin and he bit her for good measure.

"My sweet love." She whispered over and over.

He gave two more hard pushes before slumping over her. They lay in the stickiness of breast milk and spilled semen, drifting dreamlessly to sleep.

* * *

Two days later a large black carriage rolled up to the front gate of Fort Independence. A thin white man emerged, dressed in a black suit. He had bulging brown eyes, thick gold framed spectacles and graying hair at his temples. When questioned, he refused to speak to anyone but Black. He did offer a missive with the request that it be delivered into Black's hands while he waited.

The missive read:

My Friend,

Some things are better never written down.

A.L.

Black stepped onto the porch to find Simon, Elbert and Jeremiah waiting. He knew the other men were already at the gate. He descended the stairs and started the trek to the front of the fort. At his arrival, the men opened the door to the left of the main gate and Black walked through first. As the carriage door opened and the man jumped down, Black heard the click of many weapons being drawn behind him.

It was a bright day and still fairly warm; the man standing before them pissed himself from the tension. Black was gracious enough to ignore the puddle in which his guest stood.

"How may I assist you this fine day?" Black asked.

"Mr. Lincoln…" it was all the poor man could manage before he passed out.

"Shit." Black muttered, turning his attention to the driver–a fat white fellow who ran deliveries for the store "Everything". Virgil must have stepped in to keep the matter private. Black said to the driver. "Be on your way. Greetings to Virgil."

The driver nodded. To his own men, Black ordered, "Pick his ass up and take him to the first available cabin. The barracks is none of the president's business. When he's lucid, send for me."

A few hours passed before Elbert and James came to his study with news that they'd given the man a change of clothes.

"He waitin' at a storage cabin by the gate." James said.

"His name is Mr. Peabody." Elbert said, grinning. "Fitting."

Black tried not to but he couldn't help it, he burst out laughing. He shook his head before giving instruction. "Have Frank and Lou guard the cabin. After I talk with Mr. Peabody, we will meet in my office in one hour."

"Yeah." Elbert said.

James went to find Frank and Lou, while Elbert gathered the men. Black went to speak with his much-anticipated guest. He found Mr. Peabody seated in a chair by the fire dressed in brown homespun trousers. When Black entered the cabin, the man stood and cleared his throat.

"Mr. Lincoln warned me that you all were a scary bunch. I–"

"I'm Black, Mr. Peabody. How can I assist you?"

Black's no-nonsense tone was an attempt to get the man to concentrate. He could see that his guest was still shaken.

Clearing his throat once more, Mr. Peabody finally said. "The president wishes to travel to New York City. He will not begin travel until after my *safe* return. Mr. Lincoln wants you in charge of his protection."

Black eyed the slighter man before folding his arms over his chest. He let his gaze roam about the storage cabin, leaving Mr.

Peabody in limbo. The windows were uncovered permitting the natural light into every crevice. Wooden crates leaned heavily against the far wall and on the floor was dried blood mixed with hay. The setting was prefect.

"Where ya from, Mr. Peabody?"

"Illinois." He replied nervously.

"Your connection to the president?" Black continued.

"He is a distant cousin and friend. No one would suspect me."

"You have a wife and children, sir?" Black pressed.

"Yes, Mr.… ahhh, Black. Three daughters and a wife."

"You understand what I'm getting at, Mr. Peabody?" Black asked while holding his gaze, until the threat became a living, breathing thing. "You will remain here until you travel back to the president. You will be escorted."

"Absolutely." Mr. Peabody returned.

Black exited the cabin offering nothing more. On the porch, he stood between Frank and Lou. Addressing the brothers, he ordered. "Have him taken to a cleaner cabin near here. Don't take him further into the fort. Have him fed and his own clothing laundered. At nightfall leave him to Anthony and Emmitt."

"We'll see 'bout it." Frank said.

Fragments of a simple puzzle were falling together, and Black felt lighter. He had been waiting for Lincoln and it appeared the president had been waiting for him. The men were agitated and so was he. He had been stalling them, essentially meeting about nothing. But now, the plan was visible, and he would execute it with his brothers in arms. Black strolled leisurely to his house in the bright afternoon sun. The idleness of indecision was over.

He climbed the front steps two at a time, walking with purpose down the long hall. Mama was seated at the table, sewing. He kissed her cheek in greeting and kept moving, stopping only when he reached his studio. In the corner was a large parchment rolled up. Black retrieved it and continued on to his study where the men waited—minus Frank and Lou.

Black walked into the study, closing the door behind him. He moved to the center of the crowd. The men, noticing the parchment, formed a circle. When Black dropped it to the floor, four of the men placed a booted foot at the edge to prevent the map from rolling up.

"Pass me that stick behind my desk." Black said to Horace.

The long stick passed through many hands before Black gripped it. Turning back to the map, he began stepping through the real plan.

"Blackwell Island lies between Queens and New York City on the East River. This portion to the right is called Ravenswood. We will set up there and take control of a ferry and the river."

"It's gon be cold as a bitch on the water." Elbert said.

"The waterfront is lined with several mansions; we will move into the one on the far end, under the guise of staff." Black explained, pausing for effect. "There is a man who owes me and will never be free of his debt."

When he didn't elaborate, Simon spoke. "Ya stalled us long enough. Let's step through the plan."

Black grinned. "We will move out by rail and pick up horses along the way. Simon, you will accompany our guest back to the president. You will take E.J., Jesse, Horace, Shultz, Ephraim, Emmitt and Jake. Once you have delivered my words, you will wait on the president and bring him to me."

7

New York City
The Hen House

LIAM HAD BEEN unorganized in his quest to find those responsible for Hugh's death. He suspected it was because he didn't care; then Mitchell Houser happened. His nemesis seemed to have bigger plans than running a whorehouse. Liam now understood that Houser was looking to work closely with the mayor at government. The problem—both Mitchell and Fernando intended greatness from his efforts.

He'd let the mayor run the investigation into his cousin's death, thinking he would eventually tire. Now, he understood that he needed to find these runaways to gain the upper hand with the mayor. If he played his cards right, he would end up with the Hen House and the coin to do as he pleased. *If he played his cards right*—the mayor wouldn't even miss Mitchell Houser when he finally went missing.

Ennis stood next to him at the bar. The Hen House was in full swing, even with the establishment being synonymous with several killings. It appeared pussy was an attraction that most men couldn't ignore. The bar area had several patrons; the drunks sat facing the barkeep, while the businessmen were seated at the tables, chatting. A stunning, young mahogany skinned woman danced about nearly naked, pushing her breasts in several of the men's faces. Opposite the parlor, patrons sat on the overstuffed couches being tended to by the women.

His cousin was reporting and whining that he was bored of watching the orphanage. "Nufin is 'appenin' there. Just some white women takin' care of nigger babies. Francis is givin' me a break."

Liam stared down into his glass. "You will watch the orphanage 'til I say different."

"I will." Ennis said slamming his glass down. "Frannie got it tonight."

Liam nodded just as his favorite whore, Peaches stepped up and whispered. "Been a while, lover."

Peaches was all done up in a yellow, gauzy gown that clung to her beautiful form. The garment both revealed and hid everything. She was the darkest with bright white teeth and thick pouty lips. Peaches was in love with him and before Alice, he was beginning to feel an interest. He turned to Ennis and ordered.

"Relieve Francis in the morning."

"Will do." Ennis countered.

Liam walked out of the smoke-filled lounge. His carriage waited at the curb and he climbed in without the help of the driver. He had a stop to make before heading home. The hour was late as his carriage pulled through the gates of Fernando's Upper Westside mansion. There was no stable boy nor staff available at this time of night, the perfect time for a meeting. The Blackwell Island incident had caused the mayor to distance himself while hypocritically wanting Liam to murder for him.

Climbing from the carriage, Liam walked around back to the secret door off the parlor that everyone knew about. He didn't bother to knock. The chamber was dark save for a small glow around the desk. He stepped in shutting the door behind him and Fernando looked up. His graying hair was coming loose from the stay at the nape of his neck. The ruffled, white shirt he wore was unbuttoned revealing a small portion of his chest. He had a drink in his hand, and he seemed a tad unsteady. The mayor appeared surprised at his presence.

"Fernando." Liam greeted.

"We are no closer to finding the killer of my cousin–my best friend. Political obligations are closing in on me."

"I 'ave been followin' a few leads." Liam offered, noncommittally.

The mayor perked up. "What have you got?"

"I'll worry 'bout it. You just remember the 'en 'ouse is mine for the trouble." Liam replied.

"Yes… yes. I'll be a silent partner."

"No."

"It's a lucrative establishment–buy me out. I'll give you a fair price."

"Ya want 'ugh's killer or not?"

"Hugh borrowed from me to start the business and he never finished repaying." The mayor blurted.

Liam glared at Fernando. Hugh didn't even like him, yet the mayor worshipped his kin. He shook his head. "I don't care what deal ya 'ad wit' 'ugh–it's dead."

"You find the killer and I'll back away from the Hen House after three years."

"One year or nothing, Mayor."

"One. But that year doesn't start until after the killer has been dealt with." Fernando countered; he was both begging and demanding.

"Fair enough." Liam said softly. "I want 'ouser removed from the whorehouse."

"He is there until you produce."

It was better than Liam thought he would get. He offered a curt nod and turned for the door. There was nothing else to discuss.

"The woman you took from—"

"Mr. Mayor, don't threaten me or shyte will spoil between us."

Fernando laughed and Liam walked away. Once back in the carriage, he realized the mayor wanted to see if Alice mattered to him. Unwittingly, he showed his hand. He shook his head trying to back away from the implication of Fernando's sudden interest in Alice. It didn't matter because not even the mayor of New York would take her from him—*no man was man enough.*

Liam let his head fall back against the plush seat taking the travel home to relax. He didn't like to be agitated when dealing with Alice; she feared him. All parts of his life were hard and violent, but with her, he achieved softness. He hadn't even known it was missing from his life.

When the carriage pulled through the gates of his property and came to a lurching stop, Liam sat for a moment. After collecting himself, he opened the door and jumped down onto the dirt path. The vehicle moved on to the stables and he stood about thinking of her. He lit a cigarette and pulled a flask from his overcoat pocket, drinking deeply. He wiped his mouth with his sleeve and stared into the night sky. There was nothing to see, but the chill felt good against his skin.

He walked around back and didn't flinch when Brian's voice floated out of the darkness. Liam expected as much.

"We went down into the colored sector." Brian reported. "No one is talkin'."

"Offer coin, everyone 'as a price."

"How much?" Brian asked.

"Figure it out—they poor like us. Shouldn't take much."

"Liam Quinn ain't poor." Brian scoffed.

"When ya find yerself doin' dirt that makes the next bloke rich, you ain't only poor, yer dumb." Liam chuckled. "I aim to change my lot."

"The mayor?"

"Yeah." Liam replied. "Continue to watch 'im."

He stepped around Brian heading for the backdoor. The house was black as ink inside as he made his way down the short hall. Liam stopped at the smaller room and pushed open the door. Alice lay asleep on the cot snuggled down in the bedding. He turned down the oil lamp that she kept burning, then scooped her up into his arms, bedding and all.

"Sir." She whispered groggily.

He carried her to the connecting bedroom and placed her in his bed. Liam didn't argue with her about where she started out the night because he came home so late. Once home, he moved her to his bed. The first night she protested, and to his shame he was rough when he took her. She hadn't fought him again. Alice slept only in a shift at his command.

Most nights Alice lay quiet while he readied himself for bed, speaking only if spoken to. He undressed after he got the fire to blaze and began heating the chamber. Naked, he climbed in behind her and pulled her back against him. Liam kissed her shoulder and whispered against her ear.

"Take this night dress off."

She sat up, doing as he bid. Liam allowed her to feign indifference because she could not fake the carnal reactions she had when he was inside her. He was familiar with the life and times of a whore. His own mother had earned a living on her back. At the Hen House and other places like it, he had fucked women from all walks of life. But never had he taken to his sheets a woman that was unused. It was a mistake that could not be remedied.

"Come ride me, lass."

Alice climbed astride him and reached down between them to angle his hard length at her core. Her hair was coming loose from the braid and he loved it. When she sank down onto him, her mouth formed a silent "O". The firelight bathed her in orange, gold and blue hues. Her breasts bounced as she moved up and down on him. Liam was transfixed; he palmed her ass to slow her down.

"Don't rush me, Alice. Ya feel good."

She leaned over and nipped his chin, out of anger he suspected. When he grunted in pain, she suckled his tongue. Alice never broke her stride. She rode him to orgasm while kissing him all over his face. He could feel her tears as her body clenched around him.

Against his ear, she begged. "Let go… please; I needs to feel it."

Liam's dick throbbed and spasmed at her plea, leaving him shaken and spent. At dawn, he woke her again, pulling her up onto all fours. He plowed her from behind, and when they both cried out their pleasure, he dropped to the bed. Shutting his eyes, he tried to hide from his emotions and her. Alice dressed, going about her day of cleaning and cooking. Liam Quinn realized he was in trouble; he loved Alice.

❊ ❊ ❊

Fernando Wood woke with a headache from too much drink and double the problems. Lincoln had sent a missive stating he would be coming to New York to discuss the draft. The president offered no date or time as to his arrival. The mayor believed the real reason for the visit was the incident on Blackwell Island. Fernando didn't think Lincoln cared about the crime happening in any particular city, when the whole country was at war. He believed this was Lincoln's attempt to discredit him before he moved on to larger government.

The president was attempting to push his own agenda and Fernando was in the way. The Emancipation Proclamation had been nothing more than a failed publicity stunt on the part of the president. How could he free slaves in the Confederacy where he had no jurisdiction? As if Jeff Davis didn't matter - the man's testicles were sizable for sure.

His mind bounced to Liam Quinn and true anger seized his

person. But Fernando had to admit that part of his trouble with Quinn was self-inflicted. Taking up with Mitchell Houser had set their relationship on shaky ground. Blackwell Island had been a message to him, and Fernando understood that. Though he would never admit it. His own smugness had worked against him, and Quinn was now giving lessons in wins and losses.

His personal manservant appeared with his morning nourishment on a rolling tray. The older fellow had been with him for years and knew how to be invisible. Jasper was elegant and flowery in his mannerisms while carrying a gun. It was the strangest of things, but the mayor figured he could do worse. Jasper was a white man of about sixty summers with silver hair and faded blue eyes.

Fernando stood on wobbly legs and managed to pour his own coffee. Jasper pulled the drapes back inviting in the powerful sunlight.

"Please have word sent to my wife that I have political obligations and won't make her cousin's wedding. Advise her to spare no expense in choosing a gift for the lovely couple. Leave me, Jasper."

"Yes, sir."

When the butler was gone, Fernando immediately closed the drapes. The mayor of New York wanted to wallow in pity, while he figured on how to take the president's actions and turn them back on him. He also needed to pay closer attention to Liam Quinn, so that he didn't end up assassinated. As it was, Mitchell Houser was going to end up missing.

8

Fort Independence
December 1862

BLACK STOOD IN his studio reliving the meeting he had days ago with Simon, Morgan and Sunday. He wanted for his wife and Morgan the luxury of tending the children without the worry of safety. But this was nothing like his situation with Will Turner and his attempt to have Sunday or Elbert's circumstance with slave trackers that didn't know they were being tracked. This wasn't even comparable to James' plight with the death of Fannie. What they had now was someone actively hunting them and killing innocent folks in the process. He had to respect his wife enough to bring her in on the matter.

"Me and the men will leave in two days." Simon said.

Black nodded, before turning his attention to Sunday and Morgan. He had expected Morgan's nonchalance at the matter, but it was his wife who shocked him. Sunday wore a wine-colored dress with a beige decorative collar. Her brown skin glowed with health, and he was thankful to Callie for helping with his sons. Morgan's hair had grown to shoulder length and was tamed into two fat braids. In contrast, she wore black trousers, boots and one of Simon's shirts.

"Me and Morgan will run the fort. You ain't gotta worry." Sunday said. "I done started weaning the boys, so's I can pay attention to what's happenin'."

Black's chest squeezed at her words, and he paced back toward the window to collect himself. Simon chimed in. "Morgan and the baby will move in here."

"Yes," Sunday confirmed. "Havin' the chilren together will take the strain off us."

"They tell me we being hunted." Morgan said.

"Yeah." Black replied.

"When ya leave, Nat?" Sunday asked.

"The goal is to give Simon time to travel to Lincoln, then we will head to New York. We should be settled when they meet up with us in Ravenswood."

His wife nodded her approval. Morgan added, "Let's hear yo' plan."

Thankful for something to do with his hands. Black unrolled the parchment, dropping it to the floor. They all placed a booted foot on the edge, while he stepped through the plan.

A knock at the studio door pulled him from his thoughts. He didn't bother to grant the person in the hall entry. At this hour of the night, he was sure it was his wife. Black watched as the knob jiggled, then turned before Sunday walked in. One of his black shirts was draped over her small frame and she was barefoot. There was a chill in the air and he feared she would catch her death.

"Barefoot," he said, disapprovingly.

"Callie and all the chilren moved in wit' Mama for the night." She answered, ignoring his scolding.

His wife moved to inspect the canvas in front of him and frowned; it was blank.

"No painting?" she asked.

"My head's too full."

Anthony: Unshackled | 119

Sunday looked over her shoulder at him and smiled weakly. "Will ya come to our bed and rest wit' me?"

The inconsistency of his emotions caused him anxiety. Black wanted to lay with his wife-he wanted inside her, but...

"Nat?"

He cleared his throat and dropped his gaze to the floor. Sunday turned to face him, leaving him no room to evade. She coaxed. "Pick me up, Nat, my foots is cold."

Black did her bidding. His wife wrapped her arms around his neck and her legs about his waist. She smelled of lavender oil and peppermints. His dick hardened when she leaned in and kissed his Adam's apple. Sunday rubbed her nose against his and the intimacy rocked his very being.

"Take me to our room," she demanded softly.

He was powerless to refuse her request. Turning, he exited the studio, walking the dark corridor until he came to their door. Once inside, he noted the fireplace blazed, and the tub was filled with steaming water; their bedchamber was cozy. Black stood her on her feet and his wife treaded on tiptoe over to the tub. She removed his shirt and clambered in. Her beautiful brown body was on display for his pleasure. Black remained at the door, as if he were not welcome in their personal space.

Sunday sank down in the water and invited. "Come bathe wit' me, Nat."

He lingered at undressing, slowly removing his guns, boots and clothing. When he was completely naked, he moved toward the tub and stepped in. Involuntarily, he groaned at the feel of the warm water against his skin. Once he settled, his wife straddled him. Sunday leaned in kissing him chastely.

"Tell me ya woes. I see ya ain't wantin' to be naked wit' me." She whispered.

Black didn't know how to articulate such thoughts or feelings. He shook his head, but no words came out. So far in this interaction, Sunday had taken the lead. Finally, he managed. "I been worried for you and the boys."

"I's well, so what else concerns ya?"

"I want to be inside you, but…" he sighed, then tried again. "I mean, I'm trying to give you a break. I—"

"I ain't needin' no break from being naked wit' you. When I needs somethin', I'll tell ya."

"Why can't we be like everyone else? We keep having two babies at once." He said, lifting his hands then dropping them, sloshing water over the sides of the tub.

Sunday giggled. Black needed her softness, her laughter—he just needed her. He continued. "I worried when we had to depend on another because you didn't have enough milk. I felt powerless."

"Benny eats a lot, but we worked out his needs. Sides, you ain't a normal man." She said, looking him in the eyes. "You is greatness."

"Sunday."

"Nat, we gon have more chilren. Anyhow, Mama put me back on the drink."

"Shit, I think I should be drinking it." Black countered.

They both burst out laughing at his declaration and the night eased. Once out of the water, they dried each other and fell into bed. Black lay on his stomach, while Sunday kneaded his muscles with olive oil. He groaned at her touch. After a time, they switched positions and Black massaged his wife. Only the glow of the fireplace danced against the shadows.

Sunday reared up on all fours and Black eased into her from behind. The heat of her wrapped about his dick made his balls draw up. He had not experienced this level of intimacy with his lady love in months. It was unmanly, but he whimpered when she pulled away only to ease back onto him.

"I—woman, I love you," he breathed.

"Ohhh, Nat… I miss ya the same."

The olive oil eased the friction, but not totally. His wife's soft skin and enlarged breasts were almost his undoing. He pulled her to sit on his lap with her back to his chest. Black turned her face sideways, so he could kiss her. Sunday tasted of olive oil and carnality. They sat that way for a time, unmoving, as he allowed himself to bask in her femininity. He felt her body clench around him, but he was in no hurry. Black wanted to remain joined to her as long as he could.

"I miss being one with you," he whispered.

Sunday panted and wriggled her ass just a smidgen.

"Damn…" Black hissed, his voice tight from their shared pleasure. "You are to take care of yourself while I'm away."

"Yes," Sunday's response was breathy. "Promise to come back to me safe."

"I promise." Black grunted. "Sunday… baby. It's good between us."

His wife pulled off him, getting down on all fours once more. When Black pushed back into her, it was with purpose; still, he allowed his wife to take control. He did not want to hurt her. Placing a palm against one of the four bedposts, Black watched as his length slid in and out of her. Each time he disappeared deep within her, it shoved him closer to the edge.

"Shit… Sunday, I can't…"

"Me too, my love." She panted.

The orgasm that hit him was sharp; his seed erupted from him in three intense bursts. The ecstasy was all consuming. Tremors wracked their bodies for moments until they collapsed in a tangled heap in the bedding. Black groaned at the loss when his softening member slipped from her. Sunday turned in his arms and snuggled against him.

That was how dawn found them, cocooned in each other's love.

✻ ✻ ✻

"Simon been gone for three days." James said to Elbert when he dropped Otis off.

"Yeah," Elbert muttered. "Jeremiah gon pick the boy up from you and Abby tomorrow."

The sun was starting to go down and it was cold, like it hadn't been in days. Elbert stared out to where the sun was setting. Behind him, he could hear Otis talking to Abby. James' new baby started crying then quieted.

"Riding out…" Elbert began, then couldn't figure on how to explain himself.

"I needs it too."

Elbert chuckled. "I love living here wit' my wife and children. But I need the ruckus."

"We ain't nothin' but two misfits what stayed when Otis got killed. It's the best of both thangs."

"Did you decide to settle to keep Black safe?" Elbert asked.

"Yeah."

"Black knows and he hates it." Elbert said.

"Too damn bad."

"He does what we do…" Elbert offered as he stepped down onto the dirt path headed for home.

James called after him. "Black is needed by many—we needed by a few."

"Tomorrow."

"Elbert." James yelled after him once more. He turned, walking backwards slowly. James continued. "Remember when Ant said Luke's death made him cautious? I understands his feelins'."

Elbert nodded, then walked away. His pace was leisurely as he made his way home. The trees lining the paths were without leaves. A breeze blew and there was iciness attached. Dry earth crunched under his booted feet. Elbert gave himself a moment to reflect. James had been correct; they couldn't bear another loss. Otis and Black had been inseparable; it had been the same for him and James. Their brother's demise had brought the three of them closer.

He chuckled at Black's disgust when Mr. Peabody pissed

himself. But what to do? For all his greatness, *Black was their baby brother*. And like James, Elbert felt the need to protect him and his legacy. Black wasn't the only one that experienced feelings of failure in dealing with Otis' death. He and James both wrestled with it. Elbert hated to admit it, but like James, he wanted Black to stay safe–stay home. But he also respected the fact that Black rolled up his sleeves and got dirty with the men.

Elbert smiled when his cabin came into view. He would make the most of the time left with his wife and children, then ride out with the knowledge that they would be safe. When he reached the porch, he didn't linger as he often did. Instead, he pushed at the door to find Anna seated by the fire knitting. The cabin was welcoming–warm, smelling of stew and cornbread. His wife looked up and smiled.

"You home early."

"Missed you. I checked on the boys. Junior is wit' yo' mama and Otis is wit' James. I dropped him off myself."

"Good." Anna said before going back to knitting.

"How you feeling?"

She offered him a weak smile. "My stomach is starting to settle."

Anna wore a yellow shift with his thick itchy gray socks on her feet. His beautiful wife was with child again and he couldn't be more pleased. She'd told him immediately and he'd kissed her senseless. They'd lain together the night she told him discussing the future. Elbert decided it best if he didn't tell Black. It would only cause his brother angst. He hadn't told James either. Shaking his head, he had to come to grips with being the father of three. Otis just made five summers, Junior would soon be two summers and now a new babe.

"You hungry?" she asked.

"I could eat."

Anna served him hot chicken stew and warm cornbread. They shared a plate and talked–gossiped really.

"I think my mama is upset with Philip." Anna said.

"Are they courtin'? I ain't been able to figure it out?"

She snickered. "They are from what I can see."

"Well Imma better biddy than you." Elbert said, shoving food into his mouth to stall.

"What you know that I don't?" Anna demanded.

"Lou done moved in with Molly, finally."

"Awww." His wife said, dreamily. "I'm happy for them."

"Yeah."

"Well, guess what I know?" Anna exclaimed and she was giddy.

"What?"

"Nemind–I shouldn't tell you," she sighed, dangling the news in front of him like a carrot.

Elbert dropped his spoon abruptly and eyed her real threatening–like. "Woman, if you don't tell me, I'm gonna tickle you 'til you pee yourself."

"You wouldn't dare." Anna gulped.

His expression was deadpan. "I would."

She giggled. "Emma can't cook."

"Shit, poor Ant."

"Anthony does all the cooking. He cooks better than Big Mama and Iris."

"Does not... I don't believe you. Ant cooks and his wife don't?" Elbert gasped, and he did so like a little old lady. "How you know?"

"I'm not telling a story. Emma let me taste an apple pie he baked. Elbert..." Anna paused, then went on. "The man can cook. Afterwards, she told me don't tell nobody. She took me into her confidence, and of course, I ain't worth nothing."

They both laughed, chatted and ate. Later that night, Elbert sat with his back against the headboard. Anna climbed astride–taking him into her tight body. Placing her hands on his shoulders, she drove them deliberately toward ecstasy. He palmed her ass feeling the wetness between them. When her muscles clenched up, the pleasure pushed him to conclusion.

In the aftermath of orgasm they did not separate. Elbert held her until he hardened again.

"I'm impressed." Anna breathed.

"Woman, you ain't seen nothing yet." Elbert chuckled.

At dawn, James woke to find Abby missing from their bed. He could hear her moving about in the next room, readying herself for the day. It had been a strained few months. Abby was fidgety in Jeremiah's presence. But James couldn't complain; the black cracker took pains to steer clear of a nervous Abby whenever possible. Lil Otis brought them together more often than not and James wasn't willing to give the boy up.

Swinging his legs over the side of the bed, he used the chamber pot before washing up in the water basin on the nightstand. He didn't dress, donning only long brown underwear. Abby was seated to the table drinking a cup of tea. She looked up when he entered the front room.

"I imagined you would wanna rest since ya riding out tonight."

"Come to bed, Abby." His voice was firm.

James realized that he had to be tough and truthful with her to alleviate some of what was disturbing her. Turning down the wick on the oil lamp, Abby stood, following him back into their bedroom. Facing her, he untied the belt to her pink robe, helping her from the garment. Abby was dressed in a blue cotton nightdress; James hated the damn thing. It hid all her beauty from him. He didn't bother to ask permission as he reached for the hem, pulling the fabric over her head.

When she was naked before him, he dropped his drawers and yanked the covers back. She scrambled in and he followed. Small shards of sunlight peeked through the heavy brown drapes. He was thankful to Big Mama for keeping the baby. Leaning up on one elbow, he faced her, tangling his leg with hers.

"I'm 'bout to tell you a story." He said with some amusement, so as not to be too rough with her.

"You are?"

"Pay attention, Abigail." He countered and she smiled. "I don't favor talkin' wit' you 'bout what goes on when I'm wit' the men. Hate you worryin'—but Imma tell ya something 'bout our last mission."

Her eyes brightened with unshed tears; he had her full attention. "We stole President Lincoln."

"You didn't," she gasped.

"We did." James chuckled. "The man almost shit himself too."

Abby burst out laughing. "Y'all is a scary bunch."

"Travel was a wary thang and by the time we reached the Hunter plantation, I couldn't wait to kill that damn Jeremiah. My skin still pulls tight in the cold weather."

"He's so menacin'. I wants him to leave here." Abby whispered. "I try for Otis' sake. I loves the boy, but I cain't… wit' Jeremiah. I don't much like being in the company of Callie neither. It angers me that she acts 'fraid of you when you the one wit' the scar."

James sighed. "When we got to the Hunter plantation, we cornered Jeremiah in his cabin. Callie rushed in wit' a full belly pleadin' for his life. I beat him wit' the butt of my rifle in front of her—knocked him out."

"Oh," Abby breathed.

"Me and Elbert was finna drag him out back and shoot him in the head. Black stopped us. Callie cried and pleaded, but I couldn't hear her—I's too far gone."

"Oh my."

"We was still gon kill him, but Black didn't want it done in front of Callie. I would say Miss Callie seen me and Elbert at our meanest. Anyhow… the plantation ended up in a shootout with deserters from the war. Jeremiah shot and killed a man that was 'bout to shoot me." James explained, hating to say such things to her.

Abby leaned in and kissed his cheek, then his lips. He went on. "I ain't proud, but I know why Callie fears me."

"You knew I's scared of you riding out wit' him–didn't you?"

"Yes," James replied, while allowing himself to be kissed by her. "Me and him worked shit out; he ain't take the boy from me. I loves Lil' Otis."

Abby fell on her back coaxing him between her thighs. James pushed into her in one rough motion to the hilt. A sob ripped from him at the pleasure of their connection and the unburdening of his conscience. They found a tempo that was intense, and Abby wrapped her legs about his waist causing him to sink deeper on the down stroke, until they both cried out as orgasm beset them.

"Damn... damn." James murmured as his dick pulsed and spurted.

"I loves ya so much." Abby whispered.

The couple lay talking and loving on one another, while James ignored the fact that he would ride out at midnight.

9

Ravenswood, Queens

TRUE TO HIS word, the ambassador's presence started paying off immediately. Bainesworth managed to secure a brand-new passenger train that was being sent to the states to begin an illustrious career. The locomotive was six cars long and luxurious in the extreme. Black and the men piled into one car where there were no other passengers or staff. The seats were black velvet, the plush carpet–red, the windows large and the scenery picturesque.

In the distance, snowcapped mountains came into view. Several of the small bodies of water they crossed were frozen over. There were evergreens dressed in icicles; as an artist Black couldn't get enough. Lou, on the other hand, didn't see it the same. The windows were his undoing.

The bridges they crossed in their quest for the states were rickety at best. One overpass groaned and swayed under the weight of the train. Frank had to pull Lou away from the glass to keep him from losing his shit. The upside to this type of travel, they were able to step through the plan–rest and step through the plan again. When Black was satisfied that everyone knew their part, he took time to speak with Anthony.

"You ready?"

"If'n I don't make it back…" Anthony replied, grabbing at the nape of his neck. "You thinks this will work?"

"I think if ever there were a group of men… The answer is yes."

Anthony nodded and Black continued. "Listen, we're going to try to avoid killing Fernando Wood. But if we can't get him to back off…"

"Yeah," Anthony said. "I sees it the same."

"New York is too close to Canada. This needs to be a clean-up."

"Worried about the fort and the orphanage." Anthony admitted.

"Same." Black replied. "I agree wit' Elbert."

"Elbert?"

"If we can't fix this, then we burn New York City to the ground."

"I sees it the same." Anthony said.

Black found a seat in the corner and took a few moments for himself. The train rocked and shook as it slowly brought them in through the top of New York state. While the men rode in style, they ate rations. Black had not allowed for anything more. The goal was to keep him and his men razor sharp. Staying alert was the key to remaining alive.

Even with the luxury, there was a downside to riding the rail. It was slow going, and the engineer stopped frequently to make checks on the equipment. The necessary and the mundane caused the men to arrive in Port Jervis, New York, a day and a half behind schedule. Still, Black made allowances for such a mishap. He also tacked on four extra days for Simon's journey.

The route the train took would have been grueling on horseback for the time of year. Black noted that Jeremiah was struggling with the weather, though he never complained. The sun was in full swing but offered nothing in the way of warmth. When they stepped from the train, the trek to the blacksmith was about two miles. Carrying supplies and the weight of his clothing caused Black to break out in a sweat.

"Shit, you sweatin'." Jeremiah said as they moved along.

"This mission will recondition you or break you." Black returned.

Jeremiah snorted. "The weather is a bitch."

"You need whiskey." Black responded, holding up his gloved hand to stop Jeremiah's protest. "You wit' me. I got yo' back–trust, man."

Black knew Jeremiah never drank on the plantation because there was only E.J. to watch his back. As he went back through his list of preparations, Black shook his head in disgust with himself. He should have recognized that Jeremiah would struggle with the weather. It was his job to think ahead – to lead.

"I don't favor the cold, but you can be sure it won't break me." Jeremiah replied.

"Good."

Port Jervis was farmland, new railroad construction and waterways, which only added to the frigid temperature. It hadn't snowed and Black considered that something to be thankful for. At half past noon they came upon a white farmhouse with two chimneys; smoke billowed from both stacks. On the left of the property stood an oversized stable with the doors thrown wide. The sound of metal striking metal drifted on the icy wind. A path circled to the front of the house and kept on to the stable. On the right of the land cows huddled together in the pasture for body warmth.

Two huge, fawn colored dogs started barking and growling as they trotted cautiously in the men's direction. Jeremiah drew both his guns and James had to intervene.

"You cain't kill the dogs, then ask for hospitality."

The black cracker glared at James for seconds before uncocking and re-holstering his weapons. Elbert chuckled and Gilbert slapped Jeremiah on the back. A large black man appeared at the stable doors.

"Daisy–Tutu! Come!" the man yelled.

Both dogs turned, running back in the man's direction. Black called out. "Hudson!"

The man cocked his head to one side as if trying to gauge Black's voice. "Hope?"

"It's me." Black replied with a grin.

The big man hustled forward into Black's personal space and clapped him on the back. Hudson was roughly forty summers and dark of skin. He had a full beard that was trimmed neatly. In contrast, his eyebrows were bushy–his salt and pepper hair, unkempt. The older man's eyes were bright with mirth. He was a laid-back fellow, standing about six feet tall. The sleeves on his homespun shirt were rolled up past his elbows revealing the letter 'H' branded into his skin. Dressed in brown trousers, black boots and an apron, Hudson looked every bit the blacksmith.

"Where are my manners? Please come in out of the cold."

He turned leading them to the farmhouse and Black wondered if all the men would fit. There were fourteen of them.

"We could take the barn."

"Nonsense, Hope. The house is roomier than it appears."

Black nodded and followed. The dogs trotted between the men as they all moved down the path. The white two-story house sat about a quarter mile from the stables and barn. As they neared the structure, he noted a green swing and a white rocking chair. The drapes were drawn on all the windows, blocking prying eyes and the afternoon sun. Once on the porch, Hudson pushed at the door and stepped over the threshold. He turned back holding the door for the men. Black was met by a gush of warm air; behind him, he heard Jeremiah groan. In front of him, a woman stood tending the stove. They all filed in standing around the front door.

Hudson called out. "Janie, Hope is here."

The woman looked over her right shoulder, then turned wiping her hands on the white stained apron she wore. She was light of skin with large round eyes and an easy smile. Her hair was braided in several small plaits. She wore a brown serviceable dress and was on the plump side. Janie looked to be about forty summers, and her skin told the story of a hard life.

"Hope, it's good to see ya."

"Miss Janie, you looking well." Black countered.

She looked at the crowd of men at the door, then back at Black. It was then that he understood who she was looking for.

"Otis?"

Black shook his head. "Gone–three years now."

"Oh," she whispered. "Mary?"

"Is still with me and doing well." He decided against explaining that Mary was now with Shultz.

Her smile weakened, but she managed to push them all beyond the uncomfortable. Moving around him, Janie looked up at the men.

"I'm glad for your company. Welcome," she said with sincerity.

All the men spoke at once, causing a low murmur to float through the great room. Black took that moment to give a roll call. He pointed to each man as he spoke their names.

"This is Jeremiah, my brother James, my brother Elbert and Tim. On the left, we have Gilbert, Frank and Lou."

"Twins." Janie remarked.

The men nodded and Black went on. "That there is Anthony, Josiah, Ralph and John. Last but not least are Herman and Bainesworth.

"I'm Janie. Please make yourselves at home. Dinner is almost ready."

Hudson and Janie were abolitionists until Janie was shot. They were educators of colored children in an underground school. Both of them had helped Black hone his reading, writing and arithmetic skills. Hudson had been afraid to lose Janie, so they settled in Port Jervis, backing away from the abolitionist life. Black was happy to see they were well. The couple never had children of their own, but like Big Mama they parented many.

A grandfather clock stood tall in the corner, its gold pendulum swinging–denoting the passage of time. Black walked over to the long wooden table in the center of the room. He seated himself on the bench facing the fire. The men, following his lead, took up space on the floor around the hearth. Jeremiah sat in front of the smaller fireplace at the opposite end of the room.

The brown couch was pushed against the far wall by Bainesworth and Hudson. Tutu the smaller of the two beasts curled up on the couch. Daisy plopped down next to Jeremiah pressing her furry body against his, as if she understood that he was chilled to the bone. Conversation struck up between the men and Hudson.

"It isn't bad living in Port Jervis. The white folks understand that all hands is needed to build the railways. I'm a blacksmith by trade, and I work the railways. They pay coloreds less than white folks, but it's a steady living." Hudson explained.

Janie chimed in adding, "And Moses don't live but a stone's throw away in Auburn. The white folk don't want no trouble."

As the discussion flowed, Black took out time to work with Jeremiah. He caught Elbert's eye and nodded toward the black cracker. They both stood and ambled over to where Jeremiah was stretched out next to Daisy–his hat thrown over his face.

In a low tone Elbert asked, "Can yo' new bitch excuse us?"

"You betta not be sayin' Callie is my old bitch." Jeremiah said, removing his hat to glare up at him.

"Callie meaner than old Daisy." Elbert replied.

"She is." Jeremiah chuckled. "Miss Anna is sweet. I ain't fixing to talk poorly about her. Imma tell Callie."

"I take it back." Elbert offered quickly.

"Let's step outside." Black said cutting their banter short.

Jeremiah stood without hesitation and trailed Black to the front door. Elbert brought up the rear. Shutting the door behind them, they all stood in heavy sweaters and hats. The black cracker attempted not to shake from the cold and failed. Elbert offered

Jeremiah his flask and the black cracker did partake. Turning the decanter up to his lips, Jeremiah drank deeply and sputtered.

The sun was about to drop from the sky and Black wondered if he should alter their travel for the next leg of the journey. Jeremiah must have read his thoughts and concerns.

"I'll make it. We ain't gotta change plans."

Black eyed him for moments before nodding.

Anthony listened as the men stood about in the barn readying themselves to ride out. Black, he noticed, had taken time to speak with each man to ensure everyone was ready. This act alone on Black's part was an indication of the challenges to come. Dawn was happening as the men checked supplies and saddled their horses. Anthony also observed Black hand Hudson an envelope. He suspected it was payment for a hearty meal and top performing animals.

Though he tried, Anthony couldn't shake the feeling of dread. The image of Luke's lifeless body played on a loop in his head. Emma's presence was jammed in with his sorrow, and he often envisioned her crying. But his biggest worry was facing Sunday should Black be cut down while trying to right his wrongs. He was still shaken to the core at witnessing Mary screaming in pain at the news of Otis' death. Anthony did not want that for Sunday— he didn't want it for himself. He didn't want it for the people of Fort Independence.

The sun was starting to paint the sky pink as it rose. When Anthony mounted his horse, the animal danced to the left defiantly. Miss Janie came to stand next to her husband with a blanket wrapped about her shoulders. She handed Jeremiah a silver flask, which he graciously accepted. Black, not one for long goodbyes, brought his horse to a slow trot and rode off. They all followed.

Anthony pushed his thoughts to nothingness as they galloped

toward the Hudson River. He kept Black in sight as he brought up the rear. The posse didn't ride as one body, tactically it was the best move in case of ambush. Gilbert and Elbert rode together, Frank and Lou did the same. James, Tim and Bainesworth were invisible. Josiah, John, Herman and Ralph hadn't been spotted since they left the farm. He and Jeremiah rode with Black.

The temperature was much improved but still cold. Except for the thundering of horse hooves hitting the earth, there was no other sound; the men did not engage in conversation. The trees were bare which aided against attack, but nothing was taken for granted. Anthony followed the position of the sun in the sky, and it was well past noon when they hit the edge of the Hudson River. The sun was beginning to go down when a dirty barge bumped the pier. When the last horse was settled, the men stood between the beasts as total darkness happened.

There wasn't much in the way of comfort to their latest mode of travel. Coal was piled high by the steam engine and there was plenty of soot. Several oil lamps offered no relief as the river barge turned into what Black explained was Spuyten Duyvil Creek. Navigating the narrow body of water that the creek flowed into wasn't for the faint of heart. Anthony heard what sounded like Jeremiah retching over the side as one of the horses took a big shit. The animal began wheezing and stomping its feet looking for solid ground.

Under the cover of night, the captain, a white man Anthony only glimpsed, stood at the helm. The water added an icy bite to the air, and the horseshit was sour smelling as if it were summer. Anthony was thankful that he couldn't see his hand before his face. When finally they bumped the dock and unloaded the horses and supplies, he heard Black begin issuing orders.

"We've reached Astoria Village. The day has been hard, but the miles in front of us are few."

Around him, Anthony heard the men swinging into their saddles as Black spoke into the darkness. They pressed on, and to his left he heard Jeremiah retch some more. As for himself, the closer they drew to their destination, he was becoming silently hysterical. Anthony was sure of it.

Jeremiah was sick that was all there was to it. The cold was in his bones and he ached with it. In the past, when they had traveled to Canada and even New York, the weather had been fair. The worst part—on this trek they had journeyed in luxury, and still he had taken ill. Whiskey was more than his belly could handle. Now he had small goals—get to the destination and try to sleep off his misery.

He was disoriented from the weak, under the weather feeling and the jarring motion of his spine as he wrestled for control of his horse. It seemed to him that they rode away from the water only to ride back to it. On the river and in this place called Astoria, the temperature held more frost. They had been riding for about an hour when Black turned down a dirt path leading to the front side of some fancy homes.

As they rounded the bend, the lighting was brilliant. Lampposts lined the cobblestoned streets and a small metropolis sprung up right before his very eyes. The rush of water had Jeremiah realizing that the blackness to his left was the river. He imagined that in daylight one could see that the properties butted right up to the rocky banks. The homes were grander than a plantation big house. A few of the front yards had lampposts every few feet. The water-front properties were a sight to behold at night; to Jeremiah's way of thinking they would be even finer in sunlight.

Black was at the head of the posse, leading the men away from the well-lit flamboyance of the other homes. At the end of the cobblestone lane loomed a large home engulfed in darkness, but for a lone candle in the front bottom window. Black swung down from the saddle, walking his beast around to the right of what could only be the front door. A ripple of sound happened, denoting that each man swung down from the saddle just the same.

"Shit… what this place is?" Lou asked.

"We 'bout to find out." Frank answered.

Elbert chuckled. "Even I got the willies and I ain't afraid of shit."

Jeremiah remained quiet, but not out of fear. His throat burned and he felt of all things, faint. The black cracker was afraid of being dead weight on this mission.

"Black is a crafty fellow. I anxiously await the light of day." Bainesworth added.

"What he say?" Anthony asked.

"He can't wait to see shit in the sunlight." Elbert translated.

James laughed and Gilbert spoke up. "How the hell you understands him?"

"I'm speaking English, gentlemen." Bainesworth added in a haughty tone. Which to Jeremiah would have been funny had he not been quietly suffering.

He had traveled to nearby places with E.J. and had even been on a ferry a time or two. It wasn't as if Horry, South Carolina, hadn't seen cold days, but not like this–not like Canada. Journeying to New York in September with his brother, Frank, Lou and Anthony had been a treat. All of it was beyond his scope of the Hunter plantation. He understood that riding out with Black would be a reconditioning of his person. Past experiences with these men told him that they would have preferred a more primitive mode of travel.

Once at the back of the house, the men stood facing an open stable door. Two colored men stood at the threshold, each holding oil lamps. An older man given the lighting stepped forward. He was bald on the top with gray hair that was also part of a full beard. The man looked to be about sixty summers, brown skinned and menacing as hell. When he addressed Black, his words held admiration.

"Hope… It's an honor to have you back.

"Charlie, good to see you." Black replied.

The other man followed suit, holding his oil lamp up to try to gauge their numbers. "Hope."

"Felix, how you?" Black asked.

"I'm well, sir." Felix answered.

Jeremiah could just make out that Felix was a young man, light of skin with wild hair. His face was clean shaven. When the black cracker would have assessed the man further, he lowered the oil lamp. Black began issuing orders.

"The horses need to be fed and wiped down."

"Sho' thang, Hope." Charlie replied.

Black moved past the stablehands to the last stall. The men did the same while picking a stall for their horses. Charlie hung his lamp on a nearby hook and moved in to tend Black's animal. Felix tended the feeding sacks. Black moved to stand in the center of the aisle.

"I shall return." Black said and held up his hand when his brother would have spoken. "James, come with me. Elbert, you are in charge here."

Jeremiah watched as the brothers exited the stable. Black shoved James as they faded into the night.

Black walked toward the back of the house with James at his side. Familiarity helped him navigate to a raised corridor at a side door. Night covered everything, then abruptly gave way to light when he pushed at another door at the top of the passage. They stepped into a well-furnished parlor where a bone-colored settee daintily faced the roaring fire. A plush green carpet ran almost to the hearth and on the left of the fireplace, two burgundy wingback chairs invited polite conversation. At the enormous windows, the drapes were pulled back, but there was nothing to see.

Through the thick panes of glass, the rush of water could still be heard. Black considered that at night the sound could be interpreted as unsettling or calming depending on the person. He felt neither; instead, what he grappled with was the need to do violence before it could be done to him. The real struggle for him was keeping Sunday, his children and his extended family from harm.

In his periphery, Black caught movement and focused on it. There in a nook between the window and fireplace stood an older white gentleman. His gray hair was pulled back from his face, his eyes were wide at the sight of Black. The man was large in stature, though not taller than six feet. He had a drink in his right hand and the other wrapped about an unlit cigar.

"Milford." Black said with mocked disdain.

"Hope."

They stared at each other for moments before the man turned to James. "Did Hope tell you that I owe a debt I could never repay?"

Black never gave James a chance to answer. "I spoke the truth."

"You didn't, but I'm used to your cunning."

"Milford, this is my brother James." Black said introducing the men. "James–Milford."

"Good to meet you." Milford said, stepping forward with a hand extended.

James reciprocated. "Same."

Once polite conversation was out of the way, a sadness washed over the older man. "Broke me, them hanging John."

Black nodded and to James he offered explanation. "This is John Brown's older brother."

"John wouldn't see reason."

"Every man has his life and death to answer to." Black said.

Milford sighed. "I had to change my surname to Church. Several of my nephews perished in that fiasco. John would have been of value at a time like this."

"I agree." Black replied.

"What you owes my brother?" James asked, breaking their banter.

"Hope thinks I owe him for *not* shooting John on sight." Milford answered. "The truth lies in the reverse–Hope owes me for not shooting John. My brother was difficult, but I loved and admired him."

"I tried to talk him out of it." Black said.

"I knew you would; his death was a waste. I broke into the jail–me and my men. John refused to leave with us. He kept spouting that he would go down in history. Summoned the jailer on us–we had to flee and lay low. Of course, you know the rest."

Black nodded, but it was James who spoke. "Seem like to me while it might be sad, John done got the country to the right place. It ain't solved, but shit ain't being ignored neither."

"I agree." Milford said before turning back to the window. Once he gathered himself, over his shoulder he said. "I hate Fernando Wood."

Milford had moved them beyond the grief and Black followed. "There are fourteen of us–the final count will be twenty-two. I have one man who is sick."

"I'm not very social, so this will work out." Milford answered. "My neighbors think I belong on Blackwell Island."

"Why?" James inquired.

"The island is where New York sends its criminal element and the broken minded."

"Of which–you are both." Black countered with mirth.

"How long will you stay?" Milford asked.

"As long as it takes." Black answered. "Ahhh—"

"Let's hear it." Milford said, folding his arms over his chest.

"Lincoln will be one of my guests."

"The president..." Milford stammered, then asked for clarity. "Abraham Lincoln–is that who you speak of?"

"Yeah."

"I'm not even going to ask..." Milford said, incredulity lacing his words.

"Don't ask." Black answered. "How many rooms you got?"

"You getting ready to rearrange my house?"

"A little."

Milford sighed again. "You'll have Dorothy to contend with."

Black laughed, then got down to business. "We will take over this floor and set up a base of operations from this room."

Milford nodded and offered. "I'm happy to help."

Black stared at him for a moment before speaking the truth. "This is not abolition work."

"Perfect, I've been done with abolition work since my brother's death. These days I'm Milford Church, aging eccentric–no family."

"All right." Black said.

"Can I ask a question?" Milford went on.

"You can–don't mean you'll get an answer."

"Is the president in New York about the Draft Act, the Emancipation Proclamation or you?"

Black stared…

"Ahhh. So the president is here because he owes you a debt he could never repay." Milford laughed outright, his hilarity bouncing off the walls.

Black's facial expression remained deadpan, which only caused more laughter on Milford's part. James joined in eventually, but Black… well, he never did laugh.

It had been a long day and night. Adding whiskey, coffee and no sleep to the mix gave Anthony the jitters. Still, he wanted to bring in the new day seeing their base of operations. He also wanted to grasp the trouble Black went through on his behalf. There would be no rest until he was able to measure the debt he couldn't repay.

"I cain't sleep 'til I see where we is." Lou's voice flowed at him from the still of the night.

"Me too." Anthony replied.

"We finna see mo' than we wants." Frank stated with a chuckle.

Anthony stood between the brothers as the three waited for day to break. It was little more than an hour before the sky started bleeding the burnt orange of daylight into the darkness. Small by small, their surroundings came into focus. Anthony had been to New York before, but only to the colored sectors and the Hen House. He had never known the state held such beauty.

The lawns for as far as the eye could see were brown from winter. And though dead from the cold, the grass was well tamed running right up to craggy banks of the East River. If one walked to the edge of the property, there was about a five-foot drop before the land went soft and the water lapped the shore. When Anthony strode out as far as the grass reached, he saw in the distance the pier they'd come from the night before. On his left was a dock that extended well over the river and curved into a wider platform. Around the pier and along the shore, boats of all sizes were anchored and covered.

Frank and Lou followed as he walked the wide expanse of the weather-beaten pier. The planks were rotted and in need of repair. Turning to his companions, Anthony spoke the obvious.

"Next shift, we needs to fix some of dem planks."

"Sho' thang. It ain't sturdy nuff to hold the weight of horses." Frank observed.

"Gon be cold but I's in." Lou added.

At the end of the dock and across the water was the real attraction. Blackwell Island sat against the backdrop of the morning sunrise. Vegetation lined the tip of the island and beyond. Anthony could just make out the shapes of small and large structures. He had been told by Black that the island was a place for people with broken minds. But Anthony considered it was probably yet another way to mistreat the broken minded, people of color, and the poor.

It was time to evaluate the land on which he stood. Anthony followed Lou back to solid ground to face the eyesore that was the house. The elegance on the waterfront was so gaudy it bordered on ugly. The homes were brown and square shaped with nothing to recommend them, other than the morning sun. In the distance Anthony could see servants moving about extinguishing the lampposts that stood in front of the properties. Signs of life was happening and so was the shift change. When the next group of men came out, Anthony, Lou and Frank went to find their beds.

Black had them set up shop in the main parlor. All the delicate furnishings were covered with white cloth and pushed to the perimeter of the room. The opulence of the situation was not something Anthony was used to on a mission. It seemed that Black meant for the cleanup to be all the men considered–another indication that life would get hectic. The men shifted seamlessly, still Black had one order to issue.

"Jeremiah, you will remain."

Anthony witnessed the black cracker's self-disgust, but Jeremiah proffered no argument. He saw what Black saw–Jeremiah did not look good.

10

Smoke Signals
Queens, New York

THE STAFF FOR the house consisted of four-two stablehands and two housekeepers. Charlie and Felix handled the grounds, animals and repairs. Dorothy, a colored woman of forty summers was slender and soft spoken. She was black as a berry with graying hair, an intense dark stare and a regal carriage. Her attire was simple brown, blue and black dresses accentuated by a white apron. She wore her hair in two fat braids pinned at the top of her head.

A young colored girl about the age of fifteen summers served Black his meals and basically tended him; she went by the name Matilda. Dorothy directed her in the proper ways of being helpful while being invisible. Tilda was thin with a mop of ebony curls pinned in a bun at the nape of her neck. She was light of skin, yet darker than his brother James. The girl was gangly and hadn't quite come into her own; still she was pretty. Black would never say, but he knew that Dorothy was Milford's lady love. Felix and Matilda were the products of said union.

Black stood in the kitchen staring out the back window. It had been two days since they arrived in Ravenswood; he had done nothing but ponder the best course of action. The sun was going down and though the men continued to work in shifts—he had not pulled the trigger on their scheme. He hadn't done so for three reasons: Jeremiah was sick and weak as a kitten. Being down a man meant it would be better to wait for Simon and third, Sunday, his children and Callie.

He promised his wife that he would come home to her; he had also promised Callie silently that he would watch Jeremiah's back. The weight of the circumstance almost made his shoulders sag. Black sighed, then turned to exit the kitchen. He found a feeble looking Jeremiah standing by the wood burning stove. The black cracker's eyes were glazed over with fever and he shivered involuntarily.

"Ya paused everything for me." It was an accusation; Jeremiah grunted. "I ain't in need of a nurse."

Black folded his arms over his chest and cocked his head to one side. He understood the things not being said. Allowing the words to fall from his lips like stone, he inquired. "You questioning my authority?"

The men glared at each other for moments before Jeremiah relented. "I'm able to do my part."

"We'll wait for Simon—that should give you another day or two to recover. Do what Dorothy tells you—rest and eat or I'll leave you behind."

Jeremiah nodded, spun on his heels and quit the kitchen. Black was about to head back to the parlor when James appeared carrying an oil lamp. Placing the lamp on the counter next to the sink, his brother spoke softly.

"Elbert and me went to the dry-goods. Got us a message from Simon."

Black held out his hand before moving closer to the light. The telegram read: December 6, 1862. He looked up at James and grinned.

"What's today's date?"

"Day is the eleventh." James countered.

"So any time now…"

"Yeah," James confirmed.

The brothers made their way past the canvas of a black stallion that hung in the main hall. On the left of the passage was yet another sitting room, but smaller than the one they'd been operating from. A lone brown couch sat facing the window. At the front door, Black and James grabbed their coats from the peg. They found Elbert taking a cigar, while watching the sun dip behind the landscape.

"Sure hope the black cracker gets to feeling better. He's a perfect shot." Elbert said without looking their way.

"Yeah," Black said. "Simon should be along anytime. He sent a telegram–they been on the move since the sixth."

"Gonna be rough workin' 'round Lincoln." James added. "I thinks the president is wantin' to keep us."

Elbert chuckled. "Lincoln ain't gonna last long. He issued that Emancipation Proclamation setting free all the slaves in the rebellious south. White folks gon kill his ass."

Black shook his head in the darkness that was happening around them. "It isn't like Jeff Davis don't exist. The slaves in the south aren't any better off than before the proclamation. Politics…"

James sighed. "Yeah."

The temperature was frigid and the inky night complete. Black stared into the dark listening to the East River as it crashed onto the shore. In the distance, lampposts came to life as the servants from the other mansions began the task of illuminating the waterfront. The action only served to press them further into the shadows.

Black followed the hot orange tip of the cigar as it hit the ground. It occurred to him, as the fire end of Elbert's smoke was eclipsed by his boot, there would be no chance to regroup or make change. Once the scheme was in place, it would ruthlessly have to play out. The word politics stuck in Black's thoughts. Grabbing the back of his neck, he was thankful for the moonless night; his brothers couldn't see his anxiety.

❄❄❄

The men passed the hours on the waterfront repairing the pier and assisting the groundskeepers. They continued in their solider duties, while Jeremiah slept like the dead. It was midnight the next evening when a commotion in the raised corridor caught Black's attention. He turned his focus from the fireplace just as Simon stepped through the side door followed by Lincoln. The remainder of the men filed in behind the president and in his head, Black heard the safety release on the plan.

"Black, my friend, good to see you again." Lincoln said, stepping forward with an outstretched hand.

"Mr. President."

Black returned the salutation while evaluating Lincoln. The president appeared bone weary and Black had to stifle a laugh. Simon had done his bidding by taking Lincoln on a spine jarring romp down the east coast, all in the name of safety. The president looked thinner; his pallor and the black suit he wore adding to his paleness. Lincoln's thick coarse hair had the imprint of the hat he held in his hand. The ceilings were high enough that the president did not have to stoop.

In his side view, Black saw Milford who had made himself scarce in the last few days. Directing the conversation toward their host, Black made the introductions.

"Mr. Lincoln, I would like for you to meet our host, Mr. Milford Church."

"Good to meet you, sir." Church replied. "You must be exhausted."

"Thank you for your hospitality. Travel was beastly." Lincoln chuckled.

"I'll have Dorothy show you to your rooms, Mr. Lincoln." Milford said.

The president turned to Black. "May I have a few private words with you after I have settled?"

"Absolutely." Black answered as Dorothy and Tilda led the president away.

When Lincoln was out of earshot, Simon and his group stepped to him offering greetings and information. Black waved them toward the alcove between the fireplace and the window.

"We took 'em the safehouse route." Simon said.

"He held up." Jake said laughing.

"Thought he was going to collapse." Shultz added.

Emmitt, Horace, Jesse, Ephraim and E. J. all nodded while laughing. Black listened while they spoke. Before the men dispersed to take up their duties, Black gave instructions.

"Hunter, your brother has taken ill. You and Shultz will tend him. The rest of you see James and Elbert for duties."

"Sick?" Hunter shot back.

Black gave a curt nod toward the corner of the parlor where Jeremiah lay conked out. When Hunter and Shultz went to see about him, Black gave Simon his full attention.

"It was as ya said it was gon be." Simon began. "Ya cain't get somethin' for nuthin'."

Black grinned. "I'll take up dealing with the president."

"We needs to keep his ass live–so we ain't hanged." Simon replied.

"Yeah," Black answered. "Rest, man. We will start at the orphanage."

The house was quiet as Black made his way to Lincoln's assigned chamber. He had inspected every crevice of Milford Church's home. The place consisted of three upper floors and a basement that smelled damp. There was a tunnel leading out to the banks of the river that was now walled up. Several of the rooms were minus any furnishings but all had fireplaces. Black walked the murky corridor of the second floor until he came upon a room with light spilling from under the doorway. He stopped and rapped twice with his right hand.

"Black?"

"Yes."

"Please come in."

Twisting the knob, Black pushed at the door. Where the hallway had a draft, the chamber was cozy. The burgundy bed covers were turned down invitingly and the matching pillows were fluffed. A round wooden table sat in the corner of the room; the president was seated facing the entrance. Lincoln wore an old beige sweater, unbuttoned and the black trousers of his suit were wrinkled. His legs were crossed and on his feet were brown leather house-shoes. The president smiled at Black–the leader of Fort Independence didn't reciprocate.

"Mr. President, I do not want the job of keeping you safe." Black's voice cracked in the air. "You seek to use my troubles with Fernando Wood to address your own agenda. If you should get hurt, it's me and my men who will swing."

Lincoln snorted. "You will not swing. In the company of you and your men... I have never been safer."

"We are here to shed blood, not abolition work."

The president nodded. "You will set up a meeting with Fernando for me."

Black glared and Lincoln continued. "I wish to discuss the Draft Act, the Emancipation Proclamation and my plans for colored soldiers. You are the best man to have at my back. My plight is your plight."

"Your trouble is a divided country–mine is remaining free. We don't bear the same burdens."

"So you wish to negotiate?" The president responded. "Name your price."

"I'll have to think on it." Black said, his voice impassive.

"I'm sure you do." Lincoln replied, mockingly.

The fireplace blazed and though two oil lamps lit the space, the chamber was still dim. Black moved to stand with his back to the window; the burgundy drapes were drawn against the night. On the table at the president's elbow was a slice of half eaten pie.

Black crossed his arms over his chest and spread his legs, widening his stance.

"You will not go to Manhattan island to meet with Wood." Black said with authority. "You will meet with him in Queens so we can control the setting."

"Here at Milford's home?" Lincoln asked.

"No."

"I sent Fernando a missive. He knows I planned to visit." Lincoln confessed.

"Did you give a time and date?"

"I could offer no such information until I met with you," the president answered.

Black nodded. "We will handle business. You, Mr. President, will remain unseen."

When Black would have quit the chamber, Lincoln said, "Fernando won't come to me. His idea of private will be to throw a gala and be holed up with me in his office for partygoers to witness."

"Let me worry about Fernando Wood."

When Black sought his pallet, his rest was unmarred by worry. He slept well into the next afternoon, while around him the men readied themselves. The smaller sitting room at the front of the house was set up with several water basins and two chamber pots. Felix and Charlie kept the waste moving–Dorothy and Tilda kept fresh water and towels in rotation.

After freshening up, Black made his way to the kitchen where they ate in shifts. The men stood about conversing and partaking. Dorothy spied him and brought him a cup of coffee. He moved to stand at the counter. Tim, Bainesworth and Shultz began forming a circle that Elbert, James and Simon joined.

"We will go by ferry and split up." Black said.

11

The Misunderstanding
New York

UNDER THE COVER of night seven men and seven horses ferried from Queens, around Blackwell Island to Manhattan. The river was choppy due to icy winds and strong currents. Black and the men with him stood in the shelter of the overhang from the engine room; it did nothing to add comfort to their journey. Still, within the hour they were bumping the pier of New York City. Colored dock workers came forward to help the men with their burdens onto dry land.

The wind eased the further away from the river they traveled. Manhattan was equal parts sophisticated and rustic. The men rode inland for fifteen minutes before Black slowed his horse. At a fork in the road, they separated. Elbert, Simon and James headed for the orphanage, while Black, Shultz, Tim and Bainesworth headed to the home of Fernando Wood.

The distance to the mayor's home was great from where they originally landed on the island. Though it was nighttime, the city was alive with people moving about. Some streets boasted of lampposts, while others were cast completely in the shadows. Black and his posse moved stealthily in the background of their surroundings. They traveled the slums and the upscale, though the smell of waste was stronger in places of poverty. The weather had eased as they rode away from the East River; but it turned frosty again as they neared the Hudson River.

Another hour passed before they came upon the well-lit estate of Fernando Wood. They slowed their horses as Black took in the wrought iron fence surrounding the property. A long drive started where the decorative gate was closed and chained together.

"Entering the property uninvited will appear hostile on the part of the president." Shultz said.

"Yeah, it will." Black said, still he had anticipated the circumstance.

"We need to leave the horses on the darkest side of the property." Tim added.

"The mayor leaves us no choice." Bainesworth replied, before asking. "You want me to approach from the front?"

"No." Black answered as he moved his horse toward the shadows.

They continued west around the back side of the estate. The brush was overgrown and thick enough to hide the animals. Black climbed the gate, jumped and landed on his feet; he made a mental note of where they were in proximity to the main house. Small structures lined the back of the mansion, and Black guessed they were for the servants and animals.

As they closed in on their target, they followed the cobblestone drive where it wrapped about the main house. But once on the east side of the property something became obvious. Fernando Wood was entertaining guests, if the number of parked carriages were any indication. Black counted ten vehicles as he considered the strain of piano music floating on the chilled air.

"This should be interesting." Shultz muttered.

Tim chuckled. "It always is."

They followed the music to get a location of the event. At the point where the music was at its loudest, Black peered through a window. The drapes were slightly parted and in his view were several well-dressed white men and women. A colored male servant moved between the party goers refreshing drinks.

"Most mansions are built with a side door." Black said. "We need to find it."

"Ah yes… the door for indiscretions," Bainesworth added. "Such passages are popular in England – usually hidden by extra brush."

It was as the ambassador stated; where the bushes were thickest, Tim found a door and Black forced the lock. The corridor was raised, leading to a well-furnished parlor. The fireplace was alive. An oil lamp sat on the end of a huge desk, the wick turned low. Black moved to the window where the drapes were drawn and pushed the fabric aside. In the distance were bare trees, a full moon and night.

"What do we do now?" Shultz asked.

"We wait." Tim countered.

"Indeed." The ambassador chimed in.

"Yeah." Black added as they settled in for the long haul.

❅ ❅ ❅

Elbert, James and Simon traveled the unlit streets to the colored orphanage on 5th Avenue between 42nd and 43rd Street. The four-story building loomed large in the moonlight. Horse and buggy traffic was light. A lone carriage pulled by two beasts was parked across the cobblestone street from the entrance of the children's home. The men didn't approach; instead they hid their animals in the brush and observed.

The front courtyard was lit by three lampposts. As the men stood about in the stillness, the flame in the furthest post went out. Simon and James went to scout out their surroundings, while Elbert stood beyond the reach of the light. Pulling his flask from his inner pocket, he drank deeply.

"Lotta trees out back. If'n someone back there… cain't see 'em and they cain't see us." James whispered.

"Who ya thank in that carriage?" Simon asked.

Ignoring Simon's inquiry, Elbert said, "I'm going in," before disappearing into the blackness.

The upper windows of the orphanage were unlit. On the bottom floor several rooms were dimly lit by flickering candles. Elbert made his way around the side of the structure headed for the backdoor. He had been to the children's home a time or two on errand for Black and knew the layout. James had been correct, it was pitch dark.

Elbert climbed the stairs to the high back porch, which was a screened in structure attached to the back of the house. The latch holding the screen door was flimsy, and he broke it with no effort. The wooden planks creaked under his weight; at the door he forced the lock, making way more noise than he intended. The hinges squeaked and before he could step over the threshold…

"Son, you finna meet yo' maker. Easy or I'll drop ya."

Elbert put both hands up. "Miss Elsie, don't shoot–it's me, Elbert."

Chancing a step over the threshold, Elbert moved into the light with his hands in the air. An older colored woman stood at the ready, pointing the business end of a shotgun at him. Next to her stood Miss Carol Sherman, an elderly white woman holding steady to an oil lamp.

"Elbert…" Miss Carol breathed, her stress was apparent.

"Yes, ma'am."

"Almost switched ya from a rooster to a hen." Miss Elsie cackled.

Elbert was sweating, men didn't get the jump on him. Yet, two old birds had; he chuckled. Miss Elsie wore a white nightgown with a coarse brown robe tied in place. The hem of her night dress hanging longer than her robe. Her brown skin announced her age to be about fifty summers. She wore her hair in many plaits and even in the soft light, Elbert could see the gray.

When Miss Elsie lowered the shotgun, he turned and grinned at Miss Carol. Where Miss Elsie was slender, Miss Carol was plump and more than sixty summers. She was dressed much the same as Miss Elsie. Her gray hair was pulled back from her face.

"I'm afraid you'll have to fix the locks." Miss Carol chided.

"Yes, ma'am."

Miss Elsie turned to the small brown faces behind her, that Elbert hadn't noticed, and spoke with authority. "All right, children, to bed."

There was muffled conversation as the young folk dispersed. When the children were gone from sight, Miss Carol spoke in low tones.

"Two of our girls are missing, Alice and Emma. Does Black have them?"

"No." Elbert responded with no guilt.

The older woman's eyes watered, but it was Miss Elsie who spoke. "We get volunteer help at times and deliveries. Tween the gossip and newspaper… we thought… we hoped the girls were in Black's care."

"If ya don't have the girls, why are you here?" Miss Carol asked.

Elbert replied with practiced reserve, "Black always comes to New York City to look in on you all. He gets the newspapers and with the war…"

Elbert's answer was simply the truth. Barring the time wasted dealing with the Hunter plantation, Black made certain the orphanage was looked after regularly. The children's home was a priority, as were Camille and Curtis. Both women nodded and Elbert changed the subject.

"The carriage out front?"

"Seems the mayor believes we know something about his cousin's death. We don't of course." Miss Carol said on a sigh.

"I don't understand." Elbert answered.

"One of the volunteers says that awful house of ill repute had a shootout. Robbie told us that he was there when a girl named Emma was stolen. Says he was painting when the gunshots started." Miss Carol paused, then went on. "Robbie said after the proprietor was killed, the talk was colored men committed this act."

Elbert had to try not to snort–*painting, his ass.* Though the lighting only went so far, he cast his eyes about the kitchen, which was bigger than most. It had triple everything: stoves, counters and several long wooden tables with benches on either side. White, chipped water basins sat atop the tables with matching kettles.

"No one's been harmed, have they?" Elbert asked.

"They watches us." Miss Elsie said. "We keep the children inside–we don't need no trouble."

"They must know the girls came from here." Miss Carol added. "They wander the property at night and like Elsie said, we don't need no trouble. Bad enough when our children get too old, they end up indentured servants. I know Emma and Alice wouldn't have chosen that house of ill repute. Something happened, I just know it."

"Who wanders the property?" Elbert asked.

"The mayor's henchmen," Miss Carol answered.

"Prolly waitin' on the mayor's signal to harm one of us." Miss Elsie sneered. "Cowards… They been terrorizing the city. Coloreds is the target."

"Fernando Wood means to set the Irish against the coloreds." Miss Carol added. "Like neckbones, it's all gon come to a boil."

"All right, ladies." Elbert said. "I'll be back to make the repairs. Black will take it from here."

Closing both doors behind him, Elbert stepped into the night. He needed to touch base with Simon and James, make them aware that the people set up to watch the orphanage may in fact be observing them. The carriage had to be a trap. At the bottom of the stairs, he made a right, going back the way he came. It was easy to be quiet; the earth under his boot was soft.

Elbert stayed close to the house, but when he would have rounded to the side, someone ran into him from behind, knocking the wind from his lungs. He found himself face down in the dirt; the cold barrel of a gun placed firm against his temple.

"Who the fuck are ya?" a menacing voice hissed. "I won't ask twice."

Elbert grunted but offered no tangible words. The man laying atop him was big… bigger than him. Still, he did not speak.

"Blow yer fuckin' head off, I will."

His opponent reared up, placing a knee in his back. Elbert knew he was fucked, but he had lived life on his own terms. However this played out, he could live and die with it. Placing his palms flat to the ground, he abruptly shoved himself up, toppling his adversary. They both scrambled and the gun went off; a big flash of light then darkness. As they grappled for power, Elbert felt restricted by his overcoat.

His muscles strained with the effort of trying to push the barrel of the gun back at the other man. Since he was on top, Elbert noted that the other man had the advantage of brute force without having to hold himself up. James' voice echoed into the night, "Elbert… Elbert!" But he didn't dare look about mechanically–he couldn't see shit.

Suddenly light spilled over the situation and his adversary became real; they looked each other in the eye. As the light drew nearer, in his side view, Elbert saw a gun appear over his right shoulder. Disoriented, he figured this would be his end. The weapon discharged with a loud *bang and flash.* His opponent stilled—hole in his head, eyes wide, his person void of life.

Elbert collapsed on his back next to the dead man. Above him stood James, Simon, Miss Elsie and Miss Carol. The women held oil lamps.

"Almost got yo' wig twisted twice this night," Miss Elsie stated.

"Hell yeah," Elbert said getting to his feet. "But almost ain't good enough."

❀ ❀ ❀

It was past midnight when the party ended, and the mayor found himself stumbling into his parlor. His hands were full of a young blonde maid, whose passions rivaled his own. He kicked the door shut, unwilling to release her tight ass. The woman in his arms suddenly screamed. It took effort to look away from red lace, kiss swollen lips, and the gap in her bodice that revealed creamy skin.

When he could finally focus on the room at large, Fernando squinted and then breathed in sharply. "What the hell."

"Mr. Mayor," a tall thin man greeted as he stood, "we've come—"

"Who are you... who let you in here?" Fernando asked, his temper apparent. Stepping back from his companion, he growled. "I demand to know who let you in my damn house."

"We have a message of great importance for you, Mr. Mayor." A muscled fellow with thick black hair added, before he boldly dismissed the maid. "Honey, why don't you run along."

Fernando snarled. "How dare you."

"I dare." The man countered.

As the mayor scanned the chamber, his eyes fell on a huge colored man standing to the left of the window; he offered no expression but intently observed the goings on. The man was dressed in all black, which only added to the menace that seeped from him. The slave was bald, with eyes that seemed to pierce. Fernando dropped his gaze to gather himself and smarted at the sight of sweat stained overcoats thrown haphazardly over his expensive settee.

Behind him, he heard the maid exiting the parlor in haste–clumsily. The slave didn't speak and to Fernando's way of thinking, he looked out of place in all the finery. He would not speak to the slave; instead he addressed the white men standing about his salon... uninvited.

"Who the hell are you people?"

"I'm Tim." The white man with the black hair answered.

"The name is Bainesworth." The Brit replied.

The other fellow didn't bother responding and neither did the slave.

Fernando was exasperated. "We're alone. What. Do. You. Want. With. Me?"

"President Lincoln requests your presence." Bainesworth stated.

Fernando had indulged in too much drink and rich foods. Now his head was spinning, and it seemed the Tim fellow and the Brit were trying to confuse him. He couldn't keep up with the changes in conversation; when he would address one, the other would answer.

"Are you telling me the president has accosted me in my own home because he wishes a private audience? No—"

"Oh, you will meet with the president, Mr. Mayor." Tim, who was dressed in brown trousers and a brown shirt, crossed his arms over his chest and glared down at him.

"And you will come alone." The Brit added, his tone hostile.

Fernando sputtered in outrage. "I will do no such thing. If the president wishes to speak to me, he will have to come to City Hall."

"Mr. Mayor," a deep raspy voice interjected, "you will meet with Mr. Lincoln on his terms or we will kill you."

Fernando followed the words to the source and found it was the nigger who spoke. His tone was matter of fact; still it held threat and promise. Fernando felt himself pale.

The mayor cleared his throat, but the slave cut him off. "You lead a public life and will be assassinated should you raise the alarm. The circles you move in put you shoulder to shoulder with your enemies. Please don't test me, Mr. Mayor."

Silence blanketed the chamber for moments, while Fernando digested the situation. A slave threatening him—ordering him about in his own home. Is this what Mitchell Houser meant when he said some coloreds don't know they're inferior? The slave broke into his thoughts.

"You will ferry to Astoria day after tomorrow. A carriage will take you to Mr. Lincoln. You will arrive at noon on dock 9."

Fernando had been about to try to negotiate when his manservant burst into the parlor. Jasper's appearance was disheveled. His white shirttails were hanging over his britches and his silver hair was uncombed. Jasper's gun was drawn.

"Mr. Mayor, you all right?" the older man asked as his voice and his damn gun hand visibly shook.

Before Fernando could dismiss Jasper, his unwanted guests all drew their weapons. The white man who hadn't spoken picked that moment to offer his thoughts. "Put your gun on the floor. I won't say it again."

Jasper clearly understood the circumstance for what it was and did as instructed. The slave spoke up, addressing the manservant. "Come in and close the door."

Turning his attention back to the matter at hand, the slave spoke. "Mr. Mayor?"

Fernando cleared his throat, then nodded, "I will take the meeting. My manservant will be with me."

The slave snorted before pointing at Jasper and mockingly asking, "Him?"

"No, Quinn and one other of his choosing will travel with me. He handles my security."

"You will come—" the Tim fellow sneered.

The slave cut him off by holding up his hand. "You will be allowed two for security."

Fernando nodded. But before he could say more, the slave strode over to the settee and retrieved his overcoat and hat. The other men followed suit, exiting by the secret door. When the door swung closed, the mayor turned to Jasper, who appeared faint and issued an order.

"Have that door permanently barred."

Black was the first to climb the fence on the side of the mansion. Alarm filled him when he found Simon standing among the horses minus his brothers. Simon spoke up immediately.

"Elbert and James is well. We ran into some trouble is all. I come alone and left dem at the chilren's home."

"Shit," Black hissed, trying to get the banging of his heart under control.

"What kind of trouble?" Shultz asked, the doctor in him kicking in.

"We killed the man what was watchin' the place." Simon explained. "Him and Elbert locked asses and we ain't have a choice."

"Sound like shit went well," Tim said. "We all still standing."

"Yeah," Simon amended. "We ain't get a chance to question 'im. He was Irish from his words."

Black began working through the matter in his head. "What did you get from the women at the orphanage?"

"The women say an Irishman named Quinn come there on errand for the mayor. They say they turned him away, but soon enuff a man start watchin' dem." Simon said.

"Quinn?" Bainesworth asked.

"That's what the womenfolk at the home say." Simon reassured.

Black wanted to get all the men hunting them in one place, but that was not an option. Still, things were coming along; they would clean up before dawn and see the problem through. He began issuing orders.

"Bainesworth and Tim will remain to watch the mayor. Fernando Wood will not sleep, he will go to this Quinn. Follow him and once you get a location, head to the ferry."

"Yeah," Tim said.

Black went on. "Shultz and I will help at the children's home."

They followed Simon down the darkest of streets back to the orphanage. Travel took about forty minutes and when they neared the home, they dismounted. Leaving their horses in the brush, they moved on foot for about a quarter mile. They approached the orphanage from the back and Black's tension eased at the sight of his brothers.

His eyes bounced around the kitchen; he spied Miss Carol and Miss Elsie seated to a table. James and Elbert were pacing.

"It couldn't be helped." James said.

Black shook his head and James heeded. He addressed the women. "Miss Carol–Miss Elsie."

The older white woman grinned before breathing his name. "Mr. Black."

"Hope," Miss Elsie simpered and giggled.

"Ladies, I'm sorry about this. When will the children rise?"

"They's up–but been told to stay put." Miss Elsie answered.

"How many children do we have?" Black asked.

"We have seventy-three." Miss Carol replied. "They will get schooling today–we will keep them occupied."

Black nodded and Miss Carol went on. "Mr. Elbert lied to me. You have Alice and Emma, don't you?"

"I have Emma. She didn't know what became of Alice. It appears Alice is dead." Black answered honestly.

"Oh," Miss Carol whispered, removing the handkerchief from her sleeve. She mopped at her eyes and sniffled.

Miss Elsie lowered her head and sobbed. Elbert's voice chimed in. "I apologize for not telling you the truth. I ain't want to speak on Alice."

Both women nodded. Changing the subject, Black asked. "Where is the nearest public stable?"

"The stables is betwix 46th and 47th Street, right chere on 5th Avenue." Miss Elsie answered.

"Black—" Miss Carol started.

"No," Black answered firmly. "I told you all I know about Alice. We will keep Emma safe."

Both women nodded again, and he went on. "Go care for the children, so we can clean up. I'll send one of the men to fetch you when you and the children are free to move about."

The women stood and left the massive kitchen. When he and the men were alone, Black asked. "Where's the body?"

"Jammed his ass under the stairs," James answered, his temper evident.

"Let's get moving." Black said. "Tim and Bainesworth should be at the docks soon."

"I hope the mayor does what we think." Shultz said.

"Fernando will do as expected; the mayor didn't appreciate me ordering him about." Black countered.

"I'll fix the locks." Elbert said.

"Yeah," Black responded. "You all right?"

"Ears ringin' from the discharge of the gun, but I'm good." Elbert replied.

Turning away from Elbert, Black stepped into the early morning with the other men in tow. The temperature dropped, and the subtle winds felt like blades against his skin. Simon and Shultz got the body while he and James retrieved the horses and buggy. The animal made nickering sounds at their approach. James climbed into the vehicle and lit the oil lamp they brought with them. The compartment was empty of anything that could identify the dead man.

Black moved the carriage to the courtyard of the orphanage. Save for the glow of the oil lamp from within the vehicle, the blackness around them was complete. Simon and Shultz could be heard grunting and swearing as they tussled with the burden of dead weight. A gust of wind caused the vegetation to rustle loudly, drowning out the squeak of the carriage door.

When the man was loaded inside, Black jumped down from

the driver's seat, handing the reins over to Shultz. Simon climbed up next to the doctor. James hopped down and Black talked them through the next step.

"I will remain with Elbert."

"Naw, Imma stay wit' Elbert. You go and move the men in place. We ain't got but a few hours 'fore someone come lookin' for his ass." James said.

Black nodded. "I was going to leave the carriage at the public stable on 46th street. We'll dispose of the carriage and the body in Queens. I'll be back by midday."

"Why would they set one man out here like this?" Shultz asked.

"They ain't thank this would amount to nothin'." James said.

"James has the right of it." Simon said.

"All the lampposts blew out–good and dark," James said. "Me and Elbert is all right."

"Stay safe," Black said before climbing into the vehicle with the dead man.

They rode the quarter mile to where the horses were left in the underbrush. Black took control of all three animals. He set an unhurried pace to the docks, and when day broke Tim and Bainesworth were at his side. While they worked to disassemble the horses and buggy, Black listened as the men spoke.

"You all weren't gone thirty minutes before Wood had his carriage brought around." Tim said.

"This Quinn fellow lives in a small farmhouse on E. 65th Street." Bainesworth added. "The mayor raised quite the fuss until his driver climbed the fence to roust a stablehand. Tim and I left when the gate closed behind Fernando's vehicle."

❊ ❊ ❊

Liam stood in his kitchen glaring at Fernando Wood. New York City's mayor woke him before the rooster to complain that he had been manhandled by a slave. It was early morning and Fernando had worn himself out trying to explain the significance of what happened the night before.

"Girl!" The mayor hollered. "More coffee!"

Alice had come to the kitchen to make coffee before starting her chores. Now she came running from the farther points of the house to do the mayor's bidding. Liam didn't like it.

"Fernando," The word was said low–menacing, "mind yer manners."

The mayor blinked, then looked between him and Alice, who was coming forward with the coffee pot. When she topped his cup off, he mumbled halfheartedly. "Thank you."

"Alice, we won't be needing you again."

She turned to him and Liam supposed she was looking for signs of his displeasure. He offered a smile and she nodded before walking away. When he turned his focus back on the mayor, there was no missing Fernando's attention to detail.

"Your maid is plumper than I remember. Is she with child?"

"I ain't a fop from one of yer damn salon parties. We ain't friends, Fernando, and we will never speak the frivolous."

The mayor held his hands up as if in surrender. "Yes… well, as I was saying. I have never seen the likes. A nigger ordering about the mayor of New York City."

"You say they came on the president's behalf? Makes sense given Lincoln's stance," Liam said.

"I don't know why, but I believe this slave has something to do with Hugh's death."

"Why would the president care about yer cousin?" Liam asked, bored with the conversation.

"If Lincoln is here, I'm sure it's about the Blackwell Island incident." Fernando responded with disdain.

"The country 'as been torn apart by war. Crime is everywhere, why would Blackwell Island or patrons from a whorehouse matter?"

"You will accompany me to this private meeting." Fernando demanded. "And don't be surprised to find it a sham."

Liam stared at him. Being in the president's company wasn't high on his list. He shook his head and was about to send the mayor on his way when Fernando made him an offer he couldn't refuse.

"I'll remove Mitchell from the Hen House."

"You will give me the whorehouse?" Liam asked, trying to comprehend.

"The original deal still stands, minus Mitchell Houser. You could start running things, but you can't have the place until my cousin's killer is caught and the one-year silent partnership is complete."

Liam stared at the mayor, measuring his desperation. Fernando's judgment was severely clouded if he thought the president was tangled up in the matter of Hugh's death. But Liam was an opportunist, so he conceded.

"Time and place."

"We have to ferry to Astoria Queens by noon tomorrow." The mayor explained.

"What proof do you have the president wishes to see you?" Liam asked, entertaining for the first time the opportunity of a sham.

"I received a missive from Lincoln prior to this situation." Fernando answered. "It was authentic, but the president didn't give a time or place. It may be a trap, set by someone who knows Lincoln's travel plans."

"Or one of your own wide range of enemies." Liam muttered. "I'll meet you on the morrow–early morn."

Fernando nodded and Liam stood. This meeting was over as far as he was concerned. There was no need to linger; the probability of ruining the new deal they'd struck was real.

Taking the cue, the mayor stood and allowed himself to be escorted to the front door. Liam watched as his carriage rumbled down the drive, through the gate and onto 4th Avenue. When Brian closed the wrought iron gate, Liam turned his thoughts to Alice.

They had not spoken on the matter, but he was sure she carried his babe. He also saw that she struggled with her feelings for him; still, he was certain she loved him. Things had changed. Now, when he got home late or early morn, Alice was in his bed. Liam considered it a win. Children never crossed his thoughts; but with Alice, he wanted a family.

He found her putting away clothes in the master bedroom. She looked up when he shut the door. "No chores today, Alice, come lay yer sweet arse wit' me."

In the daylight her shyness was visible. There was nowhere she could hide her nakedness from him. Liam began stripping to help her understand there was no room for refusal. Alice removed her dress, boots and undergarments. Liam strode to the bed and pulled back the covers.

"Get in," he instructed.

When she was settled, he followed her under the bedding. Placing his large palm on her belly, he leaned in and kissed her. A small sob escaped her, and he leaned back to search her face. The heavy drapes he favored were tied back allowing the natural light to flow through the chamber.

"I ain't happy 'bout this, Liam." She whispered.

He knew it, but he was pleased. "You are stuck wit' me, lass."

"I ain't yo' whore."

"Ahhh, my Alice, from the moment I found ya unused, you were mine. Ya never were my whore." Liam countered.

"Ya shouldn't have kept me. I's a free woman."

He hated the insecurity he felt in the face of her dignity. "Do ya love me, Alice?"

She closed her eyes and still the tears leaked from them. He studied her beauty and distress in the sunlight. She turned her face away from him, trying to stifle her anguish.

He went on. "Yer angry because ya love me."

She nodded, but Liam needed her words. "Say it damn you."

"I's mad cause I loves you and I ain't want no children. I comes from a place where colored children is tossed away," she hissed.

Liam would take what he could get; he pushed her no further. Leaning down he shoved his tongue in her mouth and she accepted. Alice whimpered and he groaned. Climbing over her, he settled between her legs and pushed into her tight heat. When he bottomed out, a guttural moan tore from him.

"Shyte–lass, I can't let ya go."

"Li…am," she moaned, as she wrapped her legs about his hips.

He pushed up on his palms and stared down at her before pulling out to the tip, and then slamming home. When her eyes rolled up in her head, he closed his own letting himself surrender to the sweetness of her body. His cadence was clumsy as he rocked into her. He couldn't manage the finesse of an experienced lover; the woman in his arms broke him and when her insides began to clamp down on him – he was done. His balls drew up, choking his shaft until he erupted with ecstasy.

Their hips stuttered against one another as they both cried out. Liam shoved himself in her as far as he could go and held on tight.

"I love you, Alice," he mumbled between kisses.

She didn't answer, but she did snuggle in close, placing her cheek against his chest. He wasn't tired and already he was hardening at the prospect of more. But Alice drifted off to sleep and he was content to hold her. In his relaxed state, his thoughts turned back to the mayor. He snorted at the concern that Lincoln was even aware of the Hugh Wood debacle.

Fernando seemed to think everything was about him. In the past, Hugh had complained about his puffed-up cousin. If for no other reason, Liam was going to witness the mayor being ordered about by a slave. The hilarious rarely happened to him and he wouldn't miss this for all the potatoes in Ireland. He could rest his person–finally the Hen House was within his grasp.

Liam found himself drifting into a deep sleep when pounding

on the bedroom door happened. Alice was shaken from a peaceful sleep, and he whispered to her.

"Rest, I'll be back."

"All right," she answered, groggily.

He dressed quickly before yanking the door open. Liam was annoyed. "What are ya wantin', Francis?"

"Ennis is gone missing."

"Missing?"

12

Moments of Clarity

THE HOME OF Milford Church was a beehive of activity from the moment Black and the men returned. There would be no down time. And though the trigger was pulled prematurely, they would stay the course. Black made provision in the event the orphanage had to become his base of operations. He would remove the children and set them up in Queens.

Standing in the parlor facing the men, Black shared information while giving orders.

"Emmitt, Ephraim, Josiah, Herman and Horace will move out. You five will go by ferry to the orphanage. Miss Elsie, Miss Carol and the children are to be brought to Queens. Milford will meet you on this side; the children will stay at a farmhouse not far from here. Herman and Josiah will remain with the women and children."

After the first set of men left to do his bidding, Black went on. "Ralph, Jesse, Bainesworth and John will guard the president. No one is to enter or leave this house."

Ralph and Jesse immediately posted up at the top of the stairs leading to Lincoln's chamber. The ambassador and John did the same outside his bedroom door. Black waited for the commotion to die down from the men moving about before he continued.

"Simon, you and Tim will meet up with Elbert and James. The four of you will see what there is to see at the Hen House."

"Yeah," Simon and Tim replied in unison.

Black stared around at the remaining men and he could see that Anthony, Jeremiah, Frank and Lou were agitated. The black cracker was still pretty sick, but he was standing. "Jake, Shultz and Gilbert will guard the orphanage; it will also be our base—if need be. Jeremiah, Frank, Lou, E.J. and Anthony will accompany me to the home of Quinn."

It was still morning and while he couldn't afford the time, Black went to speak with the president. He found Mr. Lincoln seated at the table working. His fingers were smudged with ink and his glasses hung from the tip of his nose. He looked up when Black entered. The sun crawled into the chamber, not touching the left of the room. Where the natural light didn't reach, the fireplace offered the relief of visibility and warmth.

"Good morning, Mr. President."

"Black, morning. I attempted to come find and speak with you last night."

"I went to do your bidding, sir." Black replied. There was no mistaking the president's vexation.

"I wasn't allowed to leave the chamber."

"You put me in charge of your safety, did you not?" Black asked.

Lincoln sighed. "Fernando Wood?"

"The mayor understands the need for privacy. He will come to you tonight." Black answered, then asked. "Is there anything else I can do for you, sir?"

"No... no, Black."

Not wishing to be questioned any further, Black turned on his heels. But when he reached for the knob, the president added. "My cousin Peabody says you kept him locked away when he visited your home. He didn't appreciate it either."

"You threatening me, Mr. President?"

"Your tone borders on treason." Lincoln countered.

Black turned back to look at the president, whose right eyebrow was raised in challenge. Clasping his hands behind his back, Black stared at the man before him for moments. When he finally spoke, his words were deliberate.

"I have figured out what I want from you, Abe."

The use of his given name shook the president and his gaze dropped. Black waited for him to acknowledge the statement.

"What have you decided on?"

"I would like for you to recognize that I am my own man—not someone you can force into your employ. The circle in which you exist is too big and unreliable for us to part as foes. I don't wish for us to become enemies, but should it happen I can live with it."

Lincoln chuckled. "You threaten me."

"No, sir, but treason doesn't carry the same meaning for you as it does for me."

"Oh," Lincoln said.

"Treason for you is a treachery that plagues the office you occupy. Treason for me would be to step away from my personal freedom and the liberty of those I love. I am unable to engage in surrender of any kind."

"Black... I—"

Cutting off the president's next words, Black continued. "I am not a boy to be ordered about, Mr. President. The favor I wish from you, sir, is that you recognize such. Let us never approach the threshold of threat again."

Lincoln nodded.

"Is there anything else I can do for you, Mr. President?"

"No."

"Good then... I will bring Fernando Wood to you."

The president nodded and Black exited the chamber. He could hear the president's laughter as he walked away to face the rest of his day. Black grinned, the damn president wanted to run the streets with his men and terrorize Fernando Wood. The very notion was absurd.

❀ ❀ ❀

The morning shaped into a cold crisp day with bright sun. James and Tim approached the Hen House, while Simon and Elbert remained invisible. The outside was in pristine condition. Still, James thought the establishment looked out of place against the backdrop of upscale shops and eateries. A colored woman swept the small porch and walkway.

"Good day, ma'am." Tim greeted.

"We ain't open, you gon has to come back later." She assessed Tim, but when her eyes fell on James, her breath caught. "The man what runs the place ain't finna serve ya friend."

The chocolate skinned woman with light brown eyes addressed Tim, while never taking her gaze from him. James grinned; he was dressed in all black the same way Anthony, Frank and Lou were the day of the shootout. Even his hat and overcoat were black. Tim also wore all black.

"Who runs the place, sweetheart?" James asked.

She stared between him and Tim before deciding she would talk. "Mitchell, but him works for the mayor. I's sho' of it. He live here–the women is tired of him thankin' he can get somethin' for nuthin'."

"The mayor?" Tim asked.

"They's fightin' for power of the Hen House—" the woman replied.

"Betty!" a white man called out, stopping all conversation.

James noticed her fear; he was subtle when he shook his head and winked. At the top of the stairs, leaned against one of the posts, stood a white man with thick black hair. He was of average height and dressed in blue trousers; his white shirt boasted of ruffles around the wrists and collar.

"Gentlemen, we're closed." The man named Mitchell said.

"Is there somewheres we can speak in private?" Tim asked never missing a beat.

The man narrowed his eyes. "And who might you be?"

"My apologies, I'm Will and this here is George." Tim answered, while pointing at James with his thumb. "I'm here about the mayor."

The man visibly paled as he looked past Tim to the street where horse and buggy traffic had begun to pick up. He didn't speak, just pointed with his chin toward the front door. When Tim started for the door, James tried to follow.

Mitchell put his hand up. "Your manservant will wait outside."

Tim nodded and didn't look back as he strode away. When the door closed behind them, James looked about before he asked. "How many menfolk is inside the house?"

"Mitchell the onlyist one." Betty answered. "You know dem what shot up the place months ago–ain't ya? They's dressed like you."

James didn't answer; instead he countered with his own question. "Who is fightin' for power of the Hen House?"

"Quinn, the mayor and Mitchell."

James nodded at that bit of information before demanding, "Show us to the backdoor."

"Us?"

He pointed to Elbert and Simon who were also dressed in all black. Betty shrugged, then turned leading the way around to the back of the house.

❉ ❉ ❉

Shultz stared out the front window of the orphanage where two white men rode into the courtyard on horseback. The children had been removed from the home in covered wagons used to lug merchandise and ferried to Queens. Gilbert was posted up at the backdoor and Jake watched the front of the house. The doctor was sweating; half hour sooner and their unwanted guests would have happened along when the children were being loaded and carted off.

Both men were dressed as gentlemen; their tan overcoats open, a sign they were strapped. Wide brimmed, brown leather hats concealed their features. Shultz studied the set of their shoulders and gait; he found them hostile. Over his own shoulder he called out, "Two."

It was obvious they expected to find the women and children in attendance. They separated with one man headed for the front door, while the other moved to the back of the house with purpose. Shultz stepped away from the window. He found Gilbert standing with his gun trained on the door.

"You got this?" the doctor asked.

"Yeah," Gil countered. "Go cover Jake."

Shultz nodded. Going back the way he came put him in a long hall between what could only be described as a family room and the kitchen. The corridor was dim, but the doctor could make out a few children's drawings hanging on the walls. He passed an unlit oil lamp that sat on a wooden table in the hall. At the entrance of the family room he noted the furnishings were a combination of desks and couches, and against a far wall was a blackboard with white chalked sketches.

Jake stood with his back to the wall at the right of the door; Shultz stood to the left. When the door opened, it would block his vision of the man and Jake for seconds. It also occurred to the doctor that they were about to do violence where innocence made a home.

The sound of the lock being forced got his attention and when the front door swung open, he heard Jake speak in clipped, deliberate tones.

"Get yo' damn hands in the air."

At the back of the house two shots rang out. Keeping his composure, the doctor stepped from behind the door, cocked his gun and pressed the barrel to the side of the man's head.

"Come in, my friend." Shultz said. As he kicked the front door shut, he called out. "Gil!"

"I's good… but my new friend ain't!" Gilbert hollered back. "You and Jake?"

"Good!" Jake responded. He checked the front window, then yelled out. "All clear!"

At gunpoint, the doctor walked his hostage toward the kitchen. Gilbert shoved him down none too gently on a bench beside a long table. Jake slapped his hat off to reveal brown hair shorn close and fear. Shultz understood the man's distress–his companion was dead, propped up beside the backdoor. Blood trickled from his mouth to his chin.

"Quinn send ya?" Jake asked.

The man's eyes widened, but he didn't speak; still it was enough.

They played the waterfront all the way down the east side of Manhattan Island. Tim and Bainesworth had given perfect directions. The sun was bright but offered no warmth. It was past noon as they made their way to the home of Quinn. Black turned over several scenarios in his head and all of them were of Fernando Wood and his henchmen. They had not been able to question the man James killed, so they were going in blind.

The mayor's superior stance had helped Black narrow down the man called Quinn. He didn't think Fernando would seek protection from a man incapable of the task. It also seemed to Black that men like Fernando Wood expected other men to get their hands dirty. He hoped he was chasing the right dog and the right fight.

Blackwell Island was to his right, across the East River, and on his left–high vegetation. Along the waterfront were clusters of shanty towns abandoned due to the frosty weather. The proximity of Blackwell Island, the docks and the direction of Quinn's home added up. If nothing else, Black was sure they could pull from him what they needed to know. They paired off and rode in silence. E.J. and Jeremiah brought up the rear. Frank and Lou rode in the front, while Black paired off with Anthony.

As they neared their destination, the underbrush gave way to a path that led to the docks. A large boat had bumped the pier and the crew could be heard yelling as they unloaded its freight. Black saw this as a good sign, for Tim had relayed even this fact. They turned down the dirt path and moved deeper into the brush away from the river. Soon the vegetation thinned, and the back of a small farmhouse came into view. Black found it interesting that no fence separated the rear of property from the waterfront. In fact, upon closer inspection, he could just make out carriage wheel marks along the path leading to and from the house.

They split up, with E.J. and Jeremiah headed for the front of the property. Black had some concerns because Jeremiah did not look good. Frank and Lou took the side of the land, while he and Anthony moved in on foot headed for what looked to be a little barn. At the front of the property a loud bell began clanking. Suddenly, two men burst from the weather-beaten structure and raced around to the front gate. E.J. and Jeremiah were creating a diversion.

Backs pressed up against the barn, Black and Anthony rounded the wall, stepping into full view of a large window. In the center of the frame, a young woman gazed out at them. She was still as a statue offering no reaction to seeing them–but see them she did.

"Shit," Anthony hissed. "We's fucked."

Black stepped out in the middle of the barnyard; his mind trained on the commotion that could be heard at the front of the property. He raised a gloved hand and pointed to the backdoor. The woman disappeared from the window and the door opened ever so slightly with a *snick*. When Black would have moved for the house, Anthony grabbed his arm.

"Careful, man."

Black nodded. "Cover me. I'm going in."

"Shit," Anthony muttered. "I got chu'."

Climbing the stairs of the back porch, Black heard and felt the wood creaked beneath his weight. He stepped into the kitchen. Gun drawn, he faced the woman. She held her hands up in surrender, palms open. Up close, she appeared void of any emotion. The sound of Jeremiah's voice snagged his attention.

"Drop yo' damn guns."

Over his shoulder Black said to Anthony. "Watch her."

Anthony gave a curt nod and Black turned his focus back to the ruckus happening in the corridor. The hallway was a busy exchange because three rooms spilled into the same place. At the opposite end of the passage four men had their weapons drawn. The sun was bright and all along the hall, pockets of light spilled in at odd angles. Black could make out enough to know that Jeremiah had both his weapons drawn and one of their would-be hostages had his gun pressed to E.J.'s temple. Shit was intense, but Black couldn't see well enough to shoot into the chaos.

As he stepped into the corridor, Jeremiah's words stopped him. "No... first door on yo' right."

Jeremiah was correct, a shadow skittered away from the doorway. Turning back to the woman, Black asked. "How many?"

She didn't answer verbally but held up one finger. Tears rolled down her cheeks, but her grief was silent. Black turned back to the tight situation unfolding in the corridor in time to see a flash of light along with an ear-splitting bang. The man standing between E.J. and Jeremiah stiffened then dropped. E.J. spun and began beating the other man with his gun. Jeremiah discharged his weapon again and their hostage screamed in pain.

Black took that moment to run through the first door on the right. He came face to face with a red headed man, who held his gun trained on the door. They were at a standoff–Black had his gun aimed at the man's head. Chancing sudden movement, Black uncocked his weapon and slid it back in the holster. He noted that the man kept looking toward the kitchen, and Black was sure it was out of concern for the woman; it was enough.

"Ant."

"Yeah!" Anthony answered.

"Have the woman taken to the barn."

"No! The lass is innocent in all this." The red head yelled.

Black heard the click–click–click of three revolvers at his back. "We ain't gonna stand down. The woman's safety is on you."

Jeremiah coughed at that statement, and Black knew he was remembering when he was in similar shoes. Black continued. "Put your gun on the floor."

"Alisss!" the man called.

Quiet settled as Black reconciled the woman's name. "She won't answer."

"Alisss!" the man called out again and this time his voice broke.

"You can't win." Black said, then shoved a thumb over his shoulder indicating the men at his back.

Jeremiah addressed Black. "Give me the girl."

The black cracker moved from sight leaving Frank and E.J. covering the door. The red head took a step forward waving his gun. E.J. shot him in the leg. When he went down, his gun spun out of his reach. Red scrambled for it, but Black was faster; he kicked the weapon to keep it spinning and Frank retrieved it.

His hostage was lying flat on his back staring up at him. Black spoke and his voice denoted curiosity. "I'm Black and we killed the mayor's beloved cousin and you are?"

"The woman is mine–I don't give a shyte about the mayor."

Black placed the heel of his boot over the man's blood-stained thigh and pressed. He demanded. "Your name."

Red head screamed, then panted out. "Quinnnnn."

Black stooped down next to his victim and asked. "Were you looking for us, Quinn? Were the dead bodies on Blackwell Island a message for us?"

Quinn turned his head studying the door. He had broken out in a sweat, still his message was clear; he was refusing to chat. Black stood exiting the bedchamber. E.J. was posted up at the window and Frank took the door. In the hall Lou had the other hostage covered, and Anthony watched over the woman. Jeremiah sat on the floor at the entrance of a smaller bedchamber; the black cracker's eyes were closed and in the natural light his skin appeared almost gray. His breathing was also labored.

Everything was at a standstill while Black wandered through the property. The house was simple–two bedchambers, a kitchen and parlor, all well-kept. The barn/stable housed several horses and the loft above had several beds. Next to the barn, another structure held three different carriages–one was a paddy wagon. The other two were black vehicles with intricate carving; all three were expensive from what Black could tell.

Walking around to the side of the house, Black's gaze surveyed the front of the property. It was fenced in and fell back from the main thoroughfare just enough for privacy. There was a steady flow of horse and buggy traffic; the clip clop of hooves kept the commotion inside the farmhouse undetected. Black sighed. It was time to bring this matter to a close. He would start with the girl and glean what he could.

As he wandered back to the house, the sun dipped behind the clouds. The weather was changing; he could smell rain but hoped like hell the conditions held. They didn't need a cover for this matter because they weren't going to clean up. He, too, was sending a message and how he planned to proceed with the mayor required only darkness.

In the kitchen, he found that neither Anthony nor the woman had moved from where he'd left them. Walking over to the table and chairs, he sat before leaning in, elbows to knees. When he spoke, he addressed Anthony, who nodded before walking away to do his bidding.

"Take them to the barn."

Anthony was gone for only moments when Lou appeared dragging the unconscious man. The man moaned but never opened his eyes. Anthony appeared seconds later dragging the dead man through the kitchen. A blood path marred the floor; besides tears, Alice offered no expression. Quinn was hauled out kicking and screaming by E.J. and Jeremiah. Alice turned her back.

"Alisss–lass, ya all right?" Quinn had yelled, but Jeremiah outted his light.

Black noted that for Quinn, she was conflicted. When the door closed behind the violence, Black asked. "So what happened, Alice?"

"We was wantin' to be governesses. We ain't wanna be no whores." She whispered.

Black waited and she went on. "Is Emma all right?"

"Yes," Black answered. "How many men?"

"I only ever seen five."

"Was Quinn the sixth man or only five?"

"Quinn was numba six."

Black nodded. "The mayor?"

"The mayor come here one time. He was mad about Blackwell Island. The mayor say it was makin' folks talk."

Black remained silent and she went on. "Hugh Wood took us to the Hen House, even though I told him we's free and we wasn't no whores."

"You love Quinn." Black wasn't asking.

Alice crossed her arms and looked to the yellow drapes. The sky had darkened, and shards of water hit the pane from the outside. Black saw her swallow hard before she asked.

"Will it save him if'n I say yes?"

"No."

"I carries his child." She breathed.

"I figured as much." Black responded. "We will keep you safe—you and the child."

She didn't answer, so Black continued. "Come."

Removing his overcoat, Black wrapped it about her shoulders and pointed to the door. She preceded him onto the rickety back steps. Rain fell in oversized droplets and the earth had become soft under his boot. They crossed the yard to the barn. Puddles had already begun forming, the weather reflecting life—one moment all was well and the next shit was happening.

Down the center aisle and against the far wall, Quinn was tied up. His arms and legs were spread wide and restrained individually. The Irishman had a black eye and a busted lip. His head was lulled forward as if he were passed out. A lantern hung from an overhead beam on a hook. The smell of hay, dampness and animal sweat assailed him. Black placed a hand to her back and propelled her forward until they stood in front of Quinn. His hostage's head jerked up and his good eye fixed on the woman.

Black didn't walk away, but he did turn his back to offer the smallest amount of discretion. Alice's soft voice broke the quiet.

"Liam…" she said on a sob.

"I'm sorry, lass."

"I's free, Liam, and I wanted to stay free."

"I couldn't let go." Quinn countered. "I want you and the babe to be well."

"I know." She whispered.

"I love ya, lass."

Black heard shuffling and turned in time to see Alice step forward and kiss the other man. Abruptly, she turned and rushed away, leaving Black to face his hostage.

"Blackwell Island was my message for the mayor." Quinn said.

"Yeah… well it made me stand up and take notice."

"Don't suppose we can negotiate?" Quinn asked.

"No… I learned early in life; snakes can't be tamed."

Quinn chuckled, then spat blood on the ground. He glared at Black and whispered. "Get on wit' it then."

And Black did–he shot Quinn at close range. Using the sleeve of his homespun shirt, he wiped the blowback from his face. Behind him, Alice wept…

"Catch her," Jeremiah said.

When Black turned away from Quinn, he found Anthony holding a wilted Alice in his arms. But he stayed the course; stepping into the stall to the left of the dangling lantern, he put down the last man in this nasty debacle. The sky opened up and rain fell in icy sheets. Black was thankful for the thunder and lightning for it drowned out his thoughts.

PART II
The Village

1

Manhattan
December 1862

TWO CHAIRS WERE taken from Quinn's kitchen and placed in the middle of the barn. A horse snored amid the evidence of violence. A second oil lamp hung from a hook in front of an empty stall. Black listened to the rain as it hit the roof. Seated in the chair that faced the barn door, he waited patiently for his guest. His thoughts went nowhere; it was better this way.

It had grown dark, but the hour wasn't late. Black could hear the muffled sound of men approaching the barn. The barn door was pulled open and in stepped Gilbert and Jake carrying a dead man. They dumped the body unceremoniously against the wall before disappearing into the sleeted night only to return with yet another body. Shultz brought in the horses and Gilbert looked about before focusing on Black.

"Been busy ain't ya?" Gilbert asked.

Black didn't answer, but he did offer direction. "Shultz, give the girl something to help her rest. Jake will tend the horses. Gil, please help the others keep watch."

The men separated. Jake remained, working with and settling the animals; he did not engage Black. About two hours passed when the barn door was once again yanked open. Simon appeared with the body of a man slung over his shoulder. Tim, James and Elbert brought in more horses. After a while, Simon and Tim went to the house, leaving James and Elbert with Black.

"I think we got 'em all." Elbert said.

"The woman said Quinn had five men–he was the sixth man." Black replied.

James added. "We took Mitchell from the pussy parlor. Don't seem like he and this Quinn fella liked one anotha."

The barn had become, to Black's way of thinking, crowded. Between the animals and the dead men, the circumstance was morbid.

"Bring the mayor to me, so that we might bring this matter to a close."

"Yeah." Elbert said, before he and James quit the barn.

Shying away from thoughts of Alice, Black went over the next few hours in his head. It would soon be time to head back to Canada. The goal had to be a sense of peace for him and his men; the message they sent needed to be unmistakable–Quinn was the example of misunderstandings. Black wanted safety for the people of Fort Independence, and he wanted it by any means necessary.

Remaining in the barn allowed him to continue hiding from the situation with Alice. What he had done to Quinn in front of her was something he would never want Sunday to face. But the man had killed innocent people and had set his sights on the children's home. All in the name of tracking them for the mayor. Quinn could not be spared. He also didn't want Anthony to be saddled with Quinn's death. Alice would need Emma, so Black endeavored to leave Anthony as blameless as possible.

It was past midnight when Black realized that he hadn't been successful in stepping away from the matter with the woman. Shaking his head, he looked about at his dead companions. The rain slowed but had not stopped when he heard men shouting in the distance. Suddenly, the door was pulled wide and a gust of frosty wind wrapped about him. Black blinked and it was enough of a lapse that he missed the sight of Fernando Wood being tossed into the barn on his hands and knees.

The mayor's demeanor was no longer haughty as it had been at their first encounter. Black recognized the exact moment his guest's eyes found Quinn, who was still tied up. Fernando seemed to take inventory of the vision before him. Quinn's head had swelled—watermelon like and there was blood dried in his nostrils. The one good eye that he had focused on Alice hours earlier was now bulging. Fernando began to shake and when it became too much, he pitched forward losing the contents of his stomach.

Black was swift in moving his booted foot from the mess that was Fernando Wood. As was his way, he waited patiently for the mayor to compose himself. When Fernando finally stood to his full height, he was sweating. He wiped at his face with the back of his hand and when he could no longer avoid the situation—looked up.

"I killed your cousin, Mr. Mayor. I understand that you're looking for me."

Fernando looked away and Black continued. "Come... come, you made quite the disturbance in your search for me."

"I knew you weren't sent by Lincoln." The mayor mumbled to himself.

"I have an offer for you, Fernando."

"Offer?"

"Yes, an offer." Black returned. "You will stop this madness and we won't kill you."

"My beloved cousin was murdered in cold blood and you would have me forget." Fernando spat.

"Your grief has you beside yourself; let me clarify the matter. Unlike you, Mr. Mayor, I see my limitations and while the fallout from your death would be great, it can be done. As for your beloved cousin—do we speak of the same person? The man I killed lures unsuspecting colored girls into another kind of servitude against their will." Black chuckled, then went on. "Please don't misunderstand, I'm no killjoy, Mr. Mayor. But do I believe in letting one pick their own poison."

"I don't know what you speak of." Fernando said, his superior attitude starting to leak through his fear. "I told Quinn you were a problem."

Black leaned back in his chair and glared at the mayor, who was anything but his put together self. His hair looked like a dead squirrel and his suit was wrinkled. His trousers were caked in dirt at the knees. Yet here he was sliding back into the privilege he was accustom to wielding. One thing became abundantly clear to Black; he needed to end this meeting, or he would slit Fernando's delicate throat.

Behind the mayor stood his brother James, who Black could see had the same thoughts. When Black spoke, he addressed James causing Fernando to whirl about to see with whom he spoke.

"The mayor will be our guest–ready the men."

James glared at Fernando before disappearing into the wet night. Turning back to Black, the mayor said on an audible gulp. "I'm a government official. You can't abduct me."

"I can and will have you as my guest, Mr. Mayor. This is me giving you time to truly consider my offer." Black explained.

When Elbert appeared flanked by Simon. Black ordered. "Bound and gag him."

Stepping into the night, Black headed for the house. The background noise was rain and Fernando Wood screaming that he could not be abducted. The mayor might come to know Alice and Emma's plight intimately.

In the kitchen men stood about waiting for instruction. Alice stood between Anthony and Lou; the woman visibly trembled at the sight of him, and Black winced inwardly.

"We will move out and dock at the pier behind the mansion."

Black said to the room at large. "The animals are all we will take from this place."

The men began to disperse, and Black was left to deal with Alice. When he spoke to her, he saw that she was holding her breath. "You will ride with me."

She was garbed in oversized men clothing, and Black was thankful she would be warm. Turning, he pulled the door open and Alice went before him. At the bottom of the back stairs, Black placed her on his horse, then swung into the saddle behind her. He made a clicking sound and his animal moved forward.

As the temperature dropped, the ground iced over; still his horse was surefooted. Alice burrowed into him trying to stay warm. Black opened his overcoat giving her better access to his body heat. James, Elbert and Jeremiah surrounded him and the woman. The mayor rode just ahead on a horse led by Simon. Fernando was blindfolded and his hands were bound; his own expensive handkerchief was shoved in his mouth.

Dock workers held lanterns that lit the way once the posse moved out of the underbrush. The ferry was already against the pier waiting for them. Each man led their own horse aboard, while Jake, Shultz and Gilbert led the extra animals to a different vessel. As his men moved about getting everyone on the two ferries–not one dock worker, white or black, seemed interested in their hostage; there could be no mistaking a bound and gagged traveler.

Black, Alice and the men stood between the horses as the ferry they occupied began to move away from the dock. There was no conversation as they drifted with the current between Blackwell and Manhattan Island. In the distance, the dock they left was no longer discernible. Black was working through their exit from this calamity, when a large splash caught his attention.

Frantic, he yelled out the names of his men. Elbert, James and Simon responded. "Yeah."

Frank, Lou, Anthony and Tim all answered as well. E.J. and

Jeremiah both spoke up before he could call their names. Black's stomach sank, for when he hollered Alice's name, she did not answer.

"Alice… Alice!!!" he called again, unable to accept the obvious.

He began moving through the animals only to encounter the cowering form of Fernando Wood. Jeremiah's raspy voice floated to him over the choppy sound of rushing water.

"The woman jumped."

"Cain't save her–cain't see shit." Lou said.

Elbert added. "It's prolly for the better. She ain't seem right in the head."

"Shit." Anthony said. "My wife thanks she dead–let's leave it that way."

Black moved around the edge of the ferry trying to peer into the darkness like a window, but to no avail. He had not seen this coming and he ached with failure. As they drifted further away from where the splash happened, Black felt the urge to demand they double back.

"We needs to press on." Simon whispered in his ear.

Black nodded. He couldn't muster a verbal response.

An hour passed before they bumped the dock behind the Church mansion. Black was shaken to his core, but Simon was correct; he had to press on, the men were counting on him. In the wee hours, the mayor was dragged by his collar off the ferry and down the pier. Fernando was then tossed into a waiting carriage. Black climbed in after him, followed by James, Elbert and Jeremiah.

When the carriage lurched forward, the mayor of New York burst into tears. It was the black cracker who put an end to the noise. "If you don't shut yo' ass up…"

While Fernando sniveled to himself, Black stayed up in his own head. Some thirty minutes later, the vehicle slowed then stopped; the door was yanked wide by Herman. Josiah held the torch. Black, followed by his brothers and Jeremiah, jumped down heading for a log cabin situated betwixt two large trees. The windows glowed with candlelight. Elbert pushed at the door, and Jeremiah shoved the mayor over the threshold.

A wooden round table sat in front of the roaring fireplace with two chairs placed opposite each other. In the seat facing the door, the president was hunched over a book–deep in thought. Lincoln's eyes went wide at the sight of Fernando Wood. When his gaze bounced up to meet Black's impassive expression, the president's lips twitched.

"You!" the mayor yelled. "The president involved with… with these ruffians."

Black noted that Lincoln fell right into step as he said, "Fernando, I'm scouting supporters for a new amendment. I expect your backing."

The mayor drew himself up, pushed his stringy hair back from his face and growled. "I will do no such thing."

"The draft will happen, and colored soldiers will fight in this war." Lincoln said with no disdain. "Might be better for your vocation if you choose the winning side."

"Do you realize what your slaves have done?" Fernando scoffed.

Black spoke, leaving Lincoln no room. "Mr. Mayor, whether you help the president or no, you will be killed should you decide wrong on the offer I've made."

"I… I accept your offer." Wood replied, never looking at Black.

"Mr. President, you have thirty minutes before we move on."

Lincoln nodded at Black's words. Jeremiah and Elbert remained to offer protection. James and Black stepped into the darkness, pulling the door shut behind them. They were quiet for a time and Black wrestled with the failure known in his head as Alice.

"I understands what ya goin' through." James said. "Alice ain't thank Quinn should live neither."

Save for the candlelight coming from the windows, darkness surrounded them. Black didn't respond to his brother's words.

James went on. "The woman say it was her fault 'bout the orphanage. Say she wanted him stopped."

"She loved him." Black countered. "Alice was with child."

"You's a leader and ya done what leaders do." James countered.

They fell into an amiable silence, and Black allowed himself to be comforted by his brother's presence and words.

※ ※ ※

"I'm not going to ask what you all did to correct the matter regarding Hugh Wood," the president said.

Black stood in the center of the chamber given to Lincoln at the Church mansion. His arms were folded over his chest as he eyed the president. There was no mistaking the other man's vexation and Black had to remember his manners, so as not to bring about unwanted problems. He suspected that the president's issue was the illusion created that he was somehow involved in the Hugh Wood fiasco. Lincoln had intended to force them into his employ and was frustrated that he had been outsmarted. Black could muster no remorse, but he backed away from smugness. A prosperous fort was his goal above all else.

"It would be better if I don't tell you, sir."

Lincoln replied. "I take it the matter will be in the newspapers?"

"Sir, let us engage in comfortable words." Black answered before changing the subject. "We will leave you with your captain of the guard—in just a few short hours."

"You dismiss me and my need to understand."

"I dismiss the possibility of you being implicated—no matter the speculation." Black replied.

"The mayor didn't accept my request for support, yet he agreed to your offer." Lincoln said, his disappointment bubbling to the surface.

Black coughed. "My proposal enhanced Fernando's goal for self-preservation."

The president glared at him for long moments before standing to walk to the window. Day was breaking and he seemed defeated after his time with Fernando Wood. His disheveled appearance said much. Lincoln wore wrinkled black trousers, a matching vest and white shirt; his clothing made the paleness of his skin prevalent.

"Fernando Wood will be moving to larger government in the coming days. His time as mayor complete." Lincoln spoke over his shoulder, and his words were premeditated. "Should Wood go missing or meet with an unfortunate accident..."

Black thought of Quinn and his answer was careful. "I have other more pressing obligations, sir. It is not my goal to hang."

They both heard what Black did not say... *A man should roll up his sleeves and do his own dirt.*

The president sighed, then nodded and Black took his leave. As he strode down the hall with purpose, he found James and Elbert posted up at the top of the stairs. He was thankful that his brothers didn't try to converse; instead the three of them moved as one readying their posse to exit the New York City conundrum.

❉ ❉ ❉

They waited for night to fall once more before transporting Abraham Lincoln by carriage to Astoria, Queens. The president was met by his captain of the guard, David Derickson and twenty armed soldiers. Anthony and James held the torches, shining light on the handshake between Black and the president. Derickson, a short skinny fellow, huffed at the respect shown between Black and the president; the captain of the guard was ignored.

In a low voice, the president promised. "I will keep you abreast of any new developments."

"Yes, sir." Black replied.

Stepping back from Lincoln, they all watched as the president's carriage was loaded onto the ferry headed for Rikers Island. Swinging into the saddle, the twenty-two started the journey back to their women and children–back to Fort Independence.

2

The Journey
January 1863

ANTHONY WAS ANGRY; in an effort to avoid Black, he worked with Jake to help separate the horses from the animals they would take and the ones they would leave behind. At Black's order, Milford would make certain the remaining horses were given to the orphanage. He, along with Jake and Milford, fulfilled yet another of Black's request—they put down the horse that had gotten sick on the ferry at the beginning of the journey. The goal was to make sure the other animals stayed healthy.

The rushing water wasn't enough to clear thoughts of Alice from his head. Anthony's guilt was large because he had secretly wished her dead to save the orphanage—to save himself. But now... now that Alice had jumped into the freezing waters of the East River, he couldn't step away from thoughts of his wife. How would he face Emma? It didn't help that Black had tried to protect him from the troubles of his own making. The very notion only made him angrier for it highlighted his shortcomings as a man. He felt strangled by his own hand.

When they loaded onto the ferry, a wave of unreasonable panic assailed him. The water added to the blackness of the night and the icy air he breathed into his lungs. Jeremiah could be heard trying to quietly lose the contents of his belly. Finally, after two hours, the barge bumped the pier and Anthony walked his horse onto dry land. Swinging into the saddle, he partnered with Black and Jeremiah as he had when they'd come. The posse split up and headed for the smithy.

Dawn was happening when they reached Port Jervis. As the first rays of light peeked through the clouds, Anthony recognized a new complication. He wasn't too young to realize that their new circumstance may be far more serious than the killing of Hugh Wood. The men merged onto the path from different directions forming a single file. Shultz was at the head of the procession and Black was number two. Hudson appeared at the front of the stable and Anthony watched as Shultz spoke with him from a distance.

As the sunlight became brighter, Anthony marked yet another issue for which he would feel remorse. Gilbert, James and Tim didn't look well, but Jeremiah seemed to be near death's door. Before he could grasp what he was seeing, the doctor rode up directing his words to Black.

"Hudson understands that we will keep on to the train. He will follow and bring back the horses."

A muscle ticked in Black's jaw, but he only nodded. Simon stepped in and began issuing orders. "Bainesworth, Frank and Lou, ride out and secure the train."

"I'll ride with Gil, Tim, Jeremiah and James." Shultz replied.

E.J. was about to protest when Black cut him off and ordered. "Go with Bainesworth."

When the men broke down into groups headed for the train, Black partnered with Shultz, so he could help with the sick men. Anthony moved in behind the doctor to do the same.

"Go with Elbert and Simon." Black ordered.

Anthony looked him square in the eye and replied. "No."

Black slowed his horse and glared, but before he could speak Anthony continued. "I's the man who caused all this–ya carried me long enough."

"Sickness isn't something you can take the blame for." Black said on a sigh.

"None of ya would be here if not for me."

"You ain't the only one that could play that game. Luke wouldn't be dead if we hadn't taken him with us." Black countered.

Anthony's eyes widened. Had Black been blaming himself for Luke's death? The thought to fault anyone with Luke's demise never occurred to him. He knew Elbert struggled with it, but Black…

"I ain't blamin' 'bout Luke."

Black's horse sidestepped sensing the tension and his horse did the same. He thought Black would still send him to Simon, but he asked. "You feeling under the weather?"

"I ain't sick." Anthony answered. "How is you?"

Black eyed him before being honest. "I don't feel my best."

"Shit."

"Go ride with Simon. You don't need this."

"Imma stay wit' you."

Anthony waited for more refusal, but Black nodded curtly. They caught up with Shultz and made the short trek to the train. Hudson appeared wearing a blue handkerchief tied about his face. He herded the animals away and did not linger. The train they caught headed for Canada was an empty freight. There was no luxury and it was cold, but they were going home.

❄ ❄ ❄

Travel to Canada was grueling for several reasons. One–the conductor had to make several stops to check the equipment. Two–the railcars were freezing and about two days into the journey, the tracks had to be repaired for the stretch of a quarter mile. But the rigorous trek was not what caught Black's undivided attention. What snared his interest was the fact that he and several of his men seemed to be suffering from some variation of a wasting disease.

As the train rocked and rumbled along, Black tried to muster enough strength to help the doctor and Anthony when needed. What he didn't understand was how Shultz and Ant were untouched by the sickness. Black was chilled from his time in the underbrush; he retched twice. Jeremiah was no longer tossing his stomach, but his bowels seemed out of his control and for the rest of the men, it was still early yet.

The doctor did his best to keep the space they shared tidy–fresh hay lined the floor of the railcar. Shultz also lugged clean drinking water to the train. Black had refused, but the doctor insisted. As for Jeremiah, Shultz forced the water down his throat, only to have it come back up. Tim, James and Gilbert were like Black–ill, but holding their own.

"Dis rockin' shit is killin' me." Gil said.

"Just when I thanks I's empty–more shit falls outta me." James whispered from his blankets in the corner.

"Keep drinking water–even if ya don't want it." Shultz demanded.

Tim and Jeremiah slept, but Black couldn't rest. He ached from the cold and he worried about the men and the fort; he feared entering the gates–Black feared spreading a wasting disease among the people of Fort Independence. The men rode in separate railcars to keep down the unwellness. But when the freight made two more stops, Jake was moved to the sick car and later Simon joined them.

Two more days passed with Shultz having more and more trouble rousting Jeremiah. Black thought of Callie and shook his head. He absolutely did not want to face her. The moments of self-pity he engaged in brought about a new type of shame. Black couldn't step away from cataloging his troubles. Sunday, Callie and Alice plagued him, but the well-being of the fort suffocated him.

"Should we camp outside the gate?" Black asked the doctor on the morning they reached Ottawa.

"We are all under quarantine. None of us can go to the women and children." Shultz countered. "But we should enter the fort and set up on the westside. There are several empty cabins and when this is over, we'll burn them."

Black would have protested, but the doctor went on. "If we set up outside the gate, the people will worry. Entering the fort will give us better conditions and a better chance."

Black nodded.

Once in Ottawa, the twenty-two were met by two covered wagons and unseasonably warm weather. Chester, a field hand and Philip drove the vehicles. When they would have come forward to help the men load the wagons, Shultz yelled at them to stay back. Both men wore puzzled expressions.

"We are under quarantine." Shultz explained from a distance. "You are to each take a horse and head back. Ready the cabins on the west-side of the fort and spread the word that we are not to be approached."

Both men looked to Black, who nodded to confirm the doctor's words. He didn't send a message to Sunday. Black didn't want anyone who even looked upon him to come in contact with his woman and children. The thought was unreasonable, but he couldn't help it. The leader of Fort Independence was giving himself over to silent hysteria.

The men piled into the wagons based on who was sick and who wasn't. Anthony drove one wagon and Shultz drove the other. The back flap of the cover was left open and Black observed a bright day, barren trees and rushing streams. And while the day was lovely, he had no doubt that he was weaker than the day before.

After a few hours of travel, the fort came into view, but the gate did not swing wide. Shultz and Anthony spoke to Philip through a portal to the left of the gate; the men listed out much needed supplies. Still another two hours passed and night was upon them before the gate opened on a loud groan. The wagons lurched forward and traveled along the large inner wall to the westside.

When Anthony brought the wagon to a bone jarring stop, Black was thankful for the ability to climb from the vehicle on his own steam. Light flickered from the windows of the four eerie cabins and Black felt his life on the fort come full circle. These rudimentary structures were the first on the land. The largest cabin was first shared by Otis and Mary. A small stream that wasn't the main water supply flowed behind the cabins.

Black turned in time to see Jeremiah climb from the wagon only to pass out when his boots touch the ground.

"Shit." E.J. said, as he reached out in time to break his brother's fall.

Jeremiah grunted then whispered something that made E.J. reply, "You'll tell Callie yourself."

Shultz broke into Black's dread. Grabbing his shoulder and squeezing, the doctor ordered. "Come this way."

Black shook his head and started on wobbly legs toward E.J. and Jeremiah. Shultz whispered, "We're gonna help him as best we can... come."

Reluctantly, Black followed.

Paul and Sonny appeared in the doorway of Black's office. Sunday looked up from the parchment she was working through at their arrival. She'd heard the gate groan but hadn't gotten her hopes up. Now she felt dread for both men appeared grim.

"Black done come home." Paul said.

"Come in and shut the door." She replied.

Sonny stepped into the office first and Paul followed closing the door tightly behind them. Sunday waited, giving each man and herself a moment. Two oil lamps burned bright as the natural light of day had faded hours ago. She allowed her eyes to fall to the children's toys in the corner of the office; a reminder of the fragility of life. When she could no longer stall...

"Nat?"

"The men is dealin' wit' illness–they's on the westside of the fort. Black and the doctor done quarantined them. Ain't no one can see them." Paul answered. "Black is holdin is own–Philip laid eyes on him."

Sunday stood behind the desk, then sat again; her peach dress rustling with her erratic movements. Sonny moved forward as if to help her, but she held up her hand.

"Has any of the twenty-two..." she couldn't make herself finish the question.

Sonny shook his head taking mercy on her. He had the blackest skin with a light sheen of sweat across his forehead. The keys at his hip jingled as he shifted from foot to foot. It was Paul who offered a verbal explanation, and Sunday felt his words like a blow to her belly; the unnatural blue of his eyes fixed on her.

"Philip say–Jeremiah done caught his death. It ain't lookin' good."

Sunday covered her face with both hands and tried to collect herself to no avail. Finally, she asked. "Do Callie know?"

The older men glanced at each other first before they turned to her and shook their heads in the negative. Sonny added, "My mama and Eva don't know neither... you's in charge. We wanted to tell you first."

Sunday didn't want to be in charge. What she wanted was to go to her husband and comfort him. Nat would expect her strength, not her weakness. She stood heading for her bedchamber where Callie was putting the children down for the night. In the kitchen she found Cora and Big Mama.

"Philip say the men is unda quarantine." Sunday said softly.

Big Mama and Cora didn't speak, so she went on. "Jeremiah ain't doin' well."

Mama and Cora followed her to the master bedroom where Callie sat rocking Miah in her arms. Lil Otis, Lil Letti–Morgan's child, and her children were sleep. Callie was smiling when she first looked up at them. Sunday figured it must have been her expression because Callie frowned and stood.

"Jeremiah?"

"Come wit' me," Sunday countered.

Callie placed a sleeping Miah in Cora's arms and followed Sunday back to the office. Paul and Sonny stood next to the window waiting. Once in the office, Sunday closed the door and spoke putting them both out of their misery.

"The men is back–but they's unda quarantine. We cain't go to them."

"Jeremiah?"

"I been told he and Nat is sick." Sunday said and she felt no shame in leaving out what Philip said. "Ain't nothin' to do but wait."

Callie whirled heading for the door, the brown skirts of her dress swaying from her speed. "I have to go to him."

"What about the children–Miah? If ya goes to him, you cain't come back." Sunday said softly.

Sunday hated having to say such a thing. It was asking her to choose between the people she loved most in the world. Callie stopped at the door–her hand on the knob, her back to the room.

"I need him," she whispered brokenly.

Sunday walked up behind her placing a hand to her shoulder. "Come sit."

Callie allowed Sunday to hug her before leading her to the gold couch. Looking up at Paul and Sonny, she ordered. "Go around to the womenfolk–tell 'em I says come to me."

After Sonny and Paul left to do her bidding, Callie broke down and wept. When she could cry no more, she whispered. "You will care for Miah and Otis–I have to go to him."

"You ain't finna listen to nothin' I say on this. Is ya?" Sunday asked.

"No." Callie countered. "And you're a horrible liar."

"Will ya wait 'til daybreak?" Sunday asked trying to stall.

"No."

The women stared at each other for long moments with no words passing between them. Secretly, Sunday agreed with Callie. But like her husband, she had the weight of the fort on her slender shoulders. Callie stood and exited the office; she didn't look back.

Sunday sighed aloud, for Callie didn't know Black as she did. Her husband would soon give Miss Callie another reason to hate him.

3

The Borders of a Man

THE MEN WERE set up in the cabins according to their level of sickness. But Black remained with Jeremiah, though he wasn't as ill. E.J. who *wasn't* sick also settled in with them. Six cots were set up in the cabin, but only three were occupied. The rules were the same for each group; every man had to strip down and wash-the process was harsh and cold. All clothing from their travels was burned and holes were dug by the healthy men to dispose of the waste.

"Nettie and Suzanne will be beside themselves." E.J. mused aloud.

Black lay flat on his back staring up at the ceiling, his belly rolling, and his head pounding. Jeremiah had taken to mumbling but they could just make out that he was calling for Callie. Black warned Shultz that if his situation worsened, Sunday was not to be notified. He even went so far as to instruct the doctor to burn his body.

"Will Nettie and Suzanne look after Callie?" Black asked.

E.J. chuckled. "Callie loves only my brother. She ain't sisterly with my women."

Black turned his head to find E.J. squeezing out a cloth to place on his brother's forehead. He was seated in a wooden chair by the cot where Jeremiah slept fitfully. Black had known Callie wasn't friendly with anyone but Jeremiah, Eva and Sunday; still, he hoped for a different answer.

The doctor came from another cabin and immediately began washing up in a white basin on the scarred table. Black's eyes followed the doctor. He tried to catalogue his symptoms to help Shultz solve the mystery of why they had taken ill. Black had been about to speak to Shultz when E.J. asked.

"Ya know Callie is gonna come here–right?"

"Elbert said the same." Shultz added.

Black was thinking on Callie when the door to the cabin swung wide. In walked Elbert and James, each brother picking a cot. When the movement settled, Black spoke and he was vexed.

"You two shouldn't be here."

"Yeah we should," Elbert countered.

James didn't bother to answer, and Black didn't have the energy to argue. He addressed Elbert when he accused. "You ain't ill."

Elbert glared at him. "No, but you and James are."

Black looked to James who appeared green in the candlelight. "How you feeling?"

"Weak," was James' only reply.

❊ ❊ ❊

Black woke to the sound of Jeremiah retching. Shultz held the bucket and E.J. wiped his face. Elbert opened both the front and the back door of the cabin. When James began retching, Black stood to help him, but Elbert beat him to it. E.J. and Elbert removed the buckets and replenished the fresh water. The doctor forced more water down Jeremiah and when Elbert threatened to do the same to James, he gave in.

As the cabin settled, Black asked. "What do you think we contracted?"

Shultz turned and stared at him for moments, before answering honestly. "I can't say for certain, but my guess is influenza."

"Damn." Elbert said, echoing Black's thoughts.

"I don't know much about this illness, but what I've read says the patient shouldn't be reduced to dry retching. Tomorrow, you all will start on broth and keep drinking water–even if you have to retch." Shultz said speaking to himself.

Black gave what Shultz said serious thought. He realized the doctor was correct–riding out meant the men could go days without eating. In New York, Jeremiah was at least still standing. The black cracker took a turn for the worse on the trek back to Canada. On the freight train, none of them had really eaten. The goal and destination was the fort. In his periphery, Black noted Shultz closing the backdoor of the cabin, while leaving the front open. In the distance, Anthony, Frank and Lou could be heard talking.

"Simon?" Black asked.

"He ain't better, but he ain't no sicker." Elbert answered.

Black nodded, then got to his feet heading for the door Shultz just closed. He stepped out into the night and Elbert followed him with a lantern. There was no wind, the night was still.

"I'm good."

"We dug some deep ditches while you was sleep. I don't want yo' ass fallin' in." Elbert said.

"I need to piss."

"Yeah." Elbert returned.

Black pissed down into a hole, then headed for the pump. After washing up, he observed the faint scent of food on the air. It made him want to toss his belly. "What *is* that smell?"

"Ant cookin' chicken soup." Elbert answered.

"I can't eat." Black countered.

"Come." Elbert demanded. "Ya need rest and ya will eat."

Black used all his strength to get to his cot. Elbert then helped James out to the hole, where James tossed up his guts. Jeremiah was given more water against his will. E.J. had blue bruises under his eyes from lack of sleep, his concern for his brother apparent. Everyone was physically and emotionally taxed. As Black drifted into a restless sleep, he was snatched awake by the sound of men yelling outside the cabin.

He sat up abruptly and was briefly disoriented. Elbert spoke through his sleep haze. "Easy, man… easy."

Black reached for the gun holster he placed under his cot. "What's the commotion about?"

"Callie is wantin' to be with my brother." E.J. whispered. "Jeremiah is out of it, but he wouldn't want her here. I know my brother… he loves that woman and would not want this for her."

Shultz shook his head. "Philip and a few men from the barracks are standing guard. They are detaining her and well… you can hear for yourself."

Black looked to Jeremiah for guidance, but he was indeed out of it. James was awake, though too weak to sit up. When Black started for the front door, he heard James' words to Elbert. "Betta go wit' Black. Eva told me Callie beat Jeremiah's ass before. Black gon need back up."

Elbert chuckled and followed him onto the porch; in the background E.J. confirmed. "That shit is true."

Black and Elbert walked down between the trees into a clearing. The darkness was cut by the light spilling from the door of an old, unused barn. As they moved toward the flickering light, Philip could be heard explaining.

"Miss Callie, it ain't safe for you to be here."

The weather was cold, but not icy and there was no wind, for which Black was thankful. Still he had to fight the chills coursing through him. As they approached the barn, Black whispered, "The woman is too perceptive. Imma have to be mean."

"I can hold her down, so you can punch her." Elbert replied on a soft laugh.

"Shit." Black grumbled.

Elbert's tone changed for the serious. "She ain't Alice… Callie has to listen to keep herself and the people safe–be mean, brother."

Black leaned against the side of the barn to gather himself before facing her. He was sure of one thing… this night Miss Callie was going to be mad as hell.

"Ready?" Elbert asked.

"Yeah."

Stepping away from the wall, Black steadied himself before walking to the entrance of the barn. At the opposite end of the aisle, Philip and Chester each held Callie by the upper arm. She was struggling to free herself. The empty barn was dusty, and hay covered the floor. Two lanterns lit the space–one hung from a hook in the overhead beam and the second sat on the floor in the far corner.

Upon seeing him and Elbert, Callie stopped her struggles. Her voice was thick with tears when she spoke. "Mr. Black, they won't let me see him–they won't take me to Jeremiah."

The lighting left some parts of the barn in the shadows, but Black could see Callie clearly. She wore a brown dress and several buttons of the bodice had come undone. The matching shawl she sported lay rumpled in the hay. Her hair had come loose from the two plaits pinned at the top of her head. All of it was the sign of a power struggle, and he saw it for what it was–challenge to his authority.

Dismissing formality, Black spoke, and his displeasure was palpable. "Callie, why are you here?"

She hiccupped under the weight of his controlled anger. "Jeremiah needs me–where is he?"

"Were you told the men were under quarantine?"

"Please… I need to see him." she pleaded.

"Answer me!" Black yelled and she jumped.

Philip and Chester backed away from her as if to disassociate from the situation. Callie wiped the tears from her eyes and replied in a tone so matter of fact that Black wanted to shake her.

"I don't answer to you. Please take me to Jeremiah."

Black actually took a step forward causing Elbert to place a restraining hand on his shoulder. "Oh, Callie, you are mistaken—you do answer to me. I am in charge on this land and you will heed me. You left the women and children—placing yourself and them in harm's way."

Callie had been about to protest when Black directed his next words to Philip and Chester. "Take her to the nearest cabin and place her under house arrest. She is to remain under guard until the quarantine is over."

Philip placed a hand on her upper right arm. "Please come on wit' us, Miss."

Callie fell to the floor in a heap. Chester reached under her other arm to help Philip carry a kicking and screaming Callie away.

"Black!" she hollered. "No... please... take me to Jeremiah!"

The men dragged her out the opposite door, and Black continued to stare at the space where she last stood. Elbert walked over to the lanterns outing them, casting the barn into nothingness. The brothers walked back to the cabin in silence. Black lingered on the porch; Elbert went inside.

His anger with Callie sapped his last bit of strength. Black moved on unsteady legs to the back of the cabin where he retched—until empty. He heard the backdoor creak on its hinges and the voice of Shultz floated on the cool air.

"Brought you clean clothes—wash up at the pump. Drink some water and come rest."

Black stripped down, tossing his tan homespun trousers and shirt into a barrel by the bushes. He splashed cold water on his person, shocking his senses. The doctor handed him a towel—he dried, then dressed. Carrying his boots and his gun, he made his way through the backdoor onto his cot. The doctor pulled a chair to his bedside.

Shultz helped him snuggle under several blankets. The front

door was closed, but the back was ajar for the mix of fresh air. A fire burned in the hearth and on the table the lantern had been turned down. E.J., Jeremiah and James were asleep. Water boiled on the small black stove in the corner. Elbert lay quiet.

When Black could get his shivering under control, he told Shultz how he was feeling. "My belly is unstable–my head spins, my body aches and my throat burns. I can't tell whether I'm hot or cold. I'm weak."

"In the morning, we will start chicken broth." Shultz said again and then… "My throat burns."

Black opened his eyes and gazed at the doctor. "Are you falling ill?"

"Yes."

❉ ❉ ❉

Callie sat in a chair by the window staring into the night. Her heart ached and because of the pain, she could not form a positive working thought. Jeremiah was probably dead, and no one wanted to tell her the truth. Black was making decisions for everyone on the fort. He would have burned the dead already and placing her under house arrest was a way to control the panic.

Chester lit a candle before exiting the cabin, which was a converted storage building. There was a small fireplace, cot and table; against the far wall sat crates stacked one on top of the other. At the back of the cabin was no door or window. She wouldn't be escaping.

Trying to control the desperation she felt, Callie leaned back in the chair and closed her eyes. Thoughts of when she first saw Jeremiah danced in her head. The first time she experienced pleasure with him, even the first time they exchanged words of love. She was going to die without him; her only solace was that Sunday had Otis and Miah. The children would be better off without her for she was no good without him.

After hours of sitting in the same position, she felt ill. Her breasts were filled to bursting and feverishly ached. In an attempt to calm her soul, Callie laid on the cot staring up at the ceiling. Blanketed in sorrow, she dozed. Later, she awoke to the sound of the door scraping the floor as it was being shoved open.

Sunlight angled through the door and window—it was a beautiful day. Callie didn't understand how life could go on; she had been separated from her love. Philip placed a tray on the table then backed out before she could ask a question. Grief had swallowed her whole 'til there was nothing left but to hide from herself.

When she could no longer live in the oblivion of sleep, she lay facing the wall. The cabin door opened and closed periodically. She rose only to use the chamber pot in the opposite corner of the room. Callie was thankful for one thing. Black had given her the space to be alone so she could wallow in sadness. The sun had come and gone two times when she heard someone speaking to her.

"Miss Callie, ya needs to eat somethin'."

She opened her eyes to find Philip standing over her and Chester standing behind him. Her voice was weak but steady. "Go away."

The cabin door closed and then there was nothing again. Sleep found her again and she was grateful. At times, her melancholy was so great that she wept in her sleep.

❄ ❄ ❄

Black sat in a chair by the doctor's bedside and worry marred his brow. In a matter of days, Shultz took a turn for the worse and was too weak to stand. He had to be assisted to take a piss and he had to be forced to drink broth and water. In a strange turn of events, Black, while still weak and shaky on his feet began feeling better. James was also feeling improved.

E.J. had gotten ill and like the doctor, he couldn't stand under his own steam. Jeremiah was experiencing longer bouts of wakefulness, but still couldn't hold anything down. Elbert for some reason hadn't contracted the sickness. Outside their cabin, Anthony hadn't taken ill, but Frank and Lou were sick. Simon, like Black was on the mend, but weak.

Tim seemed to be getting better, but Gilbert hadn't changed. While Gil wasn't any better, he hadn't retched in days. Black didn't know whether that was good or bad, because when he retched, he actually felt stronger. Ephraim, Jesse and Horace joined the ranks of the sick. Elbert went between the cabins assisting the men and spreading Shultz' instructions to drink plenty water and eat the soup Ant made. Every man did as he was told.

Black couldn't make out what to do with Jeremiah. The black cracker drank water and the broth, but he seemed to toss up more than he consumed. While Black was trying to figure on how to help Jeremiah, Anthony appeared in the doorway of the cabin, his expression grave. Black stood going to him. Anthony backed out onto the porch and when Black stepped into the sunlight, he saw strain etched deep in the younger man's face.

Anthony reached passed him and shut the cabin door for privacy. "Jeremiah's woman is ill."

Black frowned. "Elbert and I didn't come in direct contact with her. I had her moved to a cabin to keep her safe."

"Been two days and Philip say she ain't eating or drinkin'. They believes she tryin' to starve her fool self."

Black was in disbelief. He couldn't be hearing correctly. "She has the children to live for... why..."

"No." Anthony said. "Phil is worried for her."

Black nodded. "I'll take it from here."

"Anythang you wantin' me to do?"

"No." Black answered, before turning to walk back into the cabin.

He stared around the one room, his head swirling with thoughts of Callie. Black felt the squeeze of woman problems and he wanted to punch something; he wanted to punch Jeremiah. The doctor had drifted back to sleep, E.J. was sleeping as well. James lay awake and Elbert was seated at his bedside. The black cracker was staring at him.

Maneuvering through the cots and chairs, Black approached Jeremiah, who looked weighed down with hair growth. He had a full beard and the hair on his head was wild. When Jeremiah spoke his voice was raspy.

"Shit, I never seen you wit' hair."

Black raised a hand to his own head and, indeed, he too had grown some hair. Taking the chair at Jeremiah's bedside, he asked. "How you feeling?"

"Like whateva I had changed to somethin' more. My belly is cramping."

Though E.J. wiped him down, Jeremiah smelled foul. Black suspected he smelled about the same. Unable to decide where to begin, Black blurted. "I had Callie placed under house arrest."

Jeremiah eyed him. "I know."

"It was for her safety and the safety of the other women and children."

"I know." The black cracker repeated.

"It seems she has bested me." Black said.

"How so?"

"She is refusing to eat or drink. Callie is starving herself."

Jeremiah's eyes widened, then he rasped. "She thinks I'm dead and you won't tell her the truth."

"I figured as much."

"Can you take me to her?" Jeremiah asked.

"You could expose her to the illness."

"She'll fall ill anyway if I don't show myself." Jeremiah replied.

Black stared at him, before conceding to the truth. "I'll take you."

"Wait–Otis and Miah…"

"Your children will be safe." Black promised, even though he wasn't sure he wouldn't take a sudden turn for the worse.

Jeremiah closed his eyes, essentially ending the conversation.

Black took the cue and stood. His eyes fell on Elbert who also stood. They headed out the backdoor and once alone.

"Have a horse and small wagon brought around. I'm moving Jeremiah to the cabin with Callie."

"Hell." Elbert breathed. "What if she catches this shit?"

"She has taken to starving herself." Black replied, self-disgust lacing his words.

"I'll ready a wagon and horse."

As he watched Elbert walk away to do his bidding, his thoughts went to Sunday, his children and Mama. Callie's actions made him think of the pressure his wife must be feeling. Sunday stepped in bearing the weight of the fort and its people with him. They could not put down the burden he carried, and the mere thought made his eyes water.

When he gathered his emotions, Black entered the cabin to help get Jeremiah ready for transport.

4

Love from all Angles

SHE WAS DRIFTING in and out of wakefulness when the sound of wagon wheels brought her fully aware of her surroundings. Callie closed her eyes once more trying to force herself back to sleep, but the sound of booted feet on the makeshift porch kept her attention. The door made the scraping sound and she remained still as she waited for one of the guards to take his leave; her name floated on the air and it hadn't come from Philip or Chester.

"Callie." Black's deep tone echoed about the cabin.

At the sound of his voice, she wept; but she didn't turn to him. She just wanted him to go away. More booted feet and shuffling sounded behind her.

"Woman," Jeremiah rasped, "I'm here and I ain't dead."

She turned slowly on the cot and sat up. In the doorway stood her love, who was being held by Elbert and Black. He was thinner and carried lots more hair–but it was Jeremiah. Callie got to her feet and rushed to him. Elbert swayed a bit trying to keep them all from toppling over.

She sobbed his name and the sound reverberated around the

room. Callie shook with emotion and Elbert grunted. "Easy, woman–you gonna cause us all to be sprawled out. Let's get him to the cot."

Elbert carried the brunt of Jeremiah's weight, as both Black and Jeremiah were still weak with illness. Jeremiah didn't even try to sit up; instead he ended up flat on his back. Getting down on her knees at the side of the bed, Callie buried her face in his neck. She couldn't stop crying, but she paid close attention when Black spoke to Jeremiah.

"You have to drink water and the broth. We ain't for sure what else to do for you. I don't want you to waste away."

"My belly is unstable. Imma try and keep drinkin'."

"Me and Elbert will come back to let you know how E.J. is doing." Black said before turning his attention to her. She sat back on her haunches, but she did not look up. "Anthony and Elbert will remove his waste–you are to drink and eat. Anthony will bring fresh water for you. It's important to keep yourself and him clean. I don't want you sick. I'll be back to help you."

Callie was knelt before Black's feet, his black boots in her line of vision. She couldn't manage eye contact with him, and he didn't push her for it. Black didn't even respond to her whispered. "Yes."

She watched as his boots turned from her and walked away. When the cabin door closed with a soft thud, Callie placed her face between Jeremiah's neck and shoulder. He pulled her onto the cot and held her. She wept.

"Shhh." Jeremiah murmured.

"I can't…" she sobbed. "I thought you were dead."

"Woman–I don't want you to be sick," he said, his voice scratchy.

"You need water." She replied, stepping over his worry.

Climbing from the bed, she found the supplies lugged in by Elbert. There was a bucket by the door. On the table was a wooden bowl and cup both marked with a 'J'. He'd placed a crate with other necessities next to the chair–she would sort it later. Right now, she would stoke the fire and give Jeremiah some water. When she turned back to him, he was asleep.

Callie pulled the chair to his bedside and marveled at the difference between yesterday and this moment. It was well after noon, because the natural light began to dim–although it was still daytime. She sat for about an hour smoothing his hair back from his face. Callie couldn't resist touching him. She had to make certain this wasn't a dream.

Another hour passed when she heard wagon wheels once more. There was a knock and then Anthony pushed the door open when she failed to answer. Callie stared at him with indifference and he gave a curt nod.

"Miss Callie."

Anthony didn't wait for a response, instead he disappeared and came back with a large tin tub. A pattern was set with him stepping from the cabin only to return with more supplies. He filled the tub with steaming water, leaving two buckets by the door. On the table he sat a basin, a kettle and a pitcher. Next to the crate, he placed a sack before taking his leave.

She refocused on Jeremiah, dismissing the other man. Callie waited to hear the thud of the cabin door. Instead, Anthony's voice broke the peace and his words were filled with empathy.

"Ya has to eat and stay clean. Ya cain't care for him if'n you gets down."

Emotion blurred her vision, but she answered. "Yes... Anthony."

The cabin door closed softly at her back, and she looked up to find Jeremiah's eyes on her. "Can ya sit up?"

"No."

"How long you been flat on yo' back?"

"Don't know." Jeremiah replied.

"Will ya try, for me?"

He stared at her for seconds, then nodded. When he pushed up onto his elbows, Callie rushed to help him stay up right. She adjusted him so that his back was against the wall.

"How is that?"

"Shit—get me the bucket." He groaned.

Callie rushed to do his bidding and when she shoved the bucket at him, he retched. The sound grated on her ears and soul; her love was miserable. Dumping the contents of the sack on the floor, she found cloths, towels—two dresses and two shifts. Also included was a comb and brush. Dampening a cloth, she wiped his face and fetched him some water. He refused.

"Rinse your mouth." She demanded, after moving the bucket to the floor.

Jeremiah rinsed his mouth and when he would have handed the cup back. Callie ordered. "Swallow two times."

He glared at her but did as she requested. Taking the cup from him, she placed it on the table. And when she turned back to him, she found that he was trying to lay back down. "No love, try staying up for five more minutes."

Again, he nodded but closed his eyes. She stood on the side of the cot staring at him. Jeremiah blinked slowly and when he finally focused on her, his eyes were watery. "You gonna catch this shit. I shouldn't have come to this cabin. You should be with the children."

"You have two more minutes, then you can lay down." She replied.

After the allotted time, Callie helped him resettle and Jeremiah fell immediately to sleep. When he woke next, she fed him broth. And so it began, the cycle of him resting, retching and glaring at her. This was the pattern her life had taken in her care of young children. She found that she wasn't out of her element. The aim would be to maintain common sense.

It was well past midnight when she heard booted feet on the porch. She knew who it was for he walked with authority. He banged on the door and like when Anthony had come, she didn't respond. Callie held her breath as Black entered the cabin. She met his intense gaze with apprehension.

"Have you eaten?" he asked.

"Yes."

"What did you eat?" Black continued to press.

"The kettle holds chicken soup. I ate the meat and vegetables. I fed Jeremiah the broth."

"Are you feeling unwell?"

"No."

Callie had never seen Black with hair, and it was unsettling; his hair was of all things curly. He wore homespun trousers with a matching shirt. The holster of his gun bunched his shirt up on the left side. He wore a brown overcoat that hung open–black boots on his feet. His slanted dark eyes assessed her, and Callie dropped her gaze. Still, she noted that he carried a saddlebag and what looked like folded clothes.

Stepping back out the door, he returned with the chamber pot and she glanced up at the scuffling. Embarrassment made her look away once more. She was pondering how she would get Jeremiah on the pot when Elbert appeared; he walked right up to the cot and asked.

"You needin to take a piss?"

"Hell if I know." Jeremiah answered.

Elbert pulled back the covers and assisted Jeremiah to his stockinged feet. Black, who had placed the pot in the corner, was now busy adding a log to the fire. Callie stared at her own stockinged feet, but she did hear Jeremiah relieving himself. Elbert maneuvered him back to the bed and Black emptied the pot into the waste bucket and set it outside.

"I'll be back." Black said, his voice sharp.

"Yes." Callie whispered, mostly because she feared the consequence of ignoring him.

Once Black and Elbert left, and Jeremiah drifted back to sleep, Callie took a moment to reflect and assess the leader of Fort Independence. She matched the man she encountered moments ago to the man who had methodically taken over the Hunter plantation. She then compared him to the man who spared Jeremiah and even the man who placed her under house arrest. Black was to be feared and there was no other way to see him.

While Jeremiah rested, she bathed quickly in the now chilled water. Callie also expressed as much breastmilk as she could to give herself some relief. Ben-Ben was her biggest drinker and she sorely felt his absence. She also donned a shift and plaited her hair. When exhaustion finally kicked in, it was close to dawn. She curled up at the foot of the bed and dozed, content that her love was with her. The sound of Jeremiah retching woke her.

He began to dry heave when she advised. "Easy love, try to calm down."

Jeremiah fell back on the bed and groaned. "Callie, I ain't gonna make it. You gotta be alright without me."

"Shhh." She whispered to him. "Don't talk like that."

"Woman." He moaned brokenly.

Callie filled the basin with fresh water and set up by the bed. She stripped him naked wiping the perspiration from his body. Jeremiah appeared equal parts cold and hot. She added another log to fire, though the cabin was stifling. He drank some broth and then a few swallows of water; but tossed it up. She did not stop tending him.

Placing the waste bucket at the door, she stole a few moments to wash up and change her shift. Jeremiah's words rang in her head and she couldn't say which was worse; not knowing what was happening to him or watching him waste away. Standing in front of the fireplace, she chanced a look in his direction. Jeremiah slept and she wept.

As she stood staring into the fire, the sound of boots on the porch got her attention. There was nowhere to hide, or room to collect herself. Black banged on the door then shoved it wide. Her only saving grace was the one candle–it left the cabin dim. Callie wiped the tears from her face and offered no eye contact.

"Are you unwell?" Black asked.

"I feel tired–I have some aches, but I am well."

"Is he drinking?"

"Very little and whatever he does manage comes up double." She answered and it was more than she intended to say. Callie kept her eyes on his boots.

Before she knew what he was about, Black reached out and palmed her chin. He was forcing her to engage him. His grip was firm but not painful. She could hear his previous threat dancing about in her head. *Oh, Callie, you are mistaken–you do answer to me.*

"You shouldn't be here."

"Jeremiah is not well–there is no other place for me." She answered, while hoping he didn't feel her trembling.

"There are only men in this sector of the fort. Who will care for you should you become ill?"

Her tone was breathy when she countered. "You will care for me."

Black stared at her and Callie could feel time pass. Finally, he replied. "Yeah."

The power of the exchange was intensified by the fact that he continued to hold her chin in his rough palm. When he spoke again, it was as she suspected–Black gave his list of demands.

"You will tell me immediately if you feel ill."

"Yes." She answered, conceding to his control.

"I will come in the early morning to check on your needs for the day. Any time after that–one of the men will be with me. You will not wear a shift–you will be fully clothed."

"Yes."

"You, Miss Callie, will not defy my authority ever again."

"Yes." She whispered.

"You didn't trust that I would try to help Jeremiah–as I trusted you with my children."

She sobbed and still he didn't release her. "I love him."

"I don't want you to become ill."

"I am tied to Jeremiah—you can't control that." She explained, her voice thick with sorrow. "Sunday is tied to you and your responsibility—that can't be controlled either. Your wife could have put me under house arrest, but she let me be. It was her way of gauging your condition based on your anger with me."

His grip tightened. "Number three."

"Three?"

"You will not defy me." Black countered and he was vexed.

"Yes."

The cabin shook with his presence and still he offered no relief from his potency. Callie went on. "My devotion to him will at times clash with my devotion to you. It is an uncomfortable place to be."

"I understand." He countered and there was no surprise in his tone or demeanor.

She noted that when Black felt he had the rules established—he added yet another condition to their situation. "You will not stare at the damn ground when you encounter me."

"Yes."

As if testing his reins on their circumstance, he released her chin and stepped back. Callie continued to maintain eye contact and he nodded his approval.

"When Jeremiah wakes, inform him that E.J. has not worsened, but he has gotten no better."

"I will."

Black turned on his heels, removed the waste buckets and quit the cabin. Callie stood for a time pondering the exchange between them. Black looked as though he had been unwell and was trying to manage his own sickness while leading the people. His was a heavy burden. As she pondered the plight of Fort Independence, she caught movement in her periphery.

Callie walked over to the bed and stared down into the wide

eyes of Jeremiah. He had been awake and heard their conversation. Callie didn't shy away or evade.

"You understand that my love for you is unshakeable–even in his presence."

"Yes." Jeremiah answered. "But Black's presence–"

"You don't have room for unreasonable worry. I love you–so much. I want to speak with you about settling your belly."

He closed his eyes trying to step away from jealousy. Callie rushed on. "I plan to stop the broth for a time."

Jeremiah never opened his eyes, but he replied. "I don't want the water–neither."

"I can't let you stop the water–I have nothing to replace it with. You will drink breastmilk in place of the broth."

If the situation weren't so grim, Callie would have laughed at his expression. He rasped. "Woman–I am no damn baby."

His words didn't carry the meanness that Jeremiah could bring to a situation, but he was appalled for sure. Her next words were unfair, still she used whatever she could to get her way. "I will not be all right without you."

Blinking slowly, he nodded, all the fight gone from him–his defeat tangible. In an effort to give him a few moments to think, she went about tending him. She set up the basin, a cloth and a hairbrush. Pulling back the covers, she washed the sweat from his body. She brushed his hair as he drifted on sleep. His mane had more strands of gray, but nothing could detract from the beauty of Jeremiah–not even illness. When she stopped touching him, he opened his eyes as if disappointed.

"I want you to sit up for five minutes."

"My belly." He groaned.

"You will drink after ya sit up for a few moments. I want you to get stronger. Lying about can't be good."

He pressed up on his elbows and she helped situate him, so his back was to the wall. Jeremiah kept his eyes closed and broke out in a sweat from the effort. As she straightened up, she cast a glance to the window realizing it was daybreak. This was normally the time her breasts filled and ached. Smiling, she made her way back over to the cot.

"How you feeling, love?"

"Tired." Jeremiah replied–eyes still closed.

"You ready to lie down?"

"Yes." His answer was simple.

Callie helped him lay back and turn on his side. Removing her shift, she climbed into bed with him. Like Jeremiah, she too was naked. His skin was hot and the feel of him against her skin made her eyes tear up. She lay facing him and he was lower in the bed–his cheek against her breasts.

"You don't have to drink much. Just enough to coat your belly."

She ran her fingers through his hair and pulled him closer. Callie felt hope burst between them when Jeremiah latched on to her nipple and drank. There was nothing she wouldn't do for this man.

❋ ❋ ❋

Sunday stood in the center of the office surrounded by the women of the twenty-two. She had no answers other than Callie had been placed under house arrest. It was the fact that Callie was under guard that gave her hope. If Nat were that angry, he must be still standing; it was all she had.

Glancing around the office, Sunday found E.J.'s women holding hands. His white wife nursed his black son, while his black wife rocked a blonde baby girl in her arms. Molly, Lou's woman kept dabbing at her eyes and Emma–Anthony's wife kept an arm around her. Anna and Abby sat together. Miss Cora sat between them, helping to manage the children. Sonny and Miss Ella, Jeremiah's grandma and uncle helped Big Mama with both her and Callie's babies. Iris and Paul helped manage Morgan's daughter. Mary hugged her daughter close to her bosom, her worry for Shultz evident. Sarah–Tim's wife rocked their sleeping daughter.

Turning slowly, Sunday attempted to offer eye contact where she could. It was hell trying to quell panic when you were panicked. She would cry later when she had the small luxury of being alone.

"Philip tell me the men ain't sure what they has–but the doctor and Nat decided on the quarantine to keep us and the children safe." Sunday said.

"How long we has to wait?" Carrie, Frank's woman asked.

"I cain't say right now. All we can do is wait." Sunday answered.

"Yo menfolk rides out to keep this place safe. Ya all has a reason to stay strong. We ain't got no choice but to run the fort." Morgan added.

It was Sunday's cue to add. "The fort has been placed on lockdown since our mens is down."

"Sunday and me has men patrolling the wall and movin' down betwixt the cabins. We's safe." Morgan explained.

"Do any of ya has questions?" Sunday asked.

"Is you all right?" Molly inquired, directing her inquiry to Sunday.

Blinking back tears, Sunday answered. "I's makin' it."

Day was breaking and Sunday had the added bonus of addressing the people. The burden she carried in the absence of her husband was colossal, but she would press on. Sunday lumbered over to the window allowing herself a moment. As the sun rose, she observed the people of the fort gathering. There could be no more delay, turning she spoke to the room.

"Follow me–the peoples is waitin."

Sunday didn't look back as she exited the study, but she heard the rustle of the other women's dresses as they made their way to the porch. Paul moved out ahead of them, pulling the door wide. Sunday stepped into the sunlight to greet the people of Fort Independence. She felt Morgan on her left and Big Mama at her right. She was strong–she could do this.

Out in front of her, the people gathered; the yellow and orange tones were beautiful as the light drenched the families standing at the bottom of the stairs. An older woman broke the silence.

"Sunday, is ya well?"

"Thank ya for askin'. I's well." She replied in a strong voice. "I ain't got many answers, but the men is on the westside of the fort in quarantine. They's set apart from us to keep us safe."

"Has any of 'em passed on?" An older man called out.

"Naw—ain't been no deaths reported and we's thankful." Sunday answered, and then changed the subject. "Wit' our menfolk down, I has locked down the fort. Until the men is back on they feet, the gate will not be opened."

A new resident of the fort—a man named Rufus yelled out. "So we's locked in?"

Sunday allowed her eyes to fall on the man. He was a big fellow with muscled arms from a life of manual labor. He wore a brown overcoat with no hat. Rufus stood taller than the people around him. His hair was knotted on his head and he sported a full beard. The man was brown skinned, and when he spoke, Sunday could see that he had missing teeth. Most important, she didn't evade.

"Yes—you's locked in 'til the quarantine is done."

"I come here causin' I was told I could come and go as I pleases." Rufus replied, his anger obvious. "I wants that gate open now. You ain't got no right to lock me in."

Before Sunday could respond, Morgan stepped forward. She wore a purple dress with her gun holstered to her left side. Her hair had grown and was braided in two cornrows—the ends hanging down her back. Threat spilled from her lips with ease.

"What yo name is?" Morgan lifted a finger and pointed to the man.

"Name Rufus, little lady," the newcomer sneered.

"Well… Rufus," Morgan responded, "make no mistake, cause we's womenfolk don't mean ya won't be handled. Mind yoself—hear."

The crowd broke into laughter and Sunday stepped in. "We meets again in a few days. If'n someone don't feel well, please let us know."

As the people dispersed and the women went back inside. Sunday and Morgan remained. When they were alone, Morgan said, "Rufus needs to be put down."

Sunday laughed. "We ain't finna kill the man."

Morgan who was part of Black's original eighteen had no problem making the decision to kill the newcomer. Sunday studied and compared the old and new Morgan. When they first met, Morgan's hair had been shaved close and her attire had been men's clothing. Though her friend was now dressed in skirts with long braids–Sunday noted Morgan was still one of the menacing eighteen.

"We don't need nobody makin' trouble cause we's women." Morgan said.

"I sees it the same." Sunday said. "Have him placed on house arrest. We cain't let him go–not now."

"We don't need him tellin' the town folk that the fort is weak." Morgan answered. "We can toss Rufus from the land when the men is betta."

Sunday sighed–that was the problem. She hoped the men were all right.

5

Ramifications

BLACK STOOD ACROSS the barn staring at Philip in disbelief. Philip was explaining how the town meeting went, and Black was sure he hadn't heard correctly. The newcomer had challenged the order of things. The man was testing the strength of the fort with the women in charge. Rufus was attempting to sow discord—he was trying his hand at divide and conquer. But his wife was an extension of him, and he would not stand for her being manhandled.

Sunday had done what she was supposed to do and locked the fort down. He'd been too ill to think of it, but he was proud when Philip and Chester reported the lockdown. It was safe to say that he was on the mend, though still weak. He had not gone back to his wife and children because several of his men were still sick.

Shultz seemed to be getting worse not better. Simon was weak but much improved. James was well, while Gilbert seemed to be on the decline. Elbert never took ill, though he never left he or James' side. Tim, Frank and Lou were on the mend. The ambassador, like Elbert and Anthony, never took ill. It puzzled Black why some of the men got sick and others didn't.

Jake, Ephraim, Jesse and Horace were on the mend and neither man retched. Black had real worries about the people and his
family. Jeremiah was still pretty bad off and though he noted some
improvement of the black cracker, E.J. showed no signs of better
health. Callie was like Elbert, Anthony and Bainesworth, she hadn't
taken ill, and Black was pleased. But his good mood was short lived,
and the newcomer was the reason. When he finally spoke, Elbert
who stood behind him grunted in approval.

"The newcomer." Black spat. "Place him under house arrest and
make a spectacle of it."

"Fuck yeah." Elbert growled.

Black was boiling and his head was wiped clean of all other thought.
"Make the message clear that my wife is not to be challenged."

"Yes, sir." Both Philip and Chester replied in unison.

When they were alone, Elbert added. "The newcomer needs to
be put down."

Black didn't comment, but he saw it the same.

The brothers left the barn but instead of going back to the
cabins, they walked through the line of trees headed toward the
center of the fort. Black moved in as close as he dared, allowing
the people to glimpse him–to see his displeasure. The area they
chose was a raised piece of land that wasn't quite a hill but gave the
advantage of looking down on the sea of cabins. The sun was bright
and in full swing, though the hour was still early.

Black paced between the trees and it felt good to have the sun
on his skin. The chill took nothing away from the beauty of the
day or the anger that seized his person. Under his booted feet twigs
snapped and small patches of brown grass crunched. He stepped out
of the trees in time to see several men from the barracks approach
on horseback. People stepped from their cabins to watch the situation unfold. Black was sorry he couldn't hear the goings on; Rufus
was dragged from his cabin and taken away.

Folding his arms over his chest, Black looked on–his stance

hostile. The people pointed at him and Elbert. Some folks waved, but Black didn't reciprocate. His message was clear; he was still running shit.

❀ ❀ ❀

Sunday was seated behind the desk holding her son Benjamin. Big Mama was seated on the couch with Daniel. Otis, Miah, Nattie and Lil Elbert were playing with the blocks in the corner. Morgan appeared in the doorway. Iris was behind her and she was holding Morgan's daughter. Once over the threshold, the women separated–Iris sat on the couch next to Big Mama and Morgan approached the desk.

"Come stand by the window."

Sunday pushed back from the desk and Ben-Ben squealed at the sight of Morgan, who took him into her arms. They moved over to the window keeping their backs to the room. Sunday smiled at her chubby baby. Benny's skin had gotten dark, and like his twin he had a head full of black curls. Unlike his brother, he enjoyed being held by other people–Callie especially.

"Did ya arrest the newcomer?" Sunday asked.

Morgan grinned as she jiggled the baby to a rhythm. "No."

"No… what all that ruckus was then?" Sunday countered.

"Black placed him unda arrest 'fore I could give the order."

"Oh." Sunday said, her eyes watering.

Morgan reached out and hugged her. Sunday heard her sniffle. "Phil tell me Simon been down. I really ain't been able to thank on nothin'."

"This gotta be a good sign–don't it?" Sunday asked.

"Yes."

Hope bloomed in Sunday's chest. Nat's message was clear; he was still running Fort Independence.

❈ ❈ ❈

Jeremiah woke to the sound of a male voice reverberating about the cabin. A man was speaking to Callie. When he opened his eyes, he found Black seated at his bedside. He couldn't see Callie, but she was present. She answered when Black asked a question.

"You are awake." Black said.

Turning his head slowly, Jeremiah answered. "Yes."

"How you feeling?"

"My belly is painin' me less." Jeremiah replied.

"I came for the waste buckets, but there was nothing to empty." When Jeremiah could focus, he asked. "E.J.?"

"E.J. is very ill–both he and Shultz."

"The doc is down with this shit?" Jeremiah asked incredulous. "Yes."

Guilt flooded his senses, and Black broke through his thoughts. "You are not to blame here. This was out of our control."

Opening his eyes, he stared at Black, while both admiring and hating him; the combination was disturbing. Callie spoke into the space between them.

"I'm going to step out on the porch. The morning is beautiful."

"Yes." Black replied, as if giving her permission.

When Jeremiah heard the door close, he was weak with relief. He didn't want Callie in Black's presence. He glared at the ceiling. "You tryna take my woman?"

Black chuckled, but he offered no response. Jeremiah went on. "She is devoted to you. I wasn't sleep."

"Callie is devoted to me and I am devoted to her." Black countered with a smile. "You knew that before we rode out–you knew it before I did."

Jeremiah grimaced–defeated, for it was true; he knew Callie felt this way before Black did. Yet, even in his weakened state, he growled. "You can't have her."

Black laughed out loud. "Callie's devotion to me is born out of my not killing you during our first clash. My devotion to her is born out of her taking my sons to her breast. It is the strangest thing I have ever encountered. She both loves and hates me. She also made it clear that her devotion for you will always come before her devotion to me. I think you needn't worry about my stealing her."

"I can feel the fancy between you two."

"When a man leads, he cannot be governed by pussy–it is the root to evil." Black said and his mirth was infectious.

Against his will, Jeremiah chuckled and Black continued. "Besides, I am second in her heart to you. Like E.J., if we formed a threesome–it would consist of you, Callie and me. It wouldn't be Sunday, me and Callie. I can't go for that."

"So you weighed it?" Jeremiah asked.

"I did." Black countered, his tone becoming serious. "I won't allow the fort to fall victim to whims and pussy."

"You ain't denied the pull betwixt you and Callie."

"Get some rest." Black said as he stood. "I'll check on you later."

The cabin door closed, and Callie appeared at his bedside. She was so lovely–his love for her was large. "I told Black he couldn't have you."

She smiled down at him. "That explains it."

"Explains what?"

"Why he looked so sad when he left here." She giggled and the sound warmed him.

"You make fun of me," he pouted.

"I do no such thing."

Jeremiah narrowed his eyes and in an attempt to shock her, he blurted. "Black and me discussed a threesome."

"Did he refuse coming to our bed?"

Jeremiah grinned. "He did."

"I figured as much." Callie replied.

"So you weighed it."

"I did." She laughed as she peered down at him. "Black don't seem the type to share a bed with you."

"Woman–you mock me." He tried to conceal his grin. "Did you consider joining his bed?"

Callie sobered. "I cannot live without you. Anyone who knows me, knows this. No, I never considered it."

Jeremiah closed his eyes; this woman was going to reduce his ass to tears. Gathering himself, he asked sardonically. "But you weighed a naked Black in our bed?"

Changing the subject, Callie replied. "How's your belly?"

Before he could muster a retort, she shimmied from her dress and shift. Naked, she climbed into bed with him. Callie kissed and caressed his face. When he relaxed, she offered her breast and he drank deeply. Jeremiah fell asleep in her arms, and for the first time in weeks he felt stronger.

❄ ❄ ❄

It was day five of the quarantine, and Black was thankful that all his men were above ground. Tim, Simon and James were much improved, and they were moving about under their own steam. Ephraim, Jake, Jesse and Horace were back on their feet as well. Elbert, Callie, Anthony and Bainesworth never got ill. Shultz, Gilbert and E.J. were better, but still bedridden. Frank and Lou were holding their own, though it was clear they had been under the weather. Try as he might, Black couldn't detect a pattern in the way the illness struck them.

None of the people reported being ill and with several men still sick, they would have to remain in quarantine. When he had a moment to himself, Black wondered at the fact that Sunday hadn't sent him a message. All the men had received declarations of love from their women, but not him. It wasn't that he thought Sunday didn't love him–he knew she did. What troubled him was that she was suffering in silence. He was sure his wife thought he needed her to show no emotion while helping him shoulder the weight of the people.

He felt further away from Sunday while at the fort than he ever did when they rode out. The worry that she or his children might become ill was more than he could bear. In order to quiet his thoughts, he began having work from the office brought to him. He also planned an exit strategy to start moving the men back to their families.

Eight of his men, plus Callie, never took ill. He knew Callie wouldn't leave, but the healthier men needed to be moved away from the sick. Black figured to set them up in other cabins for a week. If no one took ill, then they could go home. As for the men that were sick, but on the mend, they could transition away for two weeks, then go home.

Black would stay and assist Callie with Jeremiah. He would also help Shultz, E.J. and Gilbert back on their feet. It was the best way to get the men back with their families. At nightfall when the doctor, E.J. and Gilbert were resting, he called a meeting. The gathering was held in the last cabin at the end of the lane. The one room smelled amazing, and for Black it was a sign of better health. Only days ago the aroma of food sent him retching in the bushes.

Anthony did all the food preparation and Black furrowed his brows; no one had told him that Ant could cook. Regaining his focus, Black stared around the room. Some of the men stood, while others sat on the planked floor. A fire roared to the left of the room, and a large cast iron pot hung over the blaze; its contents bubbled rhythmically.

Black cleared his throat. "I have devised an exit strategy so that we can start integrating back with the people."

"Exit?" Anthony repeated as though the word tasted vile.

"Imma stay 'til dis ova." Josiah said. "I ain't finna leave ya."

They all started talking at once, and Black had to hold his hands up to get the room to settle down. "We have to end the sickness. If you all stay, we run the risk of passing it back and forth. The goal here is to keep our women and children healthy. We don't want this to spread to the people. It's our job to keep them safe."

"What you's sayin' is fair, but you alone cain't care for Shultz, E.J. and Gil." Simon said.

"And ya cain't cook." Anthony added. "You needs me."

Black folded his arms over his chest and waited. He wasn't going to try to be heard. Letting his displeasure bounce around the cabin, the men quieted, and he went on.

"Those of you who have not been sick will be moved to a new set of cabins. You will stay for one week before moving back to your families. Once back with your families, you will see only them for one week before integrating back with the people. If you become ill at any point, you are to return."

The men grumbled, but they didn't argue. Black continued. "We will start the transition in the morning. Philip will meet you all in the barn at ten o'clock."

Black stared around the cabin, waiting for protest. When none came, he took his leave. He made it down the three stairs and onto the dirt path when Elbert called his name.

He turned back, surprised to find that James wasn't with him. "Yeah."

"I need to speak wit' you." Elbert said.

"You are going back–you need to help the women."

Elbert chuckled. "You runnin' shit from quarantine. I'm staying wit' you."

"Listen—"

"Anna is with child. I'd rather wait this out. I'm afraid to be with her too soon. I ain't worried about Anna and the children, they are safe. The gate is locked down. You need me and Anthony–yo' ass can't cook." Elbert said.

The cabin was behind them and the door was open. It was the

only light on the otherwise dark path. The night was chilled, but not icy. Black sighed.

"I'll tell Ant we're staying." Elbert said.

"You didn't tell me Anna was with child." Black countered on a grunt.

"You worry too much." Elbert replied. "I'm tellin ya now."

Black grabbed at his neck and shook his head. "Surprised James ain't out here complaining."

"James ain't gotta complain. He been sick so you can't send him away. Sent me out here to make sure Anthony stays, says he ain't finna eat yo' damn cooking."

Black shook his head. He had to swallow twice before admitting, "I was afraid when James got sick."

"James said the same yesterday. He was scared when you got sick."

Both men stared at each other for moments, then turned walking back to the cabin where Shultz, E.J. and Gilbert were resting.

❄ ❄ ❄

Both the front and back doors of the empty barn were pulled wide. The morning cold carried bite as Black and the men who hadn't taken ill stood facing Philip and Chester. The sun poured in on an angle allowing Black to gauge Philip's words and mannerisms. The older man looked stressed, and Black wanted to know why. Frost laced his words.

"What troubles you, Philip?"

When Black's voice rang out, his men recognized his agitation. The small pockets of conversation at his back stopped, leaving the barn quiet. All eyes were on Philip.

"Miss Sunday…"

Alarmed, Black growled. "What about my wife?"

Elbert placed a hand on his shoulder to calm him. Philip was visibly shaken when he answered. "She was wantin' to see me in yo' office. I refused her. I know you and me ain't been close to one another, but me and Chester been staying away from the barracks and the women. I cain't understand this thing and I's scared to spread it. I ain't seen Miss Cora and Chester ain't seen Miss Mamie or the boys. We think it best."

Black blew out a breath. "You are handling things as I would. Thank you for that."

Philip and Chester breathed easier. Elbert, realizing that Black needed a moment, stepped in. "Are the cabins ready?"

"They is." Chester answered.

The men started forward, crossing the barn and filing out the opposite door. Black, Elbert and Chester remained. The field hand had a message for Elbert.

"Amos and Mamie was worried for ya. They's wantin to see ya when the quarantine is ova. I ain't been able to tell her that you's well. But I knows she'll be pleased."

Elbert smiled. "I'll come to them when this is over."

Chester nodded, spun on his heels and disappeared through the other door. Black and Elbert exited the barn and began walking. It had become routine for Black to appear on the raised piece of land that overlooked the cabins. Once there, he paced in and out of the trees before standing to soak in the sun. The walk served two purposes; he gained strength and the people witnessed him daily. He didn't engage them, but he made it known that he was moving on his own steam.

During these jaunts, Black was quiet, reflecting on Sunday, Callie and Alice. His wife still hadn't sent a message, but she would have squeezed Philip for information had he complied with her wishes. He was thankful Philip hadn't gone to Sunday. As for Callie, he wanted her to transition with the men. But he had three problems where Callie was concerned. She wouldn't leave Jeremiah and if she did transition—she would be the only woman. Most importantly, the black cracker wasn't strong enough to be without her.

He sighed when Alice popped in his head. It never occurred to him that she would have jumped. If there were any good to come from his being sick–it was that he had been comfortably numb to thoughts of Alice. Now that his health had improved, the conversation he had with her played on a loop in his thoughts.

"You love Quinn."

"Will it save him if 'n I say yes?"

"No."

"I carries his child."

"I figured as much."

Elbert broke into his thoughts while he paced. "Alice?"

Black stopped, shook his head and replied. "It never occurred to me that she would do such a thing."

"You can't think of everything."

"I hate to see a woman suffer." Black countered.

"Yeah." Elbert responded. "Ya still can't control everything."

As the brothers stared out over the cabins and the people, Black thought he heard the school bell ring. Life at the fort had finally settled, which gave him too much time to think. He even had ponderings of Emma and worried how Anthony would face his young wife. All his musings weighed heavy; but he would press on–it was all he could do.

They went to look in on Callie and Jeremiah. Moving out of the trees, Black stepped onto the path and strolled past the four cabins to the structure that was more a storage/guard house. Elbert followed him onto the porch. Black banged on the door.

"Come in," Callie yelled in a sing song voice.

Black shoved the door open to find Jeremiah seated to the table. Callie had shaved him and was cutting his hair. The black cracker was much thinner, and his eyes were larger in his face due to the weight loss; but he was out of bed. Around the feet of the chair and under the table were tangles of hair. Callie had clipped most of it off.

"You're up." Elbert said, his appreciation obvious.

"Yeah, but I'm weak." Jeremiah answered.

"You have to start somewhere." Black countered, and he too was grateful.

"E.J.?" Jeremiah asked.

"Still in bed, but he has stopped retching." Black explained.

"Same for Shultz and Gilbert." Elbert added.

Callie backed away from the men, seating herself on the bed. Black knew she was trying to remove herself from the interaction–from him. Jeremiah was dressed in brown trousers and a tan homespun shirt, on his feet were gray wool socks. Again, Black thought it good to see him upright.

"You need anything?"

"Yes," Jeremiah grumbled, "some sleep. Callie won't let me lay down for another fifteen minutes."

Black's back was to Callie and he turned to engage her. "Can I get you anything?"

Her head was down, but at his words she looked up. Black assessed her and Callie appeared tired. She wore a brown serviceable dress and a pair of Jeremiah's gray wool socks. Her hair was neatly braided in two cornrows and her dark eyes were bright. Black could feel her happiness at Jeremiah's slow recovery.

"Yes," she replied never breaking eye contact, "I would love some soup with no chicken–just vegetables. If it isn't too much trouble."

"I will see to the vegetable soup." Black said. "Anything else?"

"A book." Callie smiled.

"I'll see to both." Black replied. "Elbert will bring you fresh water."

"Thank you, both."

Turning back to Jeremiah, Black found him staring at the floor. "Me and Elbert will come back later to check on you?"

"Yeah." Jeremiah answered, his eyes bouncing up. Black felt no hostility, but jealousy emitted from Jeremiah into the space between them.

"Would you prefer I send Anthony to check on you later?" Black asked.

"No." Jeremiah said without hesitation. "My loyalties are the same–jealousy hasn't clouded my judgment."

Behind him, Black heard a soft intake of breath. He grinned. "We'll check in with you later."

Jeremiah offered a curt nod and Black took his leave. Once back on the pathway, the brothers doubled back to the barn to get two wooden crates that had been left for him. Black had requested all correspondence and packages be brought to him. The goal was to take the pressure off his wife, so she could tend his children and the people. Black knelt to sift through the crates.

"So, Callie both loves and hates you, huh?"

Black stood and eyed Elbert. He knew his brother would eventually get to the Callie situation. "You are entertained?"

"A little."

"What you are seeing is a woman who is happy the man she loves is alive and well." Black replied.

"Is that what I'm seeing?"

"Yeah."

"Oh…" Elbert responded. "I thought I saw Miss Callie smile at you. I ain't never saw that."

"You and James are a couple of hens." Black said, kneeling to the crates once more.

"What James gotta do wit' this?"

Black replied. "Because I know ya told him."

"Told James what?" Elbert pressed.

"Hell with you." Black shot back. "Grab one of these crates and shut up talkin' to me."

Both men laughed before heading back to the grim tasks that awaited them.

6

The Applecart

ANOTHER FOUR DAYS passed with no reports of illness among the people. Black was seated at Shultz's bedside; the doctor *was* alive, but weak. He had rehashed the exit plan for the healthy men in his head over and over. In the background, Elbert could be heard at the pump with E.J., who was none too pleased with the coldness of the water. Tuning out their bickering, Black broke the silence between he and Shultz.

"Can you eat something?"

"I don't wanna do shit but lay here." The doctor countered.

"I'll get you some chicken broth."

Shultz eyed him. "How is Jeremiah?"

Black grinned. "Callie has him out of bed and eating vegetable soup. He ain't been retching."

"Good."

"None of the healthy men took ill. They'll be moving in with their families in another day or so. The men who have no families will stay on at the cabins a little longer before going back to the barracks. You, E.J. and Gil are the only ones down at this time. I was worried about Gil, but he is looking better." Black explained.

"If the men who are on the mend will be moving out, you should go with them." Shultz said.

"No," Black responded. "Elbert, Anthony and I will remain. It looks like Jeremiah may have been the source. He will be the last to go back home. When he is restored to health, we will burn these cabins and cover any new waste holes."

Shultz nodded. "The plan you have is a good one."

Black helped the doctor and E.J. eat and drink a bit. Gilbert, who was set up in the cabin next door, was helped by Elbert. When the cabin quieted, Black sat to the table and began working through the new correspondence left by Philip. It seemed the owner of the store "Everything" had personally delivered a package to the fort. Black surmised it was from the president, and Virgil was attempting to maintain discretion.

Using the silver letter opener, Black slit the brown packaging. Folded neatly inside was a copy of the World newspaper and it was almost fifteen days old. On top were two missives and Black had to read both several times in order to see the full picture. He looked up to find Elbert staring at him from the doorway.

The first missive read:

My Friend,

I hope this missive finds you in the best of health.

A.L.

The second missive read:

Regards Sir,

I wish this correspondence were about the weather and other frivolous matters. Alas, I have a pressing inquiry. I would like the names and whereabouts of your undesirable associates.

F.W.

Black extended a hand, and Elbert took both letters before wandering out to the porch to stand in the sunlight. Turning his attention to the newspaper, Black pushed back from the table and began reading. The headline said much: **Hundreds Die from Illness in New York**

The first few pages blamed the poor for the spread of an unknown illness, and the second few pages blamed the poor for the political unrest on Manhattan Island. As Black read on, he was disenchanted with every printed word. On the back of page four, his eyes were drawn to a caption that read: **Woman Found Dead on the Banks of the East River**

Black couldn't be positive, but he thought the article spoke of Alice. The paper described the frozen body of a young woman who washed up on the east side of Manhattan. He stood abruptly and stared around the cabin as if looking for an escape. Shultz lay on the cot before the fire wrapped in several blankets. On the left of the room, E.J. lay on the cot in front of the window; both men were asleep. Maneuvering between the cots Black stepped onto the porch to face Elbert.

"I need a moment." He said, before continuing to the pathway.

His pace was brisk as he made for the line of trees, and he was grateful Elbert didn't follow. The day was bright and the temperature frigid. Every puff of his breath was frosty as he headed for the raised land overlooking the center of the fort. Miss Elsie and Miss Carol from the orphanage popped in his head and he wondered if they had seen the paper. Chances were slim that they would know it was Alice–if it even was her. He stood with his arm folded over his chest as he watched life happening in the distance.

He could see children running and playing, while the womenfolk hung laundry. A wagon rolled onto the path below pulled by a donkey. Men from the barracks wandered between the cabins making certain all was well. Everything felt too tight–even his skin. He felt jumpy and unable to calm down. His thoughts were loud, intrusive and sorrowful. He figured the best thing to do would be to keep moving until he tired or froze to death. When he would have turned to walk away, the slender form of a woman stepped onto the path below. She wore a brown wrap; he couldn't see her face because of the distance and the hood she wore, but Black was sure it was his wife.

They stood for a time gazing at each other–Sunday didn't wave but he felt her strength. When he could no longer take being so close and yet so far, he stepped through the trees going back the way he came. Once at the cabin, he set about running the fort–working through all the latest correspondence. When night fell, he helped settle E.J., Shultz and Gilbert. Later, James appeared followed by Elbert. His brothers didn't attempt conversation; instead, they each picked a cot and laid down. Black was glad for their presence.

Over the next five days, the healthy men moved back to their families. The men who lived at the barracks remained in transitional quarantine. They would slowly be integrated back into the population. The men who were on the mend would begin moving away from the original quarantine. Eventually, they would be placed with their families or at the barracks. Soon there would only be Shultz, Jeremiah, E.J. and Gilbert. All was going according to plan, until James was informed that it was his time to transition. Black and he fell into a nasty disagreement.

Shultz, E.J. and Gil were resting when James stormed into the cabin. Black had been seated but stood making his way around the table. James had come to accuse, which caused the situation to escalate.

Elbert had to step between them, but it did no good. "Ya both need to calm down."

"You are part of the process—you have to go." Black yelled.

"I ain't finna leave." James countered and his tone had bite.

"You will do as you're told." Black growled. "And you will stop undermining my fuckin' authority."

But James was refusing compromise. "I ain't part of no damn process. When we rides out, you in charge, but not here—not betwixt us brothers."

"You betta mind yo' words, brother." Black replied, his tone soft.

"You thanks only you is scared to lose someone. You thanks Otis is only yours to mourn. Ya thanks I cain't see ya wantin' a message from Sunday—but ya leaves her no room. You, Nat, cain't control every damn thang." James sneered, his chest heaving with anger.

Black couldn't gather himself and his level of anger took even him by surprise. He reached out and flipped the table, sending the parchments and ink flying. The table cracked when it landed against the wall.

"Shit." Shultz whispered.

"Calm down." Elbert pleaded.

An unimpressed James added just a bit more kerosene. "So, Hope is mad."

"Quiet, James." Elbert demanded.

"You will transition, or you will be placed under house arrest." Black promised, before exiting through the backdoor.

No one followed him and Black thought it was for the better. The sun was starting to go down when he reached the place where he watched over the fort from a distance. When night and the temperature fell, Black remained. He could see when each resident began lighting candles, the sight was both fantastic and troubling. The chill had numbed him, helping his anger to recede.

After a time he heard the crunch of booted feet. He didn't

bother to look around, the darkness was complete; he knew it was Elbert.

"His words have some merit."

Black countered. "Careful."

"You will not place him under house arrest."

"I am in charge here. Brother or no—" Black snapped.

"Me and James stayed because we don't want to lose you–little brother." Elbert responded. "We handled shit wit' Otis wrong– left him to watch yo' back alone. Like you, we have learned from our mistake."

At the term *little brother*, Black snorted. Still, Elbert went on. "James will not transition."

Black turned in the direction of Elbert's voice. "So you have chosen sides."

"Yes," Elbert replied without hesitation. "I am with James; our job is to keep you safe. He nor I will step away from the task. You will learn to do better at understanding that–you are needed by many and we aim to protect you so you can lead the people. Do not fight us."

Black had no response and soon he heard Elbert walking away. He lingered in the darkness for another hour before heading back to help with the men. Upon reaching the cabin, he found Elbert standing on the porch. The rich smell of cigar smoke greeted him, and candlelight flickered from the window onto the porch. He didn't continue inside–he stood with his brother. After a time he cleared his throat.

"I can't ask shit of the men I'm not willing to do myself."

"You never do that." Elbert said.

"I can't have you and James placing my safety above your own."

"You are important to many." Elbert explained.

"You both are important to me–to the family."

"Shit–you smarter than us. Ya think of things that we would

not. Me and James is smart because we accept it. Let us protect you while you keep the fort safe. We are tryna give you room to lead."

"Yeah." Black said.

There was nothing else to say, it was clear that Elbert and James were overriding him on this matter. Black wasn't quite sure how to feel. He turned and walked into the cabin to find James seated before the fire. Gil, E.J. and Shultz were all staring at him. Black addressed his patients.

"Shultz, did you eat?"

"I had broth with bits of chicken and vegetables." The doctor answered. "Tossed it back up."

"I'm stickin' to the broth and water. My belly cain't handle that shit." Gil said.

"Same as Gil." E.J. added. "Jeremiah?"

"Jeremiah is on the mend, being with Callie seems to have helped. He hasn't retched in days." Black answered.

James remained focused on the fire. E.J. and Gil quieted. Black took a seat by the doctor's bedside. He was concerned because Shultz started retching again.

"You haven't retched in days. Are you relapsing?"

The doctor whispered. "All of us ain't as lucky as Jeremiah, and no I'm not getting sicker. Still weak is all–my belly is tender."

"Jeremiah–lucky?" Black countered. "I didn't think he would make it."

The doctor chuckled. "I pay attention to the men's habits in case I need to help them when we ride out. Jeremiah don't really care for meat or strong drink. I gave this some thought after you said he was doing better with Miss Callie."

E.J. rolled on his cot to face them. "My brother saw a cow slaughtered when we was much younger. He retched for days… I teased him. He ain't really cared for meat since."

"Callie requested vegetable soup." Black said. "I guess for Jeremiah, now that I think about it."

"Miss Callie is clever." The doctor said. "I'm thinking she fed him breastmilk to settle his belly before starting him on the vegetable soup."

Black was both flummoxed and awed. He had no comment for the doctor's words, but E.J. did. "I felt better when he was taken to Callie, but I was worried she would become ill."

"She's like Elbert and Anthony. Callie is well." Black assured them.

"Good." Both men said in unison.

When Shultz, E.J. and Gil finally slept–there was James. Elbert entered the cabin and Black was sure it was to intervene if necessary. He stood, about to head for the door, when James began speaking.

"Black—"

"I accept your apology." Black said, cutting James off.

"I ain't finna 'pologize–little brother." James countered; Elbert started laughing, Black did not.

7

The People
February 1863

THE MEN HAD survived the illness and were set up in three different quarantines. Jeremiah remained isolated with Callie. All the other men went to their families or with the group waiting to integrate at the barracks. The cabins were burned in a controlled fire and all the waste holes were covered. Life had been difficult but the twenty-two pulled through.

Anthony walked back to his cabin along with Frank and Lou. They were all to remain in quarantine with their women for a week before venturing out among the people. Anthony was both fine with being quarantined with Emma and afraid to face her. Alice had been the background noise in his head for weeks. He hadn't felt he could go to Black about the matter; Black appeared to be struggling with too many issues.

The hour was late when he stepped onto the porch and pushed at his door. Firelight danced about the chamber and his eyes smarted. They had been through much, and Anthony felt himself succumbing to the emotions he'd barely held in check for months. His wife rolled over and sat up when a gust of wind shoved in past where he stood in the doorway.

Rubbing at her eyes in an attempt to banish the haze of sleep, Emma whispered. "Anthony."

"Yeah—"

Before he could say more Emma was out of bed and on him. She wrapped her arms and legs about him and burst out crying.

He eased the door shut behind him and paced the cabin while holding his trembling wife in his arms.

"Shhh." He crooned.

"I's afraid for ya." Emma said on a hiccup.

"I's well." He assured her. "I ain't take ill, but I stayed in quarantine to help Black."

Emma leaned back to stare in his eyes as he spoke. She caressed his face, then leaned in kissing him deeply. He groaned as her tongue pushed past his lips. Loving the feel of her, he began pacing again. Anthony couldn't get enough of his sweet wife.

"Come let me help you undress." She said, as she tried to untangle from him.

Squeezing her once more for good measure, Anthony placed her on her bare feet before the fire. Taking him by the hand, Emma led him to a chair by the table. Kneeling at his feet, Emma helped him remove his boots, then his overcoat and shirt. Stepping between his thighs, she caressed his face again and smiled.

"Ya has plenty a hair on yo' head–ain't ya?"

Anthony laughed and it felt good. His wife never ceased to amaze him. "We all has too much hair. Even Black got hair."

He had shaved earlier in the evening, but the hair on his head was another story. Emma retrieved the comb and brush from the small table by the bed. She lit the oil lamp that sat before him on the dinner table. Anthony could think of many things he wanted to do right now, and getting his hair braided wasn't one of them. Still, he understood she was trying to get used to having him home.

He sat quietly, while she repeatedly worked the comb through his unkempt mane.

Although his hair was rough, Emma's touch was gentle and soon his eyes were drifting shut. Her softly spoken question brought him out of his relaxed state.

"Ant, do ya knows what become of Alice?"

He had played this scenario over and over in his head. There was no remorse in him when he replied. "It was like we figured, ain't no way to say for sho'."

"Will ya tell me what happened in New York?"

"I can say the orphanage is safe. Miss Carol and Miss Elsie was happy to hear you was well." He said.

"Ohhh, I's happy to hear they's well too." Emma said and there was a smile in her voice.

"Sorry I ain't got more about Alice for you."

Emma sighed. "Alice was a sad girl. Miss Carol used to say—some folks is unhappy in they head. Alice was like that, but she was also kind and smart."

While she chatted, his wife plaited his hair in five fat cornrows to the back. When she was finished, he tugged her by the wrist around in front of him, then pulled her to straddle him. As was her way, Emma wore a white shift and no pantaloons. Cupping her bottom made him groan.

"Wait—lemme remove my trousers." He said, voice strained.

Backing away, Emma shimmied out of her shift, while he shucked his trousers and long underwear. He plopped his bare ass back on the wooden chair and yanked his wife forward to straddle him once again. His dick stood at attention between them, but it was the nearness of her that pleased him.

"I missed ya." She breathed.

Anthony had to slow himself down. He wanted to savor the feel of her brown skin against his own. "What you been doin' while I was away?"

"I ain't done nothing special," she replied shyly. "Been helpin' with the babies; Miss Sunday is wonderful."

"Hmmm." He countered.

"Tried to bake some biscuits–like to burned our cabin down. Molly and Carrie say I cain't touch the stove 'til you come."

Anthony buried his face in her neck. His wife smelled clean; the scent of lavender clung to her. He allowed his hands to roam over her slender back. Being with his wife like this was a heady feeling and Anthony feared he would spill his seed without being inside her–he did not want that. Emma wriggled and he swore.

"Damn."

"We put the blaze out fast enough," his wife hurried to explain.

"What fire?" he asked.

"Is you even listenin' to me?"

"I am." he lied, before whispering. "I love you, Emma–so much."

She searched his face and held his eyes with her own. "I love you–more."

Leaning in, she offered him a chaste kiss. He didn't see her next move coming. Emma reared back just enough to wrap her fingers around his length, giving him a rough tug. A full-bodied groan escaped him.

"Emma." It was all he could muster.

"Take me to bed, Ant."

Anthony needed no further prodding. Pushing her hand away, he stood and moved with purpose toward the bed. Easing her onto the mattress, he climbed between her thighs and braced himself on his palms over her. Emma spread her legs and reached down, angling his hard member at her core. Squeezing his eyes shut at her tightness, he pressed forward into the heat of her tight folds.

"Ya feels so good." She whispered as she wrapped her legs about his hips.

"Woman," he grunted.

Abruptly he pulled all the way out, but she tugged him forward with her legs and arms. He wanted to be gentle, but he couldn't get his hips to mind. Anthony slammed into her over and over. Emma clamped down on him like a vice, causing his balls to tighten. He had no room for thought–his dick jerked, pulsed and erupted. Anthony was trembling when he kissed her, while riding the wave of bliss.

"Anthony," she whimpered.

He didn't separate from her; instead, he remained inside her until he hardened again. Their lovemaking was slow–good. Anthony couldn't help himself… he wept.

❊ ❊ ❊

The men had been turned loose from the quarantine late. There were no fort people milling about, and E.J. suspected that Black had done it this way on purpose. As he headed home, a sadness blanketed him. Black had forbidden him access to his brother. Jeremiah, who was now considered the original quarantine, would not be integrated back into the population for another two weeks.

"You have two women and two babies." Black had said. "Wait 'til this is over."

While he knew Black was right, he missed his brother. E.J. wondered if Jeremiah would opt to stay on at the fort. He knew his brother didn't want to leave his son. They'd bought land about ten miles away to be near Lil Otis. Now, it no longer felt like Jeremiah wanted the same things he did. It was clear that Black tolerated his presence for Jeremiah's sake. Even mean Callie had endeared herself by taking Black's babies to her breasts. Neither his brother nor his woman would be sent away if they chose to stay. Jeremiah was his brother and friend–he feared the loss of family as his brother discovered himself.

E.J. was weak. When he turned onto the path leading to his cabin, his eyes welled up. Leaning over, he braced his hands on his knees. Being ill had taxed him in every way possible. It was pitch dark and while the chill wasn't bone deep, it was uncomfortable. At the end of the lane, he saw that his cabin was lit up. As he drew nearer, he heard the cries of a baby. Reaching the stairs of his porch, E.J. smiled–his son was yelling the house down. He froze in place for moments, the worry of making his family ill–real. E.J. almost went back the way he came.

He wiped at his eyes, then climbed the steps. Before he could knock, Suzanne pulled the door open. Her heart shaped face was pale in the candlelight. E.J. realized she thought it was someone come to give her bad news about him.

"Noooo," he crooned. "I'm here."

His wife threw herself at him and it took effort to remain upright, given his weakened state. Suzanne was dressed in a pink shift with matching pantaloons. Her brown hair was loose about her shoulders. He kissed the top of her head, and she squeezed him tight. Over Suzanne's head he spied Nettie, who had tears rolling down her cheeks. The same fear that had Suzanne pale, had Nettie's eyes wide; his chocolate skinned beauty had been afraid for him. She held his son to her breast and still he beckoned to her.

She stood crossing the room to him. Nettie wore a powder blue shift with matching pantaloons. Her hair was plaited in two braids and pinned at the top of her head. When she reached them, Suzanne took the baby so he could hold her. Nettie shivered and he realized the door was still open; stepping over the threshold, he let it slam shut behind him.

"Edward, come sit." Suzanne said.

"Yes, Masta, come rest yoself." Nettie added.

As he stared about his rudimentary surroundings, E.J. realized everything he held dear was here at Fort Independence. His women, children and brother were all that mattered. He was a man of means, but he could think of nothing he wanted. The new life he lived was simple and he could see no other way; he took inventory. They had a small round table that sat three and a black stove at the back of the cabin. The bed they shared was larger than most, built by his own hand. He had also fashioned the crib his daughter was fast asleep in. A fire blazed in the hearth, and he smiled when Suzanne placed his son in his arms.

Edward III had a head full of curly black hair and a skin tone that was lighter than Nettie's, but darker than his own. His sweet son stared up at him, then burst out crying. The baby reached his chubby arms out for Suzanne and she took him. His daughter heard the racket his son was making and joined in. Nettie plucked Lizzy up and began rocking her. Both women spent the next hour settling his children. E.J. stared into the fire, deep in thought. When the children were finally down for the night, Nettie broke the silence.

"Sunday tell us ya wasn't well."

"Jeremiah was ill—we didn't think he would make it." He evaded.

"Oh, Edward." Suzanne said, her sincerity caressing him. "I know how you love your brother. Is Jeremiah better?"

"He is." E.J. replied. "We got separated in the quarantine. He will remain isolated a little longer."

"You ain't looking so well, neither." Nettie countered, undeterred.

E.J. sighed, Nettie wasn't going to let him sidestep. "I was ill and still weak, but I'm better than I was."

At his confession, his women helped him undress and led him to the bed. Suzanne brought a basin of water and wiped him down. Nettie made chicken soup and fed him as he sat propped up with pillows. When he began drifting off to sleep, both women undressed and joined him. E.J. groaned at the heat they offered at his front and back. He was too weak for coupling, but they kissed, stroked, crooned and massaged him all over.

E.J. couldn't live without Suzanne and Netti.

✻ ✻ ✻

While the men had moved into different stages of isolation, the quarantine was now reduced to the source–Jeremiah. Black remained in a self-imposed exile to handle fort matters before integrating with his family. He set up in a different cabin away from Callie and Jeremiah; he still brought them fresh water and food left by Anthony. Elbert and James tried to stay, but Black refused. His argument was simple.

"Jeremiah is the source. I will deliver food and water to him and Callie while handling fort issues. In my home there are many children—not just my own." Black then counted off on his fingers. "There is also Iris, Cora, Paul and Mama. I will not interact with them while dealing with Jeremiah."

"We can stay with you." Elbert responded.

"We are safe, and I am well. Go—both of you. I will need your help on a few issues, but you are only to see me. You are allowed no contact with Jeremiah."

"I'll come to you in the mornin' then." James stated, holding his breath.

"Yeah." Black answered. "I will also limit my exposure to Jeremiah—though I think this is done."

James visibly relaxed. When his brothers finally left, Black spent the evening making a list of the problems that needed to be addressed. Number one on said list was the newcomer—number two the men of the fort. His anger boiled anew and wouldn't settle until the men understood his plight. Life on the fort was about to become uncomfortable for everyone.

He stood and began pacing the one room, coming to a stop in front of the fire at times. He turned the oil lamp down over the stack of parchments on the table. It was an attempt at shutting his thoughts down. A small fire danced in the hearth and his pacing caused the flames to sway. James' words about Sunday popped in his head.

"Ya thanks I cain't see ya wantin' a message from Sunday—but ya leaves her no room. You, Nat, cain't control every damn thang."

He tried to stay away from thoughts of his wife. Sunday made his life brighter, but he wondered if he did the same for her. The New York debacle caused him a kind of fear he couldn't show. His men had killed the family member of a government official, and he still wasn't sure if leaving Fernando Wood alive was the best course of action. But getting correspondence from Lincoln about Hugh Wood meant the president would look to him if Fernando went missing.

While there was no love lost between the mayor of New York and Lincoln, Black couldn't give the president control over him or the fort; thus Fernando remained upright. The president understood that Black couldn't engage in blind trust. He had to tread lightly when it came to Lincoln–the goal was to keep his men free of obligations that would enslave. Black saw that as part of his job as the leader of Fort Independence–freedom.

He sighed before turning to the bed and lying flat on his back. He closed his eyes preparing himself to fight with sleep, but when he opened his eyes again dawn was upon him. The sound of two sets of booted feet woke him. Rolling from the bed, he washed his face, rinsed his mouth and donned a clean homespun shirt. When he was presentable, he yanked the door open to find James and Elbert waiting for him. He didn't speak, instead he stepped into the cold morning and made his way to the line of trees at the back of the cabin. Black took a long relieving piss.

Returning, he stepped past his brothers and continued into the cabin–they followed. The door wasn't closed five minutes before an awkward banging got their attention. Elbert pulled it open to find Anthony standing on the other side of the threshold with his arms full. Lumbering forward, Anthony placed a basket on the table. Three bowls were settled carefully inside covered by cloths. There were grits, eggs and biscuits. Turning back for the door, Anthony returned with a medium sized black pot.

"The pot for Miss Callie—vegetable soup." Anthony said.

"Yeah." Black answered as he stared at Anthony. "Does Big Mama know?"

"Know what?" Anthony shot back.

"That you's a betta cook than she is." James clarified.

"Ain't no reason for her to know." Anthony replied, snickering.

Elbert laughed and James grinned. Black remained dead-pan when he replied. "I don't know if this should be kept from my mama."

Anthony hooted before disappearing through the door. James ate with him, but Elbert had already eaten with Anna. When they were done, Black stood heading for the door. He strapped on his gun, shrugged into his overcoat while grabbing for the basket and pot meant for Callie. Exiting the cabin, he spoke over his shoulder.

"Meet me on the path leading to where the newcomer is under house arrest."

Elbert chuckled. "Yeah."

As he walked through the early morning, a light fog blanketed the fort. Daybreak was still happening, but it looked as though the sun would make an appearance. The chill that settled in the air was bearable. Off the beaten path was a lone cabin surrounded by trees and overgrown vegetation in the backyard. Black made a mental note to have this side of the fort cleaned up. Reaching the cabin, he stepped on the porch and banged on the door.

"Come in." Jeremiah called out.

Black shoved at the door and at the same time Jeremiah pushed to his feet. Callie was seated to the table reading the book he'd requested for her. She looked up and smiled at him. Black assessed and she looked well. Callie wore a blue dress with three large buttons on the bodice.

"Good morning." Black greeted.

"Morning, Mr. Black."

Jeremiah was dressed in tan homespun trousers and a brown shirt. Strapped at his upper left side was his gun. Black measured him. Jeremiah was thinner, and still had dark smudges under his eyes, but he looked better-well.

"I can't get used to you with hair." Jeremiah said.

"It's cold." Black answered. "I figured to keep my hair for now."

"How much longer for me in isolation?"

Black placed the pot and basket on the table. "Come with me."

They stepped back onto the porch, retrieved the buckets and headed for the pump just up the lane. When Jeremiah began working the arm, the pump gave an irritating, high pitched hum before the water started dripping, then gushing. Black let the water gush for moments before filling the pails. The task complete, the men stood for a time in the mud now surrounding the pump. It was Black who broke the silence.

"I can't say I understand what happened to us, but I think you were the source."

"I see it the same." Jeremiah conceded.

"There are the children and the elderly to consider."

"The barracks as well." Jeremiah said in understanding. "The men are the protection."

"Yeah... I would say about a week more."

"You trying to make sure Callie don't take ill?" Jeremiah asked.

"Yeah."

"E.J.?"

"Is home with his women and children. He is angry that I forbid him to see you." Black answered.

Jeremiah turned away and sighed. He looked to the distance avoiding Black's scrutiny. "He worries that I will part from him. Callie doesn't like him, and my brother thinks it will change our relationship."

"Doesn't it, though?"

Jeremiah laughed. "It doesn't. Callie don't like E.J., but she understands he is my brother. She don't engage him or speak of him. It seems I have a fixation with strange women. Her only concern is that I love her."

Black folded his arms over his chest and stared out to the distance as well. "I don't think she will take ill, but I have to deal in caution."

"Yeah." Jeremiah replied. "Shit, I wouldn't be able to take her falling ill cause of me."

"She didn't want anyone else to care for you."

Jeremiah's eyes bounced up to meet Black's gaze. "I will ride out with you again…"

It was a statement and a question. "It is Callie and E.J. you will have to contend with–not me. A man who can shoot with both hands is an asset."

"E.J. forgets he is younger."

"Elbert and James forget I'm in charge."

Both men laughed as they headed back to the cabin. Jeremiah parted from him at the porch and Black continued on to the business of being the man in charge. His blood thrummed as he made his way through the early morning. The sun was beginning to rise and the fog lifting. The air was thin–cold, his breaths invigorating as he stepped onto the path where the newcomer was under guard.

His brothers were standing on the dirt trail in front of the cabin; both wore tan overcoats with matching fur hats. James was handing Elbert a flask and they appeared to be leisure as they conversed. On the makeshift porch stood Chester and Philip, they too were in some kind of discussion. As he drew nearer, all chatter stopped when the men spied him.

Black reached the men and continued onto the porch. He stared out around him. Rufus was being held in the same cabin that Lincoln's cousin had once been held. The structure was several paths back from the main gate, but the activity at the entrance could still be heard. Men laughing, arguing and handling the business of watching the entry points. It was beyond daybreak–the morning was well underway.

Tall trees lined the pathways along the front of the property, while providing privacy to the cabins nestled between them. The structures along the entrance were mostly storage units and places for the men to escape the cold. Occasionally, they housed unwanted guests and the rogue tenant that had to be brought to heel. This morning would be about the latter.

Black offered direction to Philip and Chester who were posted up behind him on either side of the door. "You will bring the newcomer's belongings to the gate."

"Sho' thang, Black." Philip replied.

Both men hurried off to do his bidding, leaving the brothers to stare at each other. James offered his thoughts. "We ain't needin' no town crier. Rufus ain't fit for fort life."

Black refrained from sharing his thoughts, such an action would only serve to exacerbate. He did not want a repeat of the evening his anger boiled out of control. Losing his temper would put the people and him at a disadvantage. Still, this was personal. Sunday was an extension of him and shame to the man who couldn't grasp the concept.

His brothers stepped onto the porch, posting up on either side of the door. Black turned, shoved the door open and stepped inside. Rufus was seated to the table, his eyes wide, his demeanor meek. Black didn't know what galled him more–the fact that the man before him could be aggressive with women or the fact that he could be docile with men. Black weighed the situation.

The windows were uncovered, leaving no doubt that Rufus saw his approach. Sunlight fell through the window caressing the harshness of the room. The wooden crates against the far wall and dried chicken blood mixed with hay on the floor vibrated with the right amount of threat. On the left of the chamber was a rumpled cot with large boots pushed haphazardly beneath the frame.

The air about the cabin was sour and smelled of unwashed man. Black didn't flinch at the odor–instead he schooled his reaction to boredom.

When he finally lent his focus to the man before him, Black didn't verbally engage him right away. It was difficult for his anger to fit in the cabin with the likes of Rufus–the rude ass newcomer. Clearing his throat, Black began the task of policing his personal borders.

"Mr. Rufus, I'm told you have a problem with my authority."

"N-noooo, sah–I sho' don't." Rufus shook his big head.

"Did you or did you not challenge the power I left in place in my absence?"

"I's just tryna go to town." Rufus said. "I's told we could come and go from here when we's ready."

"When you first came to the fort, like all newcomers, were you not told at times the fort will be locked down?"

"Nawwww… I guess–I ain't for sho'." Rufus replied, his responses bordering on sniveling.

"Which is it?" Black snapped.

"Philip may a said somfin 'bout lock down."

"Not only have you been rude to my wife and the women I put in place–you are attempting to handle me."

"Handle… nawww. I ain't tryna handle a thang–not one thang."

Black weighed the unkempt man in his stained brown shirt. Rufus wiped a large ashy hand over his knotted hair and beard. Black noted his scuffed knuckles, missing teeth and crooked nose. He wasn't fooled–the newcomer was a brawler, standing six feet-five inches easy. Rufus was after thirty, but before forty.

Tired of the cat and mouse game, Black asked. "Do you know who my wife is?"

"I hearda Miss Sundee."

"So you are clear on why you are under guard?"

"I figure dis a misunderstandin'." Rufus replied.

"Ain't no misunderstanding." Black spat. "You attempted to manhandle me through my wife."

"Mr. Black—"

"I consider myself a reasonable man, except where my woman is concerned. The gate is open, and you will pass through on your own steam or by mine; the choice is yours. No man will live on my land and insult my wife." Black countered, his tone low–menacing.

"I's sho sorry—"

"Let's go." Black sneered.

Rufus stood, going to the bed to retrieve his boots from beneath the frame. When he would have sat to pull them on, Black continued in his nastiness. "I'll not wait on you."

The newcomer nodded before stepping around Black who stood in the doorway. Rufus carried his boots, overcoat and hat in his arms. Elbert and James led the way; Rufus followed, and Black brought up the rear. The men working the front of the property pulled the gate wide. A crowd gathered to watch as the newcomer was tossed from the fort.

Philip and Chester were at the gate as requested. Philip led the nag that Rufus rode in on months earlier and Chester carried his saddle bags. Black, along with the help of his brothers, threw Rufus, his horse and his belonging out the gate. The morning sun was bright as Black stood at the entrance of the fort with his arms crossed and his stance wide. The act gave him no satisfaction.

❈ ❈ ❈

Jeremiah lay in the bed watching the fire and Callie as she sat before the blaze. He was still weak, but he was better than on the mend. Now that he wasn't prone to bouts of oblivion, he studied Callie for any sign of illness and there were none. Over the weeks, he had not been able to stay awake past late afternoon. He woke at the oddest times of the day and night to find Callie curled up at the foot of the bed. Being coherent became his new goal.

She would have slept on the floor to keep him comfortable, but he wouldn't allow it. Being ill had stripped him of his dignity. Everything he wouldn't have done before another person, happened to him involuntarily. Callie handled his being sick with grace and care, for his bodily fluids were splashed all over the cabin. The worst part of it all was watching Black come and go—he was the picture of health.

Jeremiah didn't want Black to be ill—certainly not, but in Black's presence he felt less than. His being weak as a kitten, while Black came back and forth to help in his care, taxed his masculinity. Living thirty-five summers on the plantation—leaving only to acquire more slaves left him at a disadvantage. Jeremiah wished to study the leader of Fort Independence. Most crucial, he hoped to measure up. He wanted to be a man his woman and children could be proud. A soft voice broke through his thoughts.

"You are awake." Callie said.

"I am."

"Is something troubling you?" she asked.

"No."

Jeremiah figured out early on that to get Callie to talk was to answer the question she asked, nothing more. She took the bait. "You're up and you look troubled."

"I ain't."

She giggled. "I hate when you try to make me talk."

He feigned innocence. "What?"

When she turned back to the fire pretending to ignore him, he fell back into thought. Some of his memories were foggy and others were quite clear. He could still hear the exchange between Callie and Black—reliving it made his chest ache.

"You will not defy me." Black had said.

"Yes." Callie had submitted before confessing, "My devotion to him will at times clash with my devotion to you. It is an uncomfortable place to be."

He had turned *"devotion"* over in his thoughts repeatedly. The meaning was implied, but he wanted to know what Callie intended with her use of the word. However, he feared asking and appearing weaker than he already looked. His conversation with Black only added to his weariness.

"You ain't denied the fancy betwixt you and Callie."

"Get some rest." Black had replied. *"I'll check on you later."*

Callie made him feel so many things and at times it was hard to breathe. When he thought he would die, he'd worried for her and his children. He tried speaking with his brother about Callie's well-being, but E.J. had refused. There were times when he was so out of it, he had forgotten he was in her care. She had washed him and cleaned up after him; he loved her.

Jeremiah remembered when she offered him breastmilk to settle his stomach. He'd closed his eyes to ward off the pain he'd seen in her face. Callie had too much hope and his body was telling him he would die no matter her efforts. He didn't want her to experience more heartbreak. The echo of their conversation was still with him.

"I can't let you stop the water–I have nothing to replace it with. You will drink breastmilk in place of the broth."

"Woman–I am no damn baby."

"I will not be all right without you," she had said.

He sighed aloud, and once again her sweet voice brought him back to the here and now. "What troubles you, Jeremiah?"

He stared around the cabin avoiding her gaze. The fire crackled and blazed invitingly–the oil lamp on the table had sputtered out, casting the cabin in blue, orange and golden hues. He attempted to back away from his thoughts and feelings, but to no avail. While he grappled with his emotions, he forgot to answer Callie.

She stood, coming to him, her concern tangible. "Are you not well?"

"What exactly does the word "devotion" mean?" he blurted.

"Oh," she whispered, but she was smiling.

He sat up, placing his back to the wall. The quilt was tangled about his hips, covering his nakedness. When he could delay no more, he allowed his gaze to connect with hers. Callie broke the awkwardness.

"Devotion means–admiration."

Jeremiah just stared at her for moments before asking. "Admiration means–what?"

"Admiration means–adulation."

He glared at her. "Adulation means–what?"

Callie giggled. "Adulation means the same as devotion."

And there it was on display–her ability to outwit him. He didn't know what any of the words meant, though he could guess from how they were used by both her and Black.

"Shit." He muttered.

"I didn't tell you this morning, but I love you, Jeremiah."

"You told me." He countered, looking past her to the fire.

"Oh…" she said, undaunted by his attitude. "So it was you who forgot to say you love me this morning."

"I didn't forget." He snapped, unable to control his temper. "I ain't yo' friend."

Callie laughed out loud, before saying with confidence. "Yes, you are."

Jeremiah grinned against his will, damn her for being so wonderful. "I ain't."

He tried to remain disagreeable, but he couldn't. Callie inquired. "If I get naked, will you hold me?"

They hadn't coupled since he'd been ill, though his dick had started getting hard and staying hard. He hadn't pushed for the sex act because he wasn't sure he could maintain the stiffness it took to get the job done. The idea of starting something he couldn't finish…

While he was thinking too much, Callie had removed her shift, pulled back the quilt and climbed into bed–straddling him. His dick was pinned against his belly and he could feel the heat from her wet folds. It was enough to make him lose his shit. Her full breasts were leaking, and he latched on to her left nipple sucking and drinking away the tension before switching nipples.

"Oooh, Jeremiah... I love you so much." She moaned.

Callie reached down between them while moving up onto her knees. Placing him at her core, she sank down on him bit by bit. Jeremiah pulled off her nipple and grunted.

"Shit, Callie, this ain't gon last."

Clutching her ass in his big hands, he helped her ride him to orgasm. He kept licking, sucking and drinking from her nipples—their fucking was clumsy and wrought with emotion. When he thought he would come apart at the seams, Callie's pussy tightened, shoving him headfirst into a sexual haze. He called out—no, he shouted as his seed burst from his body.

"I love you." Jeremiah said, and his voice broke.

8

Full Circle

BLACK SAW NO way around it. He would have to go to his house, but he wouldn't venture inside and if he knew Sunday, she wouldn't come out. It was for the better because he still had fort issues to deal with before he could address the matter of his wife. He was sure that by the time she came to him, she would be concerned he was addle minded.

Dawn was upon him. Black had requested some comforts be added to his cabin. Philip and Chester would handle his current living situation, while he and his brothers dealt with fort business. He was deep in thought when Elbert banged on the door.

"Enter." Black called out.

When Elbert shoved the door open, James stood behind him. It was James who spoke first. "What you finna do wit' that hair, man?"

Black laughed before running his fingers through the wiry strands. He kept his jaw shaved, but the hair upon his crown was wild. It was curly, knotty and it hurt to be combed. He decided it could only be brushed–for his damn head was tender. There was no question he hated having a bunch of hair, but it kept him warm.

He also had to admit that while being bald made him look mean, he now appeared sinister.

"The hair is keeping my body heat."

Elbert grinned. "Ya looks addled."

"That's my aim."

Shrugging into his overcoat, Black followed his brothers into the early morning chill. The men walked in silence–each in his own thoughts. As they turned onto the path, they were met by more fort men headed in the same direction. Day was breaking, but the sun wasn't happening–it was overcast and gloomy. Black thought the weather suited his mood.

In the distance, his home loomed imposing and cold. He had been in quarantine for so long and now in a self-imposed exile that he had to take a moment to weigh his circumstance. Black needed to reassess his life. What was of value to him now was different than ten years ago. He saw his failings as a husband and a man–clearly. He cringed with the realization that he had failed Sunday.

This morning, he felt strangled by his anger and his hope to find satisfaction. It was as he had requested only the men of Fort Independence were in attendance. Black kept his head and gaze lowered as he listened to the murmurs and conversation around him. He stood shoulder to shoulder with his brothers and a good amount of time passed before he was recognized. It was the hair to be sure.

The crowd parted leaving a path all the way to the front of his home. As he climbed the stairs, he noted a slight movement of the window curtain. Black couldn't see her, but he knew it was his wife. His brothers stayed with him step for step. When they reached the landing, Elbert leaned in and whispered. "Have you seen Sunday?"

Black locked eyes with his brother. He allowed his hurt to be naked when he answered. "No, I haven't seen my wife or children."

Elbert simply nodded. It was neither the time nor the place, and

Black wouldn't elaborate if the setting were different. James chimed in. "He tryna give her room."

"Yeah." Black responded.

His brothers were attempting to push him toward calm before he addressed the people. They stood for moments in a tight circle, leaving the throng of men at the bottom of the stairs to wait. There were about one hundred men in attendance. Still these men didn't include the men in the barracks—no, these men were the newcomers, the long-term tenants and the field hands. Black weighed the matter and even in anger, he could see where he had failed the men before him. He would rectify the problem with grace and threat.

"You ready?" James asked.

"Ya look mad as hell to me." Elbert said.

Black didn't answer his brothers; instead, he stepped back from the circle and walked to the edge of the steps. All conversation and murmurs stopped—all eyes were on him. Daylight without sunlight was the scene before him. His eyes bounced around the crowd, sharing his displeasure without words. Finally, he cleared his throat and in a strong tight voice he yelled out.

"The newcomer Rufus was removed from the fort."

Low chatter and side discussion ensued, and Black waited. He would not fight to be heard. When the men quieted, he went on. "If you are a field hand, you feed the fort. If you are a carpenter, you provide shelter to the fort. If you are a blacksmith, you provide the tools needed in day to day life."

Behind him, Black heard the front door to his home open. Leaving the crowd in limbo, he turned to offer greeting. "Good morning, Paul."

The older man smiled. "Black."

Turning back to the gathering, he waited while his brothers spoke to Paul. This helped him to calm all the more. When the polite conversation at his back ended, Black continued.

"There is no job that a man or woman does that is more

important than the next. This is about survival while providing a safe place for our women, children and elderly; all hands are needed. We are ex-slaves who are benefiting from our own labor."

At his last statement, conversation broke out in small pockets around the crowd. Black waited and when a hush fell over the men, he spoke. "How many of you have families?"

Almost all the men raised their hands. Black surveyed the gathering with a quiet disappointment. His voice was softer when he asked. "Would you have allowed the newcomer, Rufus to speak to your women the way you allowed him to speak to my wife?"

When Black paused this time there was no chatter. A rat could have been heard pissing on cotton. He didn't expect an answer. He continued. "Morgan stepped forward in defense of my wife–the women–in defense of you; but you men did nothing. In case you are wondering, this is why I leave the women in charge."

Still nothing from the crowd. Black stood, arms at his sides, overcoat pushed back to reveal his gun. He was dressed for his name this morning. The hair on his head was huge and moved at his every gesture. Black's slanted eyes blazed with his frustration of the situation. At his back, Elbert, James and Paul stood at the ready. When he studied the crowd once more, he saw that some of the twenty-two had begun mixing in with the men.

"I aid you in providing protection for your women and children. I expect no less. My wife is an extension of my authority in my absence–to challenge her is to challenge me; to manhandle her is the same as asking for my gun hand."

Black paused for impact, lingering with the men in silence. He was giving each man a chance to understand that they would never again meet about this issue. There would be repercussions and consequences the next time. When he spoke again, more threat fell from his lips like stone. In the background, the gate could be heard yawning as it was being pulled wide.

"The gate is open." Black sneered, unable to help himself. "Any man who doesn't see it the same can take his family and go."

When no man spoke, Black pushed for acknowledgement. "Is there any among you who has a problem with my words?"

"No," the men responded in unison.

Black didn't signal an end to the meeting. Instead, he descended the stairs and the crowd parted. He moved with purpose through the men back to his cabin. Elbert and James went to man the gate—their orders were to shut and lock it after thirty minutes. The men dispersed, going back to their chores.

Back at the cabin, Black noted the changes made at his request. A desk was brought in, though not as grand as the one in his study. It was loaded down with parchment, ink and packages that needed his attention. The table had two matching chairs and could now be used for eating. A rocking chair sat before the fire and at the back of the cabin sat a white porcelain tub. In the corner was a small black stove used mostly for heat—not cooking.

Anthony was now delivering food directly to Callie and Jeremiah. Seating himself to the desk, Black began the task of going through his missives. The one that caught his eye was in a bold familiar hand. Using the letter opener, he pulled two letters from the envelope. The first read:

My Friend,

I hope all is well with you and yours. I wanted to share the concerns of a mutual acquaintance.

A.L.

The second missive read:

Regards Sir,

I take offense that I have received no response regarding my concerns. Your judgment is obviously clouded. I implore you to see reason. I would have the names and whereabouts of your undesirable associates, posthaste.

F.W.

Black stood and began pacing until he could decide on a course of action. He would send Anthony, Frank and Lou to the dry-goods store. The telegram was just a few words, but to the point. It read:

I WILL HANDLE ALL THE CONCERNS OF OUR ACQUAINTANCE–ONE WAY OR ANOTHER

❋ ❋ ❋

It was late afternoon when Sunday left the study to hide in her husband's studio. She didn't understand what was happening–she didn't know why he hadn't come to her. The thought occurred to her that maybe Nat didn't love her anymore. Losing his love was more than she could bear. Sunday burst out crying; it was a soul wrenching and shoulder shaking sob. She just needed a damn minute to be weak.

Nat had thrown the newcomer from the land and had even threatened the men on her behalf. But this had nothing to do with love, this was about his ability to lead being questioned. He wouldn't stand for it. Nat would address such a matter with or without a wife. What stabbed was his compliment of Morgan. Sunday wondered if she'd failed him and the people. More tears flowed and she wondered if he had found another.

"Shit." She muttered on a hiccup.

It appeared he intended to leave her in the house and live separate from her. He wouldn't move the children or Mama… it made sense. She wandered to the window replaying his words.

"Morgan stepped forward in defense of my wife–the women–in defense of you; but you men did nothing. In case you are wondering– this is why I leave the women in charge." Nat had said.

The hinges creaked, there was no knock. She knew it was Mama; the door clicked softly behind her. Sunday wanted to be alone.

"So you's in here feelin' sorry for yoself."

"I's allowed to take a moment from my troubles." Sunday countered.

Mama laughed. "I suppose you's right."

Sunday could hear Big Mama shuffling forward. She refused to turn and face her–she didn't answer. Mama went on. "Yo' man lookin' addled with that heap of unkempt hair, threatenin' the menfolk."

The mirth in Mama's voice was unmistakable. Sunday sniffed. "He come right up to the damn house and ain't come in to see me."

"He sho' did." Big Mama agreed. "You ain't go out neither."

"Me!" Sunday exclaimed, whipping around to face Mama. "He was speakin' wit' the peoples. What should I have done?"

Mama wore her gray hair cornrowed in two. Her dress was peach, and the decorative collar was a bone color. The focus in her knowing brown eyes made Sunday squirm. "Ya coulda gone on out there and stood wit' him–Paul did."

Sunday stared at her for seconds. "It ain't that easy being his wife. I cain't make a mistake."

Mama scoffed. "Dat ain't true, ya made a mistake today. You ain't go out there."

"I don't think Nat wants me no mo'."

"Girl, you really tickles me." Mama said. "James tell me he and Nat had a bad disagreement."

"James?" Sunday replied. "When you seen James?"

"He and Elbert come at different times." Mama said. "They stands at the bottom of the steps. I stands on the porch; they tell me thangs."

"You ain't tell me."

Mama look tired when she explained. "Chile–I's tellin' you now. Is you listening?"

"What they be tellin' you?" Sunday asked.

Mama started for the door and Sunday yelled after. "Where is you goin'?"

"I ain't no gossip like Elbert and James." Mama giggled. "Go on to the cabin where Nat is if'n you's wantin' to know something."

"Mama!"

Big Mama stopped and glared at Sunday. "Did you know the men is sayin' Anthony cooks betta than me?"

Sunday was trying to figure out what the hell Big Mama was talking about when she disappeared through the door slamming it tight behind her. She stood in the silence of the studio trying to piece together her understanding of life around her. Brows furrowed, Sunday was clear about one thing, she was confused.

❄ ❄ ❄

Lou had major anxiety when they were called on to run a telegram to the dry-goods store for Black. He understood his duties, but Molly didn't. She was happy to see him that much was clear; still some awkwardness had crept back between them because of the amount of time that he had been away. Another unease that sprang up between them came from his being sick. Molly wasn't in the best shape when he brought her home and he worried about her taking ill on account of him.

It felt as though he'd only just won her, and circumstance had stolen her from him again. Lou limited the physical contact between them in terms of kissing and the like. They did spend time together, but coupling had been taken off the table. Worse yet, he wasn't sure if it were by him for health reasons or Molly because she wasn't interested in the sex act. The week had passed between them in a tension that made him ache from within.

Night had fallen when they reached the outside of the fort. Anthony went straight to Black to confirm that the telegram had been sent. Their horses had been taken away by a stablehand leaving

Frank and Lou to wander slowly toward their cabins. They strode away from the torchlight into the murkiness of the evening. Frank broke the silence.

"What it is, man? You's troubled."

"It ain't nothing." Lou returned.

"You has Molly–what you got to be sad about?"

Lou shared everything with Frank, but their discussions about coupling had never included a woman he loved. He didn't know how to speak on his intimacies with Molly. She was so delicate–it seemed wrong. But this was his brother–his twin, he could tell Frank anything.

"Molly and me ain't exactly…" Lou hesitated. "She ain't let me inside her–not yet."

"I's thinkin you was workin' up to it."

"She and me was… we left, then we took ill." Lou said.

It was quiet for a time before Frank said. "Took me and Carrie some time to get to know one anothern. Being gone from her ain't help none. Almost like ya has to start over."

"Yeah." Lou said, feeling better that Frank understood.

"You has to leap back into knowin' her."

"I worried when we come home, worried for Carrie and the baby. It's why I ain't come to yo' house yet." Lou said.

"Is you avoidin' Molly wit' the same reasonin'?"

"I reckon." Lou answered.

The brothers started walking again. They knew the fort like the backs of their hands, and soon they were standing in front of Lou's cabin. Candlelight flickered from the window and Lou could see an outline of his brother. He wanted to turn and run away, but Frank must have read his thoughts.

"Pussyfootin' around gon' leave you on top of the quilt while Molly under the quilt."

"Yeah." Lou responded.

"Is you still feelin' ill?" Frank asked.

"No… but—"

Frank cut him off. "Stop stallin'."

"All right." Lou replied.

There was no more conversation to be had–Frank walked away. Lou turned, then climbed the few steps to his porch. He faltered briefly before shoving the door wide to find Molly folding clothes. As always, their cabin was spotless and smelled of apple pie. A fire blazed in the hearth, making their home warm and inviting.

On the table in front of her were stacks of folded clothes. The chest at the foot of their bed was open. Molly was obviously putting their things away. Dressed in pantaloons and a white shift, she appeared relaxed. She smiled when she looked up at him in the doorway. He hung his overcoat on the peg by the door.

"You's home." She said, and there was happiness in her voice. "Is you hungry?"

"Not yet, Molly-girl."

She nodded and he set about trying to share personal space with her. He placed his gun holster on the night table, then sat on the edge of the bed to remove his boots. But she spoke before he could get his boots off.

"I can help you bathe, if you's wantin'."

His hands were still on his left boot when she spoke. He let his gaze bounce up to clash with hers. His heart suddenly became too big for his chest. Lou felt faint. Molly was offering to bathe him. During her first days at the fort, he washed her body many times– but the reverse had never happened.

"I … ahhh… I could use a bath." He managed.

"I has water boiling, but ya needs to bring some from the pump."

"Yeah."

Lou needed a moment and bringing in water would give him time to collect himself. He didn't bother with his overcoat; instead, he reached for the bucket by the woodburning stove and the bucket by the door, then disappeared into the night. As the chill of the evening wrapped about his person, he found he needed the cold. He wanted to calm himself so the next hour wouldn't be awkward. Sadly, he knew his dick would embarrass him.

He made three trips, filling the large tin tub with a combination of hot and cold water. When he could no longer hide behind the chore of lugging water, he sat and removed his boots. Molly came forward with a basket pushing him to finish undressing. Lou felt weighed down by shyness and concerned for her sensibilities. He stood shucking his shirt, trousers and long underwear. Bending, he peeled off his socks. When he was completely naked, Molly started chatting–casually talking as though he weren't bare assed in front of her.

"I only has rose soap. We gotta get you some soaps for just you."

"I ain't carin' about that." He countered.

As Molly lit the oil lamp on the table and turned the wick down low, Lou stepped into the tub. He sank down into the water and groaned. In the background, Molly could be heard moving about. Closing his eyes, he enjoyed the feel of a private bath. He opened his eyes only when he felt her presence on his left. Molly stood between the tub and the fire, gazing down at him. She dropped a brown cloth into the water along with the rose soap, then knelt beside the tub.

"Can I tell you somethin'?" She asked.

Lou tried to hide his anxiety by responding. "Acourse ya can."

"Took me some time, but I figure you ain't wantin' to kiss me cause ya thinks Imma catch my death."

"Yeah." He sighed.

Molly had sat back on her haunches, allowing the fire light to dance over her lovely skin. Her hair was plaited perfectly in two cornrows. It occurred to him that she had already bathed and would get wet assisting him. He had been about to tell her that he would take care of his own bathing when she shocked him with her words.

"I thought I lost you when Sunday tell me you wasn't well. Ain't no one ever cared for me like you do. I's so glad ya home, just ain't know how to say it."

"Shit, Molly-girl." It was the best he could do.

"You's uneasy wit' me cause you's fearing scaring me off." Her words were matter of fact.

"I don't want to ruin thangs wit' us." He countered.

"Yeah," Molly said. "I know."

"We could be as slow as ya like." Lou said trying to put her at ease.

"Emma says it's all right for me to ask you for coupling. She used to live at a whorehouse–I figure she must know."

"Huh?" Lou was flummoxed.

She rushed on, blurting out. "I's wantin to try havin' you inside me. I's more afraid of losing you and never knowin what that trollop Katie knows about you."

Lou's eyes widened. Molly lowered her gaze trying to hide her jealousy. He tried–he really did, but he burst out laughing and couldn't stop. She coughed, then continued primly. "I's jealous… I's so green wit' it, I stinks."

He slid down in the water, unable to stop his mirth. When he could finally gather himself, he said. "Ya got nothin' to be jealous of Molly-girl. We will go slow."

She looked hurt when she whispered. "Don't ya wanna be inside me?"

"Yes, woman, so bad."

She smiled again. "It's settled then."

Lou didn't answer, but he did hurry and bathe himself. When he stood from the water, Molly was there with a towel for him. He dried with the quickness before yanking her to him. Their kiss was long and deep–Molly tangled her tongue with his and moaned into his mouth. His dick jumped from the contact and he pulled away, his chest heaving with excitement.

"Undress." He said, his voice rusty to his own ears.

Molly didn't dither at removing her undergarments, but her shyness won out. Once naked, she threw herself in his arms in an attempt to hide. Lou allowed it–she was offering him the world. Her skin was soft against his own, and though he was desperate to penetrate her–he was also desperate for connection.

"Come." He said, leading her to their bed.

She scrambled in first and he climbed in after her. When they were settled under the quilt, he pulled her into his arms. Molly whispered against his chest. "I love you, Lou."

Her breaths tickled his skin, igniting a need that rocked him to his very core. Lou had to relax, so he could make the experience good for both of them. The stress of possibly hurting her quelled his lust. He turned the word "gentle" over in his thoughts again and again. Untangling himself from her, he pushed her onto her back. Bracing himself over her, Lou kissed her forehead, her eyes and then her lips. He wanted to be worthy and he didn't want to give her a reason to rule out being one with him.

As he hovered over her, Molly shocked him by locking gazes with him. Even in the firelight, he saw *welcome* in her beautiful face. Leaning in, he kissed her neck and collar bone; he licked between her breasts before taking her left nipple into his mouth. Bringing her nipple against the roof of his mouth, he sucked hard. Molly's breaths became labored–he switched nipples, replicating the action.

"Lou... Lou." She panted.

The sight of Molly's wet nipples and legs spread wide was beautiful. She lay trembling from his kisses, a dazed expression on her face. His woman was perfect in arousal. Lou was on his knees between her thighs; he leaned in placing his forehead against her belly. "Gentle" still ringing in his head, he took a moment to collect himself. He licked the scar leading to her navel, but he didn't linger. Lower still, he shouldered her thighs wider, then buried his face in her core.

He savored the taste of her nectar on his tongue. Lou cherished the smell of her impending release. Molly soon cried out, but he didn't leave her. The aim was to let her peak–more than once, so her body would slick his way. He plied his tongue to her clit so thoroughly he had to pin her down to keep her in place. Lou was submerged in the smell, taste, feel and sight of her pussy; he wasn't going to last when he got inside her. But stamina wasn't the goal tonight–fitting up in that pussy was the objective; everything else be damn.

"Ohhh, Lou, please."

Pulling back, he licked his lips. "Turn on yo' side."

Molly did as she was told, and Lou settled behind her. Placing his hand on her belly, he pulled her against him–his chest to her back. Lifting her leg, he strummed her clit while murmuring more instruction. "Let me in, sweet woman."

At his urging, he felt her relax; he angled his dick at her core and pushed in. When the head of his shaft slipped between her heat, Lou started babbling.

"You all right… Molly-girl, you's tight… shit, dis some good pussy…"

He shoved in a bit more and unable to stop himself, his dick throbbed, then spurted–once. He was shaking and to his wonderment, he was still hard. More incoherent talk. "Too tight… too slow–love fuckin' you, woman."

Lou kept his fingers on her button and his shaft was only halfway when Molly tightened–then cried out. He shoved all the way to the hilt in time to experience her orgasm. Lou was only able to manage three good pumps before he flooded her with his seed. While his dick jerked, pulsed and spasmed, Lou was begging for more.

"Molly, canna has some more pussy? Please don't take it from me yet."

And she did–Molly gave him more.

❄ ❄ ❄

Black was seated behind the desk in the cabin working through ordering supplies. The hour was late, but he couldn't find rest. The quiet of his surroundings left too much room for troubling thoughts. Fernando Wood had climbed to the top of the list in terms of matters that couldn't go unaddressed. He would pace himself for the most impact when dealing with the ex-mayor of New York. His most pressing issue was Sunday and his children.

He would step away from fort business long enough to let his wife be. She deserved his strength. Even though he knew she wouldn't come out of the house when he addressed the men, it still bothered him that she didn't. His home was a base of operations and that was necessary. But Black also wanted the simple with her and this cabin would be that place—the place where he would allow her to just be Sunday.

Life on the fort was humming with tension. The men were angry with him for his words, but he would not back down from protecting the women and children. Either the men were with him or against him; he could accommodate whatever the choice. In the end, no man took his family and left—so they were all closer to the truth.

What Black did was ponder—contemplate and while this benefited the fort, it also drove him slightly mad. He chuckled to himself, then shook his head and all his damn hair moved with him. His thoughts tripped and snagged on Alice, but he didn't stay with the musings of her tragic end. Instead, he pressed on, the beginnings of yet another plan hatching in his head. But before he could sink into the role of tactician, carriage wheels rumbled in the distance.

The vehicle squeaked as it lurched to a stop in front of the cabin. Black put down his pen and leaned back in his chair. As suddenly as the carriage stopped, it was moving again. A nothingness filled the space left by horse hooves, wheels and the creak of the vehicle. Black waited as the sound of unsure footsteps landed on the makeshift porch. Quiet happened and then a soft knock.

"Enter." He called out.

The door opened slowly, before the slender form of his wife stepped over the threshold into the light cast by the fire and oil lamps. Black made certain the cabin was well lit for he had not seen Sunday close up in months. She wore a black shawl wrapped about her head and shoulders. The blue dress she wore swayed just above the black boots on her feet.

When his gaze locked with hers, Black felt the blow physically. Sunday's eyes were wide with pain and unshed tears. The shawl fell back from her head revealing two braids pinned at the top of her head. He rubbed his jaw and took in a deep breath, but he did not speak.

❃ ❃ ❃

Sunday didn't know how Mama set it up, but when the hour grew late a carriage stopped in front of the house. She had been at the sitting room window staring into the night, looking for him–waiting for him to come to her. When the vehicle appeared out front, Mama's voice floated to her out of the dark.

"Go on, chile–he waitin' on ya."

"My babies."

"Is sleepin through the night–go."

She grabbed her shawl and stepped into the chill of the night. Philip was driving and Chester held the torch. As the carriage rocked into motion, Sunday worried he would reject her. But she was moving and there was no turning back. The vehicle smelled of leather and saddle soap; she leaned back against the seat and closed her eyes.

After ten minutes, the vehicle lurched to a stop. Sunday didn't move, even after Chester pulled the door open.

"Ya all right, Miss Black?"

"I–I's well." She replied, but still she didn't move.

"Let me help ya." Chester said as he reached out a hand. "Dis the cabin, Miss Black."

The medium structure glowed in the darkness, as if there were more than a simple candle lighting her way. Gathering her courage, she stepped onto the porch and knocked. Her husband's deep voice responded.

"Enter."

Sunday pushed at the door, then stepped over the threshold into the brightly lit cabin. Afraid to see rejection in his eyes, she gave herself a moment to take in his surroundings. There was a table with two chairs and a large box frame bed pushed into the corner. It was the tub at the back of the cabin that made her eyes smart; her husband intended to live apart from her. When she could delay no further, she allowed her gaze to bounce to him. Blinking slowly, she tried to reconcile the man she was seeing with her husband.

Nat was seated in a chair behind a wooden desk and like the one in his study, it was weighed down with his work. His mane was a huge, thick, kinky cloud upon his crown. He had so much hair, Sunday almost couldn't see his beautiful slanted eyes as they assessed her in return. Nat wore no shirt and the tension in his muscled arm was visible when he lifted a hand to smooth it over his jaw. He breathed in deep, but he didn't speak—so she did.

"Why hasn't you come to me, Nat?"

He didn't respond verbally, but he did push back from the desk and stand. The cabin seemed to be medium in size until Nat made his way around the desk. He leaned against the edge crossing his arms over his chest and his feet at the ankles. The muscles in his arms, chest and belly bunched and released with his movements. He wore black trousers and black boots—her husband was intimidating. Her shawl fell from her head, when she stepped back from him.

"I had taken ill and feared you becoming ill because of me." He answered.

She searched his expression, his eyes—Sunday searched his demeanor. He seemed unchanged, but his actions were different than she had ever seen from him. She furrowed her brows in confusion, and he went on. "We have the children to think about and we have at least four old folks living with us. Mama, Iris, Paul and Miss Cora. Jeremiah almost died and I was still helping Callie with him. I was afraid to come home."

"Ain't the quarantine over? All the men has gone home–why didn't ya come to me then?"

"James and I had a bad misunderstanding." His exhalation was sharp; he continued. "He said I don't leave room for you to come to me. Do you feel that way?"

She dropped her gaze in an attempt to disengage from his pain. But her husband wouldn't have it; his tone was rough–hitting her ear wrong. "Sunday?"

"I… ahhh." She stammered before getting her response right. "I was wantin' to come to ya. I ain't place Callie under house arrest cause I's tryna see yo' condition. When ya placed her under guard, I had hope. I tried to be like you and think of the peoples, but I just couldn't."

"Oh, Sunday." He whispered, dropping his gaze. "I wouldn't have wanted you to come. I don't ever want you in danger."

"It's hard being yo' wife." She said, honestly. "But I cain't live without ya neither. If I woulda come to ya like Callie done for Jeremiah…"

"I would have placed you under house arrest to keep you safe." His answer was swift.

"I figured so." She answered. "Callie must still be in love wit' you though–ya let her help wit' Jeremiah."

Nat's eyes bounced back up to meet her own, and Sunday offered a weak smile. His head leaned to the left as he assessed her. "You know how Callie feels?"

"You might be in charge of the menfolk and the fort, I's in charge of yo' house–I sees and hears all."

Her husband laughed and it lightened the mood. His hilarity rolled about the cabin, and Sunday couldn't help it–she giggled.

When he finally sobered, he said. "Callie bested me. She refused food and water–we had no choice but to take Jeremiah to her."

"It ain't often someone bests you." Sunday shot back. "I sees yo' fondness for Callie."

"Sunday..." he whispered.

She held up her hand. "The fort is yo' other woman. I understands that much, Nat. Anyhow, Callie wants Jeremiah and you. If'n I know you, you cain't go for that."

"Stop it." Her husband said, but he was grinning.

"I understands because I loves Elbert. He has his own place in my heart." She said with honesty. "I's glad for Anna, but I know he left away from here cause of his feelings for me–and cause he loves you. He don't say much to me and I knows why, but I loves him just the same."

"Easy, wife... I ain't as strong or as reasonable as you." He growled.

Sunday giggled and he opened his arms to her. She went to him and he squeezed her tight. His skin was hot to the touch. She kissed his chest and he groaned. He went on. "This cabin is a place where you get to just be Sunday. I can't take away our responsibility, but I can start making sure we have time alone."

"I loves you," she whispered against his chest.

He untangled them and held her away from him, causing her to look up into his troubled eyes. She was too anxious to let him speak first. "Nat... what is it?"

"If you stay here in this cabin with me..." he trailed off as if collecting his thoughts.

"What? Of course I's wantin' to stay with you."

His gaze was intense. "If you stay with me, you are going to end up with child. I need you and I don't want to think about anything else but needing you."

"I sees it the same." He searched her face for sincerity. Sunday grinned at him, then changed the subject. "Nat, what is you gon do with that heap of hair on yo' head? It's unsettling."

He shrugged. "Makes me look—"

"Addled." She supplied and her husband chuckled. Venturing on to another issue, she continued. "Morgan—"

"Is your right hand," he explained. "You have not failed me or the people. Elbert and James serve the same purpose along with the eighteen. I hate it at times, but it is the way of things."

"Before I could place the newcomer under house arrest, you had 'im drug off."

Nat stepped around her, his anger crowding them. He began pacing, his booted feet echoing as they struck the planked floor. "No man will handle you. The newcomer is lucky I didn't slit his damn throat."

"The newcomer is gone—calm down, my love. You's plenty angry." Sunday said, gesturing to the table so they could sit and talk.

"No," he said, shaking his head at her. "I want to be naked with you. No more discussion about the fort."

"Oh."

She removed her shawl, boots and dress laying them over a chair. He leaned against the edge of the desk to watch her undress. When she was down to her pink shift, she stopped. "Can we turn the lamps down?"

"No. I need the light to be just right."

"For what?" She asked—his hair was too much.

"I want to draw you," he said with a grin.

"Really?" She said, her tone breathy. "I been wantin you to draw me naked."

He didn't reply; instead, he reached down, yanked off his boots, then shucked his trousers and long underwear. "Take off your shift and get on the bed."

Sunday removed her underdress as she headed for the bed. Boldly, she asked. "How is you wantin' me?"

Nat walked to the table in all his naked glory. He retrieved a chair, a tablet and a thin charcoal. Turning, he stepped around her, placing the chair on the side of the bed with a thud. "Come, I'll show you what I want."

She went to him, noticing for the first time all the pillows. Since the bed was pressed against the wall, the pillows were also situated against the wall. "Lay on the pillows the short way."

After she got comfortable, she saw his intent. His voice was thick with arousal when he directed. "Open for me, Sunday."

She allowed her legs to fall open and he groaned. His eyes fell between her thighs and he murmured. "You are so beautiful."

Sunday wished she could draw because Nat was a sight to behold. He was seated with his legs spread wide, his sack resting on the edge of the chair and his erection standing tall. His black skin radiated beauty and power—the hair on his head fell just over his slanted eyes. He was her everything.

"You gon be able to draw in that condition?" She asked, motioning to his erection.

"Imma try—but I may need some assistance."

"I can help—if'n ya needs me." She answered letting her fingers trail down to her womanhood. Sunday pressed on her sensitive button and moaned.

"Shit, Sunday."

Sunday met and held his gaze, but she didn't stop teasing him. Her husband growled before tossing the tablet and charcoal on the bed. Dropping to his knees in front of her, he buried his face in her wet folds. At the first touch of his tongue, her eyes rolled up in her head and her breathing became labored.

"Nat… Nat… Oh, Nat."

His mouth was magic and though she wanted the sensation to last forever, Sunday equally couldn't take anymore. As she orgasmed, she reached down grabbing a fist full of his hair to keep him in place. And soon, she was overstimulated with the need to shove him away. But her husband held fast until she was spent.

Sunday lay back against the pillows and came down slowly from bliss. When she could muster the strength, she opened her eyes to find her husband looming over her. Nat wiped at his wet lips with the back of his hand, his mane swaying with his movement. She let her eyes trail down his perfect body until they fell on his jutting erection. He was fisting himself; the bunching and releasing of his muscles wonderful to witness.

She scrambled to the edge of the bed and without preamble, she pushed his hand away and wrapped her lips about his crown. Sunday twirled her tongue along the thick vein under his shaft, then took him deeper. He reached down, palming her cheeks–trying to control the way she sucked him. She maintained eye contact; she needed to see him come undone. His mouth fell open, while at the same time his eyes drifted shut. He tried pushing her away, but she sucked harder.

"Ohhh damn." Nat groaned; his tone strangled. "Woman, back away."

But Sunday didn't back away, and his seed erupted from him in four strong bursts. She sucked–swallowed and repeated, still she couldn't catch it all. His release dripped from the sides of her mouth onto her breasts. She grinned up at him, his stare intense. Before she could know what he was about, Nat tackled her onto the bed and kissed her thoroughly.

Later, when the only light in the cabin was the fire blazing in the hearth, Sunday lay content in her husband's arms. She couldn't stop touching him. His voice was groggy when he asked.

"You all right?"

"I's well…" she answered. "I was thinkin'…"

Nat leaned up on an elbow. "Thinking what?"

"A lot of seed comes from you in just one go 'round–I feels like I dodged a bullet. No wonder you make two babies at once."

Even in the firelight, she could see his shock at her words. Her husband fell back in the pillows and barked out a laugh.

"Where you learn such talk, woman?"

Sunday giggled. "Emma tells us women 'bout what she seen at the pussy parlor. It is the pussy parlor, right?"

"Sunnnddday." He said, but his mirth was all consuming.

While he was weak with laughter, she climbed on top of him. His shaft immediately started hardening. Rocking against him, she whispered. "I wanna feel you inside me."

Leaning over, she tangled her tongue with his and it made her moan. He panted. "Woman, you sure? It won't be no dodging me if I'm in you."

Sunday reached down and angled his shaft before sliding down onto him. They both groaned with abandon. His next words spurred her on. "I love you, wife—I can't live without you."

She rode him to ecstasy and that was how dawn found the lovers.

9

Gentlemen's Agreement
June 1863

BLACK STOOD AT his study window holding his son Daniel. The boy was napping against his shoulder, while Nattie, Ben-Ben, Lil Elbert, Miah and Lil Otis played in the corner of his office. Tuning out the noise of the children playing, Black ruminated over two problems. The climate on Manhattan Island had reached a fevered pitch with the upcoming Draft Act. Being the major benefactor of the orphanage meant he needed to move the children before all hell broke loose–but where to put them.

He could bring the children to the fort, but the fact remained that the orphanage was needed. It couldn't be shut down, such a place offered hope where there was none. He also didn't want to have to deal with quarantining of children. The orphanage would have to be relocated until New York settled. They would have to ride out.

His next issue was Fernando Wood. The ex-mayor continued to badger the president on the whereabouts of the slaves who had accosted him. Black chuckled and his son squirmed in his arms, then dozed off again. Daniel wore only a cloth nappy with a green shirt. Summer had just started, and the study was stuffy. His twins were like Frank and Lou-they looked exactly alike. But Daniel wasn't like Ben-Ben, he liked no one.

As he inhaled the scent of talcum and baby, his mind wandered back to the president and the ex-mayor. Any letter of inquiry sent to Lincoln by Fernando was forwarded to the fort and they were all in the same vein. What bothered Black was the tone in each missive seemed to be escalating. The time had come–Fernando could no longer be ignored. It seemed the president understood Black's position, because he forwent fancy parchments and envelopes, sending instead a telegram.

Lincoln's message read:

I WISH OUR ACQUAINTANCE LONGEVITY

Black was vexed because Lincoln's spite was visible. The president, who had once asked him to assassinate the ex-mayor, was now attempting to bring him to heel. Black's response was swift.

LEAD POISONING

Lincoln had countered:

ABOVE GROUND

Black understood the message loud and clear, but in an effort to be defiant, he replied:

CLOSED CASKET

There were no more telegrams, but the president did continue to keep him abreast of the goings on in New York. Black was also privy to Fernando's schedule; he smirked–Lincoln was still an ally. In the background, he heard his wife and Callie enter his office.

"I'll take the baby." Sunday said softly.

Black passed his sleeping son to his wife, then kissed her cheek. "The twenty–two will meet here in about an hour."

"See ya this evenin'."

"Yeah."

Callie ushered the other children out the door without looking his way. It was back to business as usual–they were not friends. He would from time to time demand that she acknowledge his presence. During those interactions, Callie offered eye contact and a smile. But when the exchange was over, she went back to ignoring him.

It was also because of Callie that Black studied from a distance the contact between Elbert and Sunday. His brother did indeed ignore his wife. The morning Elbert showed up to the cabin where he and Sunday were staying, popped unbidden into his thoughts. He could still see the exchange and it was vivid. Elbert had deep feelings for his wife–there was no mistaking. He was sure of his brother and so as he had done in the past, he backed away from jealousy and Elbert went back to ignoring his wife.

"Hold still."

"Use the brush." He howled. "It pains me when you use the comb."

Sunday laughed. "When ya gon shave? I ain't hardly touched yo' head and you's whinin'."

"I'm ready... you can use the damn comb."

But when she started combing his hair, he let out a loud yelp. The door to the cabin burst open and Elbert appeared, gun in hand ready to assist him. Only to find that he was getting his hair combed and braided. Sunday, who was unfazed, turned and smiled at Elbert.

When Elbert holstered his gun, Sunday went to him–hugging him tight. His brother hesitated for a brief moment, then Elbert's lifeless gaze met his own. Looking away, Elbert wrapped his arms around Sunday, kissing her forehead. She pulled back, placing her palm to Elbert's cheek.

"Nat tells me you ain't take ill. I's thankful. I worried for you."

"I'm well." Elbert replied, giving her his full attention. "The newcomer... I couldn't take it–his damn boldness..."

"I know." Sunday whispered. "He's gone–you ain't needin' to think about him."

"Rufus needed to be put down." Elbert had grumbled, his anger filling the cabin.

Sunday smiled, hugging him tight again.

Jeremiah's voice floated to him, breaking him from his musings. Sunday, Callie and the children were gone. The men were starting to file in, and he turned his mind to the matter at hand. Leaning against the edge of his desk, Black waited until the men settled.

"The president has forbidden me from killing Fernando Wood."

"But we could sho' scare him." Lou said.

"We could." Black replied. "But how effective will that be?"

"As good as we make it." Jeremiah countered.

"It's the end of June. I say we rides out within a fortnight." James added. "Ain't no sense in waitin' to scare his ass—we can start now."

Black chuckled and the men joined in. It appeared the issue with the mayor was resolved. Moving on to the next problem, Black said, "The children of the orphanage need to be moved until after the draft. Manhattan Island is experiencing much unrest. It could get dangerous—if you don't want to go, I *will* understand."

The ambassador yelled out. "I'm ready, my good man."

All the men laughed; Black shook his head, then offered direction. "We will deal with our women and children, then leave. When we return, we will live in quarantine for a week before we blend back into fort life."

"Yeah." Elbert responded, before the men stood and filed out.

New York City
July 11, 1863

Two barges carried the twenty-two and their horses across the Hudson River. As Black stared through the thick of the night, his worst fear was realized. Based on the noise and the random fires springing up, they were too late. Riot was happening and the children were still on Manhattan Island. The ferryman, an older white man with wild gray hair, spoke; his voice scraped Black's concentration.

"Seen some coloreds hangin'. You sure you wanna go to the island?"

"Yes." Black's reply was sharp. "We have an agreement and you will keep it."

James stepped forward holding the torch, casting light on their exchange. Elbert stepped up behind him offering threat. "If you ain't in place, old man, we will slit the throat of you and yo' son."

"No... no–we'll be here. We gon stay out 'til y'all come."

Black stooped just a bit to get eye contact. "Ferryman, there will be no place you can rest if I don't get my coins worth."

"We got us a boat–we gon float 'til you come."

"We have only a few hours 'til daybreak–be ready." Black countered.

They bumped the dock by torchlight, which was no easy feat. The men leapt into action unloading the horses and saddle bags from the barges. At the other end of the dock, small fires, crowds and mayhem could be seen. The men turned in the opposite direction–their goal to maintain life. They remained in the trees and the high vegetation until they had no choice but to step out in the open.

The temperature by the waterfront had been tolerable–cool, though the smell was rancid. As they moved inland, the heat became stifling. The twenty-two broke down into four groups, with Black, Elbert, James, Simon and Jeremiah riding together. They moved in units, securing each block so the next group could pass safely.

In the distance, and sometimes close up, Black heard screams, gunfire and glass breaking. Complete darkness helped their cause to remain undetected; but that wouldn't last long, for it was early morn. They moved in alleys and down the murkiest of side streets until the orphanage came into view. The bottom floor was lit up and to Black that was a bad sign.

The courtyard was dark as the men made two lines on either side of the large structure. They filed into the backyard and high vegetation, leaving the horses. The twenty-two spread out on foot taking their positions. As they moved about the night, Black's words floated through the air.

"We're moving children, that is the aim here. But you are all to remain upright. Life is also the goal–for the children and for us."

Black climbed the back stairs and the third step creaked. At the top of the landing, he heard Elbert say. "Careful, Miss Elsie will peel them braids back."

He knocked twice in rapid succession, then repeated the knock two more times. Miss Elsie pulled the door open and exclaimed. "Mista Black, ya come, but it might be too late."

She stepped back from the door and he moved into the kitchen. A sea of small brown faces stared at him. Miss Carol sat among them; her greeting was strained.

"Good morning, Mr. Black. I'm afraid Elsie may be correct."

The children all wore tan; the girls wore dresses, the boys matching shirts and trousers. There were now eighty children and they all looked frightened. He didn't address the women's worries, but he did step back onto the porch to give orders.

"We're ready."

At Black's statement, Simon and Tim followed him back into the house. They kept going, posting up at the front window. Elbert and James remained at the backdoor. E.J. and Jeremiah moved in past where he stood in the kitchen. They went to the second floor. Black directed his next words to the women.

"Do you still have the wagons?"

"We has the wagons, but we sold the horses." Miss Elsie answered. "Why you got hair?"

Black grinned but didn't answer. He needed her to stay focused. He countered. "We have horses."

"We has one ass–the chilren call her Joan." Elsie explained. "The chilren worried for her the last time we had to go."

"No worries." Black said, but he was worried. "Break the children down into two groups. We'll take… Joan with us."

The children started clapping and Black's concern escalated. Turning his thoughts to the exit plan, he moved out of the kitchen and into the night. The shanty of a stable was lit up as the men hitched their horses to the wagons. Behind him, the commotion of the children being separated into two groups could be heard.

Black stood between James and Elbert at the top of the landing. Elbert broke the silence. "Guess we takin' Joan wit' us."

"Seems like it." James replied on a chuckle.

"Old biddies." Black added.

Frank's silhouette appeared at the bottom of the porch. "It's a mob done turned down 43rd Street. They's movin' dis way. Don't seem like they's thankin' 'bout us, but that'll change."

"Yeah." Elbert said.

"Ready the men to stand and deliver." Black ordered.

"Sho' thang." Frank said before disappearing into the night.

"I thanks we made it in enuff time." James added.

Anthony and Bainesworth posted up on the back porch, while he, Elbert and James headed to the courtyard. Once out front, Black noted it was as Frank had reported. A mob was indeed coming their way and given the number of flames floating at them, it was sizable. The noise level also indicated the crowd was bigger than he could see. Black's eyes bounced up to the sky and in the distance, he could see that dawn was upon them.

"Shit." Elbert said. "We 'bout to have us some fun."

"When they finds dis ain't no easy mark, they'll move on." James said.

"Or… they could become more aggressive." Black replied.

"Then there will be dead bodies." Elbert said.

It seemed daybreak was ushering the throng of angry men ever closer. A group of five white men broke from the crowd and rushed the courtyard. The first shots rang out, leaving two men injured and one man dead. Jeremiah and Simon were in place to pick off the crowd as it approached. The other two men dragged the injured off.

Chants of "Die, nigger, die" could be heard as the crowd backed off to reassess the threat they couldn't see. Another throng tried the same tactic, but when the smoke cleared four men lay injured in the courtyard and another dead. As the first rays of sunlight broke through the clouds, the crowd had thinned. The covered wagons were brought to the courtyard; the children and the women were loaded inside. Black stood guard along with Elbert and James between the vehicles. When the children were settled, the men mounted up and moved toward the waterfront on the westside, each gripping a shotgun across his lap.

Eleven men rode with the wagons, while eleven men forced their way through the crowds. They traveled streets with little to no activity but the evidence of violence remained. Black observed a white mob hoisting the dead body of a colored man to dangle from a tree. Several cobblestone streets over, two colored men hung from the same tree but different branches–their eyes dug out and dicks cut off. The smell of burned wood and flesh blanketing the air.

As they neared the waterfront, a white man stood in the doorway of a ransacked flower shop and began shooting at them. Jeremiah swung down from his horse, weapons drawn and returned fire, nailing the aggressor between the eyes. Black had to keep a steady head to remember they all had a space to cover. If he tried to help Jeremiah that would leave his space unprotected. Simon covered Jeremiah until he was back in the saddle.

They picked up speed traveling the streets where the violence had already happened. When the wagons rumbled onto the docks, two barges and a boat floated just out of reach. The dock was still smoldering from the previous day's fires. There were throngs of colored people trying to get off the island. Ferries were coming and going taking as many as they could. The colored ferrymen weren't charging–but several white ferrymen required coin. The river traffic was high, but when their boat bumped the dock, the men got in place to escort the children.

The twenty-two stood shoulder to shoulder in two lines with their backs to the children. Miss Elsie walked them down the middle of the men and Miss Carol brought up the rear. Black stood between the wagons helping the children down. One brown faced angel with no front teeth asked.

"Is we taking Joan on the boat too?"

"Joan will ride wit' the horses on the next boat. She will be there when you get off." Black's answer must have worked because the little girl nodded, then moved on.

When the children were settled, Jeremiah stepped away and yelled. "We have room for women and children!"

Frank and Lou took a white ferryman hostage allowing colored folks to board for free. Anthony and E.J. did the same. Simon watched for mob activity, and Black was sure the scene was the same on the East River. The horses and Joan were moved onto one barge, while his men took control of all barges attempting to exploit for coin.

Hudson and Janie had traveled from their farm in Port Jervis to help. The couple was in place when the boat bumped the dock. Miss Elsie, Miss Carol, the children and the ass named Joan were moved to safety. The twenty-two spent the rest of the morning and the better part of the afternoon helping folks move from Manhattan Island to the mainland. When night fell, the men moved to the next part of the plan.

✵ ✵ ✵

Kingston, New York
July 17, 1863

Black and the men arrived in Kingston, New York, and set up camp in the woods surrounding the small estate of Fernando Wood. A colored stablehand was questioned and in exchange for coin, Black received the layout of the house.

"The Mista and Missus don't share sleepin' quarters. Mista Mayor on da westside of da house."

The stablehand was a stoop shouldered fellow who was dark of skin. He had a head full of knotted hair and creases around his perceptive eyes. The twenty-two kept the old man busy–not letting him return to his duties. They wanted nothing to ruin the element of surprise.

Black observed from a distance the comings and goings on the estate. According to the stablehand, the property had six servants–all of them colored. When night fell and the temperature eased, Black stood at the back of the house with his brothers and Jeremiah. Elbert forced the door and Jeremiah boldly lit an oil lamp. They traveled a long corridor until they came to a closed door at the far end. James tried the knob; it wasn't locked.

The wick on the oil lamp was turned all the way down, casting the hall back into darkness. Under the door, light flickered, and Black surmised that at least one candle was lit within the chamber. James worked the door silently and when they stepped into the stuffy room, Black's blood began to thrum. A colored woman lay tangled in the sheets with Fernando–both were asleep.

It was the woman who stirred first. She was after twenty, but before thirty. Upon seeing Black standing on the side of the bed, she startled but didn't speak. Raising a hand, he pointed to the door. The woman scrambled from the bed and gathered her clothing. Elbert followed her into the hall. At her movement, Fernando, who was propped up by many pillows, removed the mask covering his eyes. His sleep fog was punctured when his gaze clashed with Black's. Fernando clutched at his chest and gasped aloud.

Jeremiah pushed a chair at him, and Black sat allowing himself to get comfortable. Taking advantage of Fernando's shock, he took in their surroundings. A lone candle sat on the nightstand to the left of the large bed; the curtains were drawn back on both sides. The rest of the chamber was murky as the candlelight didn't reach far. Jeremiah and James stood just beyond the light. Black spoke first, because it seemed Fernando couldn't.

"Good evening, Mr. Mayor."

"I am no longer the mayor." Fernando countered. "What are you doing in my home?"

"You will always be the mayor to me." Black answered with a chuckle. "Why am I here, Fernando? You tell me."

"I have no earthly idea." The ex-mayor said, his fear visible.

"You have stepped up to the line that borders the end of my patience. I think you need your fuckin' throat cut before you cross me." Black replied, his demeanor now icy.

"No… no, I haven't broken our agreement."

"I received your missives." Black sneered.

Fernando's eyes widened from that bit of news, and Black went on. "It appears you have been looking for me."

Jeremiah stepped into the light and the mayor whimpered. Fernando stammered. "I–I h–have kept our agreement and there will be no more letters."

Black didn't respond for moments, allowing the mayor to wallow in terror. Leaning forward, elbows to knees, he glared at Fernando Wood.

"Get dressed, Mr. Mayor, so that we might catch up."

Behind him, Black heard the hiss of a matchstick followed

by the brightening of the chamber. Fernando looked pale, but he hadn't moved to dress. Black would not ask again, he needed to impress upon the mayor his feelings without speech, while stopping just shy of killing the man. In the blink of an eye, Black sprang from the chair. Reaching the side of the bed, he grabbed a naked Fernando Wood by his hair and yanked him from where he was perched to his feet. Against the slighter man's ear, Black gritted out.

"You will not test me, Mr. Mayor."

"P-Please… I have seen the error of my ways. You'll not have reason to seek me out again." Fernando begged.

Black shoved the mayor down into the chair he had just vacated. Looming over the man, Black found it a struggle not to slit his throat. Chest heaving, he eyed the mayor. Fernando would have continued pleading for his life, but Black reared back as far as he could, punching him in the face. The chair toppled from the impact spilling the limp bodied mayor onto the chamber floor.

The bedchamber went silent, until James said, "He's gon be out for a while."

"It's for the best." Jeremiah added. "Seem like Black forgot we can't kill 'em."

"Shit." Black grunted. "His ass will be hollering soon enough. Tie him up and meet me in the kitchen."

Turning, Black headed for the door. Jeremiah was of course correct; it had almost slipped his thoughts that Fernando was to remain upright. Black outed his light to keep from hearing the smugness emitting from the man. It was his attempt at sanity. In the darkened corridor, Elbert and the woman stood quietly.

"The kitchen," Black demanded.

"Yeah." Elbert replied.

Once in the kitchen, the woman lit an oil lamp, then sat to the table. Black didn't engage her, instead he watched the entrance leading back to the hall. Jeremiah and James appeared fifteen minutes later with the mayor in tow. Fernando was bound and gagged, his eyes wide; still, he seemed dazed.

"The oak tree at the front of the estate." Black ordered.

James and Jeremiah didn't stop; they carried the struggling, bare assed Fernando out the backdoor. Black chanced a glance at the woman seated to the table, she grinned before dropping her gaze. He heard Elbert address her.

"Come."

At the front of the estate, Black made a spectacle of stringing the mayor up—torches and all. Fernando's arms were pulled tight and hoisted above his head. His legs were yanked wide and stabilized with more rope. The gag was removed so he wouldn't suffocate. Stakes were driven deep into the earth to keep the mayor positioned just so, and all the while Fernando begged and yelled.

"No… no please! I understand the error of my ways. You'll not hear a peep from me. I swear it."

Black didn't speak again to the ex-mayor of New York City, but he did keep direct eye contact. James held the torch steady allowing him to witness Fernando's fear. When leaving the man alive became more than Black could bear, he turned and walked into the darkness leaving his men to monitor the situation.

Later, the twenty-two rested in shifts as they readied themselves for the long journey home. When day broke, the sun was bright—glorious. The men stayed long enough to witness Fernando Wood's utter humiliation. Black watched as the mayor was cut down from the oak tree where he was strung up tight. Fernando was covered with a blanket, then helped to his feet by his wife and servants. Black and the men turned their mounts toward Canada and rode out.

COMING SOON:

THE FORT

Fort Independence
March 1864

BLACK'S EYES POPPED open from a dead sleep at the sound of booted feet in the corridor just beyond his bedroom. Sunday was pressed into his side with an arm thrown over his chest. Slowly, he untangled from her before swinging his legs over the side of the bed. Once on his feet, he moved about in the darkened chamber. His wife groggily murmured his name as he was strapping on his gun.

"Nat?"

Walking to the bed, Black leaned over and kissed her. "Go back to sleep."

"What time it is?"

"Almost dawn," he answered, then kissed her again.

When his wife began dozing, Black turned and headed for the door. Stepping into the unlit hall, he pulled the knob until he heard a soft click. James broke the silence.

"Ant come to me and Elbert. He was gon ring the bell, but we told him no."

Elbert added. "Ain't no since scaring the women and children."

"It's a carriage in front of the gate. Ain't no one got out–it's just there." James continued.

"The men patrolling?" Black asked.

"They say when they come 'round one time it wasn't there–next time, it was." James explained.

Black nodded. It was dark, they couldn't see him. "Let's go to the gate."

The brothers moved through the house as though it were daylight. In the hall leading to the porch stood Paul with an oil lamp and shotgun. Once they stepped onto the porch, the old man locked the door behind them. At the bottom of the stairs, the twenty-two waited; Frank, Lou and Anthony held torches. Black descended the steps; Elbert and James followed. The men moved as one to the front gate.

The temperature held frost and though it was after winter, it was still before spring. As they walked the path to the front of the fort, Black tried to think through every scenario. He was drawing a blank. When they reached the gate, the men on guard looked agitated. Philip stepped forward to explain.

"Morning, Black. The carriage been out dere a hour–ain't no one got out. We called out–nothing."

"Thank you, Philip." Black replied, as he moved to the door beside the gate.

His brothers stepped out behind him. James carried the torch and Elbert, his gun–the hammer already cocked back. Black reached for the torch and James relinquished the dancing flame in favor of his own gun. When Black heard James cock his weapon, he approached the vehicle. The two horses attached to the carriage didn't seem uneasy or skittish. Black stepped with caution toward the door of the vehicle. Under his boots the ground crunched. He did no more than glance around the darkness to see if anyone lay in wait. His mind considered ambush, but his men were patrolling.

Torchlight, though better than nothing, offered limited

visibility. Breathing in sharply, Black placed a hand on the door handle and James hissed. "Now!"

Black yanked the door wide at his brother's command. The cab was empty; still, closer scrutiny shook him to his core. It was Elbert who summed up Black's racing thoughts. "Damn."

The brothers leaned forward in one fluid motion: the sight before them gruesome, even in the absence of a body. Blood soaked the interior of the carriage. As Black tried to process what he was seeing, James added. "Whoever was in there ain't make it."

Black agreed, but he could find no words. He began working through the questions floating around in his head. Who had been in the carriage? Where did the carriage come from? Why was it left outside the gate? How did his men miss the arrival of the carriage? What the hell did all this mean? He had begun recycling the questions, when James spoke his name.

"Black?"

"I don't know." He answered, before his brother could say more. "I don't know…"

The twenty-two took control of the gate, while the brothers stood about in complete darkness. Black had extinguished the torch, so they wouldn't be vulnerable to attack; still, they did not leave the carriage. Two hours passed in silence and daybreak found Black standing on the side of the vehicle, arms folded over his chest. As the sun chased away the murkiness of night, Black began to circle the vehicle. He noted the obvious, while thinking out loud.

"The carriage came from the east and there are no wheel marks leading away."

"Shit." James mumbled.

Black examined the horses. Lifting their hooves, he looked for the groove placed on all the shoes by their smithy; there were no identifying marks. Next, he assessed the driver's seat and found a sizable blood stain. At the back of the vehicle, he stooped down to look beneath the frame. He found an "F" branded into the undercarriage.

Standing, Black faced his brothers. "The horseshoes have no marks from our smithy. Looks to me like someone went through the trouble of re-shoeing the animals."

"What is you sayin'?" James pressed.

"I'm saying these are our horses. The animals came home." Black clarified.

"The carriage?" Elbert asked.

"Belongs to us." Black replied.

"I figured as much." Elbert said, as he looked to the trees.

"What next?" James asked.

"We count the people." Black replied, his tone grim. "See who's missing."

30123339R10176